THE HUNGRY AND THE LOST

THE HUNGRY
AND THE LOST

Bethany W. Pope

Bethany W. Pope has an MA and a PhD in Creative Writing, and has won many literary awards. Their poetry collections include: *A Radiance*, *Crown of Thorns*, *The Gospel of Flies*, *Undisturbed Circles*, *The Rag and Boneyard*, and *Silage*, which was described by *The Guardian* as 'literature as salvation'. Their debut novel, *Masque*, was published in 2016. Bethany is an American who undertook their postgraduate degrees in Wales, and currently lives and works in China.

To Matthew: my husband, my love.

And to Xeno: may you grow in love, laughter, strength, and kindness.

Parthian, Cardigan SA43 1ED
www.parthianbooks.com
© Bethany W. Pope 2021
Print ISBN: 978-1-913640-20-0
Ebook ISBN: 978-1-913640-44-6
Editor: Carly Holmes
Cover Design: Syncopated Pandemonium
Typeset by Elaine Sharples
Printed by 4Edge Limited
Published with the financial support of the Books Council of Wales
British Library Cataloguing in Publication Data
A cataloguing record for this book is available from the British Library.

CONTENTS

Prologue

THE HOUSE

Florida, 1910. The swampland rises uninterrupted, swirling in stinking mist, redolent of ancient bird droppings. The herons have departed, leaving behind mangrove-tea waters, silt, the faint tang of salt. There is the skeleton of a town along what could be called a river, the houses rising on stilts to allow airflow and prevent the floors from rotting in a flood. As the herons are gone, so is the plume-trade. The northern rich will have to decorate their hats with something else. A racoon pelt will bring a man less than a dollar, the panthers are gone, the gators and manatees have made their retreat. All that remains are the people, fewer of them every summer, clouds of mosquitoes, and the odd, water-logged cow.

There is a church in the center, its steepled roof caving, ruined by time, the weather, neglect. There is a cemetery beside it filled with lead-weighted coffins, to keep the bodies from rising before Christ, upthrust from the mud.

No one misses it.

The last parson died near on ten years ago, hacking up blood and chunks of his lungs. His portrait in oils hangs in the manse next door, fungus and river mold creeping in at the corners, obscuring the paints. You can still, just about, tell what he looked like when he was very young. A yellow face rising out from dark wood and black robes, very open around the eyes, though by now he has seen too much.

The manse is not uninhabited.

Two women live there, his wife and his daughter. They crowd together in that place, the walls throbbing blood-veined with their voices, building in strength and timber until the house seems to heave with it, breathing as they do, until the house, standing there, stolid, mock-Victorian, hovering on stilts like legs wanting flight, seems to hum with a sort of almost life. The same kind you can find in any hospital, the kind that you see in what remains of a body after the head has met a sharpened hoof. Idiot, struggling, blank eyes staring round, searching in vain for some vague memory of life.

And they are dying, too. Dying with the ruinous town. In their own sullen way. Daughter and mother: Joy-Marie, Rose.

Rose is tall, prone to wearing silk dresses in bright, lapis blue, to bring out her eyes, training the green out of them. Now she wears what she has worn for years, fading, rotted out at the armpits, the cumulative effort of humidity and her own rank sweat. Her hair was blond once, bright, the texture of spun silk. It is blond now, but fading, like the dress, not quite white, the years having made it coarser. She stands there; you can see her, at the head of the stairs leading up to second-story darkness. She stands there, vital, erect, the white handkerchief she lowers spotted.

There is light in her eyes. She calls out, down the stairs, the passage to the kitchen, her daughter's name.

Joy-Marie, Joyce, as her mother will call her, is kneeling in the kitchen peeling potatoes over a pot next to the Sears and Roebuck oven, a leftover from the minister before her father. This is the last food in the house. She shall have to think of something. Later.

Her hair is dark, near-black, wild. There is no reason for her to comb it, though she bundles it into a loose, untidy bun. Her arms are thin and white. She does not tan, even in the harsh sunlight on the river where the trees cannot obscure it, nor does she burn. She peels with passion and intensity, as though angry, gripping each spud hard enough to imprint it with her fingers and cause the veins underneath her skin to bulge. Her eyes are dark, penetrating, and she keeps them focused on her knife.

Her mother's voice reaches her, low, deep-water calm, but still the sound would seem to startle her. Her knife slips, the silver, short blade grazing her wrist.

She stands up slowly, holding the injured arm away from the raw elements of their meal, laying the bloodied potato in the bucket. She pauses a moment to bandage her wrist with a swath of rag she plucks from a bin beneath the standing pail that serves for a sink. Rose's voice calls again, meandering, and the girl does not answer. Her mother knows that she is coming.

Doctored, she makes her way through the long hall, past the library filled with books damp but readable, classics and theological texts clad in leather that is slimy to the touch. She has read them all, every one. She passes the lounge with Hepplewhite tallboys and Chippendale settee and chair-partners, all un-sat in for over a decade; she doubts that by now they could support human weight. And certainly, there are no ghosts to test them, now. She travels past the room she sleeps in. It was not meant for her bedroom. That room is across from her mother's at the top of the stairs. She sleeps in the death-room, where her father spattered his last, bright breath against the wall. You can still see the spots. The door is open. She closes it as she passes, without knowing why.

Then she is at the root of the stairs, those noisy, wood-creaking slats of mahogany that sound when touched, like axons and dendrites firing thoughts.

This is where they meet most often, mother and daughter. Standing on the middle stair, the meeting of territories, passed most often by food bowl, by night pail, the occasional dress.

Joy is silent, arms dangling, waiting, her bandage hanging like hibiscus bouquet, limp from her wrist.

Rose removes the handkerchief from her lips, it sports a blossom of its own, her blue eyes flashing. She opens her mouth and the stairwell is washed by a new infusion of words.

There is life here, of a kind, a half-life at least. And, if you are strong enough to follow, you shall feel its raging pulse.

Town

EXTINCTION

In the decades that closed the nineteenth century great flocks of enormous, white-plumed birds (so prized by haberdashers and ostentatious decorators of human homes), heron, and egrets that were almost their twins, sent up raucous cries from their collective nests set high up in the close-woven mangrove swamps. These birds gathered in hundreds, their guano spattering the floor beneath the trunks; a strong ammonia-scented mass, white and liquid as whitewash lye. It collected in piles, a foot high underneath the larger collective nests, mingled with the calcium rich discarded eggshells and the occasional deceased chick.

All of this waste, foul as it is to think about, had a purpose, an important role to play in the life of the wetlands. The ammonia and calcium lent richness to a marshland soil that is otherwise unfit for any growing thing save for mangroves, poison ivy, boab and the saw-tooth palmetto, a vegetable shaped like a small palm that was named for its stiff, cellulite-edged leaves which drew blood from any thin-skinned animal foolish enough to push, unthinking, past its crowded groves.

The birds used their long orange bills, spear-shaped and hard, to pierce the bodies of venomous snakes, swallowing them down in one fluid gulp, their long necks silently undulating as the stilled creatures slithered down, never more to poison or to sting.

These birds inhabited a world painted in blinding shades of blue and green, the water and swamp surging all around them, sending reflected light up to dance among the leaves, and all of this was punctuated by the snowy white of their own plumes. That color shone from the fine-crushed sugar sand dunes, the detritus of a millennia's work on fossil shells, reducing the skeletons of soft-bodied molluscs and the occasional crab to a fine, delicate powder. It shone from the mists that rose in clouds from the secret forest waterways, drawn upward by the sun and dyed by that great open eye the color of gold which has been washed by the blood of sunrise.

And throughout it all, the great birds swooped, feather-splayed and with glistening pinion, soaring or making their slow, Jurassic way by foot through water that rose up to their jointed knees, pursuing toxic meals in the tannin-laden soup.

Then the men arrived. The hunters who brought them down in droves, like their plains-bound ancestors who left buffalo corpses scattered throughout the ravaged grasslands, so many stinking knobs of bone. They came with birdshot and fine-woven nets, to kill, the air so full of their shrieking prey that an unaimed shot could send two birds spiralling down to earth at once.

The men formed camps, then towns, ordering desperate gingham-wearing women from ads placed in adventure magazines with chattel descriptions; twenty-seven, good worker, child-ready hips; thirty-one, even-tempered, good teeth. Women usually, though not always, too plain for wedding, or without sufficient dowries, who had sat too long upon their local shelves and needed, more than anything, free air to breathe away from hurtful gossip and dissent. They were delivered with the other mail-ordered supplies, riding with the farm and hunting equipment, the new nets and the plows, their new husband's names on slips of paper, pinned like receipts to their shoulders or chests.

Sometimes the marriages were happy.

There was a boom that lasted many years. The men built fine houses, filled with great treasures, oil paintings, and silverware wiped and dried every day to keep them free from slime and bluish creeping mold, the same kind that appears in damp vaults, creeping over the faces of the dead.

There was a general store, filled with quality things, more variety than a hunter's bride would usually ever think to want. Finally, they built a fine, steepled church of the protestant persuasion and hired a minister and his lovely wife (oh how the women envied her blond hair that flowed like sea foam along her shoulders) and they made a manse to keep them in, tall, its beams carved mainly from hardwood and not just soft and rot-prone pine. It was a house meant to outlast generations, even in this water-sodden place.

Eventually the couple had a child.

The town experienced nearly three decades of seemingly endless supply meeting with incessant demand, but as in all good displays of economics, the product gave out before the desire. The birds, save for a few token breeding pairs (eventually protected by Roosevelt in 1901, long after the slaughter) were reduced to denuded corpses.

The bodies littered the marshlands until the time came when some desperate boom-and-bust hunter who had spent the last decades moving from scrabbling potato-eating poor, to land-and-servant rich, only to cycle back to poverty again, made his way in cracked and rotted boots through wetlands that were taking their bird-feed one last time. And if they crunched down on the fragile carapace of one more rack of ribs, who would notice? The sound was soft enough to hide behind the wailings of the ever-rushing moon-drawn tide.

The sound of death is often lost.

Death came to them, to the whole town in a manner such as this, and there it lingered. For a while.

HOME

The first room that David decorated when he brought his wife down from the North was the library, an act that reflected the parts of his life that he felt were by far the most important. He would never know what a gift this room would be to his child in later, darker, times. He was a minister with vast, romantic aspirations, seeing symbolism in everything, or placing it there. A walker between worlds was David, fancying the places where the visible and invisible meet and myths may sometimes still come alive and wander, almost breathing, through passageways and the hidden channels where a mortal mind would be afraid to enter.

These are not bad qualities for a person whose job it is to converse with God.

The books on the shelves were mainly Greek; myths, poems and theological texts stacked together in fine, red-leather bindings, all neatly printed, disclosing some variation of the truth. The balance was paid out in stories told in Latin, everything from Aesop to Boethius, a vast selection chronicling philosophy, theology, a loose, mythic history, and even the occasional bawdy Rabelaisian romp.

The Bible, a large and ancient hand-lettered thing in a case of silver gilt, pages opened to The Revelation of St. John, a passage describing the rise of a star-crowned woman who was the mother of dragons, had pride of place on its own neo-gothic stand. It was like one that could conceivably be found in a medieval English church, but which really hailed from the workshop of an ancestor of Chippendale's.

The stand stood underneath the small stained-glass window he had installed, which bore a variation of the image of Persephone as Rosetti conceived her. Her hair, tinted reddish-black, strong, disdainful features, and royal-blue robe glowed with a deep undertone of flame, no matter the light. The fruit that she held, blazing skin and ember heart, was unlike any mortal pomegranate. The small bite she had taken had reduced her, like Eve, to some lingering half-life among the gray groves and the damned.

The small remainder consisted of smaller books, green varicose with cheap binding and pages, all well-thumbed. These were fairy tales and a few choice modern novels that he had read and loved in his early youth and still retained a secret passion for even now. He was a man who knew what childhood was, knew the darkness and the light, and loved it anyway in a way that was both brilliant and unashamed. And people gleaned this from him, quickly, as the knowledge of this well, this deep trove of joy, was visible in his impish eyes.

Needless to say, all of the local children loved him.

They would show up at the doorstep in the hour after suppertime, after cleaning their father's egret nets and guns, arranging the blood-quilled feathers in their shipping boxes by quality and size. His wife Rose would admit them, smiling over a swelling pregnancy, her dress a bright and radiant azure, trimmed at the hem with lapis silk.

She was one who was as conscious of effect as fashion. A pious woman with the hint of the theatrical wafting from her like perfume. She wore her hair down in a waterfall of naturally platinum Scandinavian curls that hung past her waist, having never met a pair of scissors, and her lips rarely formed themselves into any shape that was not a variation on a smile. This was a trait the plain-tending local women secretly thought a bit scandalous, though they never had any but a kind word for her when they passed her on the street.

The children would enter, decorous on their first visit, rushing thereafter – past the more classical lounge with its Hepplewhite settees, chairs and piano, whose limbs were always decorously covered by handmade lace leggings, washed once a week to quell mold – before skidding round the corner, fast as they could, into that wonderful, book-lined land.

David would be waiting for them there behind his enormous leather-topped desk, having already hidden great lumps of candy and the occasional small toy in hide-holes placed around the room. The children, both girls and boys, would gather round his desk in rows, waiting, as he removed his pince-nez, polishing them while staring at the children hard down the long length of his nose. They would stand there, solemn, shifting foot to foot. Always unsure if his severity were meant, no matter how many times they'd played it; always slightly, deliciously afraid that it were real.

The silence would reel out.

David staring, the children shifting, Rose looking on inconspicuously from around the tapestry-hung door, her eyes among the embroidered pomegranates and thread-plucked branches. All of them enjoyed it immensely, holding their breath.

Finally, after moments that felt to the children agonizing hours, David replaced the lenses on his face and, as though their reflections gave him a lighter countenance, one more prone to brightening joy, he smiled, waved his hand, sketching out the signal. Go.

The children let out a loud whoop, cacophonous and echoing, that sent the books to shudder on their shelves. The hunt was on.

They tore through the room, pulling out tomes that cost more than their parents could make in a day, wealthy as they were just now, setting them crashing, splay-spined, to the uncarpeted floor. No damage done, thank God, those books were tough. The only one they did not touch was, of course, the ancient, stand-bound Bible, left unmolested in its highly-honored place.

Dirty fingers dug through unlocked drawers, scattering paper, pens, upsetting an inkwell that sent tint spreading out on the blotter in dark red tendrils, seeking the treasure, hidden there somewhere especially for them. They went everywhere, finding candies, small toys, even riffling through the minister's deep pockets. The man and his wife stood with their heads thrown back, rocketing laughter the whole time, until the children had uncovered every last, well-treasured piece.

And before they left, sucking on fruit pastel jubejubes and peppermint sticks, winding up a waddling penguin or fondling a bright, perfect aggie marble in a small and ink-stained hand, they formed back into rows (the only neatness left in this hurricane-addled room) and solemnly shook the preacher's hand. Bursting into grins again as they left when Rose, radiant with tears that stemmed from pleasure, placed a cheek-bound kiss or ruffled soft hair.

And when they had left, in a flood of laughter, each child holding a gift and each of them content, Rose and her husband stood in the wrecked room and embraced, their fingers finding tender places on each other, their lips taking in the sweetness of their mouths, better than any sugar product ever made. David moved his hand down to her taut, expanding belly to feel the new life that they kindled there, a warm spark that set his Rose alight, until she seemed to burn in air.

They took an hour, after finishing what that touch started, cleaning up the room, setting everything to rights in preparation for the game again tomorrow night.

Soon they would be three and this building would be home.

VISITATION

It is evening now, the brief span of time when sunset paints the sky in bright, hot colors, shades from salmon to crimson in wavering striations, edged a dark and tarnished gold along the bottom and deep, plumy blue-black where the upper limits of the horizon melt into the deepest reaches of interstellar void. There are no clouds tonight and so the stars are showing, one by one, the bright white constellations shining down like holes in space interrupted at their lower extremity by the twisted, full-leafed branches of boab and mangrove interspersed with the occasional small-foliaged oak.

This time, the day's last phase, is always brief, as though even such atmospheric blooms as this cannot last long in this much heat, wilting away into blackness, complete after only a very few minutes. Things fade fast here, losing whatever beauty they have after lives brutal and brief, but oh, when there is life it is good indeed, flaring up, intensely epigrammatic as an alcohol fire igniting in an airless room.

David is out walking now, in air less boiling than in the heat of day, though never here precisely cool. He is on his way to visit the members of his parish too sick or feeble to come into his office to see him. The sick are mainly women, their illness described by their husbands, depending on the amount of affection remaining in the relationship, if ever there was any, as either 'a bit punkish' or 'she's malingering again. Could work like a mule if she wanted.'

Though there is a doctor still in town, most of these men would never think to call him for their children or their wives. Sawbones are good for when you get the gangrene infection from a hunting cut wet through by the swamp or when you accidentally trap your leg in one of the small boy's clamp-down raccoon traps, not for muley little woman's illnesses.

The symptoms range from sunken-eyed exhaustion to thin cheeks and blood-coughing (accompanied by a peculiar smell) that seems to be contracted purely by luck, drinking bad water or breathing foul air. The first group have a high rate of recovery, after a few days' rest, provided they can achieve some peace when the men are in the room, ordering them up to wash and cook and fetch. The second never seem to linger very long, they snuff out quickly, like flames without fuel, sweating out blood, their skins seeming to glow bright and vivid in their last few hours, as though flaring out in defiance of the coming eternal dark.

They die fast and are buried as soon as possible (even the best embalming cannot add any halt to decay, and after two days the stench of the corpse, even one swollen and drowning with formaldehyde, is unbearably intense). The new brides, ordered from magazines to replace the previous one, now defunct, arrive a few weeks later. They are brought with the other groceries on carts down from Tampa, usually after longer journeys from the North.

It is David's job to wed them there, directly after their arrival on the cart. The new bride rarely has enough time to wipe the road dust from her heels before the wedding. This speed is necessary so that she may immediately move into her master's house and begin the work of clearing out the previous occupant's belongings, caring for the children who are usually still glaze-eyed with grief, and getting a fair start on the maintenance work needed to keep the building afloat after a month of neglect. The chances are good that she will earn her first black eye within the week, her first pregnancy soon after, and her first illness will strike a few months after that.

It is a very ordered life.

It is a lot of work for the wives. But as they all confide to David on his visits, speaking to him separately and in groups, it is ever so much better than sitting on the side-lines forever; unmarried, dried up, unused. At least as wives they are given respect and not that bitter tincture of pity that they were forced to drink before, when they lived as millstones around the necks of their fathers.

On his first visits, David enters the houses and the sick women, well trained, would try to get up and make him welcome, no matter how sick they were or how difficult it was for them to move. It took three months of rounds and many, many visitations for David to convince them that it was his job to minister to *them*. And that includes making the tea. Once that distinction had been made, once the ladies accepted it, these meetings became suddenly much more pleasurable for both parties concerned.

In the North his visitations had a decidedly more religious air, a heightened sense of formality with everything done, quite literally, by the book. In this case The Book of Common Prayer. Here this is far less likely. He decided within a week of arriving that the best spiritual aid he can give to his parishioners, the female ones anyway, is a free ear to listen. He has found that if he lets them spend a good hour talking to him, without the fear of interruption or denial, they take it as the best gift he can give them. Even the dying ones agree with that.

And when they are dying he will sit with them in silence, offering up his own quiet prayers for their freedom from pain, before anointing their burning heads with oil that sits there, thumbed into a cross on the heated forehead, simmering until the final breath is drawn and the soul taken up into whatever there is that lies beyond.

Sometimes he can see it go, the soul a bright white light that causes the air to shimmer around the body, as though the walls of the known world were bursting, straining to withhold something of greater strength and reality than its own, like a dream figure struggling to lift a real brick.

Luckily there were no deaths tonight, just three ladies broken down under terrible exhaustion, the burden of maintaining society where no human habitation should have been able to form. He sat with them an hour each, making them tea and listening to their constant stream of talk, before leaving with a brief informal prayer. He left the women smiling with temporarily lightened hearts.

These visits also have some benefit for David. They remind him to continue to treat his wife as his equal, lest he get caught up in the hell of hierarchy where there can be respect and order, but absolutely no real love. And now David is on his way home, exhausted but happy. He has done what he can, what he will continue to do for the rest of his life.

The minister is young, a bit past twenty-five, his wife a few years younger. He looks older because of his elongated features, made handsome by kindness, and the extreme thinness of his limbs. An ungenerous person would describe him as storkish or egret-like, resembling in his form the creatures whose corpses keep the town alive and thriving. They have been married for a little over a year and a half; most of that time has been spent here. They moved down six weeks after the wedding, taking trains until Tampa and then hiring coach and carts for the rest of the journey.

This is David's second church since his ordination at twenty and while he likes it here, he does not plan on staying long. He wants his children to grow up in a place where books are valued and academic intelligence is considered a benefit, and not a peculiar form of deformity, to be discouraged by good parents and completely obliterated by great ones.

No, they will stay here five or six years, eight or ten at the very most, and then they will file a transfer request to the Bishop that will, hopefully, land his family someplace a bit more civilized. Where they can thrive.

Still, he thinks, his gum boots sloshing through the root- and branch-infested slog, disturbing lizards and the occasional scavenging rat. The motion of his walking raises a deep and tannin-rich scent from the watery swirl; it is beautiful here, in a way. If we had remained where we were, there is so much that we would have missed. Sunsets like that one just ended, for example, the joy of good friends.

About a quarter-mile from the manse house he reminds himself that he must continue interviewing for housekeepers (he is not going to allow his wife to become one of those sunken-eyed creatures he visited tonight). He has a feeling that when the baby comes they are going to need all the help they can get.

The manse is in sight now; he has just passed the locked church, its windows dark as dead eyes, passed the yard with its many graves, both sunken and raised. There is his favourite tree for reading, a wide-spread boab surrounded by tombs and growing from what, in this country, passes for a hill-like rise.

And there is his home.

He feels a flutter, a warm spread of joy, for up in the window he can see his young wife.

But oh, he has never in his life seen her like this.

She is standing in the window, her long hair down and golden in the light, gazing at her reflection in the large full-length mirror her mother gave her. That of course is business as usual, it takes an effort for her to keep looking so good. That is something that David files under maintenance and proper care rather than the sin of vanity. But what causes his pulse to race, sets his heart hard to hammering, what causes that feeling of unbelievable joy to rise in the secret root of him, is that she is as unclothed and unashamed as Eve before she bit the fruit and took the fall.

He hopes she does not see him looking at her, he senses somehow that this thing that she is doing is something very private, and not meant for any other eyes, even his own. Thinking this, feeling something deeper rising unsummoned from depths he has never known anything about, or even that he had, he retreats to a stand of trees on the other side of the house, to spare a few minutes in prayer and contemplation, and also to give Rose a brief breath of time to finish whatever it is she has been doing.

Something, on reflection, must not have been right. For while her form was undeniably lovely, beautiful beyond anything he has ever witnessed or read about, especially in that glorious light, her face was fierce and the intensity that shone out of it into whatever she could see in the surface of the glass, was terrible and wroth.

But his concern for what she was scrying in the glass was limited at best.

David is a man in love, in both the passionate and romantic senses. But he is also a man who was raised in an extremely rigid culture when it comes to topics of sexuality, inhabiting the kind of realm where a young girl is told never to take a seat just vacated by a fully-clothed young man, lest the chair, warmed by his body, deliver her into the type of excitement that will lead to damnation.

David is sitting there in the mangrove copse, the seat of his trousers becoming moist from the water-drenched moss that covers the branch that he has taken for a chair. He is breathing fast and with great difficulty, experiencing a rush that would be completely alien to an observer from a different time.

He has been married for a year and a half, they are expecting a child, and tonight is the first time that he has ever seen his wife completely naked, without even a robe. Usually the things that happen between them take place in the dark or between small gaps in their clothes, unseen, fully covered, denied as fully as possible. As is right and decorous.

It is taking all of David's strength, all of his great force of will, to allow Rose her privacy. Everything inside of him, after seeing what he has witnessed here, wants to hurl himself forward, through the doors and up those stairs, to burst into their room. And he will do just that eventually, even so. But he will do it on his terms, not giving in randomly to his animal body. He will go after five minutes, when he has collected himself. And when he returns to her he will be civilized, unfrenzied, ready to love her gently without the desire he feels now, to ravish her completely.

He can only hope that in the process of forcing a calm, his shunted passion does not tear him apart, that his new lust does not consume him as completely as a woman feeds upon a grape.

After five minutes the storm has passed. David breathes deeply, catches sight of his wife in the window. She is a streak of blond hair, the blue shimmer of a robe. He smiles and begins, with his heart hammering, the climb up the stairs' long flight to the bright tower room where his lady waits, swathed in deep silk. Waiting for him.

EXPECTING

The rules of current culture dictate that Rose never be naked, even with her husband, or washing alone in her copper-plated tub (even for that she wears at least a shift which clings but does not reveal). When they come together in the night it is through layers of petticoat and night-dress. This is correct, the vastly accepted good. Victorian rules have had it such that she has been as fully clothed as Eve, post-Eden, since her first cleaning from the womb.

Yet she is naked now, and staring, amazed at her body's pregnant swelling, as the skin brightens, the infant grows. She wonders, briefly, what she looked like before the baby took root and started growing but her heart is racing far too fast to allow for much analytical thought. She does not know where this sudden need, so like an immolating hunger for her own flesh, sprang from. Only that it's there, and so she must submit to it, or crave on.

She can see the outline of her baby, the form that distorts her skin, depicted in her mirror. That huge, high oval, standing in a Queen Anne frame, the silver mercury reflecting moonlight that makes her round swelling seem to glow, a convex bowl, turned and cleaned in preparation for the scrying.

There is some other force at work here, more than mere nature would allow.

David is gone tonight, out visiting, giving the communion sacrament to the sick, the suffering, and the damned. He left her here to commune with herself, with moonlight and glass.

What she sees is death.

In the depths of the mirror she falls into a silver-lighted vision. There is a full moon, as pregnant and swollen as her belly glittering through the tattered rags of a storm that has but lately passed. She is looking down on a ruined town that seems somehow familiar. As it should.

It is hers.

At her feet a battle rages. Bloodied dark men, howling, and in a raging swirl around them, moving in hurricane patterns, huge dog-like creatures roving. They may be wolves; it is too difficult to tell in this odd light.

There is a tall female figure standing, robed in a bloodied sheath of white, at the crossroads between boab and store. She is all in shades of light and dark, her black hair swirling in the remnants of wind, and her skin is glowing, cracking at the seams, as though she were much larger inside it. Bristling black hairs and the gleam of teeth. Her hands hold a ewer, filigreed white metal, which is somehow horrific, though it is one Rose knows. It came from the church.

Rose would run now, if she could. If the lightning firing all around her did not hold her, if she could tear her eyes away before she has seen what she must. There is a fire glowing, huge and high even in this bright-lit wet, above the robed woman's shoulder, visible even through the thick branches of the tree, and something somber and familiar tickles at the farthest reaches of her mind.

Something else for Rose to ponder in her heart, and hide.

But she is rushing upwards now, back along that twisted path, to her body which stands there, cradling another, on the other side of the glass.

Before the scene vanishes completely, before the final battle-crash of night, the foul dream deepens. The robed woman looks up from serpentine hair, her face a moon carved in miniature.

She has David's eyes.

And then Rose is back, in the room which holds her marriage bed; white bleached sheets, a garnet spread, pillows soft as breasts, and the only image in the mirror is herself, weeping.

Rose says a prayer then, just as she stands, her hands cradling the unborn infant that rests beneath her skin. She is given an answer, though only she could tell if it came from God or from herself.

She decides to forget.

Not entirely, no one has ever been capable of that, but there are caves deep within her mind where terror can be hoarded, until some use for it comes clear. And so she takes the vision of her husband's transformed eyes and buries it where it might lay seed, or even send a few roots, spreading. Burying it deep where it cannot blossom yet, in its true form.

In that instant, it is possible for her to mistake the rush of her mind's first cracking for the sensation of relief. She is, after all, essentially fine, though dreaming awake. And a small mental fissure can easily be hidden, for a while.

A sound outside her window shakes her, footsteps cracking against gravel. She shifts a blue curtain and peers beneath the hem, outlining her lapis eye.

It is David, finally, home again.

She is filled, this time, with joy. She spares a second to think, grinning; there is a good name for my daughter, and a name like that can be a prophecy. Our child shall be happy. She sets her will against something she can no longer see, shoves hard. She thinks, I do not care what it will cost me. Our child shall be happy, with David and I.

But she can spare no more time on thinking; her husband will be here soon. Picking up her underthings, her silk cobalt robe. I must look my best.

She is wearing all her garments, though un-corsetted, her long hair streaming, when she hears the creaking movement of the door. She turns to David. Smiles. Meets his rejoicing eyes.

She takes him in.

BIRTHDAY

The manse is a riot of sound, from top to bottom, so loud the walls echo with it. People are running, shouting, there is a long, drawn-out wail. There is the rippling clamor of water boiling in copper pans, the meaty sounds of sheets being torn. Malda Freeman, the new housekeeper, wipes her three-quarter sleeve across a sweaty forehead. Her silver bracelets jangle bright against her cocoa skin.

Even down here in the fogged and misty kitchen, the thing going on upstairs sounds more like a battle than a birth.

How could that white girl make so much noise? she wonders, plunging more rags in the frothing water, ready for when the doctor calls. My own mamma had ten in rapid succession, silent as the night and no trouble at all. But not this lady. Already the nurse is back with her other basin, filled up with watery blood.

Malda takes it from her, throws it out the door, not bothering to even try to salvage the pinkish rags that float there. This house is filled with sheets, there will be more. Let the vultures deal with these.

And then Cook is standing, large-boned, beside her and settling her water-roughened hands on Malda's left arm. 'The lady. Yeah. She call you.'

When Malda goes to answer she finds herself addressing a wide behind, the cook bent over the stove again.

Well, she thinks, we've got to eat.

The nurse is gone, upstairs already. Malda follows wondering why she, of all people has been called. The lady (she refuses to think of her as 'mistress') has treated her with vague kindness since she was hired, as though apologizing for a pregnancy which made a necessity out of luxury, but they have never been close.

How could they be, separated as they are by clothing, class, the tone of their skin?

On the way up the stairs she admires the wallpaper, flowers in jewel tones. She wonders at the lungs that can make that sound, and at the state of the mind behind it. The bedroom door is open, David pacing in front, still in the hall, pipe-smoking furiously, gnawing at the stem like a dog on a bone. The dictates of culture will not stand to admit him lest he see the undoing of parts he has fondled but never laid eyes on, even at night.

'Are you okay, sir?' She likes this man; it is difficult not to with his deep brown eyes and careful hands. She would like to comfort him, a small touch on the shoulder, but she does not quite dare.

He does, however, in kindness never thinking. He grasps and squeezes her hand. 'Thank you, Malda. I'm fine, just worried.' His smile is boyish, his clerical collar glimmers, white. 'Go on in to Rosie. She needs you more than I.'

Oh how she longs to call this man David. She has only worked here a few months, but her mother said that she was ever fast to love, although for Malda that passion has until now been reserved for children and her female friends. The depths of this desire, its growing, hidden roots, will remain buried inside her, never ever admitted. Instead of making the response she wants to, she nods at him, smiles, then turns to enter the noisy, sweltering room.

The doctor is bent before the altar of Rose's womb, at that place where flesh is rent, torn and made bloody in order to admit new life. The infant's head is visible, just barely peeking out from between the tender labia; the crown of its head is covered in a thick, black thatch of hair, the blood beading in the waxy vernix that covers the visible scalp.

The doctor does not notice Malda entering and so she spends an uncomfortable few moments standing in the very center of the room, listening to the wailing and the hurried orders of the nurse.

Eventually the starched lady sees her and reaches out with stained, white cotton gloves to grip Malda on the arm just below the lace edges of her three-quarter-length sleeve, leading her to the head of the bed and the writhing lady lying there. Malda sees pain-darkened eyes in a sweat-stained face the texture of chicken skin, surrounded by blond hair that falls in a nimbus bunched up behind her, tangled into knots.

The woman, Ms. Rose, looks at Malda from her vacant eyes, as though she were seeing another scene entirely, as though she were not really present in this little room or witnessing the center scene that she has formed. She smells of unwashed sweat, of blood, the unmistakable odor of shit and human skin. Underneath it all, rising up, Malda can detect the sickly-sweet scent of perfume, Lily of the Valley, David's favorite which Rose had applied to her bosom and hairline this morning, as usual, before the pains had really set their teeth in at the labor's start.

There is a calm moment, before the next insistent wave of pain, when the two women are joined together, blue eyes to brown. And then the wave comes and, wailing, lifts them up, joining them in deeper, primal ways. Malda cannot help but raise her voice in union with the ululations of the agonized Rose. Welcoming new life in pain and sorrow, and beneath all that, an inexplicable joy.

Already, Malda feels drained.

Before she can take another breath, to satisfy her craving for the oxygen she's lost, Rose's hand shoots out and grabs her wrist, closing down with surprising strength on the bangles that decorate her arm, forever ruining them. Later, when the dust has settled and the fresh blood cleared, Malda will find them flattened hard enough to leave their bright floral impressions tattooed in violet upon her skin. They will take months to fade completely. Tomorrow she will have to have the smithy cut off the bracelets with his shears. This is a loss that she will mourn bitterly for years, but will never ask David to replace. Although he would.

Right now Rose is gripping down hard enough for Malda to feel the small bones grate, hard enough for the pain to sharpen her senses, heightening them until she feels as though she could name the individual hairs on her lady's arm. When Rosie pulls her close the sensation gets worse. Malda can see the wild panic in her eyes and smell the sour carrion stench of fear in every labored exhalation.

When her voice comes it is ragged, exhausted by long hours of pushing, 'Malda. Help.' Rose is still gripping Malda's left arm in a hold that leaves no option for escape.

Malda knows her cue to action when she hears it, and positions her body directly in front of the lady, straddling her. She swings one leg onto either side of Rose's curved body so that she is kneeling on the mattress, her rear end hanging suspended over Rose's pregnancy, hiding both it and the doctor (his cruel forceps scissoring like the arms of a crab) from the frightened mother's view.

Rose peers at Malda, shocked and grateful, ignoring the exasperated mutterings of the nurse. She is thinking in her exhausted, disconnected way, What does she matter, anyway? That woman isn't any part of this. Her eyes, already more alert, meet Malda's and for now the two of them are sisters. Their future rivalries will birth themselves later, on another, less vital day. Rose lets slip her housekeeper's wrist.

Malda does not notice the pain yet, nor the way the silver manacles have been driven into her skin. Her attention is elsewhere.

She takes Rose's face between her hands, making and maintaining contact with her eyes, saying 'Now you listen here, Miss. My momma birthed ten children, one by one, myself included, quick as can be without missing a beat. She was a picker-woman,' a faint smile, remembering, 'born a slave in Georgia, way up North.'

Rose is focused now, her breathing hitched, but regular. Malda has no plans to stop.

'When I was born she was outside working, picking cotton, row on row. The war was on, but far from us. It might as well have been on the moon. All I know is by the time I was five we were free. Whatever that means. I do the same thing down here that I always did, but then it was without any money and now I get paid.'

The tale is working, calming her down. It is a good story and it does what the best of them are able to do. It makes the mind grow distant from bodily pain.

'Now I was the ninth baby, but my momma was younger than you, and you younger than me by a good seven years. But that doesn't mean anything.' Her forehead creases, thinking; she forms her words, 'Like I said, she was picking cotton, bole on bole, filling up those bags, being real careful cause her fingers were sore and she didn't want no blood on the fiber.'

Malda shifts her weight above the heaving belly, maintaining contact with eyes grown wide and luminous as though seeing the images painted by her words. 'When she started cramping, my momma squatted down and spread her head shawl over the furrows. I was born inside a minute, without trouble, without her even uttering a sound. Five minutes after that I was cleaned up and bundled in the shawl. She held me like a sling over her shoulder and went back to picking, row on row. If she could do it, so can you.'

The doctor is saying something now, but neither one of them understand it, or even really hear. Rose is too busy pushing, trying to shift this mass within her, this thing that feels like a ten-pound kidney stone, serrated. After a few minutes Malda finds herself pushing too, and the story stops while they wail together, in voices equal parts pain and relief, welcoming the new life who, after waiting just a moment to collect her breath, joins in the wailing too.

The doctor holds the baby, tying off the cord while Malda clambers over her boss and onto the side of the bed. She stands there watching while the doctor hands the child (a girl indeed, and lovely. You can tell by the crack) to the nurse who waits for it with a sterilized wet cloth from the pots that Malda set to boiling a lifetime ago.

The doctor gently closes Rose's legs, discreetly covering that torn and unrepaired hole with a swathe of white towel that soon blooms with poppies. The nurse, who has been staring intently at the infant's mobile face, slowly peels off the hanging caul. Malda makes a note of this, as the nurse hands child to mother for that first kiss, and notes too its position a little separate from the other afterbirth. Malda will fetch it later, and bury it in the ground below the stilts, underneath the high threshold of the manse's kitchen door.

David has entered, admitted at last by the beaming doctor, who says, 'It's alive and healthy, though not a son.' The medical man's blood-rimmed hand pats the new father's shoulder, gently. 'Do not let it worry you. She shall have another.'

But David is already rushing to the bed, not noticing anyone or anything around him but the mother and the girl. He is kissing his wife on her sweat-matted hair, and cupping the child's head in his palm, looking from one to the other as though his time were short, his fast long, and they the only food that could sustain him.

Finally a voice breaks through. It is the nurse, birth certificate out and ready to be filled in, 'What are you to call her?'

Rose looks up, really bright and alert for the first time since

Malda entered the room. She does not hesitate. 'Joy Marie. For pleasure and protection.'

David kisses her again, decorously for the sake of their servant and their guests, and gently squeezes her thin shoulder. The nurse looks at him, seeking approval and permission which he gives with a small nod.

The nurse inscribes the title, her fountain pen scratching illegibly until David hands her over his ivory one, the one with the real silver nib. The name is set down, permanent, made real with the ink and inscription of words.

They are all relaxed, celebratory, even Rose, who is utterly exhausted. Malda feels almost anemically drained, as though she had given something other than story. For everyone except the mother there will be fine beef tonight, Cuban cigars, the best champagne. For the mother there will be imported strawberries, ordered from the North, and soft, silken cream. For the infant, the bared feast of the breast. All will celebrate tonight, in their own ways, and the baptism will be held tomorrow, which is Sunday, in the rapturous, hunter-packed church.

The birthday has begun.

COMPROMISE

Malda brings the laundry down, cradling the basket full of baby linen, amazed at the stink of it, wondering: how can something so small create so much waste? And does the momma clean it up? No. Her hands are too white, too lily delicate to handle such a human chore. That's why they hired her.

She isn't resentful, not really, and she knows it. Jealous is what her momma would call it. She can imagine the look that big woman would give her. Momma with the strong arms, wide hips and shoulders a pillar for any child to lean upon, dressed in a floral print faded pink from so many washings and a kerchief on her head that began life as a pair of the Master's blue jeans, leftover from when they still had a master. It was one of the few things they brought with them into freedom, that and the set of silver bangles Mistress gave her, that Malda inherited and Rose destroyed.

Malda walks, carefully navigating the long stairs, trying not to spill the foul contents of the wicker basket or smudge the expensive flower-patterned wallpaper on her way down. Ordinarily the colors in such things are set and firm, remaining where the printer left them, but there is so much water here that it is difficult to take anything for granted. Take these diapers for instance. This is two days' worth of girl-baby waste, and already it is mildewing. Lovely. Just another odor for the stew.

Malda has worked here for nearly three months and she is already experiencing a great deal of difficulty, but not in the areas one might expect. She was originally from Georgia, her mother was a picker owned by an old man with many slaves and many acres. Sometimes she moonlighted in the kitchen when the

Masters were having an especially large party. Her mother had the potential to be an excellent cook, all of the elements were there: taste, a good sense of balance, a passion for fine things and an eye for presentation, but she never received the proper house training when she was young.

The prettier little girls were the ones usually chosen to learn the ladies'-maid manners and culinary arts, and Reeny Josephson (given her master's surname, which she changed to Freeman after her emancipation) was a thick dark thing with childbearing hips by ten years old, used as a picker from her earliest childhood and made into a breeder from the time of her first blood. But as she got older the slaves around the compound noticed that her cornbread never burned and always remained fluffy and light. So she was brought in to the kitchen whenever she was needed, returning to the fields when the hard work was done.

She wanted better for the daughter she was able to keep and when freedom came, she did her best to provide it. Though she could not arrange a proper reading education, she apprenticed her pretty little girl and set her up to trail after a maid of all work who served in one of Savannah's nicest houses.

Since Malda was a smart girl, a quick learner with excellent retention, she rapidly improved in manner and skill, and by the time she was twenty she was in high demand among the Georgia elite, used to working for a high salary and able to choose her own employers. But she soon tired of Georgia.

The Jim Crow laws there were harsh and strictly enforced. She had absolutely no reason to suspect that things would be any easier even further south, but they could hardly be worse. From what she'd heard about life in Tampa and the surrounding swamp no one was likely to spit on her just for walking on the sidewalk instead of in the street.

And that was a good part of the problem.

People here treated her like a human being. And it was giving her pretentions.

When one of her friends, a nice high-yellow girl working as head cook for a family called Dawson, heard that the family's minister friend from the North was heading down there with his expectant wife to service a swamp church and that they would soon need a qualified maid of all work, Malda jumped at the chance. Her friend warned her that the life in the swamp would be pretty primitive, but then, Malda reflected, this almost-white girl did not spend her childhood sleeping on a scrubbed dirt floor. She doesn't know what primitive is.

So, her confidence at a high and her desire for adventure rising swiftly after it, she sent off her letters of recommendation (all, most assuredly, excellent) and awaited her expected reply, which came three weeks later on gilt-edged linen paper in lovely masculine hand.

And now she should be happy.

She has a good job with a truly excellent salary and a little cottage all her own a few streets down (no attic room for her). The walls are freshly painted (no whitewash or lime either) and the furniture is plain, but in good order. She has been informed that the table, desk, the bed and chairs, are hers to keep even after she finishes out her term of employment, and this generosity lambasts her. She has never in her life owned so many things. And all of them are fine.

And still, still, it is not enough.

Her mother would be appalled at her. She's come down to these good people, in this place where people are polite to her; even if none of the townsfolk treat her precisely like a lady, Mr. David does. And that is the thorn at the crux of it.

David.

A white man, and married to boot (to a woman who she is

trying her hardest to like), with a new-born child. And she a maid who has kept her heart caulked tight and airless as the deepest vault. Well, the seals are broken, her doom spilled out and her job is suffering for it.

She is in the kitchen yard now, kneeling before the well-oiled pump that works with a minimum of priming, shooting cool, clear water over the soiled diapers to wash away the filth. She is pumping furiously, much harder than needed, in an effort to get herself under control. It doesn't seem to be working, her thoughts are coming fast and hard, the water rushing with it, in bursts like blood thrust with the pulse, and all furiously directed at herself.

Couldn't just have decency, needed honor too. Couldn't just take care of herself, no, Malda needed pride. And now she has gone and fallen for, but no.

She cannot say it. Her job is suffering, best just to leave it at that.

David is her superior, his lovely wife, too. They are her employers if not her masters. (She will never have another master – decided that long ago.) She must do her best for them. But if she is to do this, she must move beyond the feelings that constrain her. The only question that remains is how can she do it?

The answer comes from her mother, as all good solutions seem to do. She hears it in her mother's voice, deep and honey-smooth, the voice of a woman who was rarely angry. Why child, all you gotta do is love. If love be the problem, the love for one man, what you need to do is spread it round a bit. If you wanna love a married fella, you gotta show it by loving the wife. And you done a bit of that already when you helped her in her birthing.

You want to be with Mr. David, honey? She asks herself in her dead mother's voice, and answers: You gotta love his wife.

She finishes the rinse, moving the diapers over to a waterproof oak basin that she fills with hot water and bleach, stirring the white cloths with a pinewood paddle, not wanting to get any of this caustic mixture on her already chapped hands. It is important, in this environment, to keep your hands as dry as possible, especially if your work generates a lot of friction. Work with wood, brushes, and powerful cleaners will scour your palms until they blister and constantly bleed.

She can do that. She must. Mrs. Rose seems like a nice enough woman, even-tempered, kind. The next time Rose enters a room where she is working, Malda will do her best to strike up a conversation. Providing, of course, Mrs. Rose speaks first. There are stranger things than friendships grown up between servant and employers, no matter the skin. Stranger things have happened, she thinks. I'll try to seal the bond we started the next time I can.

That opportunity comes later that day, when Malda is ironing. Rose asks for her help in selecting the pattern of the new drapes for the dining room. Malda answers her, adding a bit of color commentary for good measure, saying, 'Just so long as you don't get nothing too loud,' fingering the vivid patterns for curtains that would be facing out. She hitches a slight smile up on the left side of her mouth, preparing for a risk, 'You don't wanna get the neighbors to mistake this for a cathouse.'

Rose laughs, and snaps back, 'Well I almost wish they would. This place could use a little excitement.'

Thus their friendship was begun.

FAMILY TIME

David differed from most men of his age. He enjoyed reading and not merely owning books, thinking them good for much more than vainglorious display. Also, he enjoyed cooking as a hobby so that whenever their cook would let him near the kitchen he would bake cookies or bread, a tendency that surprised the lucky few who could partake in them (though the town children knew how delicious his brownies were), and he had a secret fondness for chocolate that belied his sparse frame.

But the thing that set him out the most, in the rough minds of his hunter townsmen, was the way he had with women: all women, regardless of station, even their own wives, even the servants. He was known for having an especially close relationship with his colored maid Malda, and though the men who sat and gossiped at the store's counter searched hard for any sign of infidelity (for Malda was attractive for one past thirty, if dark) they found nothing much beyond the yearning printed on the maid's fine face.

He did not limit his female-inclusive speech to the topics of laundry or children – his strangeness went far beyond that. He would converse with them on the same level as he questioned the men. He was always courteous, overtly respectful of the laws of marriage and culture. As a minister it would have been strange if he had not been. In fact he had counseled several of the men into marrying girls they would otherwise have been quite happy to string along.

The surprising thing was that the marriages that resulted from his talking sessions were known for being unusually happy ones, much more satisfying for the couples involved than they otherwise would have been. And whenever anyone thought to ask David why that was, he would say nothing, drop his eyes a bit and smile.

But still, the men thought when they were speaking in groups, elbows up on the shop counter sipping soda water stirred into the sugary rum they made in their stills, what kinda self-respecting fella talks politics with his wife or asks for financial advice from his housekeeper? And, while we're on the subject of his purty little blond-haired woman, wasn't it funny that she never seemed to be marked? She never walks with a limp or acts especially tender with one of her arms. In fact, they say with exchanged glances and raised eyebrows, if you reckon it right, we've never seen that lady with a single black eye or split lip. It's downright disconcerting. If he don't want to apply some discipline how long can he reckon on going before being disobeyed?

Every fella knows that sometimes discipline is necessary. Can't be helped. Women just seem to get into trouble, they're like kids that way. Always running off their mouths or arguing. Burning the supper or serving it late. Even if you've got servants they still somehow put the food on after you're ready for it. And when stuff like that happens, well, it's sad. The hunter speaking would shake his head, take a mournful sip of rum from his flask, continuing, it's sad, but you got to train them. Can't do nothing else. It's even in the Bible; you know the place, spare not the rod. A preacher should know that.

But then you look at him, out there talking to lady folks like they actually knew something, all the while his wife makes out like she's the queen o'Sheba or something. Strolling around with her hair all loose, like a, well never mind what it's like. They shake their collective heads, shrug the compelling image off. They say, never mind. She's a good lady and he's a fine man, and the best damned preacher we ever had. Collectively, they grunt. A form of agreement.

And that was usually where they left it, moving on to other subjects. Plume prices for the season (going up) or the current struggles of the hunt. How to combat the numbers of bird corpses that seemed a bit lower this year than they had been the last. Nothing to worry about, the flocks must come back sometime. But it was still discussed.

As for David himself? He was for the most part oblivious of their storefront ruminations. He married them, buried them, and prayed for them all in his secret heart, in his office and at home, before meals and bed. And anyway, over the last couple of years he'd had better things on his mind than some worry over gossip.

His little girl was three years old and getting more interesting by the day. Not that she was ever boring. No, she was his dark-eyed pleasure from the very first day. From the time she slipped from his wife, all deep hair and wide eyes, questioning the world. The men at the store counter would be completely appalled if they knew how often it was David who shook himself awake at night responding to the sound of crying. It was such a pleasure to soothe her. They have a special smell, babies. A soft powdery scent that fades when they are old enough to be noticed by most men. It was an odor that David loved, and when he held her up to his night-shirted shoulder, he would pat her back, gently, until the crying ceased. Breathing her in.

He loved to play with her when he wasn't busy at work. He would marvel over how quickly she was developing, how quickly she moved from grub-like sleep and feeding cycles, to rolling over, crawling, speech. The moment she said her first word, baba, signalled for David her shift from creature to child. And finally standing up and tottering around unsteadily for a bit, her fat fists gripping the steadying chair legs until the moment when she took her first shaky steps to her father across the well-polished library floor.

He fed on her beauty. His love a strange mixture of proud parent, artistic connoisseur, and disciplined anthropologist. And now that she was, as he judged, old enough, David would settle down and teach her how to read. He left his office early today set on this very purpose, and now he seeks them out, his daughter and his wife.

He finds them, mother and daughter, in the library, sitting on the ground together and rolling around a bright red ball of India rubber. He smiles at the look of joy that moves between them. Rose's smile is a reflection of the pleasure experienced by their little girl. Every time Joy sends the ball rolling away from her she is so taken by the motion that she just has to squeal and clap her hands together, amazed by the motion taking place before her on the wooden floor.

He smiles at Rose, asks forgiveness for interrupting to commandeer their daughter while he scoops the red-dressed little girl up into his arms, all the while drawing a green-bound book of fairy stories down from the shelf. It is his favorite. It was a gift from his father and one that he has had for the great length of his life. He settles with her in the deep stuffed chair, sinking into the comfortable leather, the same shade as the book he has selected, finally ready to give young Joy her first true lesson.

As for Rose, she knows how lucky she is to have married this man.

Most fathers couldn't be bothered with babies, unless they were boys, happy to shift all of the work onto the children's nanny or mother, content also to miss the best, most interesting parts of their children's lives. She watches them there in the green leather wingback, the color of leaves, beneath that unsettling picture-window. Why did he select such a dark subject for a room meant to be filled with life, with light? Rose has never asked. It is burning like a shared aura over their identically-bent heads, father and daughter drawn together, in feature and in purpose, lost in their own small world.

Rose cannot help but feel just a little left out.

She knows she should not feel so. Watching David's long fingers trace the shapes of words in a book, opening up new possibilities for their girl, but still it is difficult. Her own father never took this much effort. She never knew what it was that she missed.

Rose can remember, just, when David used to direct such all-encompassing, passionate attention solely towards her, towards the contemplation of her perfect, never-naked body. Though the looks he gave her then had some other, darker fascination in them than are present in the tender, gentle kisses he bestows upon their daughter. And thank God for that, she thinks. David feels the right kind of love. She just wishes he would direct some more of it to her.

No, there is no denying it. Rose is hungry for her husband. Well, she thinks to herself, it is only correct. I am his wife, we are meant to feed each other. I suppose there is but one solution.

Rose smiles to herself, closing the library door behind her as she leaves, setting the tapestry that covers it swaying like a wind blown through the branches of a tree.

There is a cedar trunk upstairs, the same one she brought with her into David's house when she left the one belonging to her father. The one that once held her dowry. Buried within it like a treasure, wrapped in sheets of fine gauze, there is a dress both translucent and small, incredibly scandalous. She purchased it, blushing, on her last trip into Tampa from a disreputable shop and has hidden it here, a sweet marital surprise designed to kindle a small fire.

She slides into it now, the silk near weightless on her body, swelling against some places, gathered in others. Her long hair clouds out, diaphanous around her, scented with sweet Lily of the Valley as Rose, all enswathed in gold and white, lays with her blue eyes open and her lips slightly parted, gently smiling, breathing softly and waiting for her husband to come upstairs and welcome the night.

She will not wait long.

And when they come together in that place, flesh upon flesh for once and wrapped only in sheets, they will know as so few ever get a chance to, what true happiness is. No matter what horrors follow this moment, they have it now. A life rich, delicately sweet, and good.

The men who gather to gossip in shops have no knowledge of this life either, or of the passion that it signifies. This is probably just as well. Such men as those, who beat their wives, are never the recipients of *this* kind of tenderness.

Oh the beauty of the night, so swiftly passed. We do with it what we can, and also what we must. And it is never enough.

COYOTES

Coyotes have myth without language, stories told in song, passed down through generations in voices ululating and long. There was a tribe of wanderers that ranged out in desert darkness, sending out lonesome melancholic voices.

This pack, a loose conglomeration of family, followed the leadership of a solitary alpha. A dusty, bitten (though still-fertile) bitch with a long, flat-muscled flank, clipped ear and yellowed tooth, who knew, as though by some secret intuition, where their game would run. She led them to rich warrens fed by streams, where they could sup to glutting on flesh, marrow-filled bone, and rich blood.

This wordless tribe worshiped in their canine way the huntress aspect of the virgin who runs with the moon. They sent their prayers up in long songs that sounded like alien weeping mingled with smoke, vast echoes of mourning and joy.

The huntress, known as Hecate by mortal tongues, sent her signs down, visible to some, in the shadows that she dug, her vast sickle scraping the silver scry-bowl moon.

The alpha of this tribe, female descendant of an ancient blood-chain of seers, saw Hectate's bone-call on the moon while out alone hunting. She was one who watched the skies as often as she took her scenting from the earth. A rover, a wanderer, aching to begin the journey she was born for, ready at all times to run wherever her beloved goddess sent, and her pack would follow close behind. She would never have a name but alpha, though her long-descended pup would.

She saw the sign while tracking a nest of still-blind rabbit kittens. She could smell them: young, hot, impossibly fresh, as

44

though they had adopted some of the flavor of their mother's new-grown vegetable food. The alpha's nose was down among the old scents, buried in the dust; owl waste, serpent skin, the rank fug of hawk spatter, the soft, faded bloom of desert rose. The kitten-scent was beneath all that, a taste fit for her master, purified blood pouring from a beating heart.

The only sound she could hearken now was the biting crunch of her own paws as her weight crushed the small ice crystals formed in this cloudless air after the departure of the sun. She was thinking of nothing but the feast at hand, and the pleasure left to spend before it. In a moment she would be digging down, claws scrape-thrusting, until she reached the warm and fur-lined den.

She would leave a token offering for her Lady of the Moon, a marrow-rich, part-gnawed femur perhaps, before feeding herself and toting the remainder back to her kind waiting on the ridge. While the thought, if it could claim that complex honor, was making its slow way from conception to deed, some ruffling of fur made the hunting alpha set her eyes glancing up.

Her mistress waited in the face of the moon. The goddess of all dogs, virgins, and hanged men. She, whose sigul is silver cast in blood, who appears at crossroads and in glades, all the deserted areas of change. The alpha coyote heard the call that emanated from that sky-bound bowl of bone, the song her people longed for over centuries of generations, the desire for it that had carried them long in desperate anticipation.

The child had been born, at last.

The alpha sent her mingled cry aloft, flavoring the sky with her vast tracings of sorrow and rapture. The pleasure stemming from the knowledge of the birth, that long waited, flowering joy. The child! The child! Sacred avatar, for them to serve in human incarnation. In smaller part there would be the pleasures of the run.

The sorrow spread from the message's other part, the dark twin to her knowing; the child was born, and she would die before she had seen it. For this would be a journey of long generations.

She shook the grief off quickly, maintained the joy. She would be the one to set her kind off, one prophecy fulfilled. It was more than she had ever wished for. She must be content with that.

The time has come for running. She sends out another call to raise her kind up, and they answer with ghostly voices, calling her home to their scratch-camp on the hill.

The rabbits are forgotten now, there is other prey close to hand, and her pack has a journey to set off on.

She can see them gathered there, already prepared, the young ones hefting the blood-drained corpses of rabbits, serpents, and the occasional carrion-scented desert foul that dripped black feathers. The old ones cradle infants with folded ears and useless eyes, sleeping in their grand-sires grizzled, loose-toothed jaws. All are ready to begin.

That lovely Lady, their own moon, lights out their trail for them as all good gods do. A bright line in the scrim and scree of desert places, and the tribe, already large and growing, sets off on a journey that will outlast generations. They run together, alive and joyous, paws falling to the rhythm of their rapturous hearts. To cross the breadth of time and space and see, at some great length, the physical desire of their innermost hearts.

Childhood

PARISH

They had a lovely time, for a while, in their manse-home in the swamp, as did the vast majority of town's folk. The hunters brought in flocks on flocks, toting light avian bodies home in bags, their lithe forms broken of all grace, poured out onto the wooden sidewalks in base piles. The children used boiling water to scald the feathers from the skin, though not enough to discolor them with heat, cleaning out the blood from quills and sorting the plumes into boxes by quality and size.

They did not have to do this work; their fathers provided more than adequately. They did it solely for the candy money, at least at first. There was no unemployment in town now. Even the drunks worked some of the time, earning at least the cost of a beer or tot of rum by collecting the pinkish denuded corpses and depositing them in a cesspit five miles out, where the rot would feed the soil and make the sugar sweeter when it grew.

The birds were naked, save for their heads which were sometimes removed to fill a special order for an ostentatious, bead-eyed hat for some fine lady in the North. And until the flocks ceased flying and the plague came to replace it, the town was a haven of plenty and warmth.

The air is almost always warm down this far south; the humidity ensures an even temperature, water being a wonderful insulator. In springtime the swamp is lovely, a walk outside feeling as refreshing as a warm bath, and the rain, when it falls, is the temperature of flesh. It is a pleasure to walk in, a pleasure to run.

Children, the minister's young daughter included when she was old enough, used to frolic in it, chasing each other, occasionally wrestling as joyous as new colts, drunk on the bare fact that they had life. They watched the rain turn to diamonds in the air, to be found and plucked up by the sun, departing in a rainbow glitter, leaving the grass, the trees, the very waterways they played in looking crisp and refreshed.

The summers were oppressive, the heat never-ending. Indoor places were like saunas, hot but with water collecting on walls and in corners, thick drops that must be immediately wiped to salvage the wallpaper. People stored bags of salt inside their closets to try to save their clothes from mold, a strategy that worked part of the time if they ignored the water-laden weak places that split seams along the armpits of the ladies' dresses and the yellowed crotches of the men's jeans. Paper was salvaged from sodden books by placing blotting pads between the leaves, and as for leather, well, one must hope for the best.

If the indoors was breathless and terrible, once you passed the porch-stoop things got worse. Outside it felt like an oven, furnace temperatures rising up from the ground in waves, turning standing water into fog. This was TB weather, when people seemed to transform into pale, anemic shadows of themselves, hacking gobbets of their bodies out into handkerchiefs and sweating droplets of blood out of their pores. Not that tuberculosis was the only disease, or even the worst one. It was just the most prolific.

There were the occasional malarial outbreaks; with that much water pooled around there were plenty of mosquitoes. But they were hardly ever a problem during the day and the smoke from kerosene lamps kept them well away at night. Though if a man or woman ventured out past sunset to visit or carouse, it was judged best to keep their jackets on, as well as their hats, in spite of the heat.

In 1906 fifteen people, all of the same family, died of cholera caused by the father fetching contaminated water from the swamplands, dragging brackish buckets of the stuff from the marsh. When David asked him why he'd done this on his last comforting visit, walking into that sweltering room that smelled of vomit and watery shit, the man said that it was easier for him, the swamp being right there and the town's filtered pump a further hundred yards down. He said this, pausing every few moments to sick into a pot, while his little ones, the nine of his own youngsters, and his brother's lads as well, were half delirious and screaming from the intensity of pain that wracked their guts. David gave them each a blessing and anointed their simmering heads with sacramental oil that beaded where it touched, thumbing out the cross above eyes that looked out, lovely as ornamental glass, and equally unseeing. The following week he buried the whole family in one long ceremony in the churchyard, consigning their well-corrupted flesh to earth and the incomprehensible mercy of God, to rest in peace at last.

He thanked God, even as he cast down the first rich handfuls of black earth, that the father had secured insurance enough to purchase coffin-caps. These were the cement vaults poured over the sarcophagi to ensure that the bodies, once buried in this shallow, waterlogged earth, would not be able to make their buoyant coffins rise like an air-filled bottle in the sea, always floating to the surface.

This had happened before, and it was never pleasant to walk to church, cutting through the graveyard, only to find a hand or skull thrust up through earth like the remnant of some half-eaten thing that had been buried alive. Especially since he, as minister, would have to re-sanctify the site and bury the body part, tying a rock to the femur or between the teeth of the skull to keep the bones held down, under the waves of semi-liquid earth.

After that ceremony he was exhausted from tears, his own as

well as the town's. The father was a lazy, stupid man (his was the only house that was never painted, though they could easily afford it on the profits from the plumes) who only made a decent living on the pleasure that he took from killing. His children had done all of the actual work, cleaning the feathers, plucking the birds, sometimes even eating the flesh when their daddy could not be bothered to go to the store. He was lazy, his children were not. And all of them belonged to God.

David felt each loss as a personal failure, holding himself especially accountable for the death of the children. He had known most of them from infancy, baptizing one a year since his arrival here in 1889. He'd had all of them over to play in his study at one time or another, and had taught the eldest elementary Greek.

He had been a smart lad, and driven, the little boy named Bob. He'd had potential. Now he was there, pale and unresponsive as clay (though not cold, never cold here) lying on a white satin pillow, soon to be stained. His oldest female cousin has slipped a purple, lyre-stamened passionflower into the box before internment, resting its petals against his too-white face, its perfume lavished on a nose that could not trace it.

It was a waste.

No matter how you looked at it, it was a waste.

The mass funeral was over and, being Monday and therefore usually his day off, there was nowhere he particularly had to be and nothing that he was required to do. But David did not feel like going home yet. How could he look at his lovely wife, at his incredible, fiery daughter after seeing all those waxy faces laid out, in their coffins, row on row?

Ordinarily, at times like this, he would retreat to the church, a quiet place, red-carpeted and incense-scented, the organ-colored pre-Raphaelite stained-glass windows depicting scenes of death and resurrection tinting the air inside to blood so that the sanctuary resembled, when the light was right, a vast and beating human heart. Which, David supposes, is exactly what it is. This is the heart of the place, the center of the town, supplying the pulse of their community along with the sacred breath of God.

Other than his library it was his favorite place to rest. But today the Women's Society, a conglomeration of bored wives and mothers, were giving it its bi-weekly cleaning, scrubbing down the pews and mopping the moisture from the walls in their never-ending battle against the damp.

He will sit beneath the tree.

It is a large boab, with generous, low-spread branches standing on a ten-foot rise, which, in this flat marshland, qualifies as a hill. It is perfect for reading under, which he does when the weather is fine and his other haunts are unavailable to him, its branches shading him from the worst of the sun. There are no graves here, yet.

It is in the far corner of the churchyard and there would have to be many deaths to bring the coffins up so far. Now he crouches on the soft grass that springs up under the branches, shaded by the sun and looking down a vast expanse of grass into the marshland where even now some birds still flit and sing. The only thing he must watch for here are serpents coiled among the rocks, cucumber-scented moccasins, their fanged mouths open, ready to spring.

But there is nothing waiting here now save for two anole lizards, looking like miniature alligators. Their skin is khaki-colored, pebble-textured, plain looking, but for the male who displays a strawberry-colored flag beneath his jaw. A flag which he unfurls in threat and, as he is doing now, as a means of attracting his small, winsome mate. Their spines are slightly ridged, their tails curled together, the reptile equivalent of clasped hands, as they twine their bodies, serpentine and rapturous, being fruitful. Multiplying.

David sits down, but not too near. He does not wish to disturb them.

In his pocket is a thin book, covered in red morocco leather, a dull-shining jewel. *The Iliad* in original Greek. This is his third time through it. He never tires of this story, the whole tragic construct; the interfering gods (appearing when they feel like it to change the course of mortal life, and almost never for the better) the lovely lady and, of course, the awful fall.

He is deep inside the story as the light sinks down, the long, unhappy day forgotten. He has become so absorbed that when his daughter, a thin but happy child of very nearly six, climbs up onto his narrow thighs, he nearly shrieks out loud from terror and surprise.

He sees her face, sharp but already lovely, surrounded by a corona of hair so dark it verges on black, staring up at him with his own eyes. He transforms his shriek into a laugh and, stuffing the book into his breast pocket, he takes and scoops the small girl up.

'Dinner's ready, Daddy.' She giggles, raucous as a little crow, as he hoists her up high over his head, so close that she could touch the boab's branches and pluck the berries hanging there. 'Mama sent me.'

He swoops her down again, making avian noises, for she is flying, imitating the hunting cry of her favourite bird, the red-tail hawk. And when he is finished landing her gently, says, 'Well then, my darling, shall we race?'

And they are off.

Father and daughter run; the girl's coltish legs pumping, David checking his stride but maintaining the appearance of effort for the sake of her pride, dodging past trees and through fence gates until they reach the high steps leading through the back door to the kitchen where they clatter past the cook and Malda. They skid around her skirts before crashing together in great heaving strides into the federalist dining room that is really too dignified for this much excitement. They find Rose sitting at table already, her blue eyes glowing, laughing so hard at their expressions that she can hardly seem to breathe.

And then of course, there is the golden light of evening, and a meal shared with love. The great sadness of the day is buried, as it should be, underneath this field of love. That does not mean that it won't rise (all things do here, given time, everything resurfaces and all things that rise must soon converge) but at least there is respite for David, a time of happiness and love, to fend off the long night, losing himself in family, food, and later, song.

Before the coming ravages of the night.

STITCHES

Rose and Malda were in the kitchen, a clean room painted yellow with a pattern-embossed tin ceiling to both add beauty and maximize the light. Soap was not yet in general usage in food preparation, but Cook was enamoured with it, especially with the lavender-scented cakes that David brought back from his occasional trips to Tampa. She washed her hands often, especially after handling a bit of pork or chicken. She did not know a thing about germs, at this time hardly anyone did, but she knew she could not stand the smell of raw flesh on her fingertips. Nor could she stand the scent of even slightly spoiled meat. She would not, like most people in the town, use anything a little rancid for the basis of a sauce. She thought instead: let the seagulls have the scraps, if they can stomach them.

This is why no one who ate the food she made ever died of it. Cook's sensitive nose.

Rose is sitting at the blond-pine table, ornately carved. She usually prefers the darker woods, and certainly something more solid than pine, but teak and mahogany hide stains and since this table is used for laundry as well as preparing food, her aesthetics must be sacrificed for necessity. Besides, this is not a room that visitors travel in often, just trade-men, the servants, and herself. She sits across the table from her maid, an unusual bending of the rules of class, but over the last six years they have become closer, joined by the blood-ties of the act of birth.

Besides, who else would she talk to, way out here? She is separate from the other women in the town by virtue of her status. The minister has to maintain a certain amount of distance from the people of the town, if he is to be able to handle the delicate fabric of their souls, if he is to remain worthy of handling their confidences. Such responsibility does not make for many close friendships, and some of that distance has rubbed off on Rose, although the theatrical nature of her appearance contributes to her sense of alienation and loneliness.

Still, whenever company arrives all of their dialogue is 'Fetch this, Malda.' Peppered intermittently with a demure, 'Yes Missus', the response delivered with requisite downcast eyes.

They are alone now though, save for Cook who does not count, and so the rules are relaxed though not completely obliterated. Rose sits at one end of the table, embroidering serviettes inside a wooden hoop, her fingers moving in a blur of emerald and lapis thread, placing passion-flower blossoms down upon an otherwise white field, laying them as gently as flowers on a grave.

Malda is on the other side of her, repairing socks.

They are both excellent seamstresses – they have to be, it is one of the few marketable skills a woman is allowed – and their fingers are equally calloused along the tips but the similarities stop there. Rose's hands are otherwise soft, smooth as cream and perfectly manicured. Malda has worn her nails away doing the wash, and her palms are rough as sandpaper from the sweeping and the butter churn.

They are mostly silent while they are working, but today Rose brings a subject up. She begins all of their conversations, though they both enjoy them. It is the custom for her to speak first, rules of class and race can only bend so far.

'Have you heard anything else about the sickness?' She speaks in a carefully neutral tone, not looking up. She knows that Malda has her own connections, an open stream of gossip and news that flows underneath the noses of the Hunting Rich.

'Some of the workers have noticed people covering coughs,

but not that many.' Malda focuses on sealing a difficult seam, finishes it, picks up another sock. 'I know that a lot of us servants are leaving, though not so you'd notice. They were the part-time people for the ones who couldn't cover full-time live-in help.'

'Are they afraid of disease?' Rose does look up at this, her blue eyes wide, her face a white circle in a nimbus of hair. She knows what she fears. Emptiness. Abandonment. A dark, ruined place. 'No, not really. Some of us, we think that the TB come from Tampa. All those sick people comin' from way up North. To recuperate. The Masters bring it back with them when they do the high-class shopping.' She looks up, her brown eyes soothing to Rose, as they almost always are. 'I don't think the sickness is gonna be a problem. They're leaving because of the feathers. Because there aren't enough of them. The big hunters are still okay, they got lots of nets and lots of shot, but the little ones? Nah. There aren't enough birds. So they cut costs. I don't expect that, after a while, there will be any but the Big Boys left. Except of course for the shop, Mister David, and you.'

She has finished the last sock, moves on to the minister's white drawers, which she handles with a special tenderness. Malda does not know why he doesn't throw the things away, they are by this time more patch than cotton. He is like a child that way, she thinks, running one brown finger tenderly across the seam that joins the legs together. So innocent. So sweet.

Malda catches a soft smile forming on her lips, and quells it. Rose is here, after all. And Rose is her friend.

Looking up, she says, 'A town will always need a minister, until it ain't a town anymore,' she catches the terror those blue eyes exude when she lets those words slip from her tongue, and does her best to shore up the rent. She lays her platitudes like stitches, a skilled seamstress of feelings as well as fabric, sealing the tear, 'but that will never, ever happen here.'

'How so, Malda?' Rose is frightened, and close to weeping, but she could not tell you why. 'Surely it can happen anywhere?'

'Because the sickness is hardly spreading, so that's no problem, and even if the birds run out, and they won't, there is always something else. Maybe they could switch to some kinda farming. Grow oranges like they do in Braden Towne.' She puts down the repaired undergarments, breaks another rule by extending her hand, which Rose takes. Malda sees their fingers interlocking, ivory white and teak brown. 'And in any case, that won't happen for years. Trust me, Missus,' she squeezes reassuringly, 'if anything does happen it won't be for years. And anyway, you got a wonderful husband and a great daughter, why you wanna worry about something that has no bearing on you now?'

Because, Rose thinks but does not say, because I have a wonderful husband and a beautiful daughter. And also I remember something that I cannot quite see. Instead of commenting further, Rose clasps Malda's hand again, before releasing it, smiling back at her friend.

The women sit together, working on related, but very different things, luxuriating in silence while Cook moves, unseen in the background, preparing them a luscious feast that all will share, in different rooms.

Life is variable but very, very good, seen in this mellow kitchen light.

MALDA WALKING

Joy has been six years old for three weeks, which makes the puppy she leads by the collar three months old. The animal was a gift from her father. A wriggling, yapping bundle of baby fat and fur, that wonderful smell that pups have, warm and irresistible, utterly indescribable, but something that once you have smelled it you never forget. A scent that, years remembered, causes a warm stirring in the chest and a smile to rise to the lips.

You could not pry the two apart now if you tried.

Joy is training Bess to follow with the lead. Malda is training her. They are only going as far as the general store across the street from the church. Mrs. Rose needed some new embroidery needles and some lengths of cobalt thread to finish the serviettes she has been embroidering as a gift for a newly-wed couple in the parish, and they will be appreciated. Her needlework is exquisite, and there are families in this town who will keep her gifts for generations, providing her with immortality, of a kind.

The Blue Tick hound puppy is new to the leash, as is her mistress but Malda thinks it is eerie how quickly they are falling into step together. It is almost as though they had some primal connection. Bess fits her growing shoulder up against Joy's calf, the indentation of the puppy's bone locking with the convex swelling of the muscle there, the two flowing together in perfect synchronicity. It is uncanny, thinks Malda as she watches Joy turn to look at something (a figure, waving) and seeing the puppy's small eyes turn as well without ever seeming to look up to gauge the correct behavior from the movement of her mistress.

A few steps more down the path through the trees, the one

that leads from manse to church, to main town road, and Malda can identify the figure. It is David, and he is beckoning, 'Come.'

Malda's heart speeds up for exactly half a beat, long enough for her reason to reassert itself. He is calling to the little girl; the maid is, is as always, incidental. She can feel the heat rising in her face, visible in spite of her coloring. She tries to quell it, then doesn't bother. White men almost never look at her closely enough to detect a blush. And while David is not like most of the men she has worked for, he might notice but there is absolutely no chance that he would be able to interpret the thing he saw.

One of the traits that first attracted her to David is also his most frustrating feature: his purity, the ever-visible goodness of his soul. He is not innocent, no one is, but he tries harder than most. David cannot consciously do wrong, though sometimes he wounds inadvertently and he is far from perfect. It is possible to be too trusting, too willing to sacrifice yourself for others (especially if you have a family, especially if they need you and you put the parish first) but still, he is good. This surety of faith seems to send a light out from him, transforming otherwise somber, rather blade-like features into something boyish and soft, lending a soft upturn to his lips and a childlike gleam to his near-black eyes.

Malda never stood a chance.

And never shall. Unlike many white employers with former-slave help, David has never looked at her in any way that would not be appropriate for an upper-class white lady. He is respectful, courteous, asking her opinions on current events as though she were his equal, while at the same time occasionally kissing her hand in greeting or dismissal. Nothing more than a thin brush of lips against skin on her way out to Negro Services (held Sunday afternoon at six, after supper has been laid, and led by a black circuit rider who makes the bi-weekly trip from Tampa). The sensation of his breath against her fingers never fails to stoke a high fire, deep down in the places where her momma used to scrub extra hard with a rough rag, to discourage the urges.

David is sitting under the low-spread boab he likes to read under, smiling up at them, red-bound book in hand, his place marked with his thumb. The title, just barely visible, reads *Wuthering Heights*.

Joy and her puppy run up to greet him, and he catches up the girl, remaining seated himself, and swings her thin body high over his head. Bess yaps furiously, forepaws low and tail up and wagging, wanting to join the fun playing out before her, just out of reach.

Malda knows just how the little dog feels. She is smiling stiffly, outside of the circle made by father and child, outside of the shade too. She can feel the heat-sweat building up in jewel-like beads underneath her armpits, in the creases where her small breasts meet ribcage, and in the hollow of her crotch. She sincerely hopes she does not stink.

Malda makes a habit out of rubbing her foul places with Arm and Hammer powder, the baking soda is supposedly good for preventing this kind of odour, if you believe the advertisements in the *Tampa Tribune*. But then, they also say that the product is good for teeth, a process she tried once and never will again. The powder was foul-tasting and the texture was vile. She just hopes the 'odour eating' action is, for once, exactly as advertised.

She can't decide if she would like for David to notice her that way or not.

Not that he is close to noticing her now. Playing with the girl like that, reading her a page from that far-too-frightening book. It is one that she had made it about halfway through before having to stop, frightened out of her wits. And the fact that she can read at all is testament to the goodness of David. He taught her, on his own time, calling her away from household chores so as not to infringe on her few private hours. He reads his daughter a section from an early chapter; the one where the idiot narrator mistakes a brace of dead rabbits for Catherine Linton's pet cats. He reads out loud and traces under the words with his finger, Joy's flashing black eyes moving with it, absorbing the words.

Soon she will be reading entirely under her own power.

Every few minutes he lets out a small cough that leaves his complexion all ivory and roses, nothing to worry about, probably. But it is a bit distracting for the girl, who looks up every time he lets one slip.

This is ghastly reading for a child, in Malda's opinion, and only an innocent or a fiend would set out to teach it. Well, that's David for you (dropping 'Mister' if only in her mind): an innocent. I must hope his daughter's purity survives his childlike ministrations.

Malda's lips quirk up, watching them, just as David chances to glance away from the book for a half-moment. Seeing her expression, he sends her a sweet smile, kisses his daughter on the forehead, and closes the book.

'Go on with Malda now, Dearheart.' He stands to take her to the maid, stopping to stroke the puppy's silken head and receive a kiss from doggie tongue. And then, addressing Malda in the same breath, 'I'm sorry to have held you back.'

She cannot seem to look up from the ground, or quell the roses in her cheeks. 'No sir, you haven't held us. We're just getting some needles for the missus, and some more fine thread.'

'Still,' he places his long, spidery hand on her thin, well-muscled arm. She suppresses a small, pleasurable shudder, 'I am sorry to have delayed you.' He reaches into his pocket, draws out a quarter, silver eagle flashing. 'Buy yourself a treat with this, a cooling tonic or one of those cocoa wine sodas, something refreshing, and also something for my girl.' He smiles down at the reflection grinning up at him, ruffling the dark thatch of hair, so laden with sweat the curls clump and seem to writhe against her scalp like snakes.

Malda takes the quarter with a small curtsy. 'Thank you sir, the day is hot and this'll help some.'

She has felt this way for six years, and she loves Rose like a sister. God help her. He'd better, she thinks, because no one else will.

And with a wave of his hand, he is down again, settled in among the branches and the roots, his book once more wide open, lost in a world of cold air, ghosts, and the wailing sound of wind on moors, lost in an alien world.

Malda takes little Joy by the wrist, the girl leads her puppy, and they, hand in hand, with wandering and slow steps, through town take their solitary way, crossing into the bustle of the store. With a fire stoked and blazing in her heart's sealed room, cannibalizing its own oxygen and feeding on her living flesh, Malda silently burns.

COUNTRY STORE

Mr. Joseph Mackenzie is a short dark man, a fastidious dresser with a penchant for monocles (he owns twenty-seven, ranging from plain brass to gold-lighted ebony, all of no particular prescription) and the inability to stomach any sort of bad news, a failing which he consistently blames on his ulcers. He has owned and run this store for over twenty years, stocking his shelves in the early days with basic staples and hunting supplies, having a great turnover on skinning knives. These range from the basic iron-clasp model, designed for work both quick and rough, breaking after only a use or two, to the exquisite ivory-handled Damascus steel version, the dense white elephant-tooth base scrawled over with silver filigree and various sizes of birdshot.

Over the years, as the wallets of the townsmen have grown heavier and deeper, as they started importing women to become their wives, his stock has developed in richness and variety to help lighten their loads. Now he has everything from a wide selection of foodstuffs, both basic and fine, to clothing goods, bulk items and even, occasionally, fine furniture, a bit battered by the time it arrives in town perhaps, but then considering that the last thirty miles of the journey are spent being jostled by mule-cart, it is amazing that he has them to sell at all. And do people buy them? Of course they do.

These people want status the same as everyone else, and the items that he sells, the ladies especially favouring the Queen Anne-style armchairs in jewel-tone red and deep sapphire, only slightly scratched, and the Chinoiserie armoires, their black lacquered smudged, of a type the rest of the nation forgot decades ago. But what does that matter? The fact that no one wants them anywhere else means that he can get them all cheap and make a good mark-up. Just so long as the market holds up here. And it will. It takes a while for the changes of fashion to make it this far south.

Now his store is bursting brimful with goods, the many shelves jam-packed, with every available pinewood surface covered with items which never sit there long. Just last year he installed a brand new chrome soda fountain at the glass-topped counter near the front, the one that still holds his wide selection of knives sharp enough to skin anything up to the toughness of gator-hide in under five minutes flat. He serves Coca-Cola, New-York Egg Creams, Barques Root Beer, and plain, ordinary soda and rum to the nearly exclusively male customers who gather there to drink and exchange gossip as fiercely as women gathered at the central pump to do the wash.

While the men at the counter, all over fifty, all worn through from work, are the main purchasers of lukewarm soda drinks (he never got the cooler working, not that anyone here ever notices) the main shoppers are almost uniformly female. They are the ones who handle the household money, taking the plume-earnings from their husbands and dividing it up into three piles: household expenses, which they keep, fun money which goes back into the men's pockets, and government cream-takers, reserved for good old Uncle Sam. Because there is nowhere that a revenue man will not go to vacuum up another dime, even down in the depths of this swamp.

Today the shop is full of the usual swell of people and chatter, the healthy signs of a prosperous town. And if there is just a bit less spending going on than usual, no one comments on it, or even notices. The slow downward slide of the profit margins is slight enough that even Mackenzie can't really track his losses when he gauges the balances at the end of the week, though he has noticed that credit buying is slightly on the rise. Well, that is easy to explain. The birds, while still plentiful, came in slightly fewer numbers this year. This is a mild setback, not any sort of decline.

The men at the counter are dressed in their usual blue jeans and chambray, still dressed like workers, even if their uniforms are clean, even though the vast majority of them are considered rich men. They are watching the ladies pass on the wooden sidewalks that stand a good few feet off the street that swills, as usual, with a good few inches of water. The puddles are composed of mean brackish stuff that swirls with threadlike white mosquito larva. Not that any of the men are particularly worried about insects now, they are too busy hoping for a lady to slip on the slick wood, and perhaps expose a sliver of ankle for them to capture with their eyes and take home with them tonight for use in their bedrooms.

By this same token, all of the men who sit patiently, awaiting a slip, are hoping that the woman who falls will not be their own wife. But such is the gamble and such is the risk taken with this sort of game. The opportunity to see flesh is balanced by the possibility that the bodies other men will see are as good as your own.

Still, Mackenzie reflects, polishing up a just-cleaned glass, it is better this game than their usual dark gossip. He would much rather put up with a little Tom-peeping than listen to unfounded tripe about their neighbors' insolvency or dangerously blood-speckled coughs, which seem to be what most of the local gossip consists of just lately, that is when the men are not looking at a woman and guessing how many times she's been had, and by whom.

This is the game they are playing now, having given up on the ankle-spotting. It is more fun for them, there are more women to choose from and the time is spent in creating and not just passively awaiting a fall. Right now they are studying the preacher's black maid, that girl Malda, who is just crossing the street toward them with Reverend David's little girl and that wee one's small puppy trailing obediently in tow.

She is, they agree, fairly attractive for a negro, and an older one at that. She must be well past thirty-five by now, edging closer to forty. But she has had no children and so has kept her figure trim. They take turns naming the men that might have paid her to spend a wild night, each name growing more and more unlikely. Ranging from Philippe the one-eyed drover, who has probably at least considered making an offer, to the parson himself, which spurns on loud laughter, for they judge correctly that he is too pure. He is so innocent, in fact, that some of them are amazed that he even knew how to father a child, in spite of the undeniable beauty of his wife. And had the child not looked so undeniably like him, you can bet that the men would have cast their dispersions on her and felt in the process completely justified.

But look, the maid they were talking about has turned toward the door. It looks like she is coming here, no long walk after all. She is bending down, her hand on the child's shoulder, saying something to the girl who smiles, nods, picks up the dog to carry it in. They must be doing their grocery shopping.

The men all fall silent, nodding to her politely enough, some murmuring a vague 'good day', but none of them rise from their seats to greet her properly, as they would do for any white woman. Even one who made her living washing sheets, scrubbing floors, or lying on her back. Malda is aware of this but thinks, at least they let me shop here. At least they don't curse me, or spit on me, throw me out on the street like they would back in Georgia. In matters such as these any progress is good progress. One of the benefits of being in a place so small and isolated as this is that there isn't enough variety to justify a Negro shop.

After a few moments, all the while feeling rows of male eyes boring small smoldering holes in her rear, thighs, breasts and back, she finds the sewing supplies that Missus Rose sent her out for. Sharp needles and dark, bright-dyed sapphire thread. When she goes up to the counter to pay she sees McKenzie's small signal and lays her coinage down on the counter rather than even trying to place it in his white hand. He bags up her purchases, carefully writing the colors and quantities down on the brown paper wrapping in spear-proof grease pen. He does this for the benefit of Rose, so that she will know if Malda were stealing.

He has no idea that the maid can read, or of the friendship that the women share. How could he? She and Rose have been so very careful. They have had to be.

Malda sees the shopkeeper write down his columns of item and numbers, correctly gauging his assumption, but she struggles not to be offended. It would do no one any good and might actually harm the families' relationship with the town. Both Rose and David are sensitive about her treatment and status, a fact which leads to Malda protecting them from quite a lot in order to preserve the family's reputation as upper-class. And she must protect the innocence of David who, if he were aware of the treatment that Malda has grown so used to receiving, would try to change it, which would be disastrous.

In any case it does not matter, even these small indignities are so much better than the treatment she received up North in Georgia, a place where if she complained, ever, about anything, she would more likely than not end the day with a broken face, severely beaten, unable to chew anything but the softest mash for days.

At least here they are nominally polite.

When she has gone again, child in tow, leading on the leaping, flop-eared puppy (a good potential hunting dog, if ever there was one) the men turn back to the counter and continue their talk, looking out the window and signalling out the ladies as they pass.

They are ascribing more and more romantic rendezvous to more and more unlikely subjects, until Lucky Reinhold suggests the pairing of seventy-eight-year-old Gladys Williamston with sixteen-year-old Buddy Eisenberg. He is a kid so young his voice only dropped last year and he has a face so ugly it makes the pimples on his ass look like beauty marks.

All of this leads to a massive bout of loud hilarity, laughter so strong it leads on to crying, which the men are forced to struggle hard to disguise when, five minutes later, three members of the dignified ladies' auxiliary strut their decorously-covered legs and harsh patrician faces through the open door. They have come to purchase soap and furniture polish so that they can finish wiping down and polishing the church's new hardwood oak pews, which are in this climate, already growing moldy.

This is what the town was like once, when it was alive.

Death

I

THE SKULL BENEATH THE SKIN

David stares at himself in his wife's oval mirror, a curve of glass high and wide enough to hold his whole frame. He leans into the silvered surface, until he is close enough for the fog from his own breath to obscure his face and he can see himself only as a body with a pair of scintillating eyes. All of his other features are lost in a gray cloud that spreads from his nostrils, transforming his head into a void. He pulls back, one hand still gripping the finely-carved mahogany frame, and wipes the condensation, watching as he reappears beneath the passing of his sleeve.

He is a man who ordinarily avoids mirrors. He finds nothing quite so fascinating about himself that it could justify such close scrutiny, knowing that a stretch of polished silver that catches light can be as much of a border place as moonlit crossroads in the night. And the thing about borders that he always remembers is that at such places things can cross. The space that most people think of as reality blurs and fogs, and other creatures, older things with deeper roots and a firmer grip on the bedrock of a deeper reality, can enter into our paper world.

Once, he knows, the intruder was God.

It was the equivalent, he thinks, of a writer forcing onto the page to move among his creatures there; a beautiful, if terrifying, concept. How could He make Himself so small? It is a question he has no desire to court. For to such creatures all attention is worship.

But the demands of necessity are never to be denied, and he must look for what he already suspects, to confirm or deny at last. And David is praying that the things he sees in that glass are lies. His heart refutes that longing.

No. It is true.

The face that stares back at him was always thin, slightly beaky about the nose with thin lips and deep eyes. He looked into the glass as a child and saw severity; he has no mental image of the way he looks wearing a smile, though Ruth could tell him, Malda too. The way his face seems to light up with the expression, as though someone were holding a yellow-glowing candle beneath his mask of skin.

His face is even thinner now, the flesh hollow, as though scooped out from within so that his cheekbones rise prominently as knobs and the skin of his nose is stretched out tight against the bone. His eyes are pouched below the lids with purple smudges, almost bruises, and there are beads of sweat at the deep hollows of his skull that cannot be attributed only to heat. He can smell himself, too, now that he thinks of it, and the odour does not belong to the soured, honest sweat of labor or unclean skin. It is a deeper odor, like the stink that rises from a shallow-dug and un-capped grave.

He tries to attribute these changes to age, but cannot. After all, he is hardly thirty-five, and even after ten years in the swamp he cannot be yet considered ancient, or even old. Just ask the Miltons, their nearest neighbors. The man is older than God, and his wife only slightly younger. They've been out here hunting since the start of the boom, and stayed these last years when the birds started to run out. Unlike the rest of the town they don't seem to be suffering for it – he must have invested in the stock market or some other Tampa-based venture. But still they remain, hale, with her apple-doll face and the gent with his four orange-colored peg teeth, living well.

No, this is something else.

He fatigues easily, just lately, requiring a nap in the middle of the morning and another past midday. And his appetite has fled.

Foods he once loved taste sour and spoilt, though it has occurred to him that that may be attributed to the taste of his mouth. He has seen the way that Rose has taken to avoiding kissing him, though she can't be conscious of it, the way she still bends toward him whenever he enters the room, like a flower inclining toward the sun, and she still is passionate enough in their dark bed, though he rarely has the energy for it any more.

But by far the most concerning things are the coughing that he can no longer suppress and, linked to it, the new prevalence of blood.

He has started finding pinkish stains on the armpits of his shirts and in the creases of his drawers. He has urinated and divulged a pinkish stream. His saliva is the color of tired roses and, when he coughs, the sputum is a dark, arterial red, a color that tells him the one hard fact that the mirror he looks in can only confirm.

David is terribly afraid.

Not of dying, no, the darker part of his nature longs for that, as most Christians do. Once dead, there will be only God before him, and who on earth could want more than that? No, he is afraid for his family, for his girls. All three of them. For his lovely wife and her white hands, for his child, the fruit of his heart, and for the woman that he has come to think of as a sister, despite her black skin (a feature that he has never truly seen, at least not the way most men do). What will happen to them when he has gone? He must think of that, not that he has accepted the fact of his going.

Before he came here, he was a rich man. His father had left him a vast inheritance, and Rose's dowry was large, but all of that is gone now, or most (there is two-hundred dollars in the locked drawer of his desk, emergency supplies), and all that he truly owns is locked up in the form of possessions inside this very home.

The last few years have been hard on the town, on the children especially, and he has bled his fortune away a drop at a time, feeding it into the economic veins of the families that surround him, of his parishioners, until business picks up again. As it must. After all, those children, some of whom are grown now, must continue to be fed. They are not like fallow earth which, left to itself, brings forth fertility and growth. Left to themselves they find only poverty and death.

Add to that the fact that the church has been unable to pay him, and he has paid for recent repairs himself, and paid the last five shipments for the grocer who has extended credit to his customers so long that he no longer qualifies for any himself.

And what have all his efforts amounted to? The town is dying, people trickling out one by one, leaving anemic houses whose shutters clap in the hollow wind, leaving behind nothing but the graves in the churchyard and a few names scratched out on sandstone tablets, a few dropped photographs lost in mud, and empty skies whose silence is hardly ever broken by the call of a bird.

All around him, the world is dying, and into his house he brings the same. He only prays he does not contaminate his family, more than he already has.

And what is he ever going to tell his Rose? Those eyes, so blue, so innocent, he cannot widen them with this knowledge. He cannot burden them with this truth. And poor little Joy. She is hardly ten.

He watches his lips firm down to slits, the mirror projecting him at his worst, so that he can trace the shape of his own skull beneath the skin. He must survive, at least another few months. He must get his family out of here, back up North. In civilized company they may be poor, but cared for. They can even, should it come to it, sell off their possessions one by one and live on that until his wife remarries, as she definitely will. A woman as beautiful as she, even widowed and without dowry, will not remain without suitor for long. And Joy is going to be a beauty too; that combined with her admittedly masculine education and vast intelligence will surely get her far.

But he must live to arrange it, and that means refining his focus and conserving his strength.

David moves away from the mirror now, swaying slightly, just a bit dizzy. He braces himself against the banister supporting the bed, his fingers caught in carved flowers, blossoms that will outlast the age.

He will never sleep in it again.

He thinks, I must move my rooms downstairs to save the walking. Rose will be hurt, but I must make her understand. That alone might purchase me another week. He moves to gather up his things but cannot seem to manage it. I will have to have Malda fetch them.

The trip downstairs takes close to five minutes, him weaving the whole way, breathing hard, but when he walks into the kitchen where the ladies are sewing, Rose on embroidery, Malda on repairs, he enters there erect, his lips stretched tight but smiling. Looking if not like the very picture of health, at least its distant cousin.

He has a lot to plan, a lot to do, but first there is this announcement. He is ill, that is all they need know, and exhausted from his work. The family could use a long vacation. After he announces his change of rooms to the women who sit, wide-eyed and with paused work, he will retire to his office and really begin to plan.

WILL

David is still lying to himself. He thinks that he has time. He has been sleeping in the small back room for days now, waking up later and later each morning with a red stained pillowcase, the cotton batting clumped and clotted, scabbed over like an over-used bandage.

It took him three days of struggle before he knew he had to quit the church and the little work left to run and maintain it. There are only a few women left in town now, and most of them are living under his own roof. None of them have any inclination towards cleaning the vestibule. He had been trying to maintain it himself, saying, when I get home I'll get started on the paperwork for moving, write my letters, and my will.

By the time he'd been out for an hour he was finished, completely exhausted. He could not stand to see his family's worried faces, all of them suffering for him. It was enough to make him want to cry. But if he did that, they would think he wept for pain, and they would waste their tears on him.

No, there was nothing he could do, except give in. Now his wanderings are limited to the path that leads from his new bedroom to his library and study, and back again after the light has fled.

It is terrible, how he reaches out in the night only to find his wife missing.

But there is no time for nostalgia. That has passed, along with the time for physical love. What remains is hard, and deeply buried, the diamond that rests in the heart of good marriages, feeding on the flesh. Rose will still have that. It will outlast her life.

The pen in his hand is carved from solid ivory, a protuberance of skull where words flow out in thick black tide. It feels right in his hand, slightly talismanic, as if this dead thing he inherited from his father were holding some incredible force, ready to be brought to life.

Son of man, can these bones speak?

Perhaps it is the fever.

Certainly he does not feel well, as if the light around him were bending, a hole in the world to let something through, a creature too big for it, like Christ was on the cross. Too big for this world. It buckled under the weight of Him, hung there on that hill of bones, and spooled us all to hell. The words on his papers waver and shine, they could mean anything.

He had better stop looking.

Instead he shifts his head, a difficult thing in this thick air, and looks at Persephone in her stained-glass room. She turns her chin, looks back, dark eyes contacting his from their nest of pale skin and flaming hair. She raises her pomegranate, red lips moist and smiling slightly, takes a bite that sends the red juice flowing.

This has got to be a fever-dream. Please God, let it be.

The air is thick, solidified light, on the point of tearing. There is something huge, immensely real, throbbing below the surface of the air before his eyes, about to break through.

David knows that he is screaming but has no idea what. He only knows the world is bulging, fit to bursting with the pressure and the joy. Maybe he can use his pen to burst it, to let the creature out from its cocoon, the ivory base, the silver nib, so sharp; surely they could puncture fabric already grown so taut? He reaches out, his arm outstretched to make the cut when suddenly a vast pressure he was unaware of, like a dammed-up tide, lets go at last, and hides the flaming air in flood.

That blood-dimmed tide is loosed, and everywhere the

ceremony of innocence is lost as a delicate vein bursts somewhere vital in the hollow chambers of his skull. His brain is flooded with a stream of liquid, cells drowning like children lost in a hurricane, irrevocably lost. David slumps across his desk, pen in hand, ink splashing everywhere in thick, black wash, obscuring all that he had written, whatever it was. The last thing he sees is light of lovely intensity, and the last thing he feels is a sense of terrific peace, a long tunnel, leading through green woods, to a soft clearing lined with moss and a small, clear stream where he can take his rest.

When Joy finds him he is slumped over, but breathing. She heard him screaming, so how could he be asleep?

And yet he is.

He is unconscious when Rose and Malda come across them a few minutes later, when all three females, struggling and grunting, shift him into bed.

He never wakes, but who knows? Bodies in this climate are well-known to rise again.

FEVER BRIGHT, BURNING

Midnight and Rose is burning, her long hair filament bright, each thread highlighted by the candles that surround her, and the room is ablaze with dizzying heat. Her David is lying in the dampened bed she sits beside, eyes rolling, unconsciously delirious, coughing up blood that spatters against the wall in mauve droplets, and against the sapphire fabric of her long dress, which she will never change out of.

The man she loves is dying, badly, and there is nothing she can do to soothe or aid, save what she does now in the flame-broken darkness, the moon wide and full as an aureole, shining through the window and backlighting her head. She runs her fingers through the furrows that sweat has planted in the hair of his scalp, feeling the concavity of his temples, gently dabbing with alcohol and cotton to soothe his heat with vapors.

David is much possessed by death; she sees his skull beneath the skin, the shadows creeping up to fill the hollows of his eyes, obliterating his light. And she is so afraid.

Over the last few days she has bitten her nails right down to the quick, feeling that fine hairline crack in the surface of her mind spreading into yawning fissure, but yes, she is fighting it. Refuting the grief. She cannot tell if the blood that rims her nail-bed belongs to David or herself. She does not care. There is no distinction.

This is what marriage means.

A basin of water, just off the boil, and a soft rag are placed on the table beside her, to clean the stains and use the heat to cool the raging head. She looks up to see Malda beside her; the maid's face is calm, her eyes weeping, as though she held a deep well inside her that she was unaware of and it has reached the surface, to flow until it's gone.

Malda looks calm because she has made a decision. If David leaves tonight, so shall she. She might as well help now, while she can.

Rose knows none of this. All she sees is her friend, who stands there beside her. She forces herself to smile, an enormous struggle, takes and squeezes Malda's hand. The effort of comfort. David would be proud. If he were conscious. Maybe part of him is.

All that Rose knows is that she is praying, as hard as she can, begging a God she does not comprehend for something that the rules of nature would make no exception for, to the creator of nature, who makes His own rules, and follows them with very few exceptions. She might as well pray to the Lady in the moon.

Probably she has tried.

The dog is whining in the hall, too afraid to enter, too afraid to leave; she paces, her head low, her tail hanging, before the open bedroom door.

All is stillness save for the rise and fall of ragged breathing, the occasional hacking cough shattering the still in this highly-wrought, opulent room. There is the body, yellowish pale, lying on the narrow bed, its head turned into the bright-patterned wallpaper, as though seeking solace from the colors. There is his wife beside him, a vision of gold and sapphire, a well-set jewel, sitting in a Queen Anne chair. There is the dark lady, returned to servant, cradling a silver-colored, blood-filled bowl.

And what is that small motion there, the red crumpled dress capped with dark hair? A little girl, just barely ten years old, her face pale, prematurely set in somber lines, though not yet weeping.

Joy.

One of her father's long-fingered hands has slipped off the

dark-covered bed and his dry-eyed young daughter cradles the tallow to her cool cheek, where it burns like a brand.

There is stillness here, the quiet sounds of falling water and air-hungry frame. Breathing that serves no purpose, postponing drowning, and the occasional cough which rends the body, the guttural sound of tearing meat.

Joy has his hand, Rose the heavy, sweat-drenched skull and the drops welling from his pores that dye her hands to match her name. Malda has nothing save his blood in her bowl. It is enough, for all three. It has to be.

There is nothing else.

But moonlight, flames, a silver basin, a road to cross, and three women gathered at last alone in the small, fading circle of family and light.

HAMADRYAD

Malda left the small back room in a daze, her eyes wide and blank, her footsteps faltering, walking as though she were the only survivor of some vast explosion, the scenes of death and battle still playing before her eyes. As they were. Her long white nightgown was spattered with blood and sputum, eye-shaped droplets running up the length of her full sleeves, and an oval smudge placed by Rose when she collapsed against the maid's strong neck after it was all over, stood out like the mark of Cain on her high collar.

She had dropped the bowl, somewhere, its silver sheen already lost to the tarnish of coagulation. But her right hand was not empty. She had picked up the long knife from the foot of the bed, one that was previously used for jointing meat, the edge honed and curved into a sickle shape. Sharp enough to de-wing a fly, mid-flight. She walks with it now, past the cemetery and church, into the mangrove swamp that leads out to the vast, uncharted sea, her numb fingers locked around the carved bone handle.

How is it possible for her to be so calm when all her world has fallen down around her, when there is such loud tumult in her breast? She must walk forward, one step trailing into another, until the moonlight leads her to the place she needs to go. Though it helps to have at least one goal.

She walks, barefoot, over root and bog hole, past hanging vine and startled, shrieking birds, the palmetto blades slicing her thighs, carving out Cyrillic words and curses in red calligraphy against her soft, sparsely-haired skin, like monk-text on ancient, time-dark vellum, messages she cannot read, written on her body for someone else.

The moon is full, desolate in her realm of sky. She follows where it leads her, never caring where that is. She died tonight in all but body, and there is nothing left to keep her here, tied to the manse-house in the swamp. Her bonds have finally been cut. She is free. Free enough, at least, to do this.

Rose did not notice when she left; after she had clutched at Malda for a while, hysterically weeping, her blue eyes disconnected; the right one looking at the ceiling, the left at the body in the bed, as though her brain had fractured straight down the middle, leaving her disconsolate, but mercifully uncomprehending.

Once Rose had exhausted herself, Malda gently detached her arms from her tear-moistened neck and, like an over-tired child, Rose crawled into bed beside her husband, curling her body close to that fever-burned corpse, as though in an effort to warm herself back into life.

Rose was almost instantly asleep, and safe for the moment, though the part of Malda that was still thinking wondered absently what life would be like for her when she woke up.

She was already moving.

Malda passed Joy on the way out, clutching to the frame of the door as though holding herself up. The girl's short nails were digging into the soft wood that held the brass latch, her face leaning into the doorknob, the one with the yawning face of a lion. Its snout and tongue were pressed up against the child's pale cheek, as though giving her a kiss, and there were deep black circles under her eyes, nearly as dark as the irises themselves, so that her infant face resembled a hollowed-out skull, prematurely wise with the understanding of death. Her expression was a reproach to David's life, lived as it was, a grown man's face with childish sheen made meaningless by a little girl with adult fears, cowering behind a pine-wood door.

Malda patted her on the head, her fingers stirring long black hairs, too infrequently washed, a rat's nest already. Her last act of kindness. The girl stared up at her, knowing, but said nothing.

There was nothing to say.

Now Malda is following a deer path in the deepest woods, out to some undiscovered country in the West, the world's last great adventure. She runs with the knife held, blade up, tip down, pressed against her surging thigh, the muscle bunching and releasing in a rhythm with each stride, until it almost seems as though she is flying, the marsh unspooling silver and black beneath her flickering feet.

For a moment, she is happy, a girl again, as she was when she first discovered what it meant to be free. Five years old and spending her first morning indoors, with no foreman's whip to summon her from sleep, and no gauntleted fists beating on the door, her face curled against the soft breast of her mother, who will rise in two hours to make bread that is meant for only them to eat.

She is forty years old, and has loved only once.

But it has lasted ten years, feeding her, a constant flame to warm her heart. She has never been kissed full on the lips, though occasionally a well-loved mouth brushed past her knuckles, and she is as much of a sealed vessel now as she was at birth. But there are worse things than the life she has lived. She knows this, and feels no pity for herself, just a gentle sadness, a quickening of the hidden places lurking in her heart.

She was never used for breeding like her mother, who never knew the man who fathered her children, only that the masters called him their 'stud'. She never had to surrender her children at seven years old, just when they were becoming remarkable people with personalities and interests all their own, never had to watch them sold out from under her at markets she was kept away from, locked into her hut like an animal in a pen. She had never had anything to sell.

Malda does not know why she stops where she does. All she knows is that the sweet running turns suddenly sour, and the moonlight reflecting in this clearing is so comforting and bright.

She stands there, feet plunged into ankle-deep water, feeling something cold and scaled slither its way between her legs, a fanged triangular head erect above the tideline of the water. The air smells of cucumbers and rot, moccasin, but she is unafraid of serpents, and too tired to even try crushing one underneath her heel, though she will swipe out with her knife if one comes too close. The water is churning with the creatures, now that she can see more clearly, knots of snakes writhing through the water like wingless birds, each one holding enough poison to kill five grown men, should the urge descend.

Malda is worried for a moment, and then resigned. She does not care.

Directly before her is a large boab, the only tree in this empty space, and it is a huge one. Its trunk hollow in the center, smooth bark riven with an entrance shaped like an enormous open eye or the top-view of a coffin, a home for a hamadryad, perfect for Malda. She fits perfectly inside, with a little room left over to move her arms, so that she and her new crevice look for a moment like a tree come suddenly to animated life.

She rests her head against the inner surface of bark, smelling the soft rot, the sweetness of desolation, cool against her fevered cheek, the moonlight silver-plating everything, the wood, the spreading bowl of water, her own dark skin. And for the first time in weeks she feels perfectly calm, at last, her body a diffused field of peace.

She has known all day what her secret mind was planning, though she had hidden it till now. Why else would she have brought the knife? The moon is singing lullabies, a harp-like plucking in her tight-wound mind. Smiling, she closes her eyes.

The knife is light in her hand, so light that the tidal moon can draw it up, raising the blade until it hangs level with her neck, a bit to the left. The moon is singing, her sad light soft, as Malda drags the blade across, painting another smiling mouth, rouged and ready for the night's hard love. Her eyes never open with the motion of her arm; the edge is honed so fine it might have been an egret feather she drew across her throat.

Her long gown darkens and the silvered ewer of the clearing becomes a basin filled with blood, a mirror for the moon to bathe in, a pool for the hunter-goddess to slake the hunger of her dogs.

The large-spread boab sleeps deeper now than it has for long centuries (at its wide roots there are a tangle of small bones, early offerings, one tendril running through the hollow socket of a feminine skull), it is whole again, its heartwood filled; a new spirit quails at this bright hell, chained into the hollow of a tree.

Eventually the bark will close around the body. Perhaps, many years from now, a wanderer will find it, a boab with long leaves, like a lady's fingers. Unbelieving, they will snap off a branch for proof. The sap will run unusually thick, unusually red, and in the outpour of that fluid, a soft voice will speak, the chained tree-spirit, with a voice full of tears and a story to tell.

But if anything like that ever happens, it will not be for a very many years.

Now there is only moonlight, blood, and a lost, bone-handled knife.

GRAVE

It was hardly a funeral. Who was there to conduct it? When David breathed his last, sending a foam-spattering of blood against the darkly-papered wall. After that last cough, the final breath expelling the last half-liter of air, flesh-scented, that the body holds in the very bottom of the lungs to stave off drowning, Joy dropped her father's empty hand and ran out into the hall.

She wanted to go further, wanted to run so far and so fast that the significance of the moment just passed would not catch up with her, as though she could outdistance time. But she knew even then, at that young age, that there was no place left for her to go. And so she stood at the threshold, one foot in that room of death, the other facing out into a place where a sort of vague half-life was at least possible, the lighter hallway leading out where her dog, shivering violently, leaned up against her naked leg.

She watched her mother wailing, drawing her long blond hair out tight as though to fiddle grieving music on those strings or pull the tresses from her scalp. Rose sat, hovering over the body, a pale Atropos without shears, as though she could prolong the life already expired there by drawing out her golden threads. There was a blank look, glassy and lost, settling into her deep blue eyes, unfocused, as though they were not looking at any one direction, but instead were wandering from place to place, divorced from one another.

Settling nowhere.

Joy reached down to fondle Bess' soft ears, and felt her anxious tongue instead. She could smell something uric, and at first suspected the dog, before noticing the warm moisture coating her legs. She was deeply ashamed, but still could not move, caught between stirrup and the ground, suspended in that place where it seems a moment could be repented, time reeled back, while all the while the hard earth hurtles toward you as you plummet from your mount. She knew then that all safety was illusion and the bedrock very hard.

She would not forget.

And all the while Malda was standing there, her face a ruin of utter calm, looking right in her cheek, brows, nose and lips but with utter devastation in her eyes. As though she were watching the stars collapsing, throwing down their bodies all around her, plunging the whole world into endless night. She carefully set down the bowl, splashing a bit of water on her sleeve, exchanging it for a long knife that had been used for bandage cutting which rested at the foot of Rose's chair.

Joy called out to her, softly, in a voice so quiet that it may have echoed only through the corridors of her mind, a place already darkening, but the woman paid no heed, she was walking off already, only stopping for a moment while passing the chair the widow sat in. That lady, gold-haired Rose, sprung up, as suddenly as a figure in a puppeteer farce, the jerky motion of wood-joints drawn by string, and fastened her arms around the high-collared neck.

Malda stood there, patient and uncaring as a hired horse, and let the widow vent her sorrow. When the body was, at last, exhausted, Malda slipped the sapphire-clothed arms back down to her sides, and Rose back into her chair, as easily as one would reposition a doll.

The knife was in Malda's hands the entire time, but if Rose felt the point of it she made absolutely no sign. That terrible blankness, those Armageddon eyes, remained on her face throughout. When Malda passed her, exiting Joy's life forever, she was not anyone that the little girl had ever known, walking like a body possessed by some sweet, far-off voice prophesying doom.

Even Bess felt the change, edging ever closer to the girl's small body as the woman slid by her until Joy was pressed so close to the frame of the door the woodwork left its mark printed underneath her clothes in blue and purple for well over a week.

With the stench of urine rising from the doorway to the hall, Joy strengthened her resolve and went out to fetch some help. She had a difficult time finding any.

The town was already a shell; people had been leaving for weeks in droves, packing up their wagons with their nets and clothes, the occasional fine thing purchased at the height of the hunt. One man last week had nailed dried vulture wings onto the side of his caravan, a bitter joke. Off, he said, to find more profitable death. The world could always use a hunter, and here there were only bones.

The houses still looked inhabited; at this time of night the people yet remaining had been long asleep, none of them had lights. Joy had to rely on the memory of which families had fled, knocking hard on doors that led to empty rooms that echoed with the shades of better times. The Mackenzies? No. Rodriguez? No. Philliburts? No.

Miltons? Yes.

The old man responded to her banging, and the frightened howling of her dog, by opening the door with his .44 locked and loaded, its black barrel staring at the door. His mouth was pulled into a grimace that displayed four yellow teeth and one squint-shut eye of cornflower blue. He was so convinced of harriers, come to raid and strip the dying town, that for a moment he really saw them there. So convincing was this half-second vision of a hoard of dark-skinned, armed men that he had applied half a pound of pressure on the trigger.

Another few ounces and the story would have ended there, with Joy gut-shot and bleeding on the porch of an old man, but his eyesight had cleared before then. No sickle-armed hoard out for murder and rape, just a frightened, pee-stained girl and a howling dog. He bent down and carefully laid the gun on the floor, praying please no accidents tonight, before opening his arms up wide enough to receive the shivering body of the child who, seeing the welcome, ran to be held.

It took half an hour to get anything out of her, she was crying so hard, and the dog would not leave her, would not sit and wait patiently on the new-swept porch. Nothing to do but carry her in and let the dog follow. Thinking, if the missus sees me doing this, I will never hear the end of it. Nor will I ever understand, the minister's pretty little Joyce all filthy and crying, not a grown up in sight, the dog howling like it's seen a banshee, and with all this noise not a single light in town, save at the manse. Where did everybody go? They must have slipped off in the night.

By then, of course, the missus had arrived and, saints-be-praised, she said not a single word about the dog. He had the girl still in his arms, seated with her in a chair in the kitchen, rocking her among the packing boxes and the crates ready for shipping. His wife, her normally cheerful apple-doll face tight with worry, dug the kettle out of its packing and used it to heat some milk for cocoa. Eventually, with love and an abundance of kind words, they pried some semblance of the story out.

'We gotta go over there, Papa, get Miz Roze.' His wife was already lacing up her high-buttoned shoes, 'It's not right to leave her there like that.'

'No, Mama,' the old man said, stroking the dark hair of the child in his lap, who snored lightly, her face calm at last, 'you heard the way poor Joyce told it. I doubt if she would notice tonight if we was there or not.'

'But what about the body? You know the preacher wouldn't leave us like that. All alone.'

'He isn't alone. His wife neither. Besides,' he glanced down at the sleeping child, 'we'd hafta leave her here and I'd hate to have her wake up all alone. We gotta think of the kid.'

In the end they had come to an agreement: stay there with the child for the rest of the night, and then one of them remain with her throughout the day while the other went over to the manse at the first shred of light to see what, if anything, remained of that horrible situation.

Mrs. Milton stayed with the girl, engaging her in cheery talk and trying to convince her to eat waffles. Joy took a few cursory bites, but left most of it untouched on her plate, smelling wonderful and dripping with rich syrup, but churning her stomach with the sight. When she thought the lady wasn't looking, she fed a few forkfuls to Bess. Mrs. Milton pretended not to notice the syrup stains on her hardwood floor.

The old man found the preacher and his wife in exactly the positions they had held when Joy had left. Rose was completely unresponsive, her lapis eyes staring in two different directions, a creepy, wall-eyed glance, as though her brain had split right down the middle, with each half taking one eye and one half of the world to stare at through it, the right completely divorced from the left. Luckily, she was as easy to move as a rag doll and as pliant as wax, not resisting at all when he put her to bed upstairs.

Next was the body. The very first thing he did was close the eyes, milky already, and constantly staring, like three-day dead fish. He found that he felt considerably easier after he did that. Less prone to running.

There was no way that he could move the body, but he knew where there was help. The offices of coffin maker and undertaker were occupied by one big man, Bluff Bill Ramone, a huge

Spaniard tanned to the same shade of mahogany he carved his boxes out of. His family were packing up but had not yet left. Milton found him in his office four doors down from the shop, packing up his wares with the help of his six sons who dropped what they were doing and came to fetch the body.

They did what they could in the time they had, but there was a boat to catch from St. Petersburg three days hence and in any case there was no embalming fluid left. Still, the Ramone women washed the body with care, and dressed it in David's Sunday best, while the youngest daughter went upstairs and tried to get Miz Rose to eat, with limited success. It was, she said, like feeding a shake-addled baby. You could get the food in, all right, but when she breathed the mash tumbled right back out, smearing the front of her pretty frock.

The girl was worried at first, but as the day progressed past sunset into night, that strange, dazed look left Rose's face and she started saying simple words mainly consisting of the names of people, lost in the night. When she left that evening, giving up her watch to Mrs. Milton, she thought that the lady would probably be able to speak and talk again, but she did not believe that she would ever again be right. She seemed, for one thing, to think that the date was two full years ago, and though the lanterns were lit and the candles were burning, she kept insisting on more lights.

As for the funeral itself, they asked the daughter where to bury him and she picked out his favourite tree, the boab that he used to like to sit and read under when the weather was fine. They laid him there in the golden afternoon light.

The six Ramone sons dug the hole as deep as they could in this marshy land, getting all of three feet down before they struck water, even on this slight rise. The coffin maker had already shipped out all of his grave liners, and the only one remaining was half-sized with a flawed side. It would hold as long as there was no storm, keeping the corpse down below the line where it could rise. It wouldn't last forever, maybe not even ten years in this hurricane-prone land, but the big man figured that the girl and her mother would be, like the rest of them, long gone by then, and the Reverend not very likely, under the circumstances, to care.

Besides, in this place all burial measures are temporary. In this soil, all dead things will eventually rise.

Ramone did have one coffin left, mahogany veneer over cheap plyboard, lined with artificial off-white silk. He had been planning on leaving this last one behind because it had sat in his stock-room for the better part of a decade, a dead-end experiment in budget burials that he did not want to bother paying to ship. It looked all right, from a distance, if you ignored the green verdigris on the fake silver handles. He wished, bitterly, that he had something better left for the minister (David had been very kind to the Ramone's, giving them the start-up money for their move and baptizing all of his lovely children from the third oldest down, though he was not Catholic) but after a moment he shrugged the feeling off. Gotta do what you can, can't do no more than that. Life moves on.

The hole was dug, the body set beside it, and the remnants of the last three families in the town gathered round to see it settled in the earth. Joy stood beside old Mrs. Milton, the girl cleaned and changed into her darkest navy-blue dress, her face pressed into the lady's soft, wide hip like a frightened infant burrowing into its mother's breast. Looking down at the top of that black head, Mrs. Milton thought, that color really does not suit her. I'll wash the dress she came in last night, put her back in lovely red. Not traditional, but what does it matter, she's mourning deep enough already. Anyone can see that. She doesn't need to signal death with fabrics or robes.

Mr. Milton read a passage from one of the Bibles in the church. He did not really know which parts were good for funerals, and he had some trouble with long words, but he figured that a happy ending was usually the best, so he read the last pages from the Book of Revelation, terrible things said with pretty words, that made him sweat and set his audience to squirming.

He regretted his choice for half an hour, all that talk of dragons and fire, the boldly woman with the crown of stars, but could not stop for fear that they would drop the body down into the dark without a single kind word to guide him there, so on he read until he reached those last few lines, 'He that is unjust, let him be unjust still; he which is filthy, let him be filthy still: he that is holy, let him be holy still. And, behold, I come quickly; and my reward *is* with me, to give every man according as his work shall be. The grace of Our Lord Jesus Christ be with you all. Amen.'

As soon as Old Man Milton had finished his verses, the Ramone boys, confused and just a little bit frightened, took hold of the coffin and lowered it in. Stepped back afterwards, shovels in hand, far enough for Mrs. Milton to have room to lead the little girl forward to hurl her clot of dirt into the three-foot wound in the flank of the earth where it hit the thin wooden top with a final, hollow thud that sounded as though there were nothing left at all inside and left Joy, weeping and shaking, pulled back by her guardian into the warm arms of the old lady into the safe shadows of the spread-limbed tree.

The boys covered up the grave in record time, not bothering to tramp down the earth, so that it would settle on its own from raised mound to thumbprint indentation. In half an hour they were finished and by sunset, after the youngest daughter had been relieved from watching Rose, the family was gathered into their two wagons and had set off down the road. They had a boat to catch, their journey already delayed far too long.

As for Old Man Milton and his wife, they would remain for another few days, perhaps a week at the most, long enough to rouse Rose out of her stupor and, if they could, drag the woman and the girl out of this dank swamp to someplace dry, with plenty of light, to begin new lives away from the rot.

They were none of them expecting to encounter the firm resolve of Rose, or the strength with which her broken mind would fight to shore her wrecked world up again, to the endless sorrow of them all.

STORMFRONT

The rains rose up three days after the remaining Miltons left, dragging their kit in a fine donkey rig, the Mrs. still bloodied from her meeting with Rose. Joy watched them go, waving sadly from her place at the window, one arm round the neck of Bess who sent her warm tongue, like a hot slice of ham, up to caress the length of her cheek, wiping off the tears. Joy was comforted by this, though the action could easily have been spurred by nothing more than a craving for salt. Joy chose to interpret it as a sign of love and fidelity.

Maybe it was.

Either way the girl and the dog were now essentially alone, unless you counted her wild-haired mother, still pacing and wailing in her room up the stairs, like some mad spirit lost in time.

Joy spent her time the best way she could: reading mostly, and wandering around with Bess. Sometimes she would dress in a walking skirt (she hadn't any trousers as Rose found them inappropriate for young girls) and a shirt of her father's. Picture her: a thin young girl strolling down the empty sidewalks before houses with blind windows for eyes, splashing through puddles, mostly silent but occasionally laughing. Becoming slowly used to solitude. Though the strain of it, of great swathes of hours alone with her dog, were beginning to show.

The town had not been empty long enough for her to justify exploring inside of people's houses yet. They still maintained the air of careful, though impoverished, habitation, and even though she was already very curious to discover what food they had left, it would take longer than a few days or even weeks (as well as considerably more hunger) to break the rules down far enough to allow for the kind of exploration that required broken locks.

This does not mean that Joy stretched that definition to include storage shacks and barns, although she found not much that was useful there but a selection of broken or outdated tools and, in one case, a puny waterlogged pullet that had hidden from the move in a pile of half-moldy hay and so missed its ride.

She caught that bird as it fled from her, a fury of feathers and thin, scaled legs. She snapped its neck in one smooth motion, a trick she learned from Malda, and that night the three of them – child, woman, and dog – ate the bird roasted to brown crackling perfection, none of them knowing it was to prove the last fresh hen they would have for years. It was a good thing, then, that they were hungry enough to justify sucking the very marrow from the bones, so that none of it was wasted.

Most of the time they were not quite that profitable in their explorations, finding nothing more interesting than the odd piece of graffiti or defunct newspaper, already well-yellowed.

This morning was no different, but still, it passed the time now that there was nothing to do and no one to speak to, and all this rambling did have the rather pleasant effect of blocking her mind, saving her from more horrifying thoughts of her parents, of what had happened to her father, poor vanished Malda, her mother, and what was still to happen, to her.

That night, Joy and Bess were curled up together in her father's green leather library wingback, the one the color of fresh leaves, reading Voltaire. This seat was always horribly clammy at first, oddly textured from the damp, but a swipe from a dry rag rendered it comfortable enough, a warm place to nestle for a girl and her dog, with space enough for both of them to snooze.

This afternoon had been overcast and so the light that shone through the stained-glass window was dusty and dull, like jewels lost and hidden underground. So even though it was yet daylight,

Joy was reading by the small flame of a candle, happily burning what she would soon learn to ration. Before many more months would pass she would be keeping a close and very detailed record of everything. But since she was young, and the reality of her abandonment had not yet set in, she was rather prone to waste.

She would learn.

The house, for once, was close to silent; the only sounds were the dog's snoring and the thin rustle of dampened pages as the words slowly turned, the low sound of her own voice mumbling French.

Rose must be upstairs, asleep.

When the rain began to fall, soft at first then rising in strength, Joy at first did not notice, but when the darkness fell, a thick inchoate blackness that spat white flashes like quick-raging fires, she could pay attention to nothing else.

Minor storms aren't unusual in this realm of hurricanes; a downpour will flourish, blooming from nothing, about once a week. Joy has known them from her earliest childhood. In fact, when she was just a little younger, the sight of those black clouds building was a signal to her and her friends of the incredible potential for fun. They used to run out in it, their clothes clinging to their bodies in that warm bathwater deluge, hurling mud like snowballs (a concept she had heard of, read of, but never known), their bare feet sliding in the grass.

But this is the first time that she has heard a storm, even one as small as this, completely alone.

The wind howls, raging around them, through the beams that bind the roof to walls and in the deep vast emptiness between the stilts that vault them aloft. For the first time, Joy knows that she has been utterly abandoned, as trapped and unstable, as lodged in this swamp as her stilt-supported house.

The thought is hard for one as young as this. She responds to it in a way that is sensible for such extremity of pain: she buries her face into the warm, fear-pricked fur of her dog, taking comfort as she gives it by soothing the whimpers that rise up from Bess when the lightning strikes and the loud winds howl.

By the time the candle burns out, streaming its wax out over the silver of the candlestick, completely obscuring it in a hard cloak of white, the girl and her dog are both deeply asleep, lost in a well far beyond dreaming.

They remain that way throughout the long night, waking in this best of all possible worlds, when the light shines bright and red-stained through the windows, and they rouse themselves, their bodies stiff and cramping, to look out onto a fresh world full of broken human things: a few loosened shingles, two shattered windows on the house down the street. The rain has beaten away the surface dirt that covered up the freshest grave, exposing a square of coffin-wood a half inch thick. Such small things, easy to forget, that they will never be repaired.

She and Bess eat a quick breakfast of week-old bread and settled strawberry jam, the homemade jarred kind sealed with a half-inch plug of wax, then leave a chunk on a plate for her mother. The sun is fully risen now, bright and glittering on the leaves, and so with the terrors of the night quickly forgotten, the two friends set themselves to go outside, ready to explore.

WEDDING

Rose is looking out of the window of her room (hers alone now, on some level she knows this, though she will not speak the words, not even here, not even to herself in the passageways of her own rapidly darkening mind). Outside in the bright sunlight that glitters on a town composed of blind-reflecting glass and cloudy pools of gathered water that sit like dead eyes, her young daughter digs a hole.

It is difficult to conceive of the bifurcated nature of her mind, save to say that it is as though the massive trauma of the last few weeks has wrenched her mind in two. One half, the one that diminishes by the day, knows exactly what has happened. Her David is dead. And so is her world. This voice, the one that says, *we are alone here, Joy and I, we are alone and we will perish here unless you do something. You are the adult, she cannot act without you, it is your responsibility as her mother to see her safely out of this God- and man-forsaken swamp.*

When this voice is in the ascent, as it is less and less often with each day that goes by, she does what she can to prepare for the moment when she must gather up her daughter and take flight. She had one of these lucid moments yesterday, a moment when she could see the world as it was, and it was as though a clarifying lens had dropped away and she could see the house as it was, suffering from a chronic case of dust and damp without Malda here to sponge the dew away, though it was obvious by the clean dishes piled in the sink and the pile of broom sweepings on the floor that Joy was trying her best.

She knew that the lucidity she wore would not last long, and so she made her moves, and made them fast, gathering up a small cache of supplies they would need to carry them into Tampa. They would have to walk, because no horse or cart remained, and she would have to hope, sincerely, that her current comprehension would hold out throughout the thirty-mile walk.

Honestly, she could not see it happening.

Though she does try. Yesterday, for example, when she was ensconced in her proper time, she packed twelve cans of tomatoes, pears, and lima beans, along with a small drum of kerosene (a full gallon, enough to light their way from town to Tampa, and a little further if they were to lose their way). She reckoned on everything save for a relapse when, moving with the blank-eyed conviction that the supplies were a trunk that she and David had finished unpacking while moving into their new home, she shoved it all underneath the bed, where the cans would corrode, the food rotting, unused, and the oil would remain, safely hidden thanks to a new-fangled zinc lining that prevented rust, for a good many years.

She knew even then that there was a limit to what she could do without losing herself again in that flood of sensory lies that has overwhelmed her in periods of increasing regularity and duration and give her the illusion of a much more bearable life, for a while at least.

It is easy to assume, from the patterns that her madness has subscribed to, that eventually these blank patches will overwhelm her life entirely, providing her entire existence with a fictive wash composed mainly of the life that she has lost. She is in the middle of one now.

Look at her there, sitting on her unwashed sheets (she sees them white and freshly laundered) moving her brush through her long, earth-scented hair. The white metal handle is already beginning to tarnish around the edges of the deep-carved flowers that run the length of it from handle to head, the one with the boar-hair bristles that David bought her as a wedding present the day before the ceremony.

And that is all the story she needs to set her on her way.

She is sitting on her mother's bed, on the day of her wedding, her dress already on, the stays drawn tight, the tulle gathered at waist and breast, her hair braided in a golden crown around her head. She has replaced the brush in its satin-lined box along with the tortoise-shell comb with floral silver back and the hand mirror, and placed the entire collection on the surface of the rosewood vanity that Rose would inherit six months from now when her mother would perish from years of the force of her blood pounding against a small and unseen flaw in her heart.

But that is something which has not yet happened at the time that Rose currently inhabits, and so she will not admit it here, in the inner sanctum of her insulating disease. No, there is no death in this cool room, no fear or pain or any tincture of dark.

There is music playing, light and soft, rising up from the parlour where a small crowd of her loved ones is gathered, her great aunt Lucinda tinkling on the harpsichord, some light and spring-like melody, made strangely discordant by the abrupt ending the instrument levies on notes, making it sound as though the tune were being somehow plucked. But this is the only disconcerting element to an afternoon of light. Besides, the lady is both spinster and old, they can forgive her for her unevenness of song.

They are down there gathered, all of them waiting for her to complete her preparations, to decorate her hair and flower-scent her skin, so that they might escort her, following behind the rented golden chariot her father ordered, down the High Street to the church where she will glide up that red-carpeted aisle, leaning on her father's arm and trailing a large bouquet of twelve fresh Lily flowers, their stems wrapped round in white and blue, the colors of the Virgin Mary.

David will be standing there, tall and thin in his black suit, looking so handsome, in his way. He will be waiting to take her in front of God and man, to slip that ring of bright white gold onto her finger, say those words that will bind them together in ways that are deeper than blood and stronger than time. And then, oh then, he will lead her, running together, out of that church and into their new life, down South in the wild, where they will make a life together in the jungle and the swamp.

And oh, will it ever be an adventure. She can feel it in her bones.

All she has to do to begin it is finish preparing. Examine her dress in her mother's oval mirror (the one that she will inherit, one day, along with the stand), looking herself from crowned, veiled top to tulle-floating bottom.

Perfect.

So perfect she looks in that white dress, it may be vanity but she cannot resist it, blowing her image a gentle kiss.

She leaves the room (that smells oddly of musk) and whirls down the stairs, running for a parlour that does not exist here, running to meet up with people long vanished, to journey to a church that is a full thousand miles north, and a man at the altar who is three weeks dead.

In an odd way it is lucky for her that by the time she reaches the bottom of the stairs time has slipped its wheel once again, like a victrola needle leaving the groove, changing songs in mid-track, or the sight of that empty, disconsolate room would bend the fabric of her heart into some obscene, irreparable shape.

Rose enters the room and starts singing, a tune from the latest edition of *Let Us Have Music* that David brought back for her as a present the last time he was in Tampa. She sings it now, bright and tuneful as a bird. Her husband is at the church right now, saying evening vespers. He will be home soon.

Outside in the heat, separated from her by a scant few feet of air and boards, Rose's ten-year-old daughter digs down a brief hole, to cover a treasure that she has been forced to discard. The song that Rose sings is joyous and light, perhaps it will tend what is covered, the notes binding it like string, to bring what has been abandoned, someday, back to the light.

BESS

The delicate morning light is soft and golden, lending a translucent cast to everything it touches, the new green leaves on mangrove, boab, oak, the tender shoots of new grass and the reclaimed collective nests of birds, just beginning to return after being driven to the very brink of obliteration by the cravings of the rich for headgear loaded down with feathers. It is just spring and the world is mud-luscious, rife with breeding and the small cries of creatures, just born.

The female alligators uncover their mulch-nests in the swamp, heeding the high peepings of their infants who hatched in the night and now want out, to taste their first free air. The eggs were laid in large clutches, thirty or forty at one setting, white leathery shells the size of golf balls but shaped like lozenges that the mothers bury in domed piles of rotting matter and leaves. The alligator's genders are decided by temperature and must be strictly controlled. Since the reptiles are cold-blooded, this must be achieved with the heat produced by rotting vegetables, and it is a very precise operation. One degree more or less and the whole clutch is lost. This is not unusual. Many things in life are so.

Now the prehistoric creatures, thirteen feet long from snout to tail and weighing up to half a ton, use their front claws to gently dig their children up. And there they are. See the small, olive-green heads, sharp-toothed already? See the little, ridged tails? In a few years those well-muscled appendages will be strong enough to snap the spine of a stag with one whip, although now they are under six inches long and needing their mother.

Listen to them cry for her, the poor little things. She scoops them up and carries them, gently, thirty at once, in a mouth large enough to hold a haunch of beef. They rest their tiny feet against conical teeth that have, in earlier days, buried themselves in femurs. They ride there, completely unconcerned and perfectly safe in a place that would, for anything else, be but the greatest of dangers, riding to their first swim in the brackish inland sea.

The morning light, stronger now, less delicate and of brassy sheen, filters down through the mangroves, over roads that are already weed-choked, over buildings that are structurally fine but look somehow blind, almost stupid, the sunshine reflecting off glass that is only beginning to be dusty. These houses look as though they have lost their minds. And it is true.

They have.

The light, acquiring a slight, but undeniable, tarnish picks out the stilted manse, the only building left with a swept porch, though there is no one left to see. Bend nearer, look a bit more closely – see the girl who's kept the whole place clean? There she is, that little one. The only moving thing in this whole place, other than a few bad-tempered seagulls and, of course, the vultures perched a few feet from her, in the trees.

What is she doing there, that little girl? What is that long pole doing in her hands?

It is a shovel – see the brass light glinting on the sharp-edged blade? The metal scratched to silver in a wedge shape on the tip, from striking a fossil or a rock. She is digging a small hole. And what are those chips of light that decorate her cheeks? Tears.

The last neighbor fled a week ago, the old hunter-man with the four orange teeth and his kind, fat, floury wife, pleading with her mother to let the girl, at least, go with them even if she would not go herself. Rose, looking haughty, her hair clumped and unwashed, her dress splashed with food, but at least able to stand, ordered them off her property and threatened the old lady with a long-bladed knife. One of the ones from the kitchen with the blade so curved it looks like a sickle. Joy remembers how dangerously it glittered in that light, a silver wound in air.

Eventually the old man and his woman left, trundling away in their little carriage, the old lady looking back over her shoulder at Joy crouched and shivering in the window, her arms around the neck of her Blue Tick hound dog. Poor, faithful Bessy.

How Joy had wanted to run after those people, just take her dog and go. She did not even know them very well – the old man frightened her a little with his carroty Halloween grin – but how could she leave her mother here, in this place, all alone?

The state she is in now, all the time wailing and crazy, babbling nonsense about coyotes in the moonlight, or hallucinating stories about what life was, it would be murder to abandon her here. Joy is only a little over ten years old, but she knows right from wrong (her father taught her, the choking lump in her throat only confirms what she knows) and leaving Mama here would be to leave her to death. Joy is not willing to do that. Not now, nor ever.

But still, maybe, if she had taken Bess and gone with those people, maybe she wouldn't be quite so alone herself.

Pretty Bessy with her black-flecked coat and brown 'eyebrow' patches above her speaking black eyes. Good Bess who slept with her at night since she got the pup for her sixth birthday, a wiggly little thing dropped into her lap with wagging tail and lapping tongue, a red ribbon tied around her head in the form of a bow. They used to run together, through the swamp, trailing the animals, almost communing.

David used to call them Symbiotes, so deep was their affinity, they seemed to know what the other was thinking, and acted accordingly without stopping for meaningless consideration. Joy remembers when she was eight, a mere two years ago, wanting to teach her the fine art of racoon hunting. It was the only scheme of hers that her father ever thwarted, saying, *Haven't there been deaths enough? Must all nature fall before us, love, like wheat before the thresher?* And then she was ashamed of her desire, though it remained there, hidden, the lust and the satiety of hunting.

And now, when she could have used her dog the most, poor Bessy died.

It was infection, must have been, from the raccoons that had come into the kitchen three days ago. They had been sleeping, the girl and the dog, curled together as usual when the crashes came from down below. Joy at first assumed that it was her mother, down there, up to some mischief, but the way that Bess was growling changed her mind. The dog's flues were drawn back over stark, glistening teeth, foam-flecked with saliva.

Joy took hold of her collar, a black leather strap, but Bess was hauling so hard, struggling to break. Together they ventured downstairs.

The kitchen was a shambles, pots overturned, jars smashed and broken, the cold pantry (and her last joint of meat) pried wide open, the flesh gnawed down to knobbly bone. The raccoons were writhing around, on the countertops, on the ground, playing and feasting on Joy's last supplies.

Later, she would have to break into the next-door house, to find enough to last her until the grocery cart came again, to stock their larder in exchange for an ever-dwindling supply of cash. It was her first break-in, and inexpertly done. There was glass everywhere, but she was grieving, and one is never cautious in that state.

Just ask Rose.

Back in the kitchen she held onto Bess for as long as she could, twining the collar around in her hands, until her fingers felt as though they were breaking and with an outrush of strength, the dog broke free.

What followed was a hurricane of fur and foam, a summer storm of gnashing teeth and injured howls. Ten raccoons had broken in and in five minutes three of them were eviscerated, their purplish intestines spilled on the blond-pine floor, and the rest of them had fled.

Bess seemed fine, at first, save for a small cut under her eye which Joy dabbed with a rag boiled in clean water, while Bess slowly wagged her tail and tried to lick Joy's cleaning hand, her voice a soft, excited whine.

The next day Joy cleaned up the mess, tossing the raccoons into the privy and mopping down the floor with bleach, Bess staying always beside, her spotted shoulder pressed into the side of Joy's knee, matching her when she moved, step for step. Bess seemed a bit nervous (and who could blame her?) but otherwise fine.

And this morning she was dead.

Joy woke to the first rays of that bright, golden light that poured through her cheerful yellow curtains like the promise of new life and found her dog curled up and cool beside her, unbreathing, the sheets below her urine-soaked and stinking. She had been dead for a while, her muscles locked and mortis-frozen, her body, fetal, curled tight as a grub. And Joy missed her passing, locked in a dream of her father, dressed in a white robe, wielding a sickle and handing her flowers the color of the full moon, rising.

Joy was burying her now.

Bess was wrapped in the white sheets she died in (Joy longed to give her clean ones, but there weren't any. She was too afraid to use the mangle and so she never did the wash. Something else she would have to learn.), the body cool and difficult to shift as mud, so heavy in death that Joy had difficulty carrying her down the stairs, though when she was alive and squirming the girl had never had a problem hoisting her. It seems that death adds gravity to things, before decay removes the weight. You would have thought that she would know this by now, having seen so much of the capacity of death over the last few weeks. Grief was a good friend, moved in for a long stay. Is it any wonder that she wept as she dug?

The hole is nearly deep enough, just a few more inches, careful to miss the shallow water-table. She doesn't want her friend to drown, nor float to the surface again some stormy night. As much as she loves Bess, she does not want her to rise again as things do here. She wants to see her well and entire, or not at all, and if that means a considerably longer wait, well, she is willing to do it.

Though maybe it won't be all that long a loiter anyway. Groceries are expensive and their cash supply is almost gone. A few weeks more, maybe, and then she'll see Bess again, and also (especially) her father. She'll wander into that clearing that waits at the end of life and join them there and then, at last, together they'll go down the long road that ends at God.

She doesn't wonder that her mother is absent from these new fantasies. She tries not to think of her mother at all. Not since last week. Though she can see her pacing through the window of her bedroom, her blue dress flashing, see the light caught up in her wild nimbus of hair. She tries not to feel it, can't help it, tries to annul the feeling that spreads like sweet rot from the fissure in her chest where her heart was three weeks ago, before everyone left. The feeling remains, it is too powerful for her, and she is so young.

She can't help cursing her mother in her secret heart.

The hole is dug, as deep as she can get it without hitting water, and she uses the motion of picking up the sheet-wrapped corpse to wipe the knowledge of her hatred from her conscious mind, if not her heart. She tries to forget her mother calling her Malda and raging at Joy for her abandonment, for the maid's unforgiveable betrayal. She forces forgetfulness as she lowers her dog into the hole that she has dug, and she succeeds. The memory is gone, and the pain buried with it (but oh, all things rise, here, all dead things return) and Joy says a prayer, sends her words dripping down into the hole that she is covering, one by one, sent from the deepest places of her soul to a God who has hurt her very badly, sent with her tears. She means every word.

When the grave is covered, the prayers all said, and her hands filthy, clotted with mud, a streak of rust, a splinter from the shovel handle buried underneath a fingernail, drawing blood, she plants down her cross. She made it from two pieces of the white picket fence that surrounds the church yard. No one will miss it. She nailed the slats together, scrawled out the name of the beloved on the lengthwise board.

She hammers it deep into the soil, using the dented shovel-blade, and stands a moment in the lovely spring sunlight, feeling a loneliness deeper and more complete than anyone now living could ever comprehend, hearing a faint music echoing, inappropriately light, from the haunted passage of her house.

She stood there for a very long time.

Death

II

LIBRARY

Joy sits in the leather armchair, her body curled into a comma, knees drawn up to her small, pointed chin. She is reading the Aeneid, that ancient chronicle of life and death, of the laying of foundations drawing her in to another, brighter existence. She has just turned twelve years old.

She is not lonely, now, with this battle blazing round her in the flickering, imagined flames that spread from cities burning. Her body sinks into the slime-textured wingback, the rest spreading above her head like the unfurled membranes of a bat. The dark red leather feels like human skin, after a decade in the water. This is exactly where it has been, here, where water and the air merge into one.

There is sunlight here, in this book-filled room, and life among the pages. At least within the tomes that have not yet become compressed to bricks by humidity and time. The girl has spent too long alone, her child's body lengthening, scraggly and wild, like a carrot growing forgotten in a root cellar, sending out its roots and pale stalk. As though it were searching for the lost, barely remembered sun.

She reads the Greek fluidly and swift, barely registering that she feels a spear of longing for her father with every cadenced word. Outside, the world is bright and verdant, the mangroves and live oak rushed to white bloom and tiny yellow blossom. It is spring, and the world is mud-luscious, a veritable riot of vegetable life. The birds and gators thrust together, like with like and kind with kind, their brief romances burgeoning in water-froth and song.

There are no lovers here for her, even if her youth did not

preclude it, no Eddie or Bill to steal a kiss (the all-important first one given, or taken) in the gold-scented hay, in a game of softball or tag among the sky-climbing roots. She can remember when there were other children around, when there were other people, servants even (though she thought of them as family, especially poor Malda, before they left her and her mother, sitting here in mire) and she was not alone in a rotting house surrounded by rich things.

The wallpaper might be a bit discolored and peeling at the edges, but it was a William Morris design. The bookcases might have woodworm, the pages they hold there might be scented through with rot, but they are made from hand-carved mahogany with teak veneers in the shape of trumpet flowers, and the books have Moroccan leather bindings. And there is a silver inkwell on the desk, filled with David's distinctive ink.

She tries her best to keep it clean, working and repairing as much as she can, but it is a struggle for her to fight the temptation to give up, to just let her massive pile of house subside into rot and twisted ruin. Part of her wants to let it go, to let it sink back down into the swamp it rose from, but then she remembers her father's dying face. He took her hands and squeezed them, lying there in the room that she is considering claiming as her own (the little-girl ruffles in her current resting place hold little appeal for her now, her dolls are nothing but blank eyes, staring, row on row). He extracted her word.

And there is her mother to think about.

Sometimes Rose seems to know her, other times not. It is as though she were wandering for half the time in an anesthetic fog, a small smile playing on her lips, remembering better times, perhaps, and happier places. She has taken to calling her daughter 'Joyce' again; that hated name the schoolboys chanted, innocuous to adult listeners, infuriating to her, when she was the good young minister's daughter, and could not strike back. The boys were egret-hunters' children, once respectable tradesmen, but their sons were running ragged by then, the last birds harvested, the few remaining feathers running out.

Joy does not know if her mother does it purposely to infuriate her, or if it is carelessness and the slow seepage of her mind. Either way she hates it. She misses her mother, the way she used to be, so vibrant and alive, moving in her bright silk dresses, her blond hair blowing out around her face diaphanous and long. Her body was made for dancing. Before the coughing started, it seemed to dance with every step, her hips swaying, her voice lilting, as though she were a lark trapped by some black spell into the body of a woman who could make laughter and the tears of sorrow sound almost exactly the same.

Joy misses her, that laughing, dancing ghost, almost as much as she misses her father.

And none of this worrying even considers the fact that they have absolutely no food.

Joy is intelligent, enough anyway to recognize her musing for what it is: a means of escaping an unpleasant thought. There is nothing left inside the house, ever since the insurance money ran out a month ago the store-men from the town have ceased bringing their carts. They must have found out about their destitution somehow. Joy guesses the bank. And she knows that they would not be persuaded to trade for any of the fine things scattered, heaped even, around this manse.

She tried to sell the man a salt seller the last time he came around, silver in exchange for food. The man, an old Mexican, smiled softly, touched her face, said, 'No.'

So maybe she told them about the money herself.

She knows that she should have asked him for a lift out of this place. That, at least, he would have given. But her mother would

119

not go. She hardly ever leaves her room (except occasionally to wander, but even that she does much less) and the stairs creak when she does. She is convinced that there will be a resurrection, somehow, a new life sent by God.

She cannot understand that the time for that has come already, and has long since passed.

And Joy's thoughts revolve again toward food.

The pantry is bare, as are all the cupboards, denuded of cans and pickling jars, the last flower scraped from every barrel. Since the last trader left, when the moon was a thin scrim, a thumbnail edge cast against the sky, she has gone over to the shop and raided it, several times. There was very little useable material left to begin with, though she did have some hopes for a large flask of flour. But once the barrel was open the truth poured out. Water had settled in through the cracks, as always will in this saturated place, and turned the powder to ferment-scented cement.

The lucky finds were dried or canned, and she fed the last of those (tin-tasting peaches, two years expired) to her mother for her breakfast. Joy drank the juice herself, avoiding the rim and the sealing gobs of lead. But who knows? There could be something left. Some small, good thing, though not quite fresh, to get them through one more long night.

The issue is decided, finally, at last. She closes up her Virgil and slides the volume back into the socket that she wrenched it from. There is much work to do, if she intends to eat tonight, and she shall do it, for she must.

Joy climbs the stairs to her hated room (she will not inhabit it much longer) to trade her pinafore for boy's work trousers in preparation for her rag-and-bone pickings in the sodden mortal dust.

GROCERIES

Joy walks out of her stilt-riding house, watching her step. Ever since the gardener quit soon after her father's death, one of the last servants to leave, the yard and porch have been falling into disrepair. At a distance the town could still pass for inhabited, if a bit ragged around the edges. Most of the windows still have their glass, and all of them stand true, their roofs for the most part intact, even if the paint is starting to chip around the corners.

Luckily there hasn't been a major storm, though Joy does not expect that trend to last. Their small patch of Gulf seems to attract hurricanes, and they have a medium to big one every five years or so. The last one struck a little under four years ago, before the town had really started drying up, when her father was still alive. There was money enough, if only just, for repairs then, and the people still sufficiently cared to make them, which explains why there is still any paint on the buildings at all. And why there won't be for long. Not even lead paint can stand up for very long in air with this much water.

As soon as she leaves the house, sweat-beads form along her hairline and in that soft indentation above her upper lip. Her armpits (where the first hairs are sprouting, black and unusually thick) send out droplets of moisture that soak through her shirt, a yellow and red striped dress front that was once her father's. He always did favour that color yellow. The boy's trousers once belonged to a long-departed neighbor, one who left a lot of things behind when they fled, expecting to come back.

She snaps the lock with a chisel; it lets go with a deep, bone-jarring thunk. It was a good lock. She doesn't think about what she's done as breaking in.

Right now, dressed as she is, her too-loose top disguising her vestiges of breasts, the gray boy's trousers, her long hair tucked up under a sun-shielding hat, she could almost pass for a male. From behind, at least. When she turns her face there is no denying the beauty there already, a rose blossoming unseen in the florid, hot-house dark, deepened by her sorrow that casts shadows but does not yet mark.

The store could almost still be open for business, the pine sidewalk in front of it a little worn, and there are grass shoots and one tenuous three-inch-high mangrove sprouting up between the slats, but otherwise the passage is intact, if empty. The worst thing about this place is the sound of the wind soughing, the lone barking cry of the occasional rook.

There is a long-necked Anhinga, or serpent-bird, perched above the door, its huge black wings spread and dripping, like some signal of a coming doom, drying its oddly oil-free wings. Water drops drip from each feather, pelting the sidewalk, one by one. In the distance, she can hear the hushed beating of the waves crashing up against a shore that lies less than five miles away, but to which she has not journeyed in years.

It is no wonder that she avoids going outside.

She reads instead, in daylight (there is no lamp oil left, in any house, at least none that she could find) and sleeps at night, behind her peeling walls, growing pale, her pupils large and dark.

The store is open, of course, it always is for her. The door sticks a little, the wood swelling a bit with humidity, but it is still moveable and strong. The air inside is terrible, but not as bad as it was at first, when the little meat left began to turn. Then it was a matter of eat as much as you can before it's gone, a task made more difficult by her mother's refusal to eat salvaged meat. Why should she, Rose argued, there was plenty around. The grocery cart was still coming from town then albeit sporadically, though they were the last people in town. They still had enough hard cash to pay.

In the end the rot moved faster than their stomachs, a fact which came as something of a relief to the then ten-year-old Joy. She still had firm ideas of personal property back then, even when the owners were long since gone. Still, she had tried her hand at jerky-making anyway, though the stench of that failure was sickening, and lasted long.

Now the store smells of ancient flesh and softer rot. There is a fermented stench rising from the water-logged sorghum and flour barrels in the back, and the mildew rising from the decaying fabric rolls where women once came to pluck a base-pattern for a Sunday dress. None of that is useable anymore.

The penny candy jars behind the counter have crystallized into solid blocks, or melted into a faecal-looking slurry, in any case there is nothing there that she would want to touch. Finding something canned is probably her best option and she had better find it soon for she is fairly dizzy now and can hear a thin high whistle inside of her head, signalling a faint.

The problem is that she has dug through all of this mess, even overturned some shelves, in her previous grocery runs, in the hope of finding something to sustain her and her mother one more day at least. There is nothing for it but to try the storeroom in the back.

This is as close as a Florida shop can get to a basement, and it is dark, wet, and even in the summertime, strangely chill, almost cold.

The shop itself is raised slightly, like every other house around, on stilts designed to prevent water seepage and enable cool air to pass underneath and cut the heat a little for the people living and working inside. The storeroom is different. Accessed by a short and downward flight of stairs, it is level with the ground. The floor is composed of that thin bluish dirt that leaves tracks like powder. The moisture does not rise from the soil, the room rests on top of the earth, and it has never been dug. The water condensates on the walls and roof, leaving droplets that stand or drip down, forming shallow puddles in places and indicating a potential for flood.

There are shelves stacked in the middle of the room, with no edge or surface touching the water-dripping walls. There are dark shapes on those planks that might be food. Joy has seen them, winking up at her tauntingly, the last few times she was here and opened the door. She has been working up to this descent for months.

Joy is a brave girl, she has had to be to survive in this place alone, but though she is brave and certainly well-educated (even if her reading has mainly been in Greek and Romantic English verse) she is still a child, and basements are where the monsters are. This is going to take some doing.

It is very, very dark.

She realizes now that the surface stock has been depleted, and she has ransacked every pantry left in town. This is the only storeroom that she has not clamoured in, and it can no longer be avoided. It is time to go down.

Steeling herself with a deep breath, a quick prayer whispered under her breath, sent up to a God she cannot comprehend, she pulls the door the rest of the way open, to let in as much light as possible. She can see, even from here, that the storage shelves are lined with row on row of sealed, brightly-filled jars. But is it her imagination or can she hear something squealing down in there?

Please don't let it be a rat.

Not that she is afraid of rats in general, she actually rather likes them, having kept one as a pet. She knows that they can carry diseases (like the one that took Daddy) and their bare feet and cold, rubbery tails are not things which one would wish to encounter in the dark.

Still, she forces herself down.

The stairs are slick, but bear her weight, slight as it is, and the banister is solid. She has no problem letting herself down. She tells herself that she is not really underneath the earth, that the chained (but not locked) doorway in the back leads up a slight rise to the rear yard of the shop. She tells herself that she is separated from the sun by only a few inches of wood. This helps, but not entirely.

Joy is hard, for a child. Life will make her harder still. There are sounds around her in the walls, though she sees nothing now, save the brief flash of a tar-drop eye, a flicker of pink paw, blurring by along the wall. There are spiders everywhere, shiny black ones with red vases on their stomachs, crouching in their messy nests and toting their pink, star-shaped egg sacks behind them like a fine lady's purse. These are very beautiful, but Joy dutifully avoids them. The nearest doctor is in Tampa, thirty miles away, and anyway she has no money, and no ride.

The shelves are tall and high before her, filled to brimming, filling her mouth with peremptory saliva and her small heart with joy.

There is food here. And plenty of it, providing the wax seals have held.

She takes what she can, all that she can carry, jars of pickle, jam, clear jars that have creamed corn stacks in them and shine like gold. Vegetables. Beans. Ten mason jars she takes at once, holding them like puppies in the hem of her long shirt. That thought makes her remember her own dog, briefly, who died a year ago of the parvo sickness. She remembers, in passing, that bitter stomach-smell. The way she looked up at her with those black, desperate eyes. That thing she did.

But the thought, and the longing (she would really like a dog right now) are banished quickly by the elation, the ecstatic realization that here, at last, is food.

She carries the jars up the stairs, into the lovely light, and lays them out across the floor, in the dancing motes of dust that paint the air in a fine, golden wash. They are all intact, the wax plugs sealed. She takes out her bone-handled pocketknife, the blade slightly curved, a moon-edged sickle; she acquired it here, from the now-rusting selection there behind the counter, and feeling her pulse race at the thought of the possibility of failure, she digs the blade into the wax and levers out the plug.

The scent of good corn rises, golden as the mote-filled air, succulent and still fresh to her perfume-hungry nostrils. Before she can even think about it the knife is folded back into her pocket and the sweet kernels are flowing, in their butter-yellow gravy, into her open, longing mouth.

She finishes the entire jar in under a minute, feeling the urge to vomit, but holding it back. The juice disperses in runnels down her chin, and she wipes it with her dirty fingers, then wipes the digits on her tongue to salvage every drop, even plunging them back in to the bottom of the jar to suck away the last few splatters of goodness there.

The guilt sets in immediately. My mother, up there, hungry, while I sit here and eat. She quickly folds the thought away. It could not be helped.

And anyway, the rest of these jars all look fine, none of the plugs have holes and there is no botulism swelling. She remembers an expanded can of tomatoes she found three weeks ago, and almost ate from desperation. She still wishes that she had not thrown it away. But there is a plenitude of food here, nine jars spread out before her, and more in the basement for her to take.

This then is the respite she's been looking for, but it is also the expenditure of her last hope and untried bastion. There is enough food down there to last her a few months more, stacked up like soldiers, row on row – but after that is gone? It is best not to think about it. Only ration, feed your mother, eat, and pray.

Something will happen, if only because something must. Whether it be life or death is something she will have to discover for herself, as the world itself will show.

CARAVAN

Mrs. Lydia Johnson sits in the front of the first of three wagons, rolling through the land of sharp-edged palmetto frond, mangrove, and live oak. She is trying not to notice the splinters that gouge into her seat. Her head is shaded by the black canvas top, but still the heat and light come pouring in, raising sweat under her clothing, slick among her folds of pale, yellowish fat.

She wishes her Randy had sprung for a carriage, at least for themselves, something with class instead of this old-fashioned thing. Like something the pioneers would use when they settled the West. And she supposes they are pilgrims, of a kind.

At least he isn't making me walk, she thinks, her ursine head turning to look at the troop of mainly black workers who trail behind the third wagon, the odd Mexican thrown in to keep up the balance. The wagons are filled like the one she rides in with a load of farm equipment and packets of seeds, a few furnishings for good measure, but it's mostly Sears and Roebuck deal items, nothing with any quality or worth.

The men are tired, they have been trudging eight hours without a rest, their whole worlds in bundles on their broad backs. Randy will not let them stop. They have a deadline to meet, thirty miles to Tampa and a storm on the way. Besides, it isn't as though these runaways have anywhere else to go, nor anyone to hire them or give them jobs. Not after the things they've done.

Randy is already beginning to consider them slaves.

He sits on the rough tongue of the wagon, not touching his wife. His predatory eyes disguised by a wide-brimmed black hat of fine leather, molded to his head. He works his mules and horses like he runs his men, having burned through four pairs of them since leaving Massachusetts two weeks ago. He thinks it's the roads. The dawn of the twentieth century, he thinks, and they call these hoof-breakers highways.

Ah well, nearly there. He'll buy more horseflesh when he picks up supplies. Buy new men as well, if it comes to that. Some more Mexicans maybe. He catches himself: not buy. Hire.

Get something for the wife also, might as well. Something pretty enough to satisfy, he knows her taste for nice things and even though she's let herself go something awful these last couple of years, she's been good for him, good to him. The fucking was only ever part of it, never the marriage entire, and he can get a firm handful of ass anywhere. He has done for years.

He looks back and shoots his wife a smile, filled with teeth. Looking past her, hard as that is with her occupying such an abundance of space, he can discern the folded, drooling lump of his sixteen-year-old son. It seems to me, he thinks with great affection, that the boy is always either sleeping, eating, or looking to fuck.

Well, one more night's camping, they'll stop for it soon, another hour of traveling to go, and then Tampa come morning. Stop a few days to rest and stock up, maybe he and I can tour a cat house together. It's about damned time. Sixteen years old and never been laid. Enough to make a nun cry. Well, I'll fix that.

Then, moving mentally from one form of conquest to another, all that land in my name, fallow and good, just waiting for a strong hand to force a crop out from the furrows. A good arm, like mine. That rich black soil. I'll plant sugar, harvest pure green. Nothing sweeter.

Under thirty miles to Tampa, thirty more after that rest stop, maybe four days total to go. And then the work, and then the harvest of all those lovely dollar bills, and all those legal issues long behind, unreachable, no longer tied like tin cans to their hypothetical tails.

And there they are, quite the family, two lost in thought, the other in dreams while the wide world unfurls around them, unheeded and unseen, save by the men (who know that they are slaves) and by the horses who must avoid the pitfalls raised by branches, and the razor edges of waist-high palmetto fronds, vibrant with the small lives of lizards and beetles. Their blades have drawn blood already, from thirty sets of naked arms.

The sky is lapis and gold-dust around and above them, filtered by mangrove, boab, and gnarled live oaks which bend down close around the caravan in their haste to see, and in doing so, block them off from human sight.

THE CITY ON THE BAY

Tampa Bay in 1900. The springtime settled hot along its long shoreline like a crown upon its brow, and the Tampa hotel, that grand minareted arabesque, is the jewel that it wields. People, mainly of the variety that is both rich and ancient, come here to hurl the TB from their lungs, spreading round the wealth. Even in its beauty, this is a realm for the dead, to remain so always.

Persephone's crown.

The humidity is worse than bad this morning, and the sun already burning high and hot, though it is barely nine o'clock. The Johnsons broke camp early, setting off at six a.m., when the light was a thin silver sickle on the edge of the horizon, broken by trees.

They spent a rough night in a clear patch of the swamp too filled with poison ivy and palmettos to be called a glade. The wagons were backed into a circle, one side facing out, the other side in, like an old-fashioned cowboy wagon train.

The family slept curled together in the lead carriage, cramped but at least warm, dry and secure. Their workers huddled as best they could on improvised beds of hard-edged palmettos, their cutting blades set face down. They shifted overnight, leaving blood-scrims behind in the morning to glitter, garnet-hued, in this early light.

All of them, family and men, were tormented by attacking mosquitoes that drained them painlessly and left large, itchy welts.

Tampa waited for them, her jeweled skirts spread out all before them like a land of dreams both various and new. And in the center of the shoreline the mosque-like hotel waited, too. The family did not really have enough ready cash to justify such expenditure, though they would have soon. Still, if they meant to do business with the local elite it would do to preserve their appearance. Besides, Randy reasoned, his wife might want something to take her mind off of what he and the kid would be up to tonight.

And even if that were not the case, nothing says 'status' like conspicuous spending. The class part comes after.

He would leave the woman and the boy a few blocks from the entrance, it wouldn't do to let the staff see them disembark from this jerry-rigged wagon and, who knows, the walk might do the lady good. Trim her down some, and tire her out. Not that she should have any trouble sleeping after the night they spent last time they settled down for resting.

After his family were deposited, Lydia carrying a signed promissory note from her husband to get them past the desk. He would wheel the wagon round to the place just outside of town, where his men and the other wagons waited, probably still fuming that they have received only a small fraction of their pay, and no matter that they've been promised the remainder later. They all know, workers and master, what that promise is worth.

Johnson knows that if these escaped criminals had anywhere else to go, they would have been there long ago. They stay here, and through worse than this, all for any shelter in the night.

The only reason he has left them anything at all in terms of spending is to save himself the trouble of locating and buying their food. They will set a watch and shop in shifts, buying what will have to be sufficient larder to last them each until a week hence, when the grocer's wagon brings its first shipment.

He has left them almost enough.

The city, that Art Nouveau gem, rises all around them, the Tampa hotel just barely visible at the edge of the wide street. He leaves Lydia and his soon-to-be-man son Randy Junior off at a turning of the road, one that traces the curve of the sea. She has her permission letter, signed in his strong hand, and money enough for rooms, their supper, and a nice enough frock to make an impression.

They will stock their larder later.

Randy lets them off with kisses, placed on forehead and cheek, tipping his black hat. When they have made sufficient progress down the street, he turns the rig back to his waiting men, to leave it there before jaunting off to solidify his plans.

The whole world is lovely, in this light.

BAY-TOWN PLANNING

The city of Tampa in the years that open the twentieth century is a bustling hive of tour and trade. The people run the gamut from German to Cuban, with a good showing of Native, Mexicans and Blacks occupying the servant positions. The guests who stay at the arabesque Tampa Bay Hotel are almost uniformly W.A.S.P, white Anglo-Saxon Protestants, down from their mansions in the North, to take the TB cure in the sunshine, sending nearly invisible red droplets out into the humid, habitable air when they cough. The organisms are very much alive and seeking solace in new lungs.

This has been the case for years and it would not be a mistake to say that the waste-waters which flow out from here contributed to the recent human migration away from the defunct, diseased towns that were once strung out around this hub like fine pearls on a chain. The water table is surface-skimming in this place and the moon-tide draws and mingles all, a fact that is easy to forget here where there are paved roads and the semblance of ground.

Absolutely none of this comes close to bothering Lydia Johnson. She is not here for the tour, nor are her lungs drowning in her own blood. She is here to make connections, line up possible clients for their future crop, and, of course, to shop.

She is in a high-end store, browsing among the chemical-dyed fabric, fingering a taffeta confection in poison green with flared shoulders and a pointed, corset-ready waist, perfect for the high society soirée lined up for tonight.

Randy has left her nearly enough this time, to do justice to her coming social station. She has never met a more tight-fisted man, though he was not this way when they were courting. Then he was all jewelry, flowers, sweetness and light.

Since that girlhood she has discovered that the diamonds were paste, the gold cheap paint, and the courtship an arrangement between her husband and her father, sealed over the fact of her sturdiness and the width of her hips, evidence of the potential for sons.

Still, her life has been very far from bad. It might have started out as business, but she has grown to love him, in spite of his catting. Possibly because of it, for every time he buys a girl it means she can avoid having to do it herself. All that sweating and grunting, so animal, so tasteless. And he is always so sweet to her, so protective, every time he gets back. Kissing her, she likes that part, without expecting it to go anywhere, bringing her pastry and chocolate to keep her fed.

She did her duty, lay there fallow, unmoving like her momma said, imagining cherubs and all the fine things she will have (imagine the status, the clothes, furniture, wealth, showing those trash girls who's boss), hardly breathing, she did her duty and gave him a son.

And what a son! So big and strong already, just like her man, and even if they have to live out there for a while, in that stinking swamp, Tampa is only thirty miles away, she can come here often as their riches increase, so that she can purchase fine things (knowing that Randy will begrudge the money, arguing even when they have it, knowing also who will win) and of course so that she can mingle with the very best people, showing off.

Lydia does not know where the land grant came from, nor the money needed to start out, though she suspects that the grant was pawned. Some once-rich fellow in a jam wandered into Randy's shop and signed it over for a loan worth a fraction of its value.

One he never repaid, one with too high interest or a close deadline for repayment.

Such happens often, though usually for smaller items than fifty acres of land. Watches, rings, and Sunday coats are the usual items, but people sometimes try other things; writers hawk their typewriters for the cost of rent or a weekend long drink, then beg for them back, their stories burning up their brains. Lovers pawn their tokens for a song, and unknown painters try shilling paintings, but Randy has no eye for those, being almost uniformly unsaleable. But all of that is over now, all that meager profit and the loss.

She has a lady's life to think of, now.

Smiling softly, an expression incongruous with her ursine face, she signals over the shop girl, a white, but dark, exotic dressed in brown and peach. Adopting her most refined voice and commanding tones, she signals for the green one, and a new corset to go with it (she misses whale-bone, these new ones are too easy to snap). With a word and a wave of her hand she orders the ill-bred creature to have the things wrapped.

Yes, she thinks to herself, this will do for tonight. I'll fit right in, make good sales. The parcel under her arm, she leaves without thanks. The poor deserve their treatment, forgetting already her former self, subsumed in new identity. If they did not they would have bettered themselves. Thinking as she clamors to the street; this dress will look well on me. And tonight, tonight I'll show them what class is. I'll show them all.

The streets are covered with the well-dressed old, the vital poor, the climbing, and she disappears inside of them, becoming in a moment a brown speck floating in that city which the marshlands soon swallow up, drowning it in distance that acts like a tide.

CONTEMPLATION

Joy is sitting up in bed. The clean sheets she washed and hung out yesterday are wrapped around her in a white froth. There is irony in this, she thinks, turning the dampened pages of her book. We ran out of food for good three weeks ago, finished off the last of the canned food rescued from the back room of the shop, but nearly every house in town forgot to pack their scrubbing soap. She estimates that at the rate things are going she can scrounge enough to keep her and her mother in clean clothes for a further two years.

It's living that long that looks to be the problem, now that they have finally depleted the shop's last cache, even going so far as gnawing on some dubious jerky she discovered in the bottom of one boarding-house drawer. Lord knows she tried her best to make it last. And she and Rose are far too thin as it is, their dresses gaping round their bodies like cheap tents, sweat-split at the armpits from the heat and the damp, displaying the shrunken remnants of their breasts that sit like deflated pads upon their exposed ribs. Luckily there is no one there to see.

But she is just barely a teenager, and it is difficult for that age group to despair. They are, by their natures, far too egotistical. No matter the circumstances, no matter what horrors she has witnessed, death has not yet become something that can happen to her. And never mind that she has watched it overwhelm so many others. It is as though she has, in her extremity of worry, blocked death completely from her conception of the natural world, at least as it relates to her.

Every book that she has ever read has told her either implicitly or directly that there is always a solution to any possible problem.

Either the right idea, some good, kind stranger, or at the very least, some act of providence that arrives at the bare last second, will come to see the hero through.

Well if this is the story, then she is hero of it, and it doesn't even matter much that she is only a girl. She may be struggling, she is definitely stranded, but hope is far from gone. After all, she thinks, in such situations one must ask oneself, what would Robinson Crusoe do? After all, are they not both castaways, sea-bound and lost, with only madmen for comforters?

She smiles for a second, at the thought, an expression bitterly flickering across the pale surface of her face. He would probably not be reduced to what she has found herself doing, setting traps for rats. She only hopes that the rain bashing against her window now will not wash away her bait. If it does, she and Rose are well and truly lost. They haven't the slightest scrap of waste left to set more to spring.

If it comes to that, she doubts that if the five she has scattered through to town are lost she will be able to find another. The store stocked them, of course, but by the time she thought to dig them out they had mostly rusted together. The five that she has armed with scraps and placed in hidden, likely places around the town, in abandoned kitchens mostly, with two settled neatly in the graveyard among eroding tombs and hollow trees, are the last.

Once they are gone? Well. She'll just have to develop some other plan.

For now all that she can do is hope. She has just about given up on the idea of praying.

The storm is really howling now, the wind runs creaking through the trees, precluding even the possibility of sleep. Not that Joy is particularly tired. It is difficult to believe that she used to enjoy storms as a child, now she finds them so unsettling.

This loose-nerved, frightened feeling is not helped by her

choice of reading matter. She cannot seem to make it past the current page, reading and re-reading, in a way that isn't like her, the passage holding Catherine Linton, trapped and wailing, lost among the wind-torn moors.

It takes the quiet appearance of wet droplets on the already discolored pages for her to realize that she is weeping. It takes the sound of her own voice rising up above the sounding storm to know that she has been calling for Bess. She always misses her dog more whenever it is raining. The sound of water pouring down, with no possibility for escape, even the temporary kind provided by a walk outdoors. She has not even entertained the possibility of her childhood frolics in the warm torrential downpour. The water does not mean fun to her anymore.

Frustrated, with herself, the weather, the vast ruins of her curtailed life, she slams shut the book and, grabbing her robe and hurling it over her shoulders (even in desolation a woman must always be clothed), she plunges out of her room without a candle into the dark and lonely hall.

She can hear her mother's voice, raised and raw, a dying rabbit howl, yelling for Malda, calling for Joy using the name her daughter despises, crying out loudly, for David. The names of the dead. Joy does her best to ignore her.

She will comfort her mother with what food she has, when she can get it, soothe her feathers with clean sheets and warm water, but she has accepted long ago that her face and voice, her loving touch, mean nothing to the lady. Let her cry. Rose will wear herself out and then she will settle into sleep, sinking down into a better, safer world.

If only Joy's problems were as easy to solve.

She has finally reached the library, having to push hard against the water-swollen door in order to stumble across the threshold. The first thing she sees is the door-hanging tapestry, the one her mother loves – it has torn from its moorings and pooled on the floor, so much blue cotton. When she picks it up, gently, cradling the strands, it unravels all at once. So much for that. All of those birds and branches, that fine woven sky, reduced to a puddle of molded thread. Frankly, remembering the humidity, it is amazing how long that poor thing lasted. It is probably just as well.

It was beginning to stink.

She moves to the bookshelves, pausing to light her small lamp, remembering to keep the flame low to conserve the last inch of fuel. There. It is just high enough for her to read by, if she strains.

Her fingers trail idly along the shelves, outlining books that she is coming close to knowing very intimately. Another few years and they will all be her friends. Finally, her fingers, all long, save for the thumb and smallest pinky, trace out an old favorite, her closest friend. A Greek named Odysseus setting off for a journey, a convoluted voyage home. It may take a long while, but he'll get there, in the end.

She loves this book for many reasons, all connected; it reminds her of her father. Lends her some hope.

She reads through the dark, warm in the chair, missing Bess, while the night passes all around her, the storm at the window at last dying out. The sun rises fresh and bright, a thick golden band bound around the treed horizon.

She rises with it, yawning and stretching, but not at all tired, slipping on her hole-soled gum boots before going out into thigh-deep water to assess the damage and check on her traps.

While the natural world looks bright and refreshed, as though every tree, every leaf, each droplet of water had been painted afresh by some unbelievably skilled artist, the human world looks worse for it. While only one building has sustained any actual damage – the white church has lost about half of its roof, only the space above the altar remaining intact – the shop and every former dwelling-place looks slightly more worn, a bit more run down, the paint more chipped, the porch and sidewalks listing towards starboard or port. Including her own.

This saddens Joy, but she can do nothing about it. Entropy is inevitable. It comes for all things, and right now Joy has not the energy, the strength or the supplies to further combat it. Things fall apart, the center cannot hold, mere anarchy is loosed upon the world. The water and the soil must have all the rest. She has enough difficult work on her plate just to maintain her own survival.

The traps she set in the abandoned kitchens were still there and sprung, three healthy males, all swamp-fed and huge. Enough for Rose and daughter to eat for two days. She moves to put them, traps and all, back into her bag, but then she thinks better of it, and grabs out her knife instead.

The ivory handle fits well in her hand, the blade silver and sharp in this light, and it slices through the rodents' taunt belly-skin like a hot wire through butter. She sets the three used traps again, and baits them with warm entrails, thinking; let's see how rats feel about eating their brothers.

She stops off at the churchyard next, checking the hollows of the boabs to see if the others there have survived the night. They haven't.

This is probably just as well, she thinks, after all even rats are what they eat. And I haven't sunk down that far yet, not far enough to eat the dead. Not that far down by a good long way.

She slings the leather satchel, now bloody at the bottom, over her shoulder and turns back to the house. She was right, something did happen. They have enough, today, to eat. And now, at last, she can afford to be tired, and she will be able to sleep with a full, or nearly full, belly without the fear of storms.

As for tomorrow? She has three more traps set. Tomorrow can take care of itself.

PARTY

The party went off perfectly, the cream of Tampa's business elite all gathered together in the hotel's massive ballroom, mauve-carpeted and with wallpaper of deep blue and bilious yellow stripes, all run round in ribbons. The ceiling was of red-tinted copper, cast in nouveau flowers and the occasional nymph with Arabic flourishes, and its centerpiece was the dazzling, crystal-dripping electric chandelier, the very latest thing.

It was dark outside, but brilliant here. The curtains were drawn, a deep rose silk thread through with gold, to close the bay life out. If they were not important enough to have been invited they had no purpose being visible to any gathered here, and the flames were not for them to gape at, nor the music to entice.

The music here was loud, though stately, and not the trash the riff-raff knew as 'the very latest thing', unless that thing was Wagner. Ralph Johnson, for one, knew which one he would have preferred. And that was not this German crap, though he had to admit the themes were good. All that sex, the rape and conquer, sentiments he could get behind and lend his full support to.

He is mingling now, making connections and promissory sales. The men are dressed, appropriately enough, for opera. All top hats and the slash of bright cravat. The women lounge in Regency chairs, drawn from across an ocean, a country five thousand miles away, nibbling canapés and waiting to dance. When Victoria was alive they would have been scandalous, but at this late date they are nearly blasé. Though Randy is from an older time and can hardly tear his eyes away from that vast expanse of white breasts. His pleasure is immense, and he is grateful that most of it remains hidden by trousers and long-cut jacket.

Still, it is probably better if he asks no one to dance. But were his son here, the boy would have enjoyed it, and for a moment he feels bad for keeping him from this swirl, a hurricane of flesh and color, before remembering their evening plans, to be enacted after these old folks have retired and his wife lies snoring in her bed.

As of now he has work to do, so he'd damned well better focus. He is speaking to an old plume hunter, still tanned and querulous in spite of his silk. He made himself rich on the stock market after the birds ran out and is, for Randy, a man to be admired, though he still talks like a redneck and every few minutes has to visibly restrain the urge to spit.

'Yeah,' he warbles, sloshing his drink, 'I know the land yer gonna be a working on.' He sips, tongue caressing a few orange teeth. 'Worked there myself till the birds ran out and I came here to make a different killing. It's good land for cane. Woulda tried her myself if I hadn't gone and got so damned old.'

Randy waits, not drinking, nodding.

'You can probly get away with spreading yer furrows around a bit, since the town went defunct, but be careful, you hear?' The old man smiles at Johnson's pricked ears. 'You ain't exactly gonna be alone down there. They some Catholics, hard people to deal with, bout twenty miles down, and some others that I would definitely avoid. But yer real problem is likely to be the old parson's wife, and her daughter.'

The old man stops talking, looks blindly away, as though seeing some specter, hovering ghostly, only visible to him.

Randy brings him back on track. 'Yeah? What about them?'

The man looks back with some indefinable expression, something in the shadow-rich place between guilt and fear.

'When the town dried up, those two stayed. Dunno why, the preacher was dead by then, but anyway they stayed. Now, the daughter ain't nothing but a button, twelve, maybe thirteen, but the momma, that widow lady, she's run crazy. Sometimes violent. She fought us when we tried to drag her out. Tooth and claw, she fought. Wouldn't let us take the girl.'

He raises his hand to his forehead, in benediction or shame. 'God knows what they're living on. We used to send food wagons, but the cost,' licked lips, 'and the grocers hated the trail. There ain't no real roads. With money it ain't no problem. But that ain't my point.' The old man looks at Johnson through muddy eyes. 'The point is you look like an entrepreneurial fella, the kind I like, but if you step one toe on their property uninvited, I'll hear about it, my friends will too and they're young and strong. If you do, you'd better be praying that God loves you then, son, cause otherwise you haven't the chance of a schooner in a hurricane.'

With that the man was gone, swirled away into the intoxicated fray. Leaving Johnson most enlightened. A widow and a young girl. Hm. Much to think about. A waiter circled like a gull at feeding, offered him a gold-filled glass. Randy smiled, living up admirably to his name under long-cut jacket fondling through his pocket, and for the first time all that evening he took a drink. Imagine, out there, somewhere, there is a young girl. All alone.

There is so much to plan.

SETTLERS

The Johnsons were camped out in tents on the driest point of their claim where the land rose up on a slight rise. Already their workers were set to work in two groups, one to clear the future fields of trees (the oak trees were saved for building the slave-huts and barns, mangrove and boab good only for fuel), while the other bent their backs to water-covered earth, scooping up buckets of river mud that will be used to raise the land that will hold the house even further, as a way of discouraging flood. As for the shacks the workers will build, after they have assembled the big house and the barns, if it floods they will be wet. Nothing more to it than that.

The raw materials of the big house have been dragged along on wagon-back from the train depot, an easy-to-assemble kit from Sears and Roebuck, all knotty white pine and machine-cut veneers, that the men will assemble once they've built a suitable foundation. Mr. Johnson wanted to purchase the cheaper one-story variety, but his missus held her ground. She wants to live someplace with class.

The next step is getting some fine things to decorate it with. A problem that Randy would solve as cheaply as he can. They came out here to make money, not spend it. Luckily, he thinks, the nearest serviceable High Street is an eight-hour coach ride away. She'll have to make do.

Still, it would be nice to do something for her, if he can do it on the cheap. Maybe he'll pick her up a plated candle stick or something next time he's in town to see the cathouses and score some sales. He can tell Lydia it's solid, she won't know the difference. It'll make her happy and earn him some grace.

But first things first, the house must be assembled, and when the land is cleared, the trees all vanished, and cane shoots planted in the water furrows. All of those things will take some time. Nothing to do then but take turns with his son supervising the men (these people are naturally lazy, tricky, it's a racial trait) and getting a reading on the land.

That reminds me, he thinks, we are only five miles from that ghost town the old fella told me about, and that crazy woman with the pretty daughter. I might as well wander on over there, meet the neighbors, so to speak, and see things for myself.

Randy Jr. is keeping up the pace with his black whip, making sure they keep to schedule. He seems to be doing a pretty good job. Lord almighty! Watch those Blacks move. Nothing like a little motivation. He can leave for a few hours; leave the work in the boy's capable hands.

He saddles up his broken mule, fitting the bite deep in the bleeding corners of the animal's mouth. Never noticing its dead eyes, they trundle through the swamp.

Mosquitoes bite and needle his flesh but he does not notice anything beyond the vast expanse of marsh, and the dollars that will blossom there, once he has removed the saw-grass and the useless trees. The five-mile journey takes a little over an hour on mule-back, but his daydreams entertain him and leave him a little disappointed when the trees thin out a bit at the entrance of the town.

Things are running down here, terribly neglected there is no doubt, but no more so yet than many other shit-poor towns he's traveled through. It's only been three years, he thinks, things here'll get more interesting as they progress, given word enough and time.

He smiles at the thought; it should be fun to watch.

There are panes missing from windows, weeds in between the

sidewalk boards, and the thin stench of decay over everything, rotten wood and the odor of wet socks curled into a ball and long forgotten. The worst damaged has got to be the peaked roof of the church. It is half-collapsed already, the steeple fallen down to the floor, the stained glass from shattered windows littering the yard-grass like Mardi Gras, the colors of a broken world.

The area over what must have been the altar remains standing yet, but it can't for much longer, it is already canted for the plummet, the only good news (were there anyone to receive it) lies in the fact that the roof is angled to fall in such a way that it should spare the Table of the Host, though no Communion will ever more be said there.

Randy likes to see it lying thus; he has no use for priests or churches. Or heaven and hell, come to that. He wants to do well now, to live, to eat, to have the occasional hot-blooded fuck and at the end of all that, sit back in his chair with his family around him, platters in hand and adoration in their eyes. It is a good life, if not quite enough, but that is another problem that time will resolve.

He has other things on his mind, right now.

First things first, where to find that lonely little girl?

This problem turns out to be not so very difficult to solve, for he can see her there standing in her rust-red dress, looking at him. She has been sweeping the porch of the stilt-born manse (now there's an idea, a house on stilts) moving toward the stairs. But now her broom has stilled, though she grips it with white knuckles and peers at him through dark, wide eyes that are reminiscent of an owl's.

Poor little girl, he thinks, smiling; three years alone and ripe for the picking. He is walking closer, maintaining eye contact, it wouldn't be good for her to run. I might have to groom her a little, break her in enough to get her ready, but who knows? A little time, a little feed to keep her from starving (and who says I have to give it to her for nothing? That's a big house, she might have something I can give the wife, to encourage a bigger, later trade) a bit of time and a few well-chosen words and, mother or no mother, she'll be eating out of my hand.

He is climbing the steps now, hands held empty out before him, smile stretching out his lips. The girl looks hypnotized, too dazed to run, wielding her broom like a weapon. In the second-story windows there is a flash of blue, gone before he can really see it, a thin voice wailing out an off-key song.

He makes his voice all brash and hearty, bristling with good cheer. 'Why hello there, little miss. Is your momma home?' he reaches out while talking, prying her hand from the broom handle and giving it a few good pumps.

The girl's voice is weak and shadow-splintery, very afraid. 'No. She is… indisposed.'

A hesitation, his heart stirs; so the story is true. This is going to be fun.

The girl has extracted her small hand, her eyes distrustful, staring. 'Who are you, sir? What do you want?'

'Why, I'm surprised you have to ask that, lady.' He sweeps off his black leather hat, genuflects a playful bow. 'I'm your neighbor, your good friend.' His smile edges wider, showing rows of white teeth. 'I want to offer you a little help.'

Of course she had to let him in.

He left after twenty minutes minus a promise and the loss of the dinner roll he brought for lunch. But the word he carried back with him more than made up for the loss. He'll have to tell Lydia to get ready for company tomorrow, get her to clear a space of honour in their tent. Even with so very few neighbors, there will be a housewarming party, and an appropriate gift.

He was not bored on the way back, either, driving his dying

148

mule through acres of mud. There was so much to think of and prepare for. Maybe, he thinks, smiling, when she is ready, he and Randy can share her. But he'll get her first. Oh, the pleasures of the young!

TOUR

Joy escorted the big man out and leaned against the thick front door. Recently the wood has begun to swell, making it more difficult to close without causing wet crumbs of once-expensive oak to gather across the threshold like the leavings of woodworm. Eventually she will stop using it entirely, reduced like a servant or a tradesman to using only the rear kitchen door.

She is trying, very hard, not to think about what just happened. But of course, when the conscious mind would leave it back, that dark interior traitor brings it ever to the fore. For the last three years she has seen no one but her mother and, at first, the trader from the store. She has been praying for someone, anyone, to come and help her. And God sent this.

A big man with a gator smile, that same dead welcome that invites small birds to peck the flesh caught between his teeth. Such animal generosity, ensuring him of a quick and ready snack when the food runs scarce, available with one swift motion of the jaws, and until that inevitability the lizard gets his teeth cleaned, free. Joy does not want to be that bird. And she cleans enough destruction as it is.

He sickened her, on some level, almost immediately. There was an attitude about him, a way of looking at the world that seemed if not entirely malevolent, at least mockingly cruel. It was in the way he looked around at everything when she led him in, his small eyes twinkling in jovial greed, as though he were surveying things already his.

He kept picking up the mementos that her family left in his enormous, thick-fingered hands; her grandmother's favourite Dalton teacup from the hearth, delicate and pink with small painted flowers, a thick carved silver candlestick, a gold-gilt cigarette box, bringing them all up close to his face to linger there in a way that would be, in any other context, highly offensive. He would stare at them for far too long, smiling.

All the while, Joy was silent.

It had been so long since she had spoken with another human being, who was not her own increasingly scattered mother, that she was torn between her own intense dislike and her longing for human companionship of any kind. Of course he asked for the tour. He wanted, he said, to get a handle on how the people used to live here, before the sickness and the mass extinction. He wanted to know what life was like in the good times. As though he were some form of anthropologist, studying the long-dead natives, and not just some farmer tired of scrimping and hungry for more.

She led him around rooms that had sunk to the level of shabby genteel, kept as clean as she could, but the wallpaper was beginning to spot along the ceiling-line, the hardwood floors grown slimy underneath her feet, the varnished shine maintained by careful waxing long rubbed off, leaving greasy white blisters in patches where the wear was worst.

He drank it all in, the highboy in the parlour, stocked with antique decanters in cut crystal with silver stoppers and a sterling George the Third coffee set (a gift from David's mother on the occasion of their wedding) carved round with vines and grapes. She could tell that he was picturing them, already, in other, fresher places where the air was more populated and less still.

She knew that he could hear the footsteps overhead, the soft murmur of one-sided, disjointed conversation, the dragging sound of something heavy being moved across the floor (Rose was moving furniture again, God only knows why). But he said nothing with his voice, though his eyes twinkled at the sounds as though at a particularly good but filthy joke. Inappropriate for mixed company.

But then, then this whole situation was a farce, wasn't it? A grown man and a little girl playing hostess in the wild? There was something inherently a little off about the situation, Joy could feel it, that went deeper than his hunger for fine things, deeper than his almost tangible greed. But she was young, and could not identify it.

She led him further on.

He lingered over the sideboard in the dining room, casually opening drawers (without a word of question or permission) carefully opening the mahogany cutlery box and fingering the wrought silver knives and forks all stacked within, edged around the scrollwork in bright gold. Joy remembers watching him reach into a drawer and carefully unwrap a bone china platter, painted delicately round with scenes of feasting done in a style after the Greek.

He lifted it above his head so that the faint afternoon light filtered through the substance of that plate, rendering it an indoor moon, and the look on his face as he stared at it was of such fierce, wolfish hunger, and of such surety of possession, that it caused the girl to feel a shudder all the way down the length of her spine and into the base of her stomach. A deep, pervasive cold.

Eventually, he lay the platter down again, setting it gently in the center of the table, not bothering to put it away. He ran his fingers along the gilded edge, softly, as though in reassurance along the face of a child. Not to worry, baby, I'll take you home soon.

When Joy led him out, intending to show him the library, he lingered in the doorway for a moment, looking back at the setting of the room, the beauty of it, the way the hardwood glimmered in the light, the white silver fittings highlighting delicate carving.

Even after three years of limited care and habitation, the room retains the delicate, mellow glow of undeniable quality. His figure is made, by contrast, even larger and more rude.

She has been alone a long time, but not nearly long enough to undo the programming of her first ten years, lived among the swamp society. She has not yet rid herself of absorbed manners or wiped away the tutelage of her mother given in other, more civilized years. This means that although she would love nothing more than to fling this man from her house, she cannot.

Besides, a small voice ponders, rising up in her mind, this man is a farmer, and that means supplies. While I doubt that he would be willing to help you out of the goodness of his heart, if he has one, he might be willing to trade.

Joy was terribly afraid of what his reaction would be to the last room on the public tour, the only place other than her small bedroom, that she still cares about at all. Imagine her surprise when he hardly glanced around at it, hardly pausing over the bound treasures piled up inside, his eyes stopping only for a moment on the cleared surface of the desk, before being caught by the large stained-glass window that glowed in this light like a jewel on fire, Persephone in flames.

But that is all he glanced at. Perhaps because it was impossible for him to cart that lady away.

The books he showed no interest in, not even the large and gilded Bible on the stand. These were things he could not comprehend buying and when Joy saw that disinterest on his face, her heart leapt in her breast, a flutter of pure, untainted relief that in no way cut the resentment forming along beside it, planted by what she knew even now was coming next.

If she had anything to offer, any tea or coffee, the time to do it would be now, and the fact that she could give him nothing but cool water in fine china weakened her position. They talked for a brief few minutes, he spoke and she agreed, in no position at this time to do any less. Before he left, lightening the air for Joy in the freedom of his absence, he slipped a fresh dinner roll, light and flaky with lard, wrapped in a white handkerchief, into her extended hand.

She tried her best to suppress the hunger that she felt, the overwhelming passionate desire to feel the whole thing in her mouth at once. It is a struggle, but in the end she succeeded in maintaining a face that was carefully blank.

The last thing he says to her as she escorts him to the porch is delivered in a voice both laughing and dangerous. 'Bring that back to the house tomorrow, with the other thing. Make sure it's washed.' He tips his fine black leather hat at her, in mocking insouciance. 'It was a pleasure, little lady. See you in the morning.'

And with a smile, he is gone.

We will leave her where we found her, slumped and breathing fast, leaning up against the crumbling oaken door. Her lips tremble slightly and there are crumbs on her cheek, wet down by tears. She is wondering about the contract signed in blood, the one usually, but not always required, when one has sold one's soul.

AID AND SUCCOR IN THE WILD

Joy is making her slow and winding way through trees and vines grown as thick and verdant as they must have done in paradise. She is going to a place where she has never been. The land spreads out all before her, a green girdle of water and moss. The deep concussive brunt of an alligator, hunting, rises up from her left. She notices enough to veer a little in the opposite direction but otherwise she holds her course, the leather satchel held over her shoulder heavy, continuously bumping the bony knob of her hip. Tomorrow there will be a bruise.

An osprey circles high overhead, angled wings and curved, predatory head visible for one brief instant through the canopy of leaves. Its beak opens, letting out an air-raid cry, the sound of some small creature's death. It plummets to the earth again, once satiated, the body of a serpent dangling from its talon; it claws the air to rise.

Joy would trade places with it in a second.

Mr. Johnson, her new neighbor, frightened her badly. Looking at her house like everything contained within it was negotiable, up for sale. Who knows, she thinks, her hand on her shrunken, three-day-empty belly, perhaps it is.

Her last store of food ran out two weeks ago, leaving her with nothing but the things she could catch. They have had two fish and one skinned rat. She is not willing to do that again, it was too messy, too bloody and cruel, but who knows? Another few days of nothing seasoned with nothing and she might set out more traps. This meeting could be a blessing.

At least his wife will be there this time, her presence discouraging him from looking at her the way he did yesterday, as though she were flesh; butcher-dressed and ready for roasting, to keep him fed. She has already decided that, no matter how this meeting goes, she will trade with these people as little as possible. Just enough to keep fed.

Her mother is worrying her. Rose's madness deepens every day, and nothing for Joy to do but keep her alive and hope for the best.

She has reached the place where the workmen are clearing, though they are not being treated like employees, judging by the red stripes that mar their many-hued spans of skin. They stare at her, gape-mouthed, as she passes, but say not a word. For her part, Joy tries to ignore them, too hungry for pity. Though the sight of the men send warning bells sounding through her too-vivid senses to echo in her heart.

The canvas tents stand up on a slight rise that more men are forcing ever higher with each slung bucket of mud. When she has climbed a quarter of the way up it, she realizes that her ankles are dry for the first time since she set out this morning.

The tents are white in this noon light; scorching hot sunshine dries the mud from the buckets and sets heat shimmers rising from the canvas, unfiltered by trees. The wagons are beside them, and crouching underneath one chassis, like a devil far from hell, she can see a rough black head, hungry eyes, and a teenage mouth: white, sharp teeth smiling.

A huge, bearlike woman stands in front of the first tent, waving.

'Why, my Lord, you must be Joy.' Her voice is surprisingly high, cracking. She takes Joy's hand in moist and meaty grip, completely enclosing it. 'Well don't just stand there, come in! Come in!'

And Joy is swallowed up.

Inside, the room is Spartan, some bed-rolls, some make-do

chairs and table crates, a pile of cheap deal-work furniture piled up in boxes, unopened, some pointed wrong-side up.

Randy Johnson is staring at her, eyes shaded by his black hat, shining leather, his mouth stretched out from side to side, a tin tea set steaming before him, plate of cookies balanced close to hand. He gestures toward a splintered soap box.

Sit. Sit.

Already she is dizzy from the sight of food, the scent of tea with cream splashed in it. An easy enough thing, buying souls cheap. It's all in the timing. Like a good tragedy.

What follows is fast, obscene and dirty, like the struggle in a dark alley. There is not, at first, much talking. Joy eats twelve cookies, stuffing more in her satchel when she thinks no one's looking. But Randy can see. He sets more out while Lydia pours fresh tea, mumbling softly. Something about ill-mannered pigs.

Once the edge is off her hunger (it would take more than cookies to shear off the base) they start talking. She brings out her silver: fine English sterling, Birmingham marks. A candelabrum carved round in cherubs and roses, fit for a queen and weighing five pounds. It came into this country nearly two hundred years ago, in her great-great-ancestor's trunk. It was sitting on the mantle yesterday, as always, when Randy came through the door.

Lydia begins visibly to drool, wiping her face with the back of her hand. Randy keeps his pawning eyes carefully veiled. He offers her a price.

'It's worth more than that in flour sir. My bag will be heavier, not lighter, when I make my way home.'

Oh, he thinks, she has some spirit. That could make this more difficult, though I know if I press her, she'll take very little. She'll have to, her momma is starving. But then, challenge adds flavor. I'll let the girl play.

Man and girl go back and forth for over an hour, Johnson enjoying every second of it, like some women treasure foreplay. In the end they settle on a workable price. One month's worth of food, to be driven there now by a slave man leading the mule-cart.

The bleeding-backed man is called in, given his orders and told what he will be loading up. The black man with rusty-sprung halo of curls nods at the girl (his tongue is missing), silent. He will give her a ride.

Randy Johnson leads her out while bear-bodied Lydia is clearing the tea, and hands her up into the cart, taking a moment (he can't quite resist) to pinch her small, already lovely chest. But no, he must pace himself, not frighten her too quickly. After all, smiling, he has nothing but time.

Joy feels more shame at that touch than at selling her daddy's treasures for a month's worth of food, but she can do nothing. Johnson is right. She and mama have to eat.

The cart starts up, the old mules plodding. Joy looks back in time to see the elder Johnson sketching out a sardonic bow, tipping his black hat. Next time, she thinks, I will bring a knife.

A girl has to be careful, her legs tired, musing as they draw off into the swamp, there are things in this forest more terrible than wolves. Heck, I'd welcome a wolf, any dog who'd be my friend, and it's men that I fear.

The cart draws off into the darkness surrounding them, green and hiding many poisons. In the air around her echoes the death-cry of a foraging hawk, warning its prey, so soon to still, sliced and bitter in its sharp jaws.

GEORGIA

The coyotes have reached the mountain lands, a part of the world named years ago by humans for an English king who ran delirious in the moonlight that dazzled on his throne and lost a nation to his madness. The dogs know nothing of this, nor would they care. They are a fierce tribe, a determined band of travelers. None but the very oldest of the dogs now living have ever seen the land they left behind, none but the very youngest will remain alive when they finally arrive, and the alpha who will lead them there has not yet been conceived, nor will he be, for a further generation.

The leader now is a middle-aged female, sleek and strong, her fur a dark umber, her teeth strong and white. She is an exquisite hunter and proud, in her own way, to know that her bloodline carries the fulfilment of the Lady's prophecy. She howls her thanks for this, every night.

Their progress has been slow, but steady, stopping every few weeks to rest and feed, regaining some of the muscle lost, burnt off like fog by the effort of flight. They stop, in places where no other tribes have left their scent, digging temporary dens in desert or sand, or wet river-mud. They stay long enough for the females to whelp and for those pups to be weaned, growing, in a few short weeks, strong enough to run.

They stop for death. When an old one begins to slow, or limp, they find a place to rest. This alpha likes to find a soft thicket, hidden by trees (her ancestor who began this journey never saw one till a week before her death. She was amazed by its height, its greenness, though it was merely a scrub-pine), these deciduous forests where small rabbits run and deer gather to sing their songs of birth and feeding.

It is lovely here, all rolling hills and loam, far from the dead roads humans carve, though occasionally they discover a small grave hidden in the woods, marked with a small cross, delicious scents, forbidden and appetising, rising from the loose-packed ground. They have resisted the temptation of that food, so far, though it is a struggle for the alpha to keep the puppies back.

When the old ones die, the tribe mourns communally, howling out the wisdom of passed lives, baying out their grief, and wishing the ones that have vanished all the pleasure of their final journey to their Lady of the Moon.

And of course, they stop for winter, for those months are sacred to Hecate, the crossroad time of stillness and death, and it is dangerous to be abroad. Who knows what a dog might meet on those forbidden, winding roads?

So the journey has lingered, despite the longing in their blood. The animals are not worried. It is not time yet, nor even close. A further few marches of years and generations will pass before they reach their final home. For the avatar is still young, a puppy really, but she is ever growing, darkening into her secret power.

They shall find her, soon enough, and love her when they do. Love her, as they love their Lady, as bitches love their puppies, as dogs love their mates. They shall sing to her the romance that predators impart to pray, in the moment before the heart stops beating, in that final, passionate struggle that is in itself a variation on the act of love.

They run, loping, teeth bared and with distended pink tongues. The prophecy has come at last. They, or their children's children, shall reach her in the end, and rise with open mouths and flagging tails, to meet their goddess face to face.

Friday

NIGHT

There are many ghosts here, though not all of them are dead. This is a haunted place, haunted by them. Joy knows this, but can do nothing about it. She sleeps, her white nightgown twisted shroud-like round her, writhing in her abandoned room. She is almost running in her sleep, as a dog will when caught in the tangles of some ill-made dream of hunting and the stalk, but that is not unusual. She has not had a decent night's sleep in well over ten years.

Her room is damp, unaccountably squalid, though she tries to keep her few things neat, her books stacked neatly on her shelf, her hairbrush and comb set, Bakelite (the tortoise and silver long sold off), set at right angles beneath the darkening mirror with algae blooming from the frame. She has stopped looking at the images there, stopped examining the progression of her own changing face, finding it more difficult to fight than to ignore.

The mold is creeping in from the corners, sending its black fingers trailing across the length of the wall, like drying scabs. The floorboards are spongy and rock beneath even her light weight, anticipating the day when they will release themselves, give way and fall, possibly pulling her down with them, as though to hell. The wallpaper, once William Morris blue peacocks, is sloughing off like dead skin revealing a new form, and the blood her father lost when dying, the once-bright spatters propelled by coughing still glimmering darkly on the wall nearest to her bed. She would not remove them, even if the rest of the house could be somehow restored. There are fewer links to him every day, why should she remove the ones she does not have to fight to keep?

But she is not thinking about any of that now. Her eyes flick, knifelike, back and forth beneath purplish lids, as though watching a play which only she can see. That is what dreams are. Her white forehead creases, her full lips purse, an expression that in her youth conveys confusion without even the far shadow of age.

Bend closer.

She is mouthing something.

Daddy. No.

In her dream she is walking down the town's long main street, walking down the center road that runs between the mercantile and the churchyard. The colors are brighter now than they have ever been, each boab and mangrove leaf etched out in shattering detail so numinously lovely in this afternoon light that it hurts her mind. She can see every detail, from the gold-glimmering dust in between the sidewalk-boards, to the cracks that maw like canyons in the rough bark of the trees, revealing their own ant-filled worlds.

There are people around her, milling, jewel-toned clothes. A man in jasper tilts his broad-brimmed hat at her, smiling from a face that exudes light like sweat. She smiles, uncertain, and curtsies back. A woman and a little girl walk by, the lady wearing lapis, amethyst for the child, each stitch and tuck of their clothing, each button, each whisper of lace appearing more real than any of their counterparts, which she has ever seen in waking life.

She drinks it in, open mouthed, breathing in the sweet, rich scent of healthy swamp in full spring blossom. The scent of oranges, mango, fresh-cut grass.

She is looking for something, someone, her father. Of course. Her mother is at home, in bed. Where else could she be? (But no, Joy, do not think of that.) She was meant to see her daddy after rounds, when he wanders from house to house with his wafer and wine, ministering to the sick. He is here. Somewhere. She must be running late.

The mercantile, a general store if ever there was one, filled to brimming with bolts of bright cloth, silver-flashes, the fresh scent of new bread, acres of sugar-candies lining the walls in huge jars, is as full of people as always. They smile out at her, peering through the wide glass windows, drowned in light. They move, almost in unison, hands up, waving.

She smiles back, and even here that feels a strange expression on her face. It isn't until she catches her reflection in the window, a glimpse caught in passing, that she realizes she is a woman now, and not a child. She is appalled by her rat-nest hair, it seems to be just piled up on the top of her head. Her red-black dress is nothing but a rag.

Why did no one tell me? Why did Mama not stop me coming out? (But yes, her mama is asleep. No Joy, shhh, do not think.) I hope I find my daddy soon.

The streets are crowded now, all those bright, clean people, all those rich clothes, like heavenly robes and her ensconced in flesh and rag, propelled by her own beating heart. They all curtsey or bow, seeming to glow softly, making her ever more aware of her thin crust of grime. Look, there is blood on her wrist. Where did that come from?

None can tell her where her father is, none even seem to speak at all. Her heart is tearing in her chest, sending up a sharp and painful ache that speaks of panic, and all she can do for the first little while is shunt herself up and down the sidewalk, calling.

Houses blow their windows open, as though in some strange mass exhalation, the shutters tearing off, the window-glass shattering, they stare with dead eyes. They lose their paint like leprous skin, coming off in swatches, the wood beneath them crumbling with rot, as though time has sped up dreadfully and all their keepers gone.

The store is empty now, the windows broken, the bread gone

to mold, the candy fossilized or turned to foul-smelling syrup in jars. There is no light, no faces inside. All the people who are still glowing, still smiling, stand outside on the sidewalk, on the street, row on row back into the ancient bone yard. She runs among them, all those bright people with their vacant eyes, calling. None of them is David.

She does not notice the sidewalk crumbling beneath her feet, does not heed that charnel smell rising from the golden flesh she brushes past, does not see the skulls beneath their lovely skin, though the bones explain the grins.

She plunges past them in her grime and rags.

The church is suddenly decrepit, the roof caved in. He cannot be inside. And anyway, when did this happen? This awful ruin? She does not allow herself to question too deeply, knowing that the ruin is right. Nor does she notice the canine length of head protruding from the hollow beneath the shattered door, watching rapt, with bright eyes. Even if she did, what of it? Her dog died years ago.

For a town so full of people, the cemetery is empty, the graves open, the people cleared out. She is alone, in a dead place, and no sign of Christ.

But no, not quite. There is another figure there.

The form of a man, tall and thin.

Her father at last.

He is leaning against the hollow tree he liked to read under, before he died, looking out at the declining sun painting its red fingers across the shadow-raising sky. One hand rests on that hollow his fingers caressing the crenulated bark as though touching the savored skin of a lover.

His Bible is in his other hand, the one he was buried with. The binding has loosened and some of the pages have fallen out. The revelation. *And a great sign appeared in heaven: A woman clothed with the sun, and the moon under her feet, and on her head a crown of twelve stars. And being with child, she cried travailing in birth: and was in pain to be delivered. And there were given to the woman two wings of a great eagle, that she might fly into the desert, unto her place, where she is nourished for a time and times, and half a time, from the face of the serpent.* They lay at his feet, curling in mud. She could read every word, though the letters they were cast in were Greek. Her father taught her how to read them, long ago.

The dog was watching from the door. She knew he was there. She did not know. Both were true somehow, and at once.

Her father did not turn to look at her, he was too absorbed by the flames spreading in the sky, their house caught as if wood for the fire, ready to be utterly consumed, reduced to ashes on the whirlwind. And look: the clouds behind the sunset, the great blackness of an evening storm.

The face he finally turns to her, at Joy's touch, is nothing but skull decorated with a few strips of flesh. She is not afraid; though her heart is rushing, it rushes with love.

He is still he, and when he speaks the words come in his voice, unaffected and unslurred, though he lacks both tongue and lips. That same deep voice that sang her softly to sleep. 'Joy,' the skeletal hand leaves off the bark, comes round to cradle her wan face, 'my Joy. You have been asleep.'

She shakes her head, no! Sending her black hair flying.

The bones trace their passage over cheek, over lip, caressing with their degradation, their mortified remnants of flesh. 'No. Joy, you must wake up.'

And he is falling, as he speaks, fading into dust beneath her grasping, longing hands, his suit unravelling around him as though composed of spider-web and whisper.

'No, Daddy. No.' The tears are falling, making clean streaks down her face, wetting her rust-red dress to black, but he is fading, fading, like a photographic image fades when left in chemicals too long, until even the smell of him, the stench of rot and dust, muddy clothes (the underscent of aftershave, fresh cream, male sweat) has vanished from the air, and she is by the tree, alone.

But not entirely. There is a canine figure slinking out from its hiding place in the desecrated church. A strong, long form with shining eyes, a rough pelt, and a long snout filled to brimming with sharp teeth.

Like Joy, this creature walks, in love.

The sky is darkening, the storms building up, the sunset throbs along the skyline. She stares, leaning up against the tree in her wind-rippled rags. The light is infected, like a sullen flame or the space around a gangrenous cut. There is lightning, and the electric out-riding current of wind.

A big storm brewing, and coming up fast. A death of fire and water to put paid to this ruinous world.

And suddenly, at last, Joy wakes up.

There are tears and a familiar keening in her heart, but she has had such dreams before and knows well how to deal with them. Get up, scrounge for food, live out what small, sick life remains. Begin again, with different expectations.

Her room is foul, but the light is fresh and new, as it can be in the mornings, after rain. She wipes the few tears from her cheeks, inadvertently touching the places where her father's fingers lingered in her dream, a thought that sends a shudder down her spine, even as desire grabs her heart.

There is no breakfast waiting for her, nor any sort of bath, but that is no excuse to lie abed in filthy, tangled sheets. She is up, her nightgown cast off, stripped away and folded on her only chair. Her dress replaces it.

The wound on her wrist looks better today, making a good start. And she had better begin herself. Even though she is getting nowhere, there is still a lot to do.

Joy closes the door behind her as she leaves, locking in her troubling bed, the pillow still embossed with the imprint of her head, waiting for the night when sleep, and hope, and death in dreams, will come clamoring again.

TRAVELER

Tampa in the decade after the turn of the century is a city of fifteen thousand, most of whom are new immigrants, fresh off boats and trains from Italy, Germany, New York. They are Catholics and Jews, natives from Mexico, the odd descendants of Spanish soldiers who arrived in 1640, the occasional longhaired Seminole hawking dried key deer meat by the side of the road.

The five-hundred-bedroomed Tampa Bay Hotel is nearly twenty years old, resplendent in the Moorish revival style, its greenish minarets in tarnished bronze glinting in the sun. It caters to the rich who come here to be cured in the sun, in health and skin tone; this is the first American generation whose elderly will choose to transform their backs into leather. There are illegal Bolita parlours in dark back alleys, church socials on sunlit streets, and restaurants at the seaport that will serve a deep-fried breaded grouper fillet on a hard Keiser roll to anyone with a dime in their pocket, French-fried potatoes spiced with pepper and vinegar for five cents more, and a broiled slice of gator flank with a glass of wine for fifteen pennies.

There are top-end clothing stores, expensive retailers of silver, gold, porcelain, a thriving art scene, new painters being discovered here every day, beggars on the streets dying slowly of syphilis and mescaline, cheap boghole rot-gut posing as moonshine, courtesans and whores walking with fine ladies on their way to dance the afternoon and night away at the Ringling mansion. It is difficult to believe that only thirty miles from here the land is still primarily frontier. In fact, less than ten miles away the unincorporated township of Braden Town huddles against the seafront, peopled mainly by itinerant workers of the new

Havana Cigar Company, the Art Nouveau train depot its only claim to fame or culture.

Matthew Ranier steps off of the Uceta Yard rail platform on a bright, hot Friday into this seething throng. He has been in America for a little over five months, long enough to naturalize through Ellis Island, to receive his settlement grant, and buy the tools and seed necessary to set up his farm.

He has spent the last week on a train, hardly any time at all compared to the six-week journey he made from his native England, not counting the four-hour coach trip to London where he caught the train to Portsmouth, traveling from his home town of Swindon where he made his stake arranging the sale of the sausages that gave his town its name.

All his life he has dreamed of this, the opportunity to own his own land and all the products from it. To pull his living from the soil and have no man carve away a portion unoffered and unearned. And now he has both means and will to make his mark on this new earth.

He will not stop here long; his bags are unloaded, his patience and his body are exhausted. He knows that there used to be a town where he is going, lost among the swamp that is so perfect for the production of sugar cane. He intends to stay in one of the derelict houses at first, until he can make something more habitable with repairs, but housing is secondary to his farm. It is not planting season yet, but he must prepare as much as possible, for the time will be short and never lingering when the season comes.

He will take his lunch at the hostel across the road, a vast building done all in Art Nouveau with a sign in front advertising the rental of coaches and horses, before making his way through the swamp, driving all night if he has to, before reaching his new home. But first, a meal, and a few questions.

The Roller Hotel is across from the station, a redbrick building in the style becoming popular in the Ybor district of the city, named for the city's largest industry after sugar. The man behind the bar certainly has a cigar roller's arms, thick in the forelimb, heavily muscled beneath the turned-up sleeves. The barman, dark, Italian or Mexican, possibly an Indian breeder, looks up with dark eyes above a moustache of heroic proportions, and is polishing a chipped glass with a rose-patterned rag made from a flour sack, the kind that is a poor recruit for a man's work shirt or a child's Sunday dress.

Matthew approaches the man behind the bar, pointing out a suitable corner to his negro porter for him to lay his baggage in and asks, 'Are you still serving lunch, or am I too late?'

The man takes a moment to process his accent, translating it into the Spanish-influenced patois used in the area. 'Yeah, we're serving. Roast beef, grouper, or pork.' He swivels a bamboo toothpick around in his mouth, not chewing or cleaning with it, just holding it there.

'How fresh is the grouper?' Matthew is running his fingers along the bar, checking for oil or dust. He finds none.

'Ship came in this morning. It's good fish. Crisp, sweet as a dream, melt in your mouth.'

Not like any of my dreams then, he is thinking. 'But yes, it will suffice. Thank you. Lemon squash to start me out.'

'No squash. Orange soda water okay with you?'

'Yes, that's fine.' He has made up his mind. 'I am heading out to Plume town.'

'Why are you going there? That place shut down ten years ago. Only people left are inbreeders or crazies, including that family of Johnsons my brother ships food to once a month. They're the only ones close to civilized out there and I still wouldn't trade a gilt piece of pig shit for the lot of them.'

Matthew is wryly taken aback, his mouth curling up in a half smile underneath his neat, close-cropped beard. 'It's lucky I'm going out for profit and not socialization. I've been given a land grant. Entitlement to a hundred and fifty acres of swampland to make a go of sugar on.'

'Well the land is good for cane, and that's the truth, but what are you going to do for help? You'll need workers, and that's a fact.'

A mulatto waiter in a pressed suit brings his fish sandwich and fried potatoes on a tray laden with salt and ketchup. Matthew tips him, shattering one stereotype at least, and tucks into his food, answering in between swallows of crisp, hot flesh, 'That dovetails nicely with what I was about to ask you. Do you know anyone to hire?'

'Well,' the bar man's moustache twitches at the corners with the rhythm of his thought, 'I suppose that if you were to leave me a deposit of suitable amount I could work through my brother and hire you, oh say, some fifty itinerant natives to go to clear and work the land for you. The cost might be dear though, not for the Indians, but for the shipping and processing fee. You understand.'

'How dear is dear?' The sandwich is delicious, the chips light. Satisfaction makes him incautious. He wipes a dab of mingled tartar and ketchup from the corner of his mouth with the hotel's monogrammed napkin.

'Ten dollars processing fee, five dollars transport of goods, arranged by my brother. He can bring groceries and supplies enough for a month at that same time for an additional eight dollars, save you several trips at once.'

Matthew crosses his knife and unused fork on the durable plate and folds the maroon napkin over top, meeting the barman with that slight, wry smile. 'Fine. And I suppose you can also arrange transport for myself and my tools, or should I say your brother can?'

The barman smiles this time, his teeth a checkerboard of black and white interspaced with generous, well-meaning gaps. 'When would you like to leave?'

'Right now, if possible.'

Five minutes pass in a flurry of loading, saddling, tire checking and lamp-oil filling. The barman's small Mexican wife prepares a packed supper of dried fish, fruit, a chunk of brown bread and half a bottle of homemade wine to sustain him on the journey. The barman loans Matthew his best driver and, fingering his payment and additional deposit, promises to arrange the delivery of supplies and workers by evening tomorrow, waving him off with a motion of his hand, his white cleaning rag fluttering as though signalling surrender.

Matthew, the travel-wrecked Englishman, settles back for a long journey and a night spent in the wild. And yet, he is well-satisfied, happy. The world, his whole vast future, lays before him, so various, so new, a land of dreams ready for him to fill and make his mark upon. The sky is bright and glittering, the trail long.

He curls his arm around his head, rests both against the paned window, and without any further thought he is asleep on that road, bumping over ruts until he seems to be nodding in agreement with some persuasive voice that cannot be heard.

BARGAIN

They meet at the center stair, mother and daughter, older and relatively young. Rose looks down at Joy with cool, clear eyes that glitter with something that might be fever, or laughter, and might be something else. Joy stands with her head bowed, chin almost touching her high, ruffled collar. Her eyes are black in the faint, struggling light.

Rose speaks first, her voice as cool as her eyes, low and deep. Even now, wrecked from coughing, it is almost unspeakably lovely. The woman is a glory in ruin, a Miltonic creation, teetering on the edge of those moisture-slimed stairs, precipitating a fall. 'Joyce? When do we sup?'

Joy answers without looking up, examining the stairs. She remembers when her mother used to sing. Years ago, now. She could imagine herself happy then. 'Oh, I should say about an hour. Potatoes don't take very long to cook, and I've peeled half of them.' She is enthralled by a crack in the step she stands on, a split where the board is pulling away from itself, weakened by the humid air and the pressure of the house slowly settling into what will be its final form.

Rose's mind stocks the cabinets with delicacies. Her wandering eye imagines shelves filled to bursting with good things. Her mind can hardly encompass having nothing but potatoes. Limited by her fractured memories, she knows not what she does.

'Really?' Her voice is humorous, somehow muddled, as though spoken through gauze. 'I thought we had at least some meat. A few tea cakes. Hasn't Malda made them fresh?'

'We haven't had meat in weeks,' Joy is still looking at the step, that one cracked plank, her fingers clenching in frustration, 'and even if we did, there's nothing to season it with. You used the salt last night.' She knows what is coming, what she will be forced to do. She wonders, hopelessly, how much of her energy is spent protecting her mother from the world outside her room.

'Oh Joy. I am sorry.' Rose raises the handkerchief, coughs, withdraws it blood-specked, her motion somehow theatrical. 'Could you run to the store?'

Joy can feel a pressure building behind her eyes, the incipient beginning of a migraine. Silently she shakes her head.

Rose furrows her lovely, clouded brows. She murmurs, 'They must have closed early today. Maybe the neighbors could help? I know that the organist owes your father some money.' She smiles at her daughter and her teeth are painted red.

'Have they not helped us enough already, Mother?' Joy is examining her fingernails now. They are dirtied from tending her wound, and from the potatoes. She knows that reason can only stretch so far with her mother. Too much truth and the lovely lady would be prone to snapping and then spend another week in bed. 'And as for trading, we have nothing left to sell.'

Rose blanches her face, the portrait of someone taken aback, ambushed by an obscenity. 'I would sell nothing in this house. But,' the smile again, lupine in that doll face, 'whatever is wrong with them borrowing a little something, here and there. God knows your father has given this town his heart. They owe us.'

'Fine.' She knew this was coming, and she cannot contain her impatience. 'I will ask.' She allows a touch of humor to creep into her voice. 'I wonder how I will repay them.'

'Oh,' Rose's voice sinks fully into vagueness, now that she has won the battle she was unaware of fighting, 'I am sure that you will find something they can use, some little thing they need.'

And with that, in a swirl of frayed silk and moldy jasmine, she makes her way upstairs, awaiting her supper of something more filling than potatoes.

Joy turns, head still lowered – she did not look up once – and traces her fingertips along the peeling roses that paper the walls. She knew this was coming. Truly, her mother is as predictable as clockwork. There must be gears in her intestines, how else could she so accurately gauge the hour before dinner? Doubly impressive, since Joy traded the clock a year ago. Both clocks, in fact. The grandfather her grandfather made from a kit, and the brass one that stood on the mantle. The one with the revolving base.

But then, she recalls, her mother is living in a dream. She has sunk so far she never noticed.

Maybe there is still something in the library. Thank God the Johnsons have no use for books or proper furniture. They do not read, their house is mostly furnished, and with Tampa thirty miles away, it is too long a distance to support a proper book trade. So she can keep her friends.

If we had any other neighbors we could trade with them and get more from it. If Papa were still alive, if the church were still open, if, if, if. If wishes were horses, might as well think, then I could ride away from here. If God can really read my thoughts, my afterlife will be spent someplace warmer than the trap I'm in now. But at least, her smile turns into a part-wild giggle, at least then I wouldn't be ankle deep in fetid water.

To be dry, for once. Imagine.

The air in here is rank with slowly rotting paper, decomposing binding glue – something small and dead lodges somewhere behind the wall. Joy does not notice it. This is the only happy space within the house. She can feel her father here. Almost see him, hunched behind his desk, his long, thin form composing some missive sent from God on curling yellowed foolscap.

She can imagine his brown eyes crinkling with pleasure, the way they used to, when he sees her at the door.

Ten years.

She was a child, then. Hard as it is to believe.

Maybe there is something in the desk.

She brushes away any sense of nostalgia or reverence, food is more important at this point than any happy memory. Besides, she reasons, memories cannot be taken away, save by injury, and even were something to happen to my brain, at least I would be insensible to pain, and soon after, dead and gone to wherever it is that I have to go.

The middle drawer sticks, cedar swollen with moisture, but at least whatever is inside should be relatively dry. She has rifled here before, of course, but she had been looking for letters, writing, some sign of a will. She has never before taken much interest in the material things. Not here. Better to get rid of the other material detritus, first.

But now the silver is gone, the victrola, the crystal, her grandfather's medical bag, and her grandma's bone china. She hasn't dared ask for her mother's jewelry, and Rose has not offered, though Joy gave up her amethyst ring a long time ago. This is the only place left where something valuable might be hidden, the last dark corner.

And there, in the darkness, underneath the well-thumbed papers and the strong, good smell, a leather box with silver hinges, heavy, and worth something, surely. She lifts it up, the skin good, well-tanned, deep oxblood.

She has, of course, seen it before, but it never really registered as something she could use. It remained 'Papa's thing', sacred. But, she thinks, any port in the storm. Let us pray it is no leviathan masquerading as an island, but something that will provide the stability of solid ground.

There is a keyhole, but no key. Thank God, again, the lock is turned and the dark lid lifts up easily. The inside is lined with velvet, kept in fine condition by the blessed cedar desk. In the darkness, something glitters.

There are three things. A chased-silver cigar case, hallmarked, solid, holding one half-smoked Cuban. Even the Johnsons will have to give a month's worth for that. There is a gilt letter opener, with a small sapphire jewel in the handle, monogrammed with Grandfather's initials, and a lovely, creamy ivory pen.

She holds the last thing in her hand, feels the weight, the heft of it, a solid fountain with a golden nib, ready for ink. Something he wrote with, something he held. It feels right in her hand. She will keep this, for as long as she can.

The rest she will sell, a piece at a time, to those awful neighbors. Sell it all, down to the lovely leather box. Cane growers, she thinks, with pretentions of glory. And, sighing at her own bitterness, why not? This is America, isn't it? Even down here. They have the right to better themselves. And anyway, another few growing seasons and they'll be gone, their Indian help scattered, off to the north with their own lofty fortune, luxuries purchased at their thrifty leisure. I only wish it did not have to be at our expense. Or at least, she thinks this last with true repugnance, that they were worthy of it.

She takes the cigar case first, fingering the fretwork, delicate and sharp, untarnished by the years so long preserved from air. The first black stains will blossom at the Johnson's house, spreading out in the shape of her fingerprints, fed from the oil on her hands.

A month of food at least, she thinks, maybe even some of Mama's ever-loving meat. Salt pork. She salivates at it, though she knows that of whatever flesh this silver buys them she will not have more than a taste. Mama needs to keep her strength up.

She places the letter opener and pen back in the box, slides that back into the drawer, covers it with its scrim of yellowed, cracked paper, the only truly dry examples in the house, and slides closed the swollen drawer.

The sun is setting now, outside of the window, a deep tropical red signalling a lovely day tomorrow, though right now the mosquitoes are out spoiling the beauty with their clouds. If she doesn't want to contract malaria, she had better cover up in spite of the heat.

She leaves the library, closing the door firmly. Her rust-colored cloak is hanging behind the kitchen door, her gum boots standing beneath it. The case is in her pocket, weighing down the tired fabric. The potatoes, all save the bloody one, are peeled and ready for the pot when she returns.

There is nothing left to hold her further, no more unexhausted excuses. She throws the cloak across her shoulders, thrusts her head into the hood. The gum boots squelch, still wet from this morning and her toes are clammy, pinched and numb.

She opens the door, pulls it closed after her.

It is time to go.

NEIGHBORS

The Johnson's farm is a little less than a mile away from the center of the defunct town. Joy leaves the manse through the kitchen, crosses the yard, the above-ground cemetery, past the roof-sunken church, the school house that closed forever the year she turned ten, and the locked and boarded general store.

There are the shells of many houses on Main Street, the only road through town, but they are empty. If you go left on the weed-strewn two-lane, you will reach Orlando in a little over a week. Tampa is thirty miles to the right.

On a map the distance would not seem over-long, but to a hungry girl it is a long way to squelch through the ankle-deep mud. She has plenty of time to dread her neighbors, swatting at mosquitoes.

The Johnsons are her only helpmeet option, as repugnant as they are. At least they can afford a goods delivery from Tampa once a month, and it takes some serious money to hire a shipper to risk those roads. The grocer comes bumping up that long, rutted road with his gypsy caravan drawn by four mules, carrying everything from staples to medicine and minor luxuries like penny dreadfuls and cheap artificial silks. Nothing of quality, nothing real.

Mr. Johnson is large and loud, unmannered, prone to gripping an elbow too hard to steer a conversation, prone to crunching the small bones of the hand in greeting. It is not malice, she thinks, he does not intend to harm anyone. Joy imagines that he would be deeply ashamed if she complained, but he injures unthinking.

He works his laborers close to their breaking. If he can work fifteen-hour days chopping cane and distilling the sugar into syrup, why can't they? Never considering that he, at least, will have a pound of cured hog and half a loaf fried in molasses waiting for him on the sideboard at the end of the day while they, if they are very lucky, will sup on a few slices of rough ground wheat slathered in gone-off lard with, perhaps, a bit of fish or a few turtle eggs, if the weather is good. He sleeps in his big dry house, built by his own hands albeit aided by a Sears kit, under mosquito nets, nestled in beside his wide, soft wife. His men sleep on pallets in the barn.

The turnover rate is lightning-fluid, and most of his staff leave in boxes, or bob along the river towards whatever comes next.

Mrs. Lydia Johnson is quite as well-proportioned as her husband, fond of the slabs of chocolate that come with their monthly shipments of whatever food they cannot grow. She orders dresses in loud silks, sewn from enough fabric to smother a cow, peppered with bright flowers like cancers. Stand her next to a hibiscus bush and she'd blend right in, always excepting the shock of her orange-hennaed hair. Mrs. Johnson entertains herself with the notion that, when she was young, she could have courted royalty. No one has yet succeeded in disabusing her of that notion, although it must be said there are few enough people around.

Still, it is entertaining enough for her when Joy calls. Pretty little thing. Spoilt by her dead father. Old Lydia could show her a trick or two. But then, it is satisfying to watch the last depths of her fall. Poor thing. Running around in rags and tatters, hawking her jewels, her pride crumbling beautifully with each item sold. A few months more and she and her mother will have nothing but her body to sell, and Lydia knows that her son would be more than willing to buy.

Randolf Johnson Jr., twenty-four, buys his whores from a cathouse on the outskirts of Tampa, in a ramshackle shack on the bright shining bay. He likes his women chocolate colored, because they are too down-beaten to look him in the eye. He likes his ripe young neighbor too; her body radiates its lines through rags. He lives for the moment when she will have nothing left to bribe him with, and he can start to break her in.

The family has been expecting Joy for a few days. They traded her three bushels of potatoes for the victrola three weeks ago and there is only so far she could make those spuds stretch, even supplementing them, as she does, with what the river brings her, the things she pulls from the swamp.

Mr. Johnson is washing his face at the pump, a quick, pre-dinner dab, quite perfunctory but insisted upon by his wife, when he sees her figure emerge, black outlined, from the red-bloodied horizon and the mangrove forest gloom. He greets her with a loud haloo and a bone-grating pump of his ham-hock hand. 'Why if it isn't little Miss Walsh here to lighten our evening.' He grins through his beard like some addled Saint Nick. 'It's right good to see you, girl. You've kept too long away. The missus likes her woman talk, though she gets it rare enough, and Randy likes it too, though for very different reasons don't ya ken?'

Joy smiles as politely as she can, massages her injured hand. 'Yes. Thank you, Mr. Johnson. May I come in?'

'Of course, girl. Of course.' He bustles her in, placing his pump-wet hands on her firm rear. She pretends not to notice. 'And how is your lovely mother?'

'She is well, as usual.' Joy moves away from his bearlike body, from the hot pressure of his hands, in as inoffensive way as possible while pulling the cigar case from her pocket. 'She sent me to sell this. It was my father's.'

His eyes light up at the sight of it, the last of the sunset dancing pinkly on the silver, catching in the floral carvings. The expression looks almost like lust. He covers it with his hand and closes her fingers around it, pushing it back to her pocket. 'Let's not talk business in this air. Come inside and have a drink.'

He does want it, Joy thinks, enough to try and buy a lower price with brandy. I shall have none of it, or very little. Any alcohol at all in this hungry state can only make me worse at bargaining, and I need all that I can get.

The house is furnished with baubles loud and bright, deal cabinets thinly veneered with mock mahogany, tall boys fronted with false marble ormolu, second-hand portraits in second-rate oils, the Janus face of new money bought with sugarcane and the sweat of near slaves. All of the quality items, she notes, the things that made the ruined manse home, were carried here by her and quietly traded for a fraction of their worth in food.

The negotiations take place in the sitting room amidst Sears settees and cabinets of carnival glass. Mrs. Johnson takes up a sofa to herself, her skirt blending in nicely with the lime green paisley. Luckily, young Randolph is off on his weekly visit to the whores. Joy has that much to be thankful for.

They argue for an hour, in wheedling tones. Mrs. Johnson heading the haggling, at first diagnosing the case pewter, in spite of the hallmarks, and estimating its value at a solid half-dollar. Joy places it at fifty, still low, she knows, but closer to the truth. No chance of a fair deal here. Lydia hitches up her estimation, allowing her five dollars, to be paid in spuds; Joy lowers her evaluation to forty-five, asking ten bushels of potatoes, half a hog and a sheet of ginger bread for Rose. At that suggestion, Lydia crinkles up her piggy eyes in folds of amused laughter. The girl, she is reminded, has some imagination.

Eventually they settle up at twenty-five dollars, American. Paid out, not in cash, but in five bushels of spuds, a quarter of a sow and a half-pound of sugar. She feels both cheated and satisfied. She will leave the cigar case here tonight and one of the

Johnson men will drive the supplies by in the morning. Long experience has taught her that there is no point in arguing about a later trade, and besides, while her neighbors might be many things, they do not cheat in business, and this *is* a business. Of a kind.

The case changes hands and takes up residence on a stamped-linoleum counter. Joy pulls on her rusty hooded cape – they never took it from her, she's been holding it this whole time in her lap – and Lydia escorts her to the door.

The night has reached full dark and the journey home is long without a lamp or candle, but Joy will have food tomorrow and there are, as yet, no wolves in these dark woods. The women face each other on the threshold, murmuring goodbyes. Joy is anxious to get home and make her thin potato supper. She gives thanks like a servant, glad to be cheated if it means more food is coming, food enough for a long month. The bare minimum, barely a kindness, a fleecing really. She expects nothing else.

This is why she is surprised when Mrs. Johnson takes her hand and slips three eggs into her palm before closing her out into the insect-haunted night.

ROOM

The room Rose spends her life in is opulent and large, redolent with the ancient scent of jasmine, rank female sweat and fresh blood. She does not notice it, hasn't for years. Her nose is trained to block out what her mind cannot accept, and that includes any hint of poverty. There is a tall oval swivel mirror standing against the wall across from the foot of her damp-sheeted bed. The silvered back is black-spotty with tarnish and there is mold creeping in along the edges, but Rose can just make herself out in the gloom. She is a body under water, smoothed of all personality by the passing of the waves.

She likes the mirror this way. The warped surface filters out what she does not wish to see. Her figure is still good, slim and strong as a girl, hunger serves its purpose, and her hair still has enough blond in it to hide the creamy white, even if the texture has gotten a little coarse. In the mirror she is the very picture of health. Her skin, so white, with rose-blooming cheeks, her lips so red, blood painted, better than lipstick. The vague light hides the holes in her blue silk and if she did not sometimes double up to cough, folding her body like the spine of a dropped book, she could fool herself, imagining that the years have fallen away like ash.

Any moment he will come through that door, take her in his arms, and slide into bed.

In the morning they will wake up late, as they did on Monday mornings, his one day off. She will make him scrambled eggs with fatback pork and serve it in bed. He will lie there, naked save for his breeches under the sheet (scandalous for a minister, but David always was a carnal man) and she will climb in with him, wearing only a clean, white shift, revelling in her nakedness.

Joyce will sleep in even later than they will, she is a growing girl after all, and little things like her need their sleep. Missing one morning of school won't hurt her. Besides, she is the top of her class, third in the whole one-room school, and that is impressive, especially considering the fact that she is in grade four and the school holds up to grade twelve.

Any minute, any second, he'll come in and tell her about his day, the parishioners he visited, the sermon he is writing. They will get down on their knees and pray together, talking over everything with God before sliding into their sweat-laden sheets. The pillow will smell of his hair-vitalize, his aftershave will linger on the duvet. And afterwards his taste will be in her mouth, on her tongue, and their sweat will mingle on her skin.

He won't be coughing yet, his skin unflushed... She stops herself there. How can he be healthy if she knows about the symptoms of this disease he does not have yet? She curses herself for a fool, allowing herself to fall prey once again to that strange, reoccurring, hellish dream of desolation and ruin in a God- and man-forsaken town.

Looking into the mirror, Rose forces herself to smile, nailing that simpering, doll-like look David loved into place by sheer force of will. Her form is slim and girlish in the moisture-stippled mirror. Her husband is gone, yes, yes, she can believe that. He is gone, but not forever. He is off on a trip.

Yes.

A trip. He is visiting the presbytery in Tampa. They are discussing the Indian problem, there still is an Indian problem. He is planning to build a school. He will be back soon. Yes.

That business with Joyce earlier, about there not being any food, that was just a misunderstanding. David left in such a hurry that he forgot to leave her the housekeeping money. He forgot, and so they have to borrow from their neighbours. Not those awful nouveau riche Johnsons with their poor taste and brash manners, no. Joyce will borrow some things, the few small but necessary things a kitchen needs to add that last delicate touch to a meal of supreme goodness. Joyce will borrow some saffron, perhaps, for the chicken Cook will make. When it is ready, Malda will lay the table with, for a treat, their fine marriage silver with roses on the knife handles and they will feast together, just the two of them, Rose and her lovely little Joyce. They will eat until they have to loosen their stays, and then when they cannot imagine forcing down one more bite of well-turned chicken or battered corn, Cook will bring out her specialty chocolate mousse. The recipe she makes with the liquid chocolate center.

And then, in the morning, after Joyce has gone off to school, David will come home, come home to his warm bed, with her waiting. He will get his fingers tangled in her long blond hair that she will wear loose just for him. This is the most erotic thing she can imagine. He will pull her close, his large hand against the back of her head, and he will kiss her with his wide, soft mouth, his eyes so dark and innocent, the eyes of a doe, and she will, finally, at last, be at peace in that warm surrender, lost in his arms.

This is how Rose lives. Editing her life into a shape that she can live with, a form she can handle. When she dreams this, dreaming awake, she does not feel her wracking coughs or see the mold spreading out across the walls like cancer. She does not notice her rotting bed clothes, or the slimy texture of her silks. She does not notice that her strand of pearls in the dish on her dresser have loosened themselves from their deteriorating thread.

Her wedding portrait looks bright to her, a painting of herself in oils, leaning against the railing of her grandmother's house, looking out into the sculpture-filled garden in long lacy sleeves, a diaphanous veil, the sunlight caught in the dew of her bouquet.

She does not notice the cobwebs or the sick green fungus that crawls across her face.

Rose is happy here, in her light, clean room, that inner-mind island in the vast sea of night.

Her reverie is ended by the sound of the door. She can hear footsteps, the latching of a door. She can hear the clink of pots, the rush of pouring water. Joyce must be home. But where is the sound of Cook? They would usually be gossiping by now. A bad habit, but Rose likes her daughter to have fun.

Cook must be outside plucking the chicken. It must be Malda in the kitchen. She and Joyce never did get along.

Supper is getting close to ready, a sumptuous feast to be enjoyed, in an atmosphere of love and luxury, with her only living daughter.

She smiles at herself, so young, so fresh, a trance in the mirror brushing out her long blond hair, prepared for her husband.

Tomorrow David will be home.

SUPPER

A bucket of potatoes and three lonely eggs. There will be more food for them tomorrow, sold for a piece of what might as well be her father's flesh. But at least they will not starve, for a month or so.

Joy sets a pot of water boiling on the surface of the stove, the round burners polished with use, the only shining surface in the room, other than the well-kept knives. When the water is really going, bubbles rising as though from some black witch's brew, she slices up thin slices of spuds and adds them to the boiling water, not much minding when the water splashes up and scalds her.

She will scramble the eggs, mix them with the potatoes as a sort of poor man's salad, and while her mother will initially be disappointed, Joy knows that given a few minutes to eat it on her own, up in that unchanging room, she will soon transmute the substances into something more palatable to her exquisite tastes.

The spuds are going well now, softening up, peel and all, in their torrid water bath. She is mixing up the eggs in a chipped glass bowl, piercing the yolks with the tines of a dull steel fork. She would wish for some tomato catsup to spice up the mix, maim for a pinch of pepper and salt. She can, just barely, remember what comfort was like, before Cook left and her world closed up. Ginger cookies in the morning with her oatmeal, thick slices of chilled ham on bread for lunch. Oranges, fresh from the trees in the garden, before the weevils killed the lot, leaving only their charred skeletons protruding from the dampened yard.

Sunday dinners with her father, with the both of them, her parents eating from fine china in the dining room after church, Royal Dalton patterned with damask rose. Roast beef, gravy dripping, a light salad, those fresh, yeasty rolls Cook made from the recipe left over from her grandmother. Her father sipping rich port after from the silver-cased, cut crystal decanter (sold long ago) that stood on the shelf in the library. And afterwards, his breath rich and sweetly innocent against her neck, his hand curled against her shoulder, they stooped together over books as he slowly taught her Greek.

A cambric passage rises, translating itself from the spuds' perdition, a scene of the *Satyricon* that she remembers clearly. *For I myself once saw with my own eyes the Sibyl hanging in a cage, and when the boys asked her, 'Sibyl, what do you want?' she answered 'I want to die.'* That passage was hard, the descriptions in Latin, dialogue in Greek. But yes, she identifies very strongly with that prophet no one listened to, to the woman who has lived far too long, shrinking with a great age that cannot kill her, fading with the years until she has become a voice and nothing else. Just that, a spirit crying in the night, alone and unanswered.

Zeus granted the Sibyl immortality, one of his sardonic double-sided gifts as a reward for saving his life, his country, his military strength. One of those important male things. He gifted her with an eternity of loss.

Joy knows the feeling.

But that moment, those after-Sunday moments when the sermon was done and the Parson's visiting hours were over and it was just the two of them translating together in that warm, well-lighted room (there was money enough for plentiful candles then, and even a few more modern gas lights – electricity never made it out this far) when they crouched together over a moisture-ridden book, those moments were heaven. She did not know that the loss she was learning was her own.

She is still learning it. The taste is bitter in her mouth: more difficult to swallow than the hard, never-ripening grapefruit she steals from the schoolyard and chokes down in winter to ward off the scurvy.

Her last sight of David was in the middle of a day that felt dark enough to be midnight. A Friday afternoon spent sweating out blood, the vitreous fluid in his eyes yellowed with it, his tongue coated intense chokecherry. He was talking about the sermon he would write for Sunday, for the sick people he must visit (there were still people even then, but they were leaving) and the people he must bury, who suffered, as he, from the bloody hack that beautifies before corruption. He ranted on, and Joy, calm already at almost-ten, wiped away the blood that trickled from his nose.

He was dead by three o'clock; his breath met the chiming of the grandfather standing near the stairwell. He coughed and then there was the final relaxation of the body, looking, not peaceful, but finished.

Eli Eli lama sabachthani?

My God, my God.

And then the nightmare started. The fast burial she handled because her mother would not stir from their bed, the coffin she made her first sale for. It was, apparently, worth her great grandmother's antique writing desk. But quality, yes. She made sure of that, lead-lined, though cheap. She could not afford a coffin-cap, that mask of concrete made to hold the body down underneath the water-logged sod; even lead-lined wood is buoyant in that soil. She knows that one day, on her walks, she might encounter her father pushing out from the earth like a new tooth, the door open, his new cold bone-hand out in supplication. But that was alright. She would not doom him to an eternity of drowning.

Whatever is waiting after this life, heaven, hell, or nothing, his body is here and he was never one to spend time in the dark.

People were kind then, after a fashion, though she was too

numb to know the kindness was running out like water in the dry season, like blood from a split vein. Her first taste of being alone.

The potatoes are cooked down almost to mush, the eggs are scorching in the pan, black along the edges. Hunger is the best sauce. Anything at all is good by now. It's not like Rose will notice.

She drains the potatoes, mixes in the eggs, and serves up her mother's portion first, leaving hers in the pot.

She carries the plate, thick clay-ware, chipped along the edges, knowing that Rose will smell the goodness and meet her at the center stair, perhaps bringing down her filled chamber pot to exchange for her meal, another thing for Joy to clean before settling down to eat herself. Hopefully the food will keep in the kettle on the range.

Sometimes she wonders how much of her mother's fantasy is willed, how much manipulation, how much of it springs from genuine need and the inability to filter pain. She can break herself out of it, sometimes, long enough to simper out an order as firm as steel. A command for Joy to suffer, like the order to sell.

Sometimes she thinks Rose is made of stronger stuff than her actions show.

But then she sees her mother standing on the step, as she stands there now, dressed in tattered blue silk, her hair down around her waist, uncombed and wild, round blue eyes glistening at the sight of food that her hands reach out for, and she thinks, No. No, the woman who was my mother is gone forever. This is nothing but the ghost of a child, that I must keep alive.

They do not speak, Rose is seeing Cook and not her daughter, and one does not converse with servants. She takes her food and turns abruptly, retreating with swaying hair to her room up the stairs.

Joy stands staring for a moment after her, watches to make

certain the latest bout of coughing does not spatter her food across the floor. It does not. She turns and makes her way down the protracted venous hall to her long-expected meal currently cooling on the stove.

MEETING

The Johnsons eat late, rarely setting down to supper before ten-thirty or eleven; there are many things that you could say about them, and they, as a family, would not refute: prideful, shifty, crass, mule-headed, but damn it, they sit down together almost every night when Jr. is around, pray, and have their dinners together, a family. As God intended.

They wait up late for Randolph.

His parents are waiting at the table when he comes in, sitting large and erect in the gas-lamp light that flickers almost like a real flame, under the watchful eye of their Florida Indian servant. He is a man who has become so accustomed to his masters that he can anticipate their needs, their wants, based solely on the slope of a shoulder or the inclination of an eyebrow. He knows what they are clamoring for almost, it seems, before they know themselves. But then, their familial needs are not plentiful.

Lydia wants status and beautiful things. She would sell her ever-loving soul for a full set of the latest, most fashionable Royal Doulton, for a vast expanse of silk that uses the latest artificial dyes to reach the exactly right, fashionable shade of poison green. And don't neglect the pink sateen fringe to edge it with when she orders it made into a tent-like dress.

Mr. Randolph Johnson, Sr. wants something a bit more complicated. Given world enough, and time, he would like to control the biggest swath of sugarcane farmland seen outside of Barbados. When he closes his eyes he sees whole leagues of it, suitable for everything from molasses and confectioners' sugar to pure, sweet rum. Acres and miles of it, out there, waving in the sunlight. After that ragged skeleton town has been torn down, the mangroves slaughtered, the swamplands seeded with swift-growing cane tended by row upon row of bent-backed, brown-skinned natives, punctuated by the occasional white man.

To his credit, he refrains from imagining whips in the hands of his foreman (those are reserved strictly for himself and his son), but it is a struggle. He would love to see them there, as a reminder. If the natives and runaways know that the white men will use it, if they, for example, see their occasional countryman riven with dripping vaginal slashes, all the better. A little humiliation makes for good workers.

He gets away with it, too. They are far enough out to be safe from any meddling. But not far enough to stop the gossip. Word occasionally filters out, and then good luck breaking into the good society when they move back up North if they cannot find some way to quench it. Never mind. There is time enough to patch that trouble later.

This is the reason he does not simply chase the women out, crouching there amidst their ruin. People *would* talk. Tampa society is happy enough to leave them there, he thinks, but woe betides anyone who turns them out cold. Even though they have nothing, not even the title of their house, not even two dresses to their name, they have their sex, and their race. Without the latter the first would be worth nothing.

The women are a problem, as is the coming threat of competition he will reckon with later. He might, just might, have a solution to both.

But that can wait, till morning at least.

Right now they sit, the slumped bear-like couple, before their empty, stylish plates, grinning at each other in the flickering light. Waiting for Jr., whose wants are simple.

He wants to drink until stupefaction and he wants to have a piece of hot, steamy tail waiting for him as a sort of fleshy dessert.

Tonight he has had both.

There is a crash, the sound of a body hitting solid pine. He made it most of the way up the front steps without falling this time. A minute of silence and he tries it again. The hall door slams. Jr. has arrived at last.

The boy is huge and dark, a Heathcliff in farm clothes. He circles the table, stumbling occasionally, catching himself on the odd empty chair, some lame-winged scavenger bird stooping to feed. Randy slaps his father on the shoulder, affectionate, admiring, and shakes his large and calloused hand. His mother he kisses with the passion of a slovenly drunk. He left for Tampa three days ago and has traveled thirty miles to be here, and yet he is still drunk. He must have a cask underneath the seat.

The father waves his hand before his face and grins, his son might as well have been bathing in rum. Must have absolutely rubbed stinking palmfuls of it into his thatch, is probably sweating it. He is, Johnson thinks, turning out to be a very fine young man. Just like his old dad.

Once the boy is seated, the servant, a native who is affectionately called Squanto, or occasionally, Squant, brings out the steaming, crisped-skinned carcass of a goose on an over-laden platter heaped with chopped slices of carrot and baked apple chunks.

Grace is said, briefly, the corpse dismembered unskilfully. Steaming flesh makes its way around the table, grease spattering the damask tablecloth like blood, hunks and gobbets are shoved into gaping orifices lined with teeth and masticated, loudly, visible through three wide-open mouths.

The dim light cannot paint a homey sheen on this, or the talk that punctuates itself with runners of saliva and flying drips of fat.

Mr. Johnson opens the gamut, wiping juice on his vast blue-jeaned thigh, 'That Walsh girl is turning out rather fine, in spite of her rags, Jr. You might want to give her a look over the next time she comes. Might have some fun with that one.'

'Oh no,' he says, grinning with meat caught visibly in the large gaps between his teeth. 'I know what you're trying to do. They don't even own that land, you know. No one does. And besides,' a look that passes for thoughtful, 'I can buy better in town, and at a fraction of the cost.'

Ma Bear raises her head, speaking her piece and spraying the elbow of her servant, who bears this, as he bears everything, in absolute silence. 'But Randy, think of the good things that a wife will do, things you can't pay for. Legally, she could never, ever tell you no. What alley cat could compare to that?'

'All of them, if you know the sheriff like I do.' He reaches his large hands into the split avian ribcage and plucks out a scrap of gristle there. 'Why are you pushing this?'

'Because, my boy, we want to see you happy, settled down.' Johnson's cheeks are red and merry, there is fat glistening in his beard.

'Bullshit.' Gnawing gristle, a wingtip like a lady's finger, the solid crunch of bone.

'Fine. You want to know?' The father is gesturing with a femur like a pointer. 'I'll tell you. Right now, and for another year or so, ownership laws down here are vague. If you're on it, you own it. Hell, Uncle Sam is paying people to settle down here.' He crunches open the drumstick, to slurp away the marrow there. 'They are sitting on that track in the middle of town. Legally, they own the whole shebang. Through a technicality. A God-damned, sorry Lord, loophole. Doesn't matter who owns the title. None of this would be a problem if no one knew the girls were there. But there are still some town folk who remember them, and trust me, while they might be fine with letting the birds starve, you had better believe there would be a ruckus if anyone tried to move them out.'

'Ok, sure Dad, makes sense so far,' he stirs the gravy on his plate with a decorative piece of carrot, 'but why all the pressure now? You've hinted at it before, but the Walshes have been there, all alone, for years. Fat sheep gone skinny.'

'They have been there all this time, you bet. Thanks hon.' His wife is heaping his plate with potato. 'But now there is a complication.'

'What kind of "complication"?'

'One in the body of a land-grant-buying Englishman come down from Missouri talking around the big town of all this land been given him, including land occupied by two crazy ladies. Tampa might know that they are there, but the government apparently doesn't. The problem is, if he comes down here waving that edict, the presence of the ladies will rebuff him, if he isn't fool enough to marry one of them. And he might. He is of a reckoning age.'

'So I'm to be the fool, then?'

'Well hell son, I'd do it myself, save for your mother,' catching her look, 'your lovely mother. The rush, as you put it, resides in the fact that if the girl is married and safely contained by the time the bastard, sorry Lord, gets here we have a legal hold on the land, can contest and win it by January and be full-planted by the spring. Bye bye competition. We'll be rich and back up North in three more seasons. Then we can ditch the mother in a mental home and you can keep up your carousing, or get back to it, after we've got at least one son.' The meal is over. Johnson folds his fat, shiny hands across his belly, his teeth luminous in his great beard, stars among the firmament.

'Well,' Junior pushes away his empty plate, takes a napkin from his mother, 'if that's the way it has to be.' His teeth are bright, fire-glinting. 'It's not like I had any other plans. Tomorrow, I'll go calling. She'll probably cream all over herself if I show up with a steak, turn all to butterflies and ashes.'

Laughing, revelling in their camaraderie, the family leaves the table for drinks in the lounge, leaving behind the plucked corpse on the table, ribcage glinting, hollow and somehow feminine in emptiness, to be cleared away by the silent, un-named man.

WANDERER

While other people plot her life in secret, Joy is sleeping in the room her father died in, lying curled on the only clean sheets in the house. They are thread-worn from washing, yellowed from sweat and stained from her body. She has tried, several times, to clean her mother's bedroom, but Rose always stops her. She cannot, even now, accept that now is now, the past is over, and yet life never seems to move for her. So Joy allows Rose to lie in her ancient filth, knowing that for her mother, it shines like the present never could.

The room is dark, it always is. The sun cannot penetrate this tree-shaded place, even at the pinnacle of day. There are other sorts of shadow than mere absence of light.

The bed is cold, even in this ever-present heat, and she is small curled in it. Her long black hair is loose across the pillow, scattering the moonbeams that filter in through the leaf-masked window. The veins in her neck throb in her troubled sleep, pulsing.

There is silence all around her, silence in the stirring air, nothing but the call of earth around her – and yet one more thing.

Hear that scratching at the struts beneath her window? Hear that moist and panting breath?

She is stirring in the night, her body, somnambulant, moving. Her head is lifting from the well-indented pillow, her eyelids sliding open over orbs, gray and dull as partly-polished lead. She moves as though walking underwater, something drowned come up to taste the long-lost air, walking slowly through the bedroom, close and familiar. She avoids the points of furniture, the hollows where the floorboards have cracked beneath her passage, weakened by water.

She walks in her moldy nightgown, stark and white against the gloom, leaving through the kitchen door, down the stairs that run past pillars, until her naked feet touch sodden earth.

She is unconscious, her pupils moving dream-jerky in her head, looking everywhere and nowhere, toward the strong, strange force that leads her off toward the mangrove-haunted woods. The trees are tall and tangled, roots rising up from the swirling filth and lizard droppings from the billions of anoles that skitter along the higher branches, moving through the swirling fog.

Joy follows the pathways through the knotted skeins of limbs, feeling her way, unseeing along the overgrown path. Along the twisted pathways where the ancient goddess waits in silence, her silver bowl a hollowed tree-bole filled with water tannin-tinted to the shade of blood.

Her feet are cold, numbed and aching, and it is the chill that wakes her, that ache in her bones, so deep, so painful. She comes to herself glimmering in moonlight, her reflection glinting in the water. And she is unsure where she stands.

She is trembling in the water, her fingers cold and shaking. She can smell something rank and living in the air, something alive, blood-tainted, setting her nostril hairs quivering. She is not alone.

The dog-shape comes before her, materializing through the ragged mist, hackles raised and snarling. A golden coyote with yellow eyes that glow like jack-o-lanterns, muscles sliding under smooth, thick pelt, tongue protruding red and moist from between jagged white teeth, breath pulsing out in clouds through the moisture-laden air.

Joy is afraid to scream or move – she stands riveted as a post, as though her feet had sprouted roots. The coyote moves toward her, panting harshly, she cannot tell in hunger or in rage, until the rough nose, like a rasp, presses against her and she feels its mouth, the sharp impress of fangs, close gently around her bruising thigh.

The jaws close, but not entirely, the hold is gentle and not unkind. She is being marked, possessed, by something ancient and very, incorrigibly, wild. The teeth press, slowly, softly, drawing blood in indents from her limb, coating the wounds in a thick patina of saliva, ingraining its scent.

And that is all.

The jaws release, the bright eyes blink, once, twice, in recognition, the body moves against her, leaving a few scattered hairs, and the creature, no monster, is gone, vanishing into the departing mist.

The girl touches her fingers to the holes in her leg, holes that she feels were made in blessing, and examines the pink-frothed substance there. Her blood, and something other. The night is bright, the moon has risen to its peaked and highest zenith, and it is well past time for bed.

She picks her way back the way she came, slowly, carefully, over branch, mulch, bracken, until she sees the steps leading up past the rising pillars to her towering, stork-like house, and her room drenched in darkness, where she can settle into bed again.

Saturday

ARRIVAL

The coach journeys through a long night of bone-jerking ruts, lurching sickly over furrows and the thick roots that have overwhelmed the rutted road. Matthew sleeps, a little, grabs what rest he can. After all, this voyage is no different than the ones he has taken before, the rocking almost seeming to sooth until a pothole catches the abused wheel and throws his head against the cooled windowpane.

The sunrise wakes him, a panoply of pink and green above the canopy of trees and he is in the ruined town. There is desolation all around him, skeleton houses of various forms, some barely standing, some almost inhabitable, outlines in stages of desecration from fresh-slaughtered to nearly ash. The coach pulls to a stop before the boarded ruin of the store, its genteel veneer sloughing off in strips of false neoclassical devastation.

Deplorable, he thinks, almost admiring, how swiftly the mark of man vanishes in this vast land. Nature will have her own, it seems, even now.

'And where should I be putting this, sah?' His reverie is broken by the cab driver who opens the door for him to stand on sidewalk boards that his boots sink into like sponge, splintered shards breaking off around his heels. The cabby is mounting the ladder to the roof luggage without waiting for him to reply.

'Oh, anywhere is fine.' Matthew is smiling, enthralled by all of this waste, though he couldn't tell anyone why. 'This shop looks the best preserved and I don't think anyone will mind.'

'No one but the haints anyway, and if you be a Christian man, they won't harm you none.' He is throwing down baggage now, disregarding the stickers marking some of them 'delicate'.

Matthew either doesn't notice, or pretends to pay no mind. 'And it's not like you won't have no neighbors. The Johnsons are still out here. His boy tips good when he come into town, though he do like cats, and not the feline kind, if you take my meaning.' His oaken eye tips shut at Matthew, slides open again, all friendliness. 'The widow and her daughter are around here somewhere. They crazy, but harmless for all I heard. And you got some other neighbors further out, but I wouldn't bother with them if I were you. Inbreeders and people hiding from the government. They like bees, those types, they find themselves a hole and stay there, won't bother no one unless some big idjit comes around and pokes them with a stick.' He is shifting the last box now, piling it onto the warped shop porch, grinning at his employer with a look half mocking, half warning.

'Luckily for me,' Matthew is bringing out his wallet to find fare and appropriate tip, more for the information than the unloading. It is good to know that he shall not be stranded out here alone, 'I don't make a habit of prodding bees.' He hands the sum, folding bills and a silver piece to the cab driver who makes it vanish without checking the amount. 'Thank you for your assistance.'

'Part of the job, sah, part of the calling.' The cabby mounts his seat again, wraps his horse-blanket around his knees, though he could not possibly be cold here, not in this weather, clicks his tongue to start the rig, and disappears in a cloud of mosquitoes and the sound of wheels squelching through thick mud.

Matthew waves his hand in a brief gesture of farewell. And then the rig is gone.

Tonight or early tomorrow he will meet his workers here when they arrive in wagons from the town. He will begin plotting his conquest of this earth, map the ways to hold it, for a while, before the soil claims its own again.

Now he will oversee his territory, impoverished king of his dominion, beholden to no man. But first, he will set up his camp.

He has not one key to open a single rusted lock, but he does not need one. The weather has made all keys obsolete, and even on this shop front all he has to do is place his hands and push, startling the small, too-tame brown lizards that sun themselves in all the daylight hours on the wood.

The door creaks open like a mummified mouth disclosing its gorge. His nostrils fill with the scent of wet sawdust, rat droppings, and the sour stench of moldy gingham fabric and a sweetish swill that must once have been sorghum. There are barrels everywhere, filled and empty, the till gapes wide and vapid. But the floor is solid and the room, if not dry, is at least habitable.

It will suffice.

He brings in his bedroll, his lamp, the supplies more vulnerable to moisture, but leaves the rest piled on the porch. No one to steal from him here. He is safe.

His gear unloaded, he makes his way back outside to survey of what he is lord. He is a short, but stocky, well-built man in middle-class dress, blond hair a bit too long but beard close-cropped and neat against his face, taking the edges off his prominent nose and wide jaw.

A fine figure, but no one is there yet to see it.

He is looking at the rickety house rising up next to the ruins of what must once have been a church; there is a cross there, visible over the sunken roof, a cemetery, must be. It looks the most habitable building, and certainly is probably better than a water-logged dry-goods shop. He will investigate it later, perhaps move in, if the air inside is clean. After all, they are all his to choose from and who could mind?

But first, he thinks, a little breakfast. He has sausage and yeast biscuits in his satchel, tinder in a box as well as Lucifer matches. Food first, then exploration.

So, content and excited, he makes his slow way back to the shop to eat and plan, as all lords do, how best to accomplish his God-granted destiny. The world is new, for him, sprouting from the fodder of previous ruin. He shall not fail here, in this lovely, rose-blushed morning. Failure is the only impossible thing.

TRADE GOODS

Joy wakes late, the sun beating against her eyelids even in the shaded room, the sound of birdcall lingering in the air, and she finds her sheets awash with blood. There is an odd tight aching in her bowels and so she at first attributes it to her woman's curse arriving with unusual ferocity, until she notices the sixteen deep indentations piercing her thigh.

The wounds are smeared, but clotted, and the ache they bring is little enough. The pain in her intestines must be something else. She moves the stained sheets back and rises from her nest, noticing that sweat has yellowed her nightgown all the way through, as though she has burned through the night in fever.

The soles of her feet are muddy, her shins and thighs scratched raw, as if she had spent the evening rolling in brambles, though she remembers nothing from the moon-times after falling asleep. She does know that she suffered odd dreams. But, she thinks to herself, winding her hair up around her sweat-dripping face, tying a bun low and loose, surely I would remember wandering out there, in the swamp, in the night. No, it must be something else, some other explanation, but how then the dog bite? Could I have made such markings with my nails?

She moves her fingers to overlay the marks, noticing that the nailed tips can cover them, with just a bit of effort. So it is plausible, but only just.

The pain rises up inside of her again and she suddenly recognizes it for what it is, a hunger denied for so long that it has been forgotten; the raw lust for equally raw dripping meat, cleaved to the bone.

Nothing doing, stomach, she tells herself, we haven't had

anything other than salt pork in a dog's years. Still, despite the irony of what she'd just said, the craving is there, remaining after she massages herself down where the pain is.

Her reverie is interrupted by the creak of the outside stairs that lead up to the unlocked kitchen door. Who could be visiting? No one is anywhere near here. It takes a moment for her to remember that the Johnsons are due to arrive after breakfast, bearing her payment. It must be even later than she thought.

There is a knock at the scullery door. She runs to the closet that still smells like her father's tobacco on dry days and jerks her once-black-now-scab-colored dressing gown off the hook, wrapping it around herself. Luckily it closes tight and covers her body from neck to ankle, modestly appropriate. She jams her narrow, tannin-stained feet into David's flannel slippers, wincing slightly as the saw-grass cuts are reopened on the rough fabric. The plaid will hide the color, she reasons, not that there will ever be anyone to see.

There is no sign of movement up the long stairs to the second floor. Rose hardly ever awakens before noon, though sometimes Joy wonders what it is that she does up there all night, alone. She knows that she would not get a sensible answer if she asked, so she remains silent.

She is expecting to find Mr. Johnson, or even his Indian servant, waiting with a few baskets to empty in the kitchen bins and take back to their barn. When she opens the door she is surprised to discover Randolph standing there, huge in the doorway, holding his hat in one hand, a small velvet box in the other. His dark, greasy locks are too long and curled against his forehead in mock kiss-curls, his brows shaggy and somehow contrite, though what wrongs he has committed against her, Joy can't even begin to imagine.

The steps behind him are loaded with goods in sacks and

baskets: food, fabric, feminine frills, even an enormous side of beef that sets the new hunger in her raging. Behind him, through the thin cracks visible between his body and the door, Joy can see two native servants unloading yet more from the wagon. Apparently, the Johnsons have been planning this for weeks. Two of them, anyway.

Joy is so shocked by this new turn that she forgets to speak. Randolph coughs twice, with his mouth uncovered, to remind her.

'Randy?' Her voice is weak and her weakness disgusts her. But the sight of all that meat is unbelievable. She half expects it to disappear if she looks away for a second. With an effort of will she calms the tremor. 'What's all this?'

'Why Miss Joy,' Randolph smiles, gap-toothed pseudo-innocent, 'how long have we been neighbors? I've gotten sick of trading and talked my dad around to viewing you like I do, on friendlier terms.' He is watching her hunger, feeding on it, for her hunger lends him power. It is a force as good as any tool, and he can use it. People in want are bought cheap, and he wants to spend as little as he can.

She is clutching the collar of her robe, sensible of his doglike eyes running along her ankles, as though sizing up the tendons, to better cull the weak doe from the herd. He does not recognize her teeth, as pointed as his own. 'I don't know if I can take this, Randy. I haven't anything more to sell.'

'No one's asking for a buyer-seller transaction, Joyce,' he doesn't see the name rankle her like a parasite burrowing underneath a collar, 'think of it as a trade, an exchange.'

Of my soul, she knows, for these goods. But she doesn't say this. She asks, 'A trade for what?'

The natives have pushed their way past her and are unloading things into her kitchen. Never mind that she has not said yes.

Everything they bring, uninvited, past her threshold they leave there, including the baskets. She is thrilled and terrified, careful not to let either emotion show.

'Friendship? Companionship?' That grin again, a predator mis-guessing prey. 'You tell me. Anyway, my dad needs my help repairing our barn. I need to get a move on, but before I go, here,' he tosses her the box, almost contemptuously, as though handling something of very little value, the action like the signature of a drunk on an unthought confession, 'this is for you. Open it later.'

With that, without waiting for her reply or checking to see that the package is caught, he turns from her, replacing his hat, his face twisted in an expression of satisfied anticipation; he knows what must happen, and leisurely decides that he wants it, but has the patience to wait. He turns from her with his helpers and re-joins the horses at the cart.

Joy stands there for a moment, the velvet box clutched in her hand, not quite ready to open it. She is almost afraid of it, the significance of what her heart says it holds. She does not like that man, almost loathes him. But surely he is better than starvation. Better for her, and better for Rose.

So much today, after years of nothing. So much trouble and confusion, and it's not even noon yet. Still... God hates a coward.

She opens the box.

It is not the worst thing, not a ring, but it is bad enough. A love token.

A simple silver cross, flat and engraved with blackened lines like the ropes binding the cross-pieces together. The chain is fine and delicate, but sturdy. It is a lovely thing in its simplicity, almost too good a thing to come from that house. She will not keep it, of course, however lovely. She will return it; not, again, for what it is, but for the true symbol behind the thing.

Still, what harm is there in trying it on? Just this once. And after this moment, never.

She has not had a lovely thing of her own since the ring she sold, all else has come from her father, and she has sold all of that save for the ivory pen she found in the desk yesterday. That, she has decided, will remain hers no matter what.

She plucks the cross from its bed of stiffened velvet where the silver glinted bright against the deep blue, and she places it around her neck, fumbling with the clasp.

The one remaining downstairs mirror is in the sitting room, its surface not yet entirely covered over with mold. The burning starts before she reaches it.

A fiery itch against her breast where the necklace lies, a rash that spreads fast like flame through dry field, becoming quickly painful. By the time she claims the threshold of the long crossing-sprung floorboards to catch sight of herself in that watery glass, the pain is unbelievable.

Her fingers cannot move fast enough, so she pulls and splits the fine-wrought chain (no returning this now, no giving it back); she drops the object, symbol-laden and weightier than it looks, back into its dark, lined case.

Her own twin image in the mirror frightens her. Her hair is down again, and wild, nearly feral, and there is a mottled rash, meaty and scarlet, but white in the center, outlining the place the cross rested, like a flash-burn.

She has read of this, an allergic reaction to silver, though she has never heard of one quite so fast moving, or so severe. She must be becoming one of those people who can only wear gold.

She stands for a moment, staring and oddly, deeply ashamed. A pity. But who is there to see her? She can wear gloves, fix the chain. Give it back. Nothing irrevocable has happened yet, nothing been said. She can cover her neck with a long scarf, if there is one; a handkerchief otherwise will have to suffice when she pays her next, suddenly necessary, visit.

Her reverie is interrupted by her stomach. There is still the kitchen to consider.

I should give this back too, all of this meat, these dry goods, but this is not jewelry. This is back-pay, and but a fraction of it, for all the things I sold, for all the cheap deals I gave them, all they owe. And all of this flesh! It has been so long.

She has not noticed that she has slid to the floor. She does not feel the knife handle gripped in her hands, or that the box that holds the unwanted, repulsed, repulsing cross has skittered under the rickety table. She does not recognize the hacking motion her arms make into the fresh meat, nor the sensation of knife scraping fat, until the ragged, bloody hunk is dangling, torn and almost untasted, from her slavering mouth.

The rest of the morning is filled with unnatural silence, punctuated by unconscious, animal slurps and moistened grunts.

The blood remains underneath her fingernails for hours.

PREDATOR AND PREY

Joy comes to herself sprawled in the moist dust underneath the blond-pine kitchen table, slathered in gristle and her own pink saliva, frothed as though she were rabid, or hacking up tuberculoid blood. Her eyes are unfocused at first, lending the sun-spattered room an eerie, almost mystical air, a golden faery atmosphere.

Before her is a tall red and white marbled column and, as her sight clears, she realizes that she is staring at the remainder of the gifted slab of half-cured beef. Her fingernails are painted rusty, her mouth bears the scent of carrion, her teeth are hungry and pointed as a harpie, and her stomach, aching and distended with part-masticated flesh, wails for more raw meat.

She is gore-streaked and exhausted, with no idea of the day or the hour. It could not have been very long since her maenad orgy-feast, or she has slept the day away to the point she left it. The sun has moved forward about an hour's worth along the floor. Flies are buzzing everywhere, around the purpled gobbets on the floor. She can clean it later, or not. Who's to see? The remaining slab is cured to keep, she need not worry about it yet, let the flies have the drips. Right now she must focus on cleaning herself.

Joy moves to the covered water basin near the ewer that serves as sink, uncovers the lid and spoons away the layer of mosquito larvae that are spawning there with her large dipper carved from a gourd. The next dipperful she drinks and the tainted water feels cool on her tongue, clearing away the feral taste of prey brought down on moonlit plains. She pours another portion into the chipped enamel basin, wets a sponge to smooth the gore from her skin.

She wonders, briefly, if she is going crazy.

No, she will not allow herself to consider that. Not now, with so much changing, now is not convenient. But then, is there ever a right time for insanity? Imagine, she thinks, what the world would be like if one could schedule madness? People wouldn't need vacations. They could pick an unneeded period from their years of time and go mad in it, returning safely when they decide, when the stress is over and the journey won.

She wonders for a moment if she has any reason to get dressed. Why bother changing at all, since hardly anyone is ever there to see? It's not like her mother will notice. Why not lose the dress, she only has the one and it is barely holding together as it is, a construct of rotten thread and half-meant prayer, why not spend her days animal naked, skin gleaming bronzed as a pelt, only resorting to the confines of humanity when it is time to get up on her hind legs and beg?

A month ago, she would never have considered it. A month ago she would have had the freedom to. But now she has attracted, belatedly, the attentions of Randolph, if not his affections. Nakedness would not be seemly, or wise. Though part of her wonders what took madness so long to find her out here, it's not like she has had anything else to do with her time.

Part of her can recognize that, with her deemed mad, the Johnsons would see them in the state hospital outside of Tampa, on the list for brain-shocking or the vibrating treatment for hysteria, or any number of horror techniques her father described when she was a small child.

She must persist in sanity; if not for her own sake, then for Rose. She would be dead inside a week in hospital. Joy has known for years that she could, if she were alone, wander into Tampa at any time and find employment, no matter how poor. She could have been a cigar roller, a fruit canner, later on, a secretary. But how could she leave Rose, while she wanders dreaming? How can she abandon her father's body, which lingers here, no matter where his spirit is?

She never could.

And now the swamp begins to claim her, too.

Joy can hear her mother moving vaguely in her bedroom above her head, and she realizes that Rose has not had her breakfast yet, nor has she called, or if she has, Joy has not heard her. She will have to see to that after she is clean.

Her arms and face are clean now and she lathers off her armpits, leg wound, and the coarse-furred space between her legs as well, for good measure. The water is tinted the burnished shade of sunset, light gleams through it as she pours her basin out the window.

She is half-naked, unused to the sensation, oddly shy, and that is why the sight of a strange man making his way towards her through the churchyard shocks her so. He is on the short side, stocky, and from this distance, fair. If he looked up he would see her, but he seems fully occupied with picking his way along the overgrown pathway, raising what must once have been fine shoes as close in time as yesterday out of the clinging mud. He is moving unquestionably towards her.

She thinks she might have two minutes before he makes it to the kitchen door, and oh, what is she going to do about this mess? Better to meet him on the porch and prevent his entry. Use whatever charm she has to steer him away.

But all of this depends on her speed of dressing.

She lets her nightgown fall to her feet beside her lost robe and sprints, naked, through the kitchen to her death-room. Her dress is pooled where it always is, like her shadow, by the foot of her bed and she slithers into it, a shedding serpent in reverse. Barefoot, she hurls herself back the way she came, setting the wind to whistling in her wind-rushed ears. She barely feels her bun let slide the rest of the way out of her holed chignon, sending lengths of black tresses down the slim span of her back.

She makes it through the door, onto the porch, just as the stranger places his foot upon the first loud step.

They freeze together, coyote and deer, the woman and the man, bound in an instant by fear and hunger. His green eyes meet her stronger black ones, and he is overwhelmed by the wild-haired beauty before him, backlit against the sun. He has forgotten his entire purpose; she has not.

With a gesture of her arm, a touch against his bicep, she steers him from the manse. She will discover who he is, and he shall learn her story, but not here. Their conversation is meant for sunlit places, away from the rank stench of shredded animal, the sour spills of blood.

She leads him, unspeaking. He follows in awe. Until they settle to converse in the treed shelter of the graves.

LOVERS

Rose is before the mirror again, running her fingers through her hair, curling the coarsened tresses into greasy curls that trail down her back like strands of bleached Spanish moss. Her eyes are vague, unfocused, drinking in the golden mote light that filters through the dusty, uncurtained windows. Her nose is bleeding, a thin trickle from burst capillaries. She does not notice. Rose has been calling for food for over an hour and her voice has hoarsened to a sick whistle that echoes in her throat, wind over a fractured reed.

If no one comes, she will have to go downstairs.

Wherever could Malda be? Cook? David left his shoes underneath the bed this morning. I wonder why. Look, they are all covered in dust. No shine to them at all. Wherever could that man have gotten to with nothing on his feet?

I shall have to go and find him.

Maybe he is in the study. She has forgotten her hunger already, as she always does when the storm of want is over. She does not need much, really. New dresses are nice, she thinks, fingering her decrepit silk, as are jewels (her hands among the spilt pearls). Good food is lovely – her feet kick a gnawed and ancient bone – but really just a frill, a passing fancy. All I really need is him, my love, the only husband of my heart.

And so she goes, to seek and find.

Rose does not see the splintered staircase, the mold that hides the roses on the walls. She does not notice the missing floorboards or catch the drifting, noxious stench of spoilt meat. She dreams the servants real around her; there is Malda in the corner, mending draperies of lime chiffon. There is Cook in the kitchen, with an expiring rooster on the block, thrashing, his head lying in the sawdust at her feet. Rose can see the tongue twitching, the disconnected beak opening and closing, drowning in air.

Where is Joyce? Out playing?

She does not see the wharf rats laying droppings on the tallboy, nor the way they scatter as she passes. Everything is perfect now, as it always was. She is out to find her man.

The library, of course, is empty even of the scent of him. Her nose does not lie about that, there is no trace of the scent of pipe tobacco lingering like perfume in the air, but neither does she catch the whiff of urine from the unemptied cistern underneath the desk.

He must be out visiting. I will join him.

She has already forgotten about the shoes.

The front door is unlocked, and even if it were not the keys are hanging, as always, in a bunch on her hip, though she has to strain to open it. The hinges have rusted, and then she has to pause to hack out the bloody flux that steals her breath. It would be painful, if she felt it, but she would be comforted to know about the lovely bloom it raises to her cheeks.

The day is bright and harsh against skin ten years hidden from it – it seems to sizzle when it strikes her, a burn like mild acid – when she lifts her arm in a crook to salvage her eyes. So much beauty out here, the air so sweet. She had forgotten the taste of it, and suppressed the forgetting of it, so that her first breath is doubly surprising. Her sinuses clear for the first time in years, though mucous trickles, unheeded, from her delicate ears and rises like sweat from her dilated pores.

Instinctively she licks the droplets that gather above her upper lip as though she had been sucking a sweetie, though she hasn't had one in years.

She wanders down the stairs, meandering vaguely through wild trees. The Queen Anne palm she planted fifteen years ago has sprouted thirty feet tall. She does not recognize it, wonders where her little pretty went. There used to be a doghouse here, and a dog. Joy tore down the shed when Bess died, five years ago. She cried for weeks and couldn't stand the sight of it. Rose does not notice the small, stone-covered mound she treads on, or the fallen, pulpy cross. She strides on over, shattering it completely, calling for her pup.

The church is standing as it was, for her, though the illusion might not hold if seen up close. On some level she must know this, for she does not try to look inside. Instead, she wanders through the open graveyard, past the two young lovers talking there, hands clasped together in the first bloom of love. Rose smiles in full, wholehearted approval.

They are a sweet couple, a well-dressed brunette who looks much as Joy might in another few years, conversing with a well-groomed young businessman. They must be new to town. She makes a mental note to find out where they live and drop in on them later, with welcome basket in hand. She promptly forgets.

She is coming to the edge of the cemetery now, before reaching town-proper, not expecting to find David here, though he often lunches under that tree, the low-spreading boab decked out in berries, its hollow trunk perfect for reading in on a hot summer day. It is after lunch time now, must be by the sun (she remembers for a second that she hasn't eaten yet today. Wonders, briefly what can be wrong with Cook), nevertheless her husband often keeps odd hours. She might as well check.

And, *yes!* There he is!

He seems tired, propped up underneath that odd, stiff blanket. On such a hot day, too! Perdition itself couldn't be warmer. Really, the only thing visible about him is his left hand, but she would know it anywhere, and besides, he is wearing the white-gold ring she gave him, proud as he is of the unusual color.

She goes to help him up.

The soil in town is waterlogged, heavy with moisture, and a human body in a lead-lined coffin is more buoyant than the dirt. Without a solid cement-cap the corpse has less chance of remaining where the mourners place it than a child's ball held beneath the thrashing waves. Though it may take years, eventually the dead will rise up.

The coffin was cheaper than the price the mortician sold it for; the lead lining occupying solely the bottom. Half of the lid has long since been washed away, the body itself desiccated by the elements, musculature liquefied like meringue, limbs pulled out of position by scavenging coyotes and raccoons. A single bone and ligament hand protrude from the opening, bearing a miraculous ring, a few paper fingernails, and the tattered cuff of a once-fine shirt.

Rose bends down to see a face nearly unrecognisable as human, and beholds nothing but the man she loves. A skull with five remaining teeth and a lot of root-holes, decorated with a few scraps of flesh and scant, dust-colored hairs. Her face lights up with love so bright it is the semblance of health.

'There you are, David! I have been looking all over for you.' She reaches down and hauls him up, his body lightened so considerably it almost seems that the bones move themselves, 'I've missed you so much. Come. It's time to go home.'

She inclines her head as though listening.

'If you are so busy, why do you have time to lie there under that tree, napping like you've got all the time in the world?' She is holding him with one arm around his non-existent waist, feeling the bones beneath the leathery skin, walking back towards the house, this time traveling over the weed-strewn road. 'You have to learn to relax, dear. You are working yourself to death.

'You are getting much too thin,' feeling, on some level, the bare ribs beneath her fingertips. 'I shall have to bribe Cook to start sneaking butter into your morning coffee, if you don't watch out.'

They are in front of the boarded general store, door gaping, with boxes full of what must be new merchandise stacked up out front on the porch. There is a crossroads of sorts here, the main road meets an intersecting alleyway that runs between the store and the cane-workers apartment beside it, to allow access to the rooms on the side. There is a boab tree where the road meets the alley and some instinct tells her to stop.

'David, I'm sorry, I have no idea what you are talking about. Who are you meeting here again?' She rests the corpse against the trunk, eye sockets tilted in the slack-jawed head as though delivering an explanation.

Rose's wide, blue eyes gleam unseeing as a doll's, glazed from within with a deeper obsession. The sweat is worse against her skin, purpling the dress she wears as it soaks through the silk. She bends down, mouth open, gaping, her breath like a dying bellows blowing against a furnace, too well stoked. She bends down and tears a strip of inch-wide fabric, the entire hem of her skirt, that parts from the body with the sound of meat being split with a cleaver. She divides the long bandage in two, a piece for each arm.

'Yes David, if you insist.' She lifts up one skeletal arm, ties it to a branch on the left of the wide-spreading trunk, blue fabric bright against the bone. 'Of course I don't mind if you stay out a little longer.' The other hand secured now, tied gently with a granny bow. 'Just so long as you come home for supper.' She bends forward and kisses the corpse, slow and lingering, her eyes shut with pleasure, tongue exploring the crevices where teeth once homed. 'You know Cook doesn't like to be kept waiting.'

She pulls away again, listening, her head tilted to the left, a cherry strand of spittle dribbling gently from the corner of her mouth. What she hears makes her burst into a bright, childlike grin, and suddenly she is lovely.

'Oh David, you know I love you too.' She runs her finger over his cheekbone. 'I shall see you at home.'

She turns, waves her hand, is gone.

She will wander around for a while, in something resembling an opium daze, before making her vague, mad way back up the outer and the inner stairs to their marital bedroom, their beautiful home.

The skeleton stands cruciform against the smooth-barked tree, bound with blue rags and almost naked. The hollow places where his eyes were gaze at the storefront's open door, empty and waiting for a body to fill it. The mouth is open, jaws parted, as though waiting impatiently with something to say to young lovers about the meaning of love, sacrifice, and the passage of time.

The afternoon is young, but moving on. The world moves with it. There is no room for stopping here. The only ending visible is the ensign of Atropos who leans there, staring, with his back against the rain-smoothed wood.

PROPOSAL

Matthew is moving in a rush of torn red velvet and female sweat, with a sweetness underneath, redolent of carrion, as though beneath this girl's white skin, just beneath the surface, something vast and predatory moves. His memories have ceased recording, overwhelmed by beauty and by shock, and he cannot remember clearly how he came to be here beneath these trees, with this girl who should not be.

The house was meant to be abandoned.

She *has* been abandoned.

They are seated together under a green, spreading tree, on a cool cement coffin-case. He brushed away the lizard droppings with his handkerchief to let her sit. There is a serpent curled around his boot, attracted to the black for the extra warmth it promises. He cannot tell if it is poisonous, and does not wish to risk the asking, unwilling to demean himself before this lovely, feral girl.

He shall have to remain very still, and hope the danger passes. If danger it is.

She is seated on the lid, hovering, ethereal between heaven and death, as comfortably as he would sit in his mother's house in Swindon, reading on a couch before the fire. Frankly, he finds the current situation more than slightly disconcerting. Her house! He nearly walked right in. If she had not been on her way outside herself, if she had been bathing, changing, or even cleaning in a house coat, imagine their mutual humiliation. Thank God, thank providence, she was already emerging, her virtue covered, fully dressed.

'Actually,' she says, her voice low and deeper than a woman's should be, 'it isn't our house. Not really. It belonged to the church. A manse. And from what you have shown me in that governmental grant, it is not even the presbyteries. It, and all of this, are yours.' That last phrase is punctuated by a look, intense, those flashing eyes. 'You could throw us out.'

'I would not, would never.' He nearly asks, what do you take me for? But refrains. She does not know him. 'But why do you stay here, in all this desolation? Surely someone in this town would be willing to help you? The Presbytery? They must make some concession for the widows and children of their ministers.'

'They do, but,' she lowers those lovely black eyes, looks to the pale fingers curled in the ends of her long hair that pool like dark water in her lap, 'you don't know about my mother.' Her knuckles tighten around a strand, as though she would break the tress in her frustration.

Unthinking, he is always unthinking, it seems, at least today, he covers her strained fingers with his broad hand.

'What about your mother?' Her face is open in its tears, unused to crying; she does not disguise her sorrow, seems almost unaware of it, detached from it, like a longing for one long dead. He cannot help but love her. He never had a chance. 'It's fine. You can tell me.'

'After Father, after he died,' she lowers her eyes, and tears drop into her lap-nest of hair, 'her mind broke. Something in her let go. Some days she does not know me. She used to wander, looking for him, barefoot, undressed, but she has mostly stopped that. I was too young, then, to get her into town, no one would take me without her permission and she would not give it. Now,' her face is pale, drawn taunt across the bone, 'now she is too far gone. It would be a madhouse for her. Me too, possibly. It's been so long since I have seen a stranger. I don't know what I would do. Besides, she has since shown the symptoms Father did, before he passed.'

He laughs at this, loud, bare and good-natured. 'But I am a stranger! And you are fine with me.' He is still gripping her small hand, squeezing it as reassurance. She tightens back, loving the feel of his strong fingers, the solid bones, in this place where nothing remains solid for long.

In the distance, a female shape clad all in blue passes like a wraith, unnoticed.

'You're different, somehow. I can trust you.'

'Then trust me to help and not to hurt you.' Matthew's passion overwhelms him, he slides off of the sepulchre to the sponge-ground beneath it, and never mind the serpent coiled underneath his heel. Her left hand, so lovely, is in his grasp. 'Stay with me now, until I am settled, let me rebuild your home, make it habitable, even as I rebuild my own.' He has told her that he is going to settle in the store house, after apologizing for his original plans.

'My workers are coming, tonight or early tomorrow. Our first task will be housing repairs, then clearing for planting. Stay on; if you will not come to civilization, let me bring it to you. Like the mountain never did for old Mohammed. And then, when you are ready, when you are used to seeing men again and I have pulled a living from the ground, come with me and live in the light with me, in the city. Let me comfort you.'

The serpent, angry at the loss of its warm boot, tired of the pressure of this man's weight against its scales, strikes. Matthew can feel its jaws collide with the bare flesh above his ankle. But it is only a rat-snake, barely marking him, and he mistakes the sensation for the jabbing of an ill-placed twig.

Joy thinks in silence for a moment. Unschooled in the art of courtship though she may be, she knows a proposal when she hears one. Two in one day, and of such different character! No fool she, Joy knows which to accept.

'So you shall let us stay here, as long as you do? You'll help us, without forcing me to trade my heritage for the favour?'

'Of course.' At the mention of trade his lip curls a bit at the edges, a twinge of disgust barely visible beneath the beard. 'I would never ask you to compromise yourself. You or any lady. I am shocked that anyone would.' The mud is soaking into his trouser leg, this discomfort, like all he experiences here, is secondary to his rash emotions. He does not feel it. 'And then, when you are ready,' he is blushing now, a bright, creeping red, 'we can move, together, into town. If your mother is still with us then, as she will be, God grant it, she can move into our house to dwell in comfort through her elder years. And anyway, before next week at the latest, I shall have a doctor down to help her.'

What is this sensation that rises in Joy's narrow chest? What is this feeling, stirring to life? It is something long dead, rising like Lazarus called forth by Christ, stinking in its grave-rags. The re-birth of hope.

She does not know if her sanity can bear it.

She does not have a choice.

Unable to speak, having spent all her words in explanation, she bites her lip, and nods a head disguised by long, unruly hair.

Matthew takes it for the acceptance it is. How can he be so happy in this hell? How can he feel such joy amidst such desolation? A new life born above these bones.

His proposal accepted, fiancée declared, he rises to his feet beside her and pulls her up to stand beside him, until they can look over the land they have inherited, in love new-minted as that found between Adam and his lady on the morning after their exhilarating fall.

The world is spread out all before them. They shall, together, bring this land to order: productive, cultivated, lovely. And when they are done, and rich in gold refined from sugar, they shall return to the world of men to live their lives, at last, in comfort and in peace.

He has a gift for her, a brooch his mother sent with him, a gold-bound cameo that he will give her as a sealing token. Later.

Right now, they stand together, talking of nothing, everything, their future, their plans, in that excited rush new lovers have, underneath the trees whose roots, untrimmed, untamed, slowly dismantle all human roads.

His helpers are far along the highway, in their wagons, on their way. When they come, the work will fall all around him in a rush. Until then, he is free to walk with this lady, dark as new-Eve in her decrepit Eden, to plan and build the dreams that will subsist far longer than the words and edifices of men.

They trod on graves in their walk, but the dead don't mind this. They grin up at them through layers of lead, cement and soil, staring in detached approval of their hopeful, mortal campaigns.

DEPARTED

Matthew and Joy spent the better part of three hours wandering around the septic ghost-town, so unaware of their nacreous surroundings that they might as well have been in Paris. The only places they avoided were their respective homes. Their conversation was deep and varied, touching on everything from family history (Matthew had a grandmother who was an orphaned foundling, adopted from the parish church step), to best childhood memory (Joy recalls her mother's fingers running through her hair before church every Sunday, combing this way to instil a curl. Her reward for sitting still was a Hershey's kiss).

Their environment never seems to touch them as they walk along the fractured street peering into old, abandoned houses, rattling the bones of forgotten ponies in the barns. They even slither into the unsafe, ruined church, startling a flight of wood doves that have made their homes beneath the fallen beams. They rise up, bright in air, scattering feathers, guano, and clumps of soft, gray down in an atmosphere of weddings.

They part ways only when the sun begins to set, Matthew escorting his new fiancée to the door, expecting to be invited in, but rebuffed on the excuse that her mother might be sleeping yet. He does not think this odd, that she would slumber through the day, not after everything that has already happened to him. Instead he kisses her, chastely, over the threshold of the disused front door, squeezing her hand once for good measure, and makes his way back to the store.

There is an evening redness in the sky, a pyrotechnic, almost volcanic umber shade, deepening steady towards spilt blood. The trees are moving, atmospheric, as though they were malevolent dryads set on dancing. In the distance, drawing closer, is the sound of many hooves.

His company has arrived at last.

There are fifty men in total, to fell and clear the land, their salaries (much cheaper than a white man's) to be paid half before, half after, food and bedding provided by themselves. The barman has come through for him after all.

Fifty strong men and one fat cook in ten large wagons loaded with sundries and tools, all heading for his camp at the shop. If he runs, he will beat them on arrival.

He breaks into a loping run.

The wagons are slowing now before the peeling storefront, drawing to a halt. There is no sound of raucous men, excited over work. They stand or sit on wagon-top, as if afraid to touch the soil. Their long brown faces drawn and tight, unnaturally pale, in an awe that seems almost spiritual, or at the least, bone-deep; frightened natives looking on a raging village god, small to the world but powerful here.

He is separated from his men by the band of trees before him, especially the massive boab across from his new home, and the rabid, strengthening light behind him. He can feel it against his neck as he flies, running, throbbing like a sickened tooth.

The boughs and branches scrape against his flesh as he pushes through the trees, as though preventing his fresh birth into the realm and company of men; still, undaunted, he shoulders through and is nearly shot for his perseverance. The men look on him as though he were a ghost, or the dead gone walking at long last; their heads are tilted as though listening for that final trumpet sound that signifies the end, the rest have raised their guns.

'No, no, don't shoot me.' He is waving his arms, noticing, but only just, the stench that rises up beside him.

'Are you ghost or living man?' The man who speaks, the obvious leader, tall and strongest with African blood.

'Your employer.' He drops his hands, risks a joke, 'I don't know what that makes me, though the greenbacks I'd give you are real enough.'

The guns are lowered, the silence remains. The men stare down at him from their nest in the carts, behind the flicking ears of mange-hided mules.

But no, they do not stare at him, but rather to the side at something tangled there among the branches, the thing wafting the stench of mortal corruption and disease.

Hands lowered, looking forward, he moves to stand beside the man who spoke. There is sweat pooling in the hollow above his lip, in the space between his legs, trickling like a living thing caressing underneath his armpits.

As in a dream, he turns, and looks upon the face of death.

Naked, gaping, tied to the tree, this thing that was once an obvious male. It is mostly skeleton and missing a foot, lashed to the branches by swaths of frayed lapis silk, its few-toothed mouth open in parody of either warning or song, the sky lit up behind him like an open wound in heaven's flank.

It is an unholy, unchristian thing, propped there standing against the bark, a grave thing, risen far too soon.

They clump together, all of them, for a moment in silence. Matthew has not an inkling what to do, does not want to admit his inequities by stating it, and is afraid of where it came from. His only consolation, the one bright, reasonable spark, is that it was not Joy who placed it here, for she was all the day with him.

The African speaks first in voice tinged by Barbados. 'We won't be staying here.' He loads his rifle, locks in the shot. 'This is a bad place. It is time to leave.'

Matthew's choice has been made for him. He must stand.

'If you leave, you get no pay, and you miss three days from working under other auspices. If you stay and help me rid of... this thing, I shall pay you fifty cents extra for every night you linger here and a share of all the profit that we pull from this land.'

'No,' the leader speaks again, 'what profit is there for us if we gain all the money in the world, but leave our souls? I say go back. This is my wagon, these my mules,' he gestures expansive with his large hand, 'all who want to can ride back with me. All who wish it, they can stay.'

Matthew knows that if he stands up to persuade them, sounds too desperate or much scared, he will lose all the help instead of only some of them. He remains firm. They heard his offer, they see where he stands.

In the end he loses all but ten men. Not enough to farm on the scale that he originally intended, but enough at least to make a start. The rest saddle up and ride away, down the long road back to Tampa.

The first thing they do, in an evening long with firsts, is remove the clattering, tree-bound corpse. They carry the body, gingerly, hesitant to come in contact with the ragged skin, back to the cemetery from whence it came, searching around to find the split grave it was dragged out of.

They find it underneath a large, cathedral-trunked tree, another boab with roots that rise up from the soil, seeking up towards heaven while still bound to earth. There is no stone to mark its head, so they cover it with leaves and strips of sod, placing a large white rock on piled soil, three feet deep above the head.

It is full dark, and the moon is glowering. There is much to do tomorrow, much survey, repairs and clearing. The men wash up for supper and for bed. The sky is clear, empty and expectant with the threat of later mist. Men move around in camp, preparing; the moon and stars look on unblinkingly.

FRIENDS

Father and son have been drinking for hours, not speaking, sitting outside their magpie house among the moss-hung trees. The shine lies heavy in the jugs, and in their stomachs, the clear, sweet taste burning their tongues. The alcohol is made from wild refined sugar, cooked and fermented in the stills in the yard, an added benefit from their chosen crop. The drink has a kick, it loosens the inhibitions. The recipe might, in fact, be the root behind the family's chosen thieving lifestyle.

The air is cooling, though the sun is not yet going down, the heat leaving the water and the rocks, leaving only a clinging layer of moisture that seals Randy's white cotton shirt to his skin like a translucent scrim. His father is kitted out in a fine foreman's suit, not seeming to sweat, cool-looking and composed, a man in power, surveying his sprawled conquest and the victories to come.

When they do speak, there is but one subject save the cane. Girls, and the dark slits between their legs.

Randy and his father share everything, figures clipped from the same swatch. It is no surprise they share this. They have journeyed together to the nearest cathouse, when the land rises hot around them, yeast-scented and warm. His father watched him the first time he lay with any woman, his lips pulled back in rictus grin, tight over teeth so sharp and white. He took in Randy's wide eyes, unbelieving, almost worshipful as he fell before the open legs of whatever whore was given him. Mr. Johnson likes to watch the look of open disgust as the girls are forced to take his son in between their tanned brown or mocha legs. The way their lips curl, the blood draining from their features, as he grunts and thrusts atop them, the occasional runner of spittle dripping from the loose and hanging lips.

The air is clear and deepening blue. Randy can see a flock of pelicans making their cretaceous way across the sky, pterodactyl-like, their wings flapping in silent ballet that passes almost entirely unnoticed by the men who drink in the trees on the edge of the sea.

The men sit in silence, planning their dark routes, looking toward their coming goals.

Mr. Johnson can picture that long plot of land and the fortune he will cull from it. He has, in a way that he will not admit fully even to himself, enjoyed the deep slow drain of the girl's last treasure, bleeding her white. He rolls a too-sweet mouthful of rum across the burning surface of his tongue, fire-drunk. That's good land there, he thinks, lip corners hitched in almost-smile, soil rich and black as a negro's ass. A year, two at the most and we'll have one of them buried, the other in a home, and be sitting rich. Society people. Up in Boston, or maybe New York. Get my boy a new and better wife after this one's worn through. Someone nice and roomy who can make sons. Someone, maybe, like mine used to be before she ran to fat.

These are as clear as his thoughts appear, and as happy. Johnson rejoices in them, silently, the light glinting on his canines, his teeth like blades.

Randy is thinking about his upcoming marriage. He takes for granted that she will give in, capitulate entirely to his greater will. What other choice does she have?

True, she is filthy, and more than half mad, but her figure is lovely, her rank hair dark and thick, animal-sexual. He would describe her as chthonic, if he but knew the word. He would not be far mistaken, given her recent midnight wanderings.

His thoughts are nowhere near this complicated.

He pictures her ass, so round and tight, muscular and tender as ripe fruit. Her breasts, small but firm.

Picturing this strange, quite sexual progression, his excitement is evident through the veined fabric of his trousers, rising like the evidence of thought.

His father sees the lump and hoots in mute appreciation, making a connection somewhere in the barely-lit corridors of his mind between his son's erection and his own fast-coming financial gratification.

The sky is darkening now, the shine running out. There are animal sounds emerging from the woods around them, canine barks and snufflings in the moist undergrowth, on the scent-trail of something, their bodies ignited in a sexual heat, the implacable urge of possession.

The grin Randy turns on Johnson is sardonic and wild, a knife-flash of bone amidst his thick black stubble. 'You know what I am thinking, Dad?'

His father's grin is malice-tainted. 'I reckon yeah, but please, enlighten me. Are you thinking of the cathouse up by Tampa?' he asks, knowing that Randy for once is not.

'I was thinking someplace closer, less thoroughly broken in. After all,' he sets the near-empty jug down upon the forest floor; the homemade clay blends in to the soft strata of river mud, down to the pockmark flaws in the firing that mimic the holes of huge-armed fiddler crabs, 'I am to be a married man.'

Without a further word the two lope off, father and son as hungry as hounds, into the forest along the rare-used path leading into the base skeleton of town, to fetch and fell the one bright thing that flutters there, flailing as a weakening heart.

The sun is setting, the moon is on the rise. All is silent, save for their footsteps and the occasional wet susurrus of a gator moving underwater, along its own foul and secret track.

The men do not care about the mosquitoes or the mud, they don't mind the hideous splashing dark, or the way the vines fall down in curtains around them, like spiderwebs encompassing prey. They have a goal, and they will reach it yet, ere the sun once more meets the lightening sky.

They do not notice, at first, when the wild dogs join their small, carousing hominid pack. First one narrow canine, and then another, trailing along behind, beside; they're moving like shadows over the variegated waterscape. The dogs match the men, paw for step, more dogs joining with every yard, until the coyotes outnumber the men ten-to-one. They travel in a knot, through the tangled branches, the saw-grass and the weaving roots conspiring to trip, the lot of them panting, gasping after the female scent that lingers in their imaginations or the air. They move together through the rising ground mist, paws setting the currents swirling in the water and the vapour, boots and bare human feet scattering the scummed surface water, mixing fresh air with the swirling fog. The dogs howl, as do the men, ghostly lycanthrope creatures screaming through the darkest hours of night.

When, at last, they reach the forest edge, they can see the few small lights set burning by scattered human hands, the cluster in the ruined store, in the stilt-born manse. The men push through to open land, led by their trouser-bulges, their wolfish grins.

The coyote escort scatters at the first breath of air freed from clustered forest, a demonic hoard pierced by the potential for salvation, a gift not granted to the two pursuing men, who hurtle onward through the wrecked cemetery and over the lawn, to burst like one welcomed through the firm-barred door to greet the girl who waits therein with something that, in a less terrible world, might pass for love.

CLEAN-UP

After the walk, when the sky has reached its blue-gray gloaming, before the thread of sunlight tinged the sky, Joy closed herself into her house amidst the slathered ruins of the meat. Her mother has not been fed, though she can detect no stirrings on the floor above her head.

Matthew left her at the threshold of the front door she never uses. The door was stiff, rust bound, and opened with grating protest. She did not notice the bright patches on the hinges where forced exit chipped the sheath of rust. She was, for the first time in a decade, something resembling happy, in spite of her numerous apprehensions.

What, for example, is she to make of her wanderings last night? What on earth can she tell the Johnsons? If she and Matthew were to leave tonight, or even tomorrow, instead of waiting for the farm to fruit and provide proper finance for a start, she would not worry about it. She would say nothing, just leave, perhaps not even bothering to pack. After all, she has little left of any worth to bring with her, besides her mother.

And she is herself another problem. Maybe there is enough time to acclimate Rose to the idea of moving, or if not quite that, time enough to weave a convincing story around her. Joy could tell her that they are meeting David somewhere, in Tampa. He has moved to a different church, and gone ahead already to prepare the way.

Yes. That could work.

She can tell the story, tell it well, and then once her greatest concern has been assuaged and Rose is safely nestled into some nice, clean rooms in town, Joy can see about bringing a doctor to her and extending, if not saving, her life. Bringing her to live for once in real comfort instead of the hallucinatory kind.

But before any of this can happen she must see to the wreck that is her house.

If she is to have a male caller, a savior of any kind (never mind that he is handsome, if a little on the short side), she must meet her rescue, must make at least some of the moves toward him. The first step to salvation, she thinks, is making a sign no matter how weak, how flailing, that there is both need and want of it on the part of the damned.

In this case that means inviting him in, no matter how painful it will be for her to let a civilized, sane person see the wreckage that has become her life. Well, she can do that. But she will disguise at least the signs of her own slippage. She might not be able to help the spreading damp, the patches of mold, but she can at least scrape the bigger chunks off, and clean her ravaged gristle from the kitchen floor. She can take the food she bought from the Johnsons out from the rest and separate the bride-gifts out to return to the groom she has rejected. Including that very troubling silver cross.

These things she can do, and do tonight, but first she must see to her mother. Twenty-four hours without food and with no clean chamber pots is hard to bear, even for the mad.

Joy makes her way up the stair, calling, without answer, passing the place where she usually stops. She will have to brave the lair tonight, see that room of false stasis. Her feet are reluctant; she forces them, through an effort of will, not to slow.

She passes the locked door to her old childhood bedroom, remembering the light pink paint and yellow curtains left up since she was a very small girl. Rose thought the room too masculine, the paint applied at a time when light blue was considered the more mild, appropriately feminine color, as pink had too much red in it. She remembers how bright it was there, in the morning, when the sunlight woke her gently and the light filtered, golden, vibrant through the windows. The sweet smell of clean linen and orange blossoms, fresh as infancy. I wonder what has become of my stuffed dog, she thinks, I never used to be able to sleep without it. It is probably too mildewed, too rotted to touch now, if it still exists at all. She has a longing for it, suddenly, that comfort of a lucky childhood.

But the door is swollen in its frame from unaired moisture. It would take a stronger hand than hers to make that passage open up again.

Her mother's door is open, not widely, but far enough for her to see into the room without effort. It is like looking into a past preserved beyond all reckoning, a moment preserved without being allowed to pass, so that it seems as though time itself has slowed and rotted here, spreading its corruption outward like a bad spot in a good apple. There is the scent of good things gone sour, fine wine vinegared, something that should by all rights be sweet plucked too early, missing ripeness, passing directly into rot.

The sorrow is palpable, unacknowledged; it catches Joy's breath in her throat.

But though there is much here to concern an active mind, there is little cause for Joy to worry. Her mother is here, undressed beneath the damp coverlet, her long hair spread, fairy-tale lovely, above the yellowed pillowcase. Sleeping Beauty, in the flesh, breathing gently, waiting for her true love's arousing kiss.

Joy stands for a moment, watching. Lost.

The chamber pot is there beside the door, filled to brimming, and so Joy takes it with her to clean and empty. She will return with it once she has prepared Rose's meal, after her work downstairs is done. She hopes that her mother will not need it before then, and failing that, she hopes that Rose will have the sense to call rather than merely letting her waste fall where it will while in the throes of vivid dreaming.

It has happened before.

Joy takes her brimming charge and walks, carefully slow, down the stairs, pausing when she reaches the bottom to pour the slop out the window, noticing the very last dregs of sunset. She can scrub it later, and right now she cannot abide the smell.

The kitchen cleaning takes a while; she had spattered gobbets everywhere in her hunger-driven madness. She scrapes chunks from table legs, from countertop, strips dried onto the surface of the range and white string of gristle dangling like party streamers from the wallpapered ceiling. She gathers every piece, removes every stain, and far beyond, sponging dust and ancient grease that had lain for a decade ingrained in the linoleum until forgotten colors bloom in this room and it, in spite of the still-persistent smell of mold, enters a re-birth.

She will continue scrubbing downstairs, tomorrow.

But Joy is hungry now, and her mother will surely be waking, stirring soon, so she empties out her filth-scummed water bucket, wrings out her over-used, stinking mop, washes her hands, and contemplates the supper situation.

The slab of beef, surely nearly half a heifer, will see them through for months. Guiltily, she recalls that her mother has not tasted of it yet. She sharpens a carving knife against the file, neither ever used before in her recollection, until the blade is keen enough to slice a hair. She cuts a small piece, of similar size to the palm of her hand, around the place she gnawed from. That will be her portion. The larger one slides from the most deeply marbled area, what might have been the cow's shoulder. She will fry them both, with onions, and potatoes cooked in fat.

The smell of onions bubbling in oil brings the spittle rising in her mouth. She hopes, against likelihood, that she has the self-control to wait, this time, until the cured flesh is halfway cooked.

The moon is out, a bright, obsessive eye, and it shines on her through windowpanes made milky by steam, the light hitting and scattering as on an aged cataract. And she can hear, above the sizzling of flesh, the distant howling of many dogs.

They wail in the mangrove swamp, like Theremin, ululating weirdly. Part of her is terrified, the areas of skin that raise the short hairs on her hackles, the knuckles that tighten around the skillet handle; part of her is longing to join in.

That part burns in cruciform shape, scarred on her chest below the clavicle. That part throbs in her whitened, bitten leg.

The meat is burning, she has forgotten to turn it, when the night song ends abruptly as though silenced with the stroke of a knife.

There is quiet outside, lacking even the sound of insects, the whine of mosquito, the call of a bird.

Joy's heart is thrumming in her chest, in fear or dark anticipation, and when the knock she knew was coming lands hollow, loud, against the solid kitchen door, she acts with unthought clarity. This could not be Matthew. It is too dark for him. She removes the skillet from the range, taking the time to turn down the flame, her hands grasping instead the long-bladed knife that is, thank God, so sharp it gleams. Her movements are slow, careful, seeming-predestined, as though the fate which set her going is holding its long breath.

The pounding comes again, shaking the door within its frame. She moves to open it, walking like a drowned corpse under water, slow, balletic, reaching for the shore that was its last long glimpse of life.

There are sounds outside: breathing, obscene, demonic laughter. The knife is gripped, long, in her hand.

Joy, breathing ragged, reaches out beyond the limit of all human reckoning, and opens the hinge-screaming door.

VISIT

The men shove inwards as the door creaks back so that they burst through into the small room like pus forced from a boil. The girl is crouching in the doorway, ready for anything, her empty hand braced as though to catch her body as she falls. Her long hair is loose and wild, the honed blade of a knife clutched in a grip loose but firm, gleams among the curls.

Part of Randolph suddenly thinks that this may not be such a good idea. The rest of him, however, can hardly be said to think at all. He is animal, hungry and raging in lust. Besides, his gifts are lined up there, where he can see them, rifled through against the wall. She sold herself by touching them.

He owns this girl, this moment, and besides as his father always told him, when a girl acts most as though she does not want it, that is when the fire's stoked the highest deep within. This theory has always been borne out for him by the behavior of the whores he's been with. Deep down, he is confident that once that shiny toy is out of her hands, this one will settle back and maybe even enjoy it. Not that her pleasure, or lack of it, matters very much at all.

His father fills the door behind him, standing large in his impeccable funerary black, his teeth white against his thick black beard, a knife-glint in the dark. The girl is crouching, fierce but afraid. The daft mother is up there, somewhere, but she is not a problem. Randy moves into the light, the candles flickering, magnanimous, smiling. He can afford to take his time.

Mr. Johnson is pleased by the virility evidenced in his son's hard stance, the way his muscles tremble below his flesh. He takes it as a compliment to his own prowess. Johnson is starting to hunger for it himself, just watching. The fear the girl is showing does more to prime him than her figure ever could. But Randy is practically throbbing for it, his own frothed spittle collecting on his cheeks. Ah well, it is the right of children and animals to be impatient. He will have his turn, when the dust has settled some.

The girl is in retreat, head still lowered, scuttling backwards, a human fiddler crab. If she meant what she was saying with the knife, if she had the guts, they would not have made it this far in. Johnson's first impression was the right one. This is going to be easier than he thought.

'Look, Joyce,' Randy is speaking with his arms open, his voice laughing, never noticing her flinch, striding through the room as though he already owns it, 'we can make this easy, or you can make it hard. You took the food I gave you, the fabric, that shiny little cross. We both knew we weren't trading for a pretty bit of silver.'

She is braced now, ready, her back against the wall. Her voice is firm and deeper than Randy would like it. Unfeminine. 'That wasn't what I put on the table. As for this trumpery,' the cross is on the side table near her, in its black velvet box; she scoops it up and throws it at him. He does not make the catch and it clatters at his feet, 'you can have *this* back. The wrong symbol, quite like you, and an empty one at that.'

He laughs. 'Nice words for a preacher's daughter.'

Randy and his father are on either side of her, Johnson's large body blocking the door, Randy gibbering at her side like some unformed daemon loosed from hell.

She does not seem to know where to point the knife, which threat is the greater.

'The cross isn't the empty thing. You are.' She makes her choice, jabbing the long blade at Randy's extended, grasping fingers, slicing off a thin scrim of tip. 'No faith, no strength, nothing.' The blood is pooling, slowly, strawberry-colored underneath the ragged nail. She swipes again, breathless, and nicks the light green veins beneath the wrist, letting that sung claret to flow. 'You are nothing,' she is breathless, and despite the small pain, the men are closing in, 'nothing. And you shall not have me.'

Her final thrust is forceful and straight, disregarding Johnson but heading directly, through ribs, for Randolph's heart. And, this time, her blade would find its home.

The fight would be ended before it began, were it not for Johnson stepping in. He sees the way the blade is flashing, and with a lithe motion that belies his bulk, he grabs her wrist and twists it upward in a motion that flesh and sinew was never meant to follow.

She can hear her tendons cracking, see the purple spread almost like magic from the fingers pressed against her wrists. She drops the long blade – how could she not? And the knife skitters, metallic and lost, across the floor, never regathered.

Joy tries to pull away and Johnson, in a motion that could be mistaken for mercy, releases her to fall. She backs herself, too terrified for feeling, into the corner where the doorframe meets the peeling wall.

Her face is blank, blasted of all evidence of thought, mouth gaping and closing in silence, the face of a fish drowning on land.

Randolph steps over the fallen blade, tracking his boot prints in the pooled shadow of his father and his own spilled blood. He is panting now, still smiling, nearly drooling in anticipation, as though his lustful hunger was freshened by the scent of her fear-pulsing sweat.

The girl is there, and she is lovely in terror. Her long hair loose, her red dress fraying, black eyes that were flashing less than a minute ago, rendered, by terror, placid and blank.

This, he thinks, is going to be fun.

He shall have no further trouble with her. This, the thought repeats, implacable, this is going to be fun.

The father is grinning over the boy's hulking shoulder. The girl's body relaxed in posture of fainting, and he can smell urine, though be it from the upstairs mother or the girl at his feet, he cannot tell.

She is prone and lovely, no further trouble. Randolph kneels down beside her. Her dress front tears as easily as a paper handkerchief, softened by rot, exposing creamy, heaving breasts tipped with nipples like ruby drops of blood. Randy rests his strong fingers on her shoulders, feeling the fine bones there, and takes a lovely nipple in his mouth.

His ears nearly burst to rupturing, it is so piercing, when she screams.

INTERRUPTION

Matthew's helpers, the few that remain, are settling in among the softening barrels in the partially-cleared general store, spreading their bedrolls out amidst the sawdust and the soil. They have lit a fire from dry wood (God alone knows where they found it) in an improvised grate in the center of the floor, and they are resting around it roasting strips of game on straightened wire hangers above the softly glowing coals.

It is a comfortable scene, oddly out of place after the end of today. Matthew is half disconcerted by the speed they have adapted. What kind of man, he wonders, remains in a place like this, with no stake but money, after seeing what we saw? His answer, when it comes, drags a wry smile across his face beneath the shaped beard. A man like me.

Of course, I do have another reason. One.

He would very much like to have Joy here with him. He imagines her body curled against his, held close, until he can hear her heartbeat throbbing against his chest, bathed in the light of the forgiving fire.

He is amazed at how deeply he feels for this woman he has known less than twelve hours. This should not be possible, this passion, this depth, but time is funny here. Compressed somehow, and drawn out, as though this abandoned town occupied some different, 'other' space. Like the paintings he saw in the British Museum when he visited last year before his current journey was barely more than a distant thought.

He is thinking of the ones on the cusp between Byzantine and true Renaissance, the holy pictures found in the scenes on icons. Scenes with human figures, magnified but recognizable, terribly prescribed, set against a golden background that delineates the division between heaven, or hell, and earth, the Holy, the Awful, and the typically mundane. As though God himself or Satan could enter in and lend a transcendent aura to any ordinary picture of a woman, reposed somewhere in a garden, or a house, decorated with twelve white lilies, her long, maiden hair spread out about her, not expecting company or distraction of any kind, but ready, and looking up to say, 'Yes. Here I am: your handmaiden.'

Joy herself is a woman who could be found in such a landscape, her dark, clear features, her odd gothic setting, long, loose hair. Hair that he could lose himself in, drinking in her rank scent.

His body is becoming heated, and not as a result of that external flame. Looking around, he can see that his men are getting settled, even as his restlessness grows. He decides that, before bedding down, he needs some clean air, a cool, brisk walk.

The air outside is humid, swirled with fog. He can hardly see where he is going, but he thinks he might be near the defunct cemetery. There is an odd wailing, some distance off, the Theremin call of howling dogs, or something more sinister.

For a moment, he imagines that he hears the sound of rushing feet that then fall silent, trailing off to nothing but the trill of cicada and the whir of night birds on the wing.

He has not gone far, but still the darkness overwhelms him. It is all milk-filtered moonlit fog and acres of black. There is the sound of falling water, somewhere, beyond locating. It is not until he decides that he had better be turning back that he realizes he is lost. The fog has swallowed him, screwed up the compass points and set the needle spinning in the vast curtain of night.

Nothing to do then but press forward.

It is not long, thank God, before he sees a faint glimmer of light, and it takes less time than that to realize that he is not looking at the gleaming from the store.

It is the manse, lit up as bright as Christmas. He wonders where Joy found the candles. What could she be doing awake so late? Cooking, cleaning? She would not need that much light to read, surely.

But what is that movement at the door, balancing on that precarious porch?

There are two figures, moving violently, forcing an entry. Something is very wrong.

Matthew runs as fast as his legs will take him over this lumping, tangle-rooted soil. Tree branches seem to descend and grab him, as though they would block him on his path, potholes open up beneath his feet. He falls three times before making the bottom step, and as his foot hits the warped pine board, he hears a terrible, blood-voiced scream.

He cannot force his feet to move quickly enough, it seems like hours before he reaches the flung-open door.

The scene that greets him is terrible, obscene. The kitchen has been thrown into confusion, plates and food goods scattered everywhere, but nowhere anything like as useful as a knife. Matthew curses his lack of a blade and scoops up the fallen iron griddle, still sliding with large pieces of beef; this will make a good concussive weapon, if nothing else.

The living room is filled with shadows that spill from the backs of monsters hulked in the center of the room. He can see a figure kneeling, britches down, in the corner like a predator contemplating meat, another stands behind him, arms crossed, grinning like a wolf preparing for a feed.

They must be the Johnsons.

The younger man is grunting, shifting a form that struggles weakly beneath him, ineffective as a kitten fighting against a storming squall, the huge black head grinning and nodding, having fun.

Matthew does not think, does not plan what he is after. There is the iron fry-pan in his hand, and he brings the metal down.

The sound is like a large, cracked bell, an ill-placed shot, but it does the job. He misses the lumbering head and connects with the broad back, between the shoulder blades, sending the massive body sprawling.

The girl takes the opportunity and rolls out from underneath the form of her assailant. Her bodice has been torn, exposing her breasts, but her lower parts remain covered. They had not, apparently, gotten to that part yet.

Matthew darts forward and pulls her toward him, sheltering her with his arm and brandishing the frying pan as threateningly as he can at the men who turn toward him, barely noticing as Joy bends down and, with a pained grunt, retrieves her long knife.

'You must be the new sugar-man.' Randolph's grin is surprisingly good-natured. 'If you'd waited but another minute my father and I would have shared her. My new filly.' He is moving forward, open handed, somehow threatening. 'I don't mind other people riding, but I'm the one to break her in.'

Joy is clutching the knife from her station beneath his sheltering arm. Matthew swipes the pan from side to side, looking from Randolph to his father who is closing in on their flank.

'She isn't yours and she isn't a horse.' Randolph laughs at that, at Matthew's accent or the sincerity in his voice. 'She is her own. And she wants you to leave. Now. I think you should.'

Randolph holds his hands up in parody of surrender, never quite leaving his father's spread shadow, but moving in the right direction, towards the open kitchen door. 'Okay, okay, keep your britches on, or don't, whatever.' He backs out through the kitchen, laughing on top as though at a joke, his anger venomous and visible just beneath the surface of the jest.

Johnson is following close behind his son. He could have moved and beaten them both, what chance have they, a pipsqueak and a female, against their strong force? But they both know that the Englishman has helpers out there and while there may be time to maim this troublesome creature, the workers would be here to help the girl before either one could dip their wicks. They are, for now, beaten. But they are large men and can be patient. He will be back, his son will be wed, and the land will be his to use as he will.

And then the lovers are alone.

'Well,' Matthew unbuttons, covers her nakedness with his shirt, 'what are we going to do now? Will they come back? What is going to happen?'

And Joy, speaking slowly, tells him.

They sit together for hours, planning, detailing, until just before the break of dawn they have arrived together at a plan. There is no way they can live like this, on edge, until the crop gets going. There will have to be a more decisive confrontation.

Together, the two of them walk out to rouse the sleeping helper men. There is safety left in numbers, and if you are intent on ever visiting the devil's house, it is best to bring your strength in men.

Sunday

PLANS

Randolph runs as best he can with his bruised back, struggling to keep up with his more rugged father, his grazed wrist dripping a thin ribbon that soaks into his moist white cuff until the fabric looks black in the moonlight. There is no word that fully encompasses the rage he feels now, not completely. He is grinning, yes, has been throughout the long disastrous encounter in the moldy vicar-house, but it always was a rictus more of anger than enjoyment, and it is very bitter now.

He is winding his slow way through the ragged trees, the thick white fog, to his parents' home. They have known about his more violent proclivities for years now, since he was a small boy, and his father at least has fostered them. Johnson took him to his first whore house the year he turned sixteen, and the first time he struck his mother for taking him to task about the state of his room (he might have been as young as five) the look she gave him was more of pride than anger. Certainly it was a far cry from disappointment.

They were the ones who came up with the whole marriage plan, they can help him salvage it. His father will know what to do with the meddling Englishman, how to handle that screaming cunt, breasts or no breasts; they can salvage this even now. A wedding was not ever the only way to get the land, merely the cleanest. People disappear all the time, especially foreigners unused to the climate, unprepared for illness, or the more animal ravages of the swamp. And as for a forgotten preacher's madhouse girl? She could disappear tomorrow and no one would be any the wiser.

And who is to say that if she and her mother *did* disappear, he would not get his fun? A body is a body, be it warm or not.

The moon is out and shining, glaring down, an open eye looking blind into the dark. His boots squelch in ankle-deep mud, branches wind and trail around his laces as though the earth would pull him down, and there is a poison ivy rash rising up against his leg.

He knows that he is damned.

His father does not speak, does not even seem to squander a harsh breath, but whenever Randy chances to look beside him, Johnson is there, hovering spectre-like, his thickly-soled boots hardly splashing where his own feet crash and send up torrents of blackened river muck to spatter his good slacks.

The wild dogs circle, howling, around them, but whether they run to protect them or consume, Randy does not know. Sometimes he can catch a glimpse of their slick yellow hides slipping through the close-knit trees, see the light reflecting off their teeth, their too-red tongues.

He does not care.

He will burn the world around him and to hell with his father's lust for money or for power. He does not need either one. All joy is in destruction, all beauty in corruption. He is a runner in the service of Pandemonium, serving Beelzebub or Pan, whichever god of rot and darkness calls him forth like a spirit in a pentagram of chalk.

The land means nothing to him, save that he can blast it. If he could set the world alight, rub salt in every furrow, take a blade to every breast, tar to every painting, and a shotgun to every new-born infant, he could die a happy man.

These thoughts are not like him, or rather, they are more like him than anything he has ever felt before. Something in the air tonight refines him, makes him glory more fully in his essential self. Perhaps the fog is serving as magnification, enlarging his natural tendencies, his normal inclinations towards mayhem and the night, until he has no other features left.

Or maybe it was the presence of the blood, serving like all sacrifices, to bring the spirits down to earth, those dark and awful forces, forcing them to settle here in this mortal self. The spirits dip their lips deep in, take a long, prophetic draught, before their lips can speak their words of comfort or doom.

His grin, if he could see it, has spread across his face, beyond all proportion, until his mouth seems to split at the corners, stretching his lips to the proportions of a demented clown. His eyes have grown a haunted look, deep set and wildly glittering, and his face seems, in this half-light, to protrude like the muzzle of some implacable, perpetually hungry, desert dog.

And his father knows nothing of this transformation. Johnson, running beside him, has left even the thought of sex behind him in the mire. All his ruminations turn on profit, all his pleasure on desire. He is thinking only of the land, of the pleasures of control, and the bliss he will find when all the trees and ruins in the town are gone, when even the grave-sites are ploughed under, never more to rise, and the whole clearing rustles with his sweet-centered cane.

They are almost to their house, that shining beacon on what passes here for a hill. Already they have reached the cleared land, walking among the stubbled leavings of last year's cane. Randy's soles are not tough enough for this rough walking (his father's are), the spikes are bruising his feet, but he has ceased to care.

His father's hand across his shoulder stops him before they reach the bottom step of the decomposing manse, the older man's voice is soft and full of care. 'Son, we are going to have to be careful here.' Johnson's wide-splayed fingers touch his cheek and feel the long stubble there. The gesture is soft, caressing. 'Your momma will stick by us, surely, but you are going to want to be careful of what you say. She's a good woman, but a woman all the same, and not capable of understanding some things.'

'I know, Daddy.' He is a large man, and strong, but when his father touches him like this he could be five years old again.

'Good. Just sit back, boy, and let me do the talking.' He smiles again, softly. 'You'll get your filly yet, and more besides. A legacy of soil, of sugar and rum. And don't forget the ever-lovely cash.' The arm moves back down from face to shoulder, becoming a conspirator's embrace. 'Acres of treasure out there for us. Just you wait.'

Randy smiles back at him, thinking different thoughts.

Luckily, half the coming battle for them is in construction of a plan.

His father, wanting land, wanting the respect that comes with power more than anything, is already turning over possibilities in his mind, counting up the figures that stand in mentally for his men. His wife hardly enters his machinations at all. She never did amount to much and is worth nothing more than decoration, like all the very best women.

They are nearly at the porch steps now, and the house is dark. As well it should be at after three in the morning. They shall rouse no one, and have hours yet to sit in comfort, to drink and plot.

None of this will be a problem.

The front door is, as always, unlocked. Stupid, Johnson thinks, turning the knob, anyone at all could just walk right in. Tomorrow, one of them, either Randolph or himself, will rally up their slave workers in their swamp shacks, to stir the blood-lust to a frothing passion through whip or words, and probably both. The other will assess and trap the lovers wherever they may lie, to stalk and watch them until the beaten men can come and bring the falling sky down around their heads. They sit and talk for hours, hammering out the basic shape then polishing until their plot gleams and not a crack can show in their designed construction, no finger-hold of hope for lovers to cling to. By the time Mrs. Johnson rouses from her sleep her men are finished planning. They sit there, red-eyed and waiting for their breakfast, a few hours' rest, and then the coming violent tumult of this one decisive night.

NEGOTIATIONS

Matthew borrows a clean work shirt from one of his men and Joy cinches it around her waist with his oiled leather belt, above the ragged remains of her scab-colored skirt. She combs her hair out with her fingers and loops it in a loose chignon, finally covering the entire length of her with that rusty, once-black cloak.

This meeting has been coming for years. She has acclimated to the humiliations the Johnsons inflicted on her, but yesterday's assault went beyond her limits. She has not seen ice for years, well over a decade, but she recognizes its formation now, crystalline around her heart. It might be shock, it might be rage fermenting this sudden coolness, but she is determined to face that family down without wavering. She will not give them the satisfaction of her tears. Joy is as ready as she has ever been to face the devil in its home.

'You know these people,' Matthew extracts his tall boot from the mud that has engulfed it, the sound is sick, like organ tissue ripping, 'how are they going to react to us? What is the likelihood they'll send off their rapist son and let us live?'

'Not good.' Joy glides over the mire like a beetle, never seeming to break the surface tension. 'These are people who made me trade my grandmother's solid-silver tableware for three bushels of potatoes. Had I refused, they would have let us starve.'

'Then why all the gifts yesterday? The fabric and food you told me about?'

It takes a moment for Joy to respond. She has just remembered that it has been over twenty-four hours since she has spoken to her mother, and that in that time Rose has eaten nothing. Another guilt to add to her lengthening skein of them.

'Hm? Oh, that was mainly because they heard that you were coming.' She catches his look of confusion. 'Not you specifically, but they knew that someone was going to claim the land, and they had been planning for years to develop it themselves. Originally they were going to wait until we had died. Yesterday marrying me seemed the easier. Who knows what they are planning now?'

'But do you *own* the land you live on?'

'No, but we have been here for so long. We are white, and we are women. If the town found out that a stranger had displaced us, well let's just say that even people in the city who had been willing to let us starve would have something to say.' She takes his hand to soften her words or to comfort him. 'So they would now be forced to move me in an acceptable way and can then lay claim to the land where I stand.'

'And my legal writ from a government thousands of miles away would not be worth the parchment it's written on.' He squeezes back, offers her help she does not need crossing over a half-sunken log.

'That's the long and the short of it, yes.'

'So now we go to them and try to make them see our reasoning. You shall not wed their monster, I shall stay and, with your permission, farm around your house. We will stay for three more growing seasons, until our financial state permits us to wed, and then we will pull up stakes and leave, to start our lives afresh in some other city far away. Tampa is lovely, but I think it is too close to this cess for our purposes.'

'Yes.' She looks at him with the wry expression of a face unused to hope. 'I have always wanted to see New York. Or London.'

'Then that is where we shall go to start again.' He can see the house, rising like some thin facade of solidity, a cardboard cut-out of a mansion used as stage dressing in some cheap play. 'Is that our Castle Dracula? Do we reach the fabled keep?'

She has not seen a new book since 1899 or so, she does not understand the reference. New publications can take a few more years to reach this far down, even if she had not been in isolation these last ten years, but she understands the bare intent, to lower fear into humor and thereby drag the darkness into light. Appropriate enough, since the sunlight rises now behind the building, almost shining through it, lending to its aura of false reality.

'That is where they live.'

'Well,' he grins at her, but it is an expression of love and humor on this face, 'let us go and wake them up.'

He signals his men, the three they brought for safety's sake, to follow close behind. They will wait out on the porch and, should either of them cry a word out loud, they will come running. Hopefully on time.

To their mutual surprise, Mrs. Johnson opens the door herself almost before the pull-bell has finished sounding. She is fully, formally dressed in a wrap of pure green poison, her bilious hair piled on her head and held with a sterling silver clasp.

'Why Miss Walsh, and with a gentleman!' Her lips are edged with arsenic, her teeth glittering beneath the rift in her lips. 'How lovely to see you both. Do come in.'

Joy can feel the muscles around her spine stiffening at the sight of that smile. By force of will she unclenches her fist, and meets her hostess with a look of level calm, dark and cool, determined to drown Mrs. Johnson's smarmy ague in her feigned tranquility.

Mrs. Johnson leads them to the sitting room where Hepplewhite rubs elbows with Sears and Roebuck, and serves them a very early high tea from a set that Joy remembers from her early childhood. Her grandmother loved to use this set on visits, holding the pot so delicately in her freckled hands, her grandfather in the soft chair by the fireside, telling bawdy stories her mother blushed at. She affects a studied lack of recognition, dulling perhaps the satisfaction of her host whose expression of malicious exaltation drops back a notch at Joy's lack of reaction. What is the use of wounding if the victim does not hurt?

Mr. Johnson enters while they are sitting, chatting, he pretends not to recognize Matthew from their struggles in the night. There is a door slam somewhere, far back in the maze. The back exit, most likely.

'I'm sorry Randy could not join us,' his teeth gleam in his rough beard, not one missing, nor one black, 'I know how much you enjoy his company. But I had an errand for him that he just had to attend to.'

'Oh, I am not offended.' She takes a sip from her grandmother's flowered Dalton cup, where the lady's lips once rested. She takes strength from that. 'We have never been what anyone would consider close. And are… less so after you and he ran your errand last night.'

'Oh good, I'm glad to know you have not been pining for the loss of him, or for our company. And not for very long, at any rate,' the man expends a glare at Matthew, his first flicker of recognition, 'though it does seem odd for you to so quickly lose your affections, to move on so abruptly, after all that we have done for you.'

Joy is breathing fast now, so quickly that Matthew can hear it over the rush of his own palpating heart. He speaks up, quickly, before the girl can lose herself, and the game with it. His voice bares the thin veneer of cold civility. He can play the ignorance game as well. 'She is grateful, sir. Not everyone would help a lady in distress, much less two of them, and for so little recompense. But you see that is only part of the problem.'

'And the rest of it?' Johnson's voice is low, dangerous.

'Well that, sir, comes down to the government.' He brings out his grant, signed and sealed by the governor of Florida, official, undeniably right. The shadow of his man Rodriguez passes at the window, sunlight glinting off of the long barrel of his rifle. Matthew pretends not to notice, but sees Mrs. Johnson's pig eyes flash knife-like to the pane and back.

He says, 'You see, sir, from these plats that I now own the entirety of the defunct township, including three hundred acres of lands that surround it, land that you are currently farming, by the way. See, here,' he gestures to a brown patch on the map, 'this is where you've got cane going. On my land. I walked through it myself this morning, on my way here.'

'The government can't give what it doesn't own.'

'No, but it owns everything whose title isn't held by someone else. And I am willing to bet good money that you cannot produce the plats for it.'

Johnson says nothing to this, glowering.

'Now, here is what I propose.' Matthew gestures at the plat. 'I can see no need for bringing the law into it and you are only infringing by about thirty acres and treating it well. I say that you should be allowed to continue farming it, the land you have already, shall we say, borrowed. On the condition that you do not infringe further on my land, including the township. Joy will work for me as secretary, for a salary and monthly delivery of food for herself and her mother, so there shall be no further need of assistance from you, and we will not be offended if you never visit.'

Mrs. Johnson's fingers are whitening against the handle of her teacup; there is a thin snap as the porcelain arc lets go that neither Matthew nor Joy affect to notice. He says, 'We shall stay for three seasons, clearing out the township, re-laying the graves and seeding the cane. After that time we will have, God willing, turned a profit sufficient for the foundation of a new life elsewhere, and for a nominal fee I will turn the grant, and the cleared lands, over to you for your disposal.'

Husband and wife look at each other, torn between lust for money and malevolence, vengeance now or profit later. The moment passes in a flicker across his forehead when Johnson realizes that it is not too late for him to have both. This blooming realization and the relief that said vengeance has begun already with the departure of his son out the back door as these two arrived, is visible on his face. Better now to smile and go along with what the fools are saying. It will make the bloodshed all the sweeter when the moment comes. Let them have their dream of three years' farming, their idiot hope for life. The dawn is coming, the dream to shatter. He shall have the land, and possibly before the day is out.

He says none of this, out loud; his expression states it for him. He extends his hands to shake. 'A good offer, gladly accepted.' His grin is manic as he looks between the lovers, meeting neither face. 'I wish you, the both of you, the very best of luck and a long, profitable, life together.' He squeezes the Englishman's hand before releasing it, dropping the appendage as though it were some poisonous reptile he cannot be rid of fast enough.

Matthew and Joy exchange a look, rise at once together. 'Thank you for your kindness and understanding.' Matthew bows to the Johnsons, the missus and the man. 'It was a pleasure doing business with you.'

'No,' the senior says, escorting them to the door, 'believe me, the pleasure is all mine.'

The pair are silent as they make their way over the mire and stubbled fields, followed by their wary men. It is Joy who breaks the silence first, when the house is but a faint unreal gleaming in the morning swirl of mist.

'If that is the last we hear of them I shall be obliged to borrow your hat, that I might eat it.'

'Yes.' He takes her hand, amazed again by the fineness of her bones. 'When do you think they'll make their move, and what sort of treachery shall it be once they have laid it?'

'I think it will happen today. Whatever it is, the Johnsons are not known for their patience, at least they have never been patient to me.' She stops a moment in the mire, bends down. She has discovered a half-drowned wharf rat gasping on its side. Three days ago she would have eaten it, now she pauses to massage it back to life, allowing it to run off to live out its small span. She wipes her hands on her borrowed frock. 'As for what they are planning, I do not know. Only that, if their previous gestures are anything to judge by, it will be swift, and hard. We had best be prepared.'

Matthew holds her thin form to him, feeling the heart beating beneath the pale cage of rib, a bird bound for now but fit for bursting, ready at any moment to fly. 'Well, then what we must do is clear. Let us go back and rouse the men. If we see a victory on this field,' he smiles a little at his military speech, 'the land will be ours to clear upon. We can still begin our lives.'

'Yes.' Her eyes are dark and bright, glittering with what might easily be either sorrow or hope, some strange tincture of both mingled therein. 'If we survive tonight.'

They pause a moment before entering town, gazing upon the various, new-seeming lands that sprawl out, tree-ridden, all before them, like the folds of a bright girdle, furled. A land of dreams, for them to live among and use.

SOLDIERS

Randolph left through the back door with the voices of those idiots echoing down the hall. That stupid cunt, that English asshole. Well, tonight he shall fix them both. The morning fog is evaporating rapidly, dazzling, going up in air like diamonds. Even diamonds, formed from coal, will incinerate if the temperature is made hot enough. The water stands in pools among the mangrove roots, up to five inches deep in places, and the fiddler crabs are crawling up to eat the rot that festers on the branches and the boughs.

He is running through the forest, moving at top speed. He leaps over fallen logs at a lupine lope. He is coming, ever closer, to the slaves' shacks gathered in the overwhelming woods. This is a lovely land, but there is darkness in it. Whether it was inborn or planted there by man, cannot be said. The clear light on river water, the deep azure sky, the way the few remaining herons look, stabbing their beaks into the brackish pools, withdrawing an impaled snake or eel that glimmers briefly, red and black, before falling into that last enduring shadowland. There are orange blossoms in the dry places, ferns with gently curling fronds, anoles engaged in mating dances, the males unfurling the strawberry flags against their throats to draw the feminine eye.

The houses stand white as bone against the black-barked mangroves, thatched in green and brown saw-palmetto, drawn together in a tight weave. The stills stand behind in the shadow of the hogshead, where the men, the Negros and the outlaws, gather to drink what draughts they can before the men who for all intents and purposes own them can come and stripe their backs with whips and set them bending to the soil again.

Some thirty men are gathered round their morning fires, setting mash to boil in enormous blackened cauldrons, crusted with the carbonized leavings of a year's worth of burnt sugar. They stand, dark bodies in bright light, diamonds of sweat standing out against their skins, sifting the cane-strands from the fructose syrup with large paddles drilled with holes.

There are no children here, nor women. Some of these men have gone five years without seeing even a cathouse girl. The youngest man is Jarnell Williams, eighteen, and when he came here he was fifteen and beautiful, with his soft, full lips and eyes dark in innocence. He had run from his hometown in the south of Georgia, made outcast by his taste for shoes that his sporadic income could not justify. He left pursued by the spectre of nooses and the baying of dogs. Now he is attractive still, but there is a hard edge to his beauty, a blade hidden in his smile, and many nights that blade is honed by the blood he loses and the grunts expelled by larger men in his cabin and the dark.

Jarnell is not the only runner here, though he is the most innocent, all the men have meant this as an escape from something, from murder, from rape. One man had a penchant for luring off small dogs owned by rich women and feeding them, for his own entertainment, bits of arsenic-laden beef. He would watch them shudder out their deaths in far back alleys, sometimes gathering a crowd around him, taking bets. He was caught by a cop in down-town Houston, surrounded by a crowd who bet on the dog's last shudder as it danced out its last in his lap. The rules they followed, the hints, the fears, have led them here, to this place, in bondage in the woods.

This is their purgatory, where they burn alive painlessly, still hoping for some lost hint of redemption, one that can usually only be glimpsed over the rim of a jug.

They spend their days in toil, ten hours at least in sweat and labor, dredging brackish land to till it for the plow, bending to sow seed or sprout, stopping occasionally at the sharp scent of cucumber to part the ravening cottonmouth from its poison-dripping head with their bluish fire-treated hoes. A battle that is not always successful, the cottonmouth viper strikes fast. Three fugitives died last year alone, legs swollen in spite of muddy poultices and the sucking lips of their companions who tried to draw the toxin out. They died in fever and gasping, with a stench reminiscent of terror and rot.

Harvest time is worse, for they must hurry, bring their scythes to order, levelling cane at the root to salvage all the sugar in the stalk before the rot sets in. There is no time for anything but work when this time comes, from before dawn to when the last long fingers of the sun have drawn out from the dense earth. The men have no time for food or rest then, no time for corn cakes or hog-fat mash. They break off stems for themselves, mid-stride, splitting the cane down the center and setting the soft pulp down over their black stump teeth to suck the sweetness there. They work with furious energy that comes from the sweet, like children in a whirlwind after Halloween, blades flying in circular arcs, culling tall plants, never stopping when the branches fall, nor when the sharp edges slip and slice a layer of skin from leg or arm, wounds that bleed slowly and are green by nightfall, and must be rubbed with salt in the dark of their cabins lest the limb be gangrenous and loose by morning.

And all the time Randy or his father are there behind them, standing in their fine boots, their white shirts gleaming and unmarked by sweat. They stand there behind their workers, surveying all they lord over, with their whips.

Randy is unarmed now, but he is not afraid of this. He does not fear these men, so long beaten, he cannot comprehend that they could ever be made of different stuff than a dog which once beaten falls ever after to the shape of your hand. He knows that even these creatures may be adverse to striking out at an unarmed girl, her insane mother and a few scattered workers, even if most of them would not balk at the thought of doing in a few lone men, especially with no fear of consequences so far out in the swamp.

Besides, he has the key to win them yet, one high card to turn over to bargain with, and he plans on dealing it now. His father has authorized him to make a promise, one they never plan on keeping, but will win them all the same. He will offer them safe passage from here and enough money to make a fresh start elsewhere, in exchange for one last small service. More fool they, if they take it. Randy has decided, on his own, to offer something else for those men whose greed is even greater. The chance to stay on here as small-hold farmers, working land they may consider themselves the owners of at a salary, in exchange for a small tithe of their labors.

He knows that soil has always been enough to murder over, some of these have killed for less, but hope can cause great things to grow in the poorest imaginations, and the fact that these are forged from air changes nothing. These men will believe, despite all they know of their masters, despite all evidence, because hope, once it has taken hold, can overpower all of reason's intimations. He grins at this, and at the pride his father would take in his complexity of thought.

Randy steps into the light.

The men look up from their pots, their faces carefully blank and clear of emotion. It is not the time for working yet, and Randy, who usually comes out to relieve Mr. Johnson in the later afternoon, after his hangover has subsided, is not who they would have expected now in this dawning, early light.

Randy grins at them, at the confusion he can sense beneath

their cautious expressions, like a man in some back alley about to offer a wayward child some awful treat. He is.

'Morning fellas,' his grin is loose, easy, he wants to keep them thrown by friendliness, 'Dad and I have a proposition for you. Come here, gather round, I'll tell you what it is.'

Suddenly he is surrounded by dark bodies. He is aware for one half instant of the vile possibilities here, of the odds of strength and power, but he shrugs his fears off like an ill-fitting robe. These are his men, and his father's. Property, even though that status is no longer recognized by the state. They will not dare to strike him now, especially with this offer on his lips.

As he speaks the men's blank faces unlock and flower. Hope has taken root at last, as planned; for the first time in years real smiles blossom there in place of grimaces and when he has finally finished speaking, the men cry out at this hint of freedom with a voice of thunder rolling over a vast expanse of sea, a sound to bring the roof beams of their white shacks down and send the nesting pelicans hurling out above glowering expanse of swamp.

He stirs and the other bodies all stir with him, staring at him with eyes awaiting orders. He stands, and they rise with him, willing and ready to follow where he leads them. He has won his army.

Now they must find weapons. For this next part, they must be armed. They will not be given guns, those will be reserved for Randolph and his father, but there are scythes gathered in the barn, sap-drenched and as yet unsharpened from the harvest. They have the day, the hours spread out all before them, to get them sharp and ready for the fray.

The slaves' cry of jubilation echoes in his veins, a separate pulse. And he knows, with a vague impression of pleasure, that he could not quit this chase now, even if he wished to. The barn is dark, hay choked and scented with the exhalation of cows. His whip is gathered, a great coil of braided leather, black and red, hanging on its hook by the wall. His father's larger one is hung behind it. Randy shoulders both as the men fall fast to sharpening, sending up bright sparks that dance in the air and sometimes land in fibrous hay to blaze a while before expiring. The process takes all day, though he allows the men to stop occasionally to drink and rest, and to take a light supper before sunset, but nothing too heavy, knowing as he does that a hungry army fights the best.

His father waits for him by now in the dooryard of their house, burying his bagful of plunder under the porch of their house, hopefully unseen by his meddlesome mother. He will rally them once more to bloodlust with false promise spewing from his mouth. It is Randy's job to lead them there. He has his dark pack gathered around him, the very human hand at the taut reigns. Together, through the dying light, they set off silently, at a lope.

GHOST

When Joy, Matthew and their scouts reach the makeshift camp inside the store they are greeted by five fewer men than there were when they left. The survivors tell them that the men left out of fear for the ghost.

'What ghost?' Matthew asks, thinking of the corpse in the tree. 'The one we buried?'

'No. There is another.' The speaker is a Seminole dressed for traveling in blue chambray work shirt and clean jeans, new from the milliners, still creased. He is holding his rough leather hat in his hands, as though in apology.

'Wait, what other?' They stare at Joy in suspicion, the woman left over from the wreck of the world. Her hair dark and cambric, frizzed out in the humidity until it forms a blackened aura around her head, gleaming in places with captured light.

'A woman.' The speaker, a man named Osceola, cannot quite meet her eye. He indicates a more shabbily-dressed man who stands prodding the ashed remains of the last night's fire. 'Holata was the one who saw her, but he is brave, and so remains.'

'Holata? Please.' Matthew reaches his hand out towards the man who stands, distracted by the fire, feeding it sticks and small dried bits of bracken, as though seeking some secret message hidden among the embers. 'Tell us about this ghost.'

His hair is long and black, his features pockmarked, making his hide resemble that of an aged alligator, reflecting the wisdom of his name. When he speaks he keeps his eyes locked onto the growing flame.

'It was a woman, white, like this one, wandering around through the trees as though in a vision of a world we could not see.' He stirs and stirs the spreading fire, building it up twig by twig. 'Her dress was sky-colored, ragged, as though from a grave. Her eyes were the same color and wide, wide open as though blasted by horrors we could not comprehend, much less look upon. She was wandering around there, dazed and babbling, her hair wild, the color of wheat.

'At first we thought she was a real woman, but when Miguel and the white man, Larry, went to fetch her, she shrieked, laughed, and called out to them as though they were some other men. Her voice sounded like coo-on-o-she, loud feline.

'When they had let go of her, she ran away, laughing and screaming, until she reached the cemetery. She was moving faster than we could follow and once we got there, she had vanished as though into the ground.'

He paused for a moment in his telling, as though reluctant to disclose so much to a strange woman and his employer. When he did continue his voice was quiet, diffident.

'We looked all around for her, in the houses nearby, including yours,' a nod to Joy, his eyes still on the flame, 'when we had checked in the fallen church and found nothing, no trace, we decided that she must have been Deghsee, the howling daemon. So the men who wished to, left.' He looks up at last, to see Joy's cheeks coloring. 'Why does she redden?' Addressing Matthew. 'What creature have you brought us here?'

Before he can answer, Joy states for him, 'That was not a daemon, or a ghost. It was my mother.'

The men recoil from her as though from one diseased.

'No, no, she isn't dead, or anything like it. She is sick in the head, wandering. She is probably starving by now.' She turns to Matthew, forehead crumpled, pleading. 'We have to find her.'

'Does she speak the truth?' Osceola, hat still in hand, seems less unsure of her humanity than the others, and Matthew suspects that if he can convince this man, at least, to stay the others will as well. He imagines, further, that this man is the only reason he has any workers left.

On some level he has, at last, ceased hoping to make a fortune here in farming. He is beginning to be satisfied with the prospect of escaping with his life. Still, he must try. He chides himself, keep that top lip stiff and avoid the word 'die'. He answers in a voice surprisingly calm for all its worry. 'What she says is true. The blue lady is no ghost, but this girl's mother. She is ill, so we must find her.' He turns back to his lover. 'Joy, please think, where would she go? Where could she be?'

Joy thinks back to the early days, when her mother was more prone to wandering, before the town rotted, when her mesh web of denial was not yet strong enough to incorporate a ruined town into her fantasies. 'She used to visit the place where we buried my father. Not that she was mourning, mind you (she still has not accepted that he is dead) but because it was his favourite place to go when he was working on his sermons.'

'Where was this place? I mean where is it?'

Joy is focusing all of her energy on holding back the tears that she has denied for almost a decade. The effort makes her face quite hard, as do the fists clenched against her thighs. 'We buried him underneath the boab tree, the huge one at the edge of the cemetery.' Her voice husks, the first long-denied droplets fall. 'He used to sit and read beneath it, or sometimes inside it. The trunk is quite hollow.'

The two Seminole exchange a look. Holata speaks. 'Where we buried the hanged corpse.'

Joy remembers what Matthew told her about that, remembers the position of the body, the bright colors of the ties. Her stomach heaves at the thought, unbidden, that rises through her mind like bubbles of gas from a waterlogged, part-digested, carcass.

Hurriedly, she leads all six of them to the tree, stepping gingerly over the newly-buried mound where her father waits for water pressure or Christ to rise him up again and, bending down, comes face to face with her mother's breath-rising lapis-covered back.

She is sleeping, gently, like a child. The men are, at first, hesitant to lay their fingers on her, terrified of daemonic wrath or holy burning, but when Osceola eventually picks her up she is as light as eiderdown, as though dehydrated, and she sleeps soundly, gently murmuring, all the way back to the store like a child.

RECONNAISSANCE

They rouse Rose from her slumber by laying her down on the floor and sprinkling cool water on her face, a baptism of a kind, bringing the potential of truth along with wakefulness. She wakes up coughing, spattering droplets on the floor where they are instantly coated gray from the layer of powdered detritus. She looks fearful for a moment, her brain partly registering the information that she is in a strange, deteriorating place, surrounded by unknown men and a ragged woman who resembles her young daughter, grown horribly older, skipping in an instant the sweetest part of her life.

And then the fantasy comes again and covers round her, and suddenly she is safe and warm, in the milliners in Tampa. David must have taken her on a trip, yes, she remembers now. And she is in here, in this modern, well-lit shop with money enough to purchase a new matching frock and hat. The men are part of a traveling Indian show, actors she befriended as part of her ministerial contribution. And that unsettling dark-haired girl? Why, that's her loyal Malda! Funny, for a moment her features looked almost Caucasian. The mind can manage some strange tricks.

The men are looking on this crazed figure with confusion. Matthew watches the almost visible revision of history with fascination. The wide eyes shift from narrow-pupiled terror to a blank, doll-like complacency in an instant, the thin white lips unfurling into a vivid smile of beatification.

Joy can see the story forming and knows what needs to be done to draw out the truth, or at least a version of it. She gestures the men to silence with a motion of her hands, pressing fingers against lips formed into a weary smile. She adopts a voice to speak in, made by long exasperated practice higher than her own. 'Oh there you are, Miz Rose! I been lookin high and low for you.'

Rose smiles in delight, finally something in the world is going the way it ought to. Malda has been so sullen lately. The Mexican, Miguel, hands her a strip of jerky on a hard yeast roll and she gnaws it ravenously, unaware all the while that the food is present and vanishing in her hands.

Joy twists her face and keeps on going, hating herself for giving in to this charade, but recognizing the potential importance of it. Besides, Malda has been gone for nine years, and even if she was still alive, she was not the type to mind lending anything, not even an identity. 'Where you been, girl? Had me tracking you all through town.'

Rose looks confused at this. 'I was in town, our town. But maybe that was yesterday.' Her forehead clouds, she rubs her fingertips against her temple. 'How did I get to Tampa?'

'Da- Mistuh David brought us up here right early this morning. You slept the whole way. I meant yesterday. I spend all day looking for you then. What were you doing?'

The blue eyes clear, the smile returns. 'Oh that's right. It was the rocking of the carriage that did it, sent me off to sleep.' She reaches over and pats the girl she calls her maid on the arm. 'I am so scatterbrained lately, Malda. Forgive me?'

'Of coas, Missus. But I still be waitin for that story.'

The men crowd nearer, unseen by dream-blinded eyes. Rose begins to speak, but is prevented by a hacking cough. She has another nosebleed, a bad one this time, letting loose a stream of blood that dribbles past her mouth and drips freely from her chin. Joy, unthinking, used to this, tears off a clean square of fabric from the hem of her borrowed shirt and uses it to staunch the flow.

The men, seeing blood, take a few steps back. 'Oh Malda, yesterday was very busy.' Her pupils have contracted into specks, even in this dark room leaving only two twin pools of lapis-colored iris that do not track as she talks. 'First, I met David under his tree for lunch, and he told me to do something, but oh, I can't remember what. And we walked over to the general store to buy some ribbon from Mr. Scalighari. I left him sitting under the tree out the front. My husband, not the Italian.

'And then I went home to have some lunch, but the grocer must not have delivered yet because I couldn't find anything in the cupboards, and you hadn't made anything.' She gives her daughter a reproachful look meant for the housekeeper.

'I sorry, Missus, but that Cook's job, and besides that was Friday,' Joy has made the connection between her mother and the corpse in the tree. It is a terrible conclusion to make, 'which, as you know, is my day off.'

'Oh that's right, Malda,' three gentle pats on Joy's naked arm, 'I had forgotten. So, I suppose yesterday, before coming here, I went and did my rounds, visiting. I went to, oh let me see,' she starts ticking off defunct names on filth-coated fingers, 'the Jorgens, Rodriquez, the Terance family, you should just see the lovely garden Mable has got going. All that frangipani, hibiscus, and even a few roses! How *does* she grow them here? Ah, and I saw that Mr. Johnson go up to the house.'

Joy's eyes widen. She looks over at Matthew, but asks Rose, 'When was this, exactly?'

'Oh in the mid-morning. I was waiting for David in the cemetery, to luncheon together as we usually do. I called out to him, but he must not have heard me. Cook must have let him in though, for some reason, because he walked right into the kitchen and stayed for a while. She must have lent him something, some of David's books or a cache of cleaning rags cause when he left he was holding an enormous bag.' Her forehead furrows again in thought. 'Or it could have been potatoes, I suppose. It sure looked heavy enough.'

'Well,' Joy says in her own voice, breaking character, 'I think we can say goodbye to whatever heirlooms we had left. Not that it matters.' The break goes unnoticed by Rose, but Matthew holds his head.

'But what possible use is it, stealing that now?' he asks the room in general, not expecting an answer. In this he is mistaken.

Osceola has been thinking about the story his employer told them all this morning, when he brought the girl half naked from the house. He asks a question that is in itself an answer, or rather part of one, 'Why do you ask reasonable questions of an unreasonable force? It may be something simple, after all, he wouldn't want goods that he thinks of already as his to wind up covered in blood.'

Joy says, sotto voce and clutching her collar close around her bosom, 'Yes. It could be so.'

'And men?' Osceola asks. 'How many men to stand beside him?'

'He has about thirty working men.' Her forehead creases in deep concern. 'He treats them about like slaves.'

'Well,' the Seminole says, 'I guess we should be expecting them.'

There is much to prepare for, much to plan, and now that they know, or are at least firm in their suspicions, the dwindled group can make their plans. They have four guns and seven useable fighting knives between them, including Joy's kitchen cleaver. They have a store that is slowly rotting into soil. They know their strengths and most of their limitations. The only questions that remain unanswered are how many of them are coming, and have they any time?

It is while they are contemplating this that Rose speaks up for the last time in that long day. 'I am tired, Malda. Do you mind if I go back and lie down in the hotel?'

'Of course, missus.' She takes her mother's pale hand and places it in the grasp of her lover. 'This is Mr. Ranier, the hostel proprietor. He has arranged a room for you in the Tampa Bay hotel, on the house.'

Rose smiles the few inches up at him, her eyes innocent as an infant's would be. Matthew leads her over to his bedroll and lays her down underneath his brand-new blanket. In a few moments she is asleep again. The rest of them, the girl and the men, gather closer together around the campfire's wavering flame, to plan.

SIEGE

Things are moving quickly now, in the forest and in town, as though there were a celestial timer winding down to detonation, until that last red fuse of sunset sizzles out into some dark oblivion.

In the town, five men work beside their employer, searching frantically for any wood that has not rotted, any plank or furniture that can form a barricade. There would be none here to shift the loads, save that Matthew has promised them that if they stay, if they win out, he will divide the land between them at the end of three growing seasons, rather than selling it. This offer, of course, rests beside their latest pay inflation. It will be a loss, but after all of this struggle one must salvage what one can.

Two men board the windows, a third struggles with the door. The others, including Matthew, are moving quickly between the storefront and the manse, bringing the supplies the Johnsons left in better times. They will leave a lantern in the window there, a small light burning in the kitchen, in the hope that any comers in the night will target there, assuming the women have been left alone.

In reality, of course, they will all of them be locked together in the front room of the store, crouched together in the darkness as far back as they can go while still avoiding the flooded stockroom whose floor is buried beneath a foot of water that teems with cucumber-scented moccasins and the occasional slime-furred rat that burrows through into the dry filthiness up front. While they have boarded and blockaded, they have spared no time to clean, and so the dust lays thick and for the most part unmolested upon the spongy wooden floor.

Rose lies curled and fetal in the corner, her blond hair dyed prematurely gray from the scattered ashes that surround her head, and those same ashes mar her dress, blurring the glacial lapis beneath a scrim of filthy snow. The woman is frigidity and flame; stasis and warped, near-constant change. None of the men quite know what to make of her. Neither, frankly, does her daughter, but a lack of understanding was never something to mar a child's love. What infant squalling understands the hands that comfort it?

Right now she is comfortable, at least dry, though she is filthier than usual. Her stomach is full of pemmican and rolls, and on her full and curving lips hovers a small, contented sigh. She could be a child or a crone, buried there in isolation, ageless in extremity, never to be mistaken for a beauty in full bloom.

Joy is sitting beside the fire in the improvised grate, reading a well-thumbed edition of the *Iliad* that Matthew was kind enough to bring her, turning pages slowly, once every minute or two, and thinking, there were times when gods directed battles, when any human life, no matter how unimportant, could suddenly be picked out and faced with the numinous. Their human substance changed forever, for better or for worse, till death did them part. I wonder if that still happens; if it has happened with us. She brings her pale hand up to touch the cruciform burn singed in shades of rose and white upon her décolleté.

Shall we see Venus, tonight, burning in the evening light? Shall Dionysus, the Great God Pan, or one of the Others, burst out from his forest dwelling place, to lead us or attack us, or order us, unprepared, to go and make a place for him in the vineyards of Jerusalem or the mountaintops in Rome?

She would have liked to be helping with the repairs or preparations but, being female, she had to fight to be allowed to carry her own knife. I have been out here, living for ten years without any benevolent male interaction, yet suddenly these men arrive and I am treated with the delicacy due a delftware figurine. Had I treated myself so carefully, I would have died here long ago. If this is what the world outside is like – she turns a page on Helen, locking her deep inside the paper cage of Troy – I don't know why I would bother with it if survival did not demand the shift.

And then she thinks, correcting herself, survival and love.

The afternoon is fading outside, the day burning out like a wick in a lamp, already the first thumbprints of night visible high above the sunset, the first vague stars appearing but not burning in their houses in the firmament. Night comes quickly here in this southern clime, there is no room for the false romance of twilight, no room for such easy atmospheric lies.

The truth is on the line between the light and darkness, easy to distinguish, divisible, drawn out in a razorblade thin line of blood.

Matthew tears his gaze away from the sunset's blaze. He will see others, if he lives, and turns his focus on the forest. All afternoon he has been expecting them, half-heartedly, more out of the conviction that whatever will happen, the moon will be a witness to it. And so, as evening comes gloaming, he has focused more strongly on the entrance to the forest, half his mind always measuring the presence, or the absence of the light.

He wishes, in his bones, that he knew how to pray. And somewhere, buried deep beneath his scepticism, beneath the thick and brittle shell of his anxiety, he realizes that he already does, and has been, since the moment he realized that he lacked the capacity for deep belief.

He tightens his fingers around the grip of his revolver, his index finger near, but not yet touching, the trigger, and feels a deep but subtle infusion of strength that does not spring from fire power. His right hand moves, unbidden, and thumbs out on forehead, lips, heart and breast the clumsy but recognisably effective sigul of the cross.

There is a voice, whispering, low and soft at his shoulder. It is the pockmarked man, Holata. 'See the stirring in the woods? Hear the coyotes calling out there?'

Matthew nods, the gun butt slick in his palm.

'I think something is out there, coming.' He puts his rough hand on his employer's elbow, directs him to look over in the edge of the mangrove swamp that creeps up to the backyard of the manse-house. 'I think it's about time for us to go inside there, boss-man.'

There is the sharp sound of a thick branch snapping, a canine's injured, protesting howl. Matthew responds, 'I think you might be right. Let's get locked in.'

In moments they are all inside, the doors locked tight and barricaded. Two watchmen man the spy holes at the corners of the windows, ready to prepare for any sort of attack. And they are left in silence, for a minute, with nothing but the sibilant hissing of rough wind for trees.

To wait for the stars to explode one by one into the visible realm from the places that they wait for night and the horrors, all of them, harsh and demonic, burst forth from their hiding places, gibbering forward painted bone-white and bloody by the flames they carry and their own dark skins, led by hard men, black-haired and shaggy, who howl like dogs.

FAMILY

Mrs. Johnson is getting worried. She knows the slaves' moonshine cabins are a mere few miles away, but her son and husband have been gone nearly twelve hours. Lydia is standing by the kitchen windows, looking out into the deepening murk, the thick white curtain stuff clenched in her hands. The fabric is patterned with enormous red blossoms in their stages of bloom and blown, and even in the extremity of her anxiety she cannot help but admire its essential quality. Besides, she has a perfect internal image of herself, standing here well-dressed and substantial, the very picture of maternal concern.

She is close to the table, its top scattered with three full ashtrays and a half-spent open pack beside them. There is an almost untouched jug of rum, and a full cup that has warmed to the temperature of her hand.

Her husband went out to the tumbling manse after the vermin left this morning, knowing that his rival and that dark-haired piece of trash would be at the store making whatever preparations they can. Not that it will do them any good. Lydia saw the train of workers leaving. She thinks that poor old Rose must have frightened them off. Still, even knowing that he is alone there, she is worried for him. But the treasure he will bring will be worth any and all danger. That little slut had to have been holding out on them; besides, Joy owes her for the teacup that she broke.

As for her son, he is out back, preparing the slaves. Or maybe they are on the move by now. In any case, it won't be long before the both of them are back and bringing glory, as all men who are real men are meant to do.

'Randy?' Lydia's voice is soft, and she cannot decide if she is addressing her husband or, theatrically, her missing son. Just whose is that nagging voice?

'Where are you, Randy?' Her mask is cracking at the corners, in spite of her perfect, preserved self-image of maternal love. Tears are sliding down her cheeks, dripping unheeded down her soft and padded chin. 'It's getting dark out.'

Mrs. Johnson is having a difficult time forcing air through her lungs. She stabs out yet another flaming butt, first lighting another Lucky from the embered tail. 'They should be home, should have *been* home. Long ago.'

She paces for a while behind the night-mirroring window, her mask crumbling for real and at last.

'He could be anywhere.' Her voice is flat, like the rasping voice of a mountain before the landslide brings it down to meet Muhammad at his doorstep. It is implacable when she uses it next. 'I've got to go get them.'

'But then,' her mouth is weak at the corners, 'I would not know where to look.' Her tongue is dead and tastes of ashes. There is no sweetness for her to drink. No sweetness for her anywhere, though her family's cane fields surround her.

She is staring out into the cleared land, at the sky that is streaked with a thin band on the horizon. Above it the heavens are green, azure, with deep black at the very dome, a few stars looking down like eyes.

The moon has not opened yet, but it would be staring soon.

Mrs. Johnson moves slowly, rises with an effort that would be required to shift a woman of even thrice her substantial bulk. She stands like an old woman on the very edge of dying. Which, she supposes, looking at the scattered butts like deadened soldiers, at the place where misplaced embers have scorched the dark mahogany, is exactly what she is.

There is nothing for her but to wait.

An old woman, old for this land. Eaten up by it, this substance that she pretended to possess. She is rendered impotent by the vast fertility of swamp.

It drinks her blood, her family's blood.

And now her boy, their flesh, is out there walking around, out there in some dark and strange communion with twisted soil.

Her own face is staring at her from the window, eyes blank and face drawn, a veritable mask of desolation that shocks her to the core.

Outside is the swamp.

She comes at last from the window and fetches up her husband's hat, old as their son, bought new the very day he was born. The shine is gone completely from the blackened leather, worn away by weather, but it fits him, so molded and battered to his body that he feels naked without it and it is hard for Lydia to picture him without it battening down his thinning hair. She wears it now herself, as though the familiarity of this battered object could call them to her somehow, summoning up her lost boys from their nesting places in the darkening mud. Once the brim has settled on her head she feels stronger, ready to face this long and desolate night.

The bell to summon the men for working in the morning is hung from a pull-chain from the rafters of the porch. It is cast of old pig-iron, cracked and pitted from the wet, but at least the tone is pure. No one comes now when she sounds it. From out in the fields there is nothing, not a whimper or a cry.

The air whips up and freshens behind her, wind playing gently at the short hairs that curl against her bearish neck. Somewhere, over her head, storm clouds are brewing. They do not yet draw their smudge across the sunset's fading band, but the clouds, the rain, and lightning promised by that gentle touch of wind, are not far off. The electricity building, even at this distance, raises goose-bumps at her hackles, sets them rising like the rough pelt of a disturbed and slavering dog.

Mrs. Johnson is alone here, some fairy tale creature, large and lost, stranded at the edge of the darkened forest that spreads out, nightmare land, where somewhere, far and hidden by the trees, an ignorant, plague-like and insectile army readies itself to clash by night.

After a few minutes, she gathers the loud stuff of her dress around her, a poor substitute for a romantic, Gothic cloak, turns back inside, and closes the door.

LOVE

The forest closes tight around them, trees reaching down with gnarled branches like ancient fingers, thick-veined and aching to grab. Glass snakes slither on their bellies through the fallen detritus of leaves, vestigial claws drawing their long bodies under the loam until they locate a pocket warm enough to keep their hearts throbbing out through the long hours of the dark.

This is the night, the hollow time, when the big cats cry out in their sorrow and longing, for food or sexual congress, all appetites sharpened beyond what mortal flesh can bear, when all is hunger and sharp teeth. There are coyotes out there somewhere, the wild yellow dogs, and they run together in packs fuelled by a vibrant raging love.

They travel beside this other pack, the one that moves on two legs through the gathering gloom, but they are not with them. These dogs have another errand here, another strong, implacable pull drawing them onward through the deepening sunset to meet the coming night. As a pack, they run with the smell of man, or something like it; some bipedal creature anyway, some creature's hour come round at last, slouching through the forest to be born into the world. The man in front is dark and wearing what must have been a fine farmer's outfit once, but has since become so filthy with the dust of cane and flaked leavings of rust that it is making its chemical retreat to earth.

This creature is following his own engorged erection, a case of priapus so severe that the bulge must throb. He is thinking thoughts of rape and murder, vaguely planning what will follow when he has the girl at last to himself. His eyes are blank, predatory, scabbed at the corners, staring ahead unseeing. His father follows close behind, the sire like the spawn in one way at least, he too is thinking of the spoil, though he would gather his reward in gold and loam-rich land. The girl's pale breasts and dark hair are just an added benefit.

Thorned branches whip Randy's arms and face as he runs, breaking a new path for his men to follow on. He is insensible to pain. His lust has grown insatiable; his mind far dimmed, operating solely from the brainstem, this onetime man is wholly lost. His hoard of men follow close behind him, thirsting for rewards all their own. Freedom is the thought common to all of them, murder trails close thereafter, and the tail end of lust. They run to drink the girl's annihilation.

They do not notice the dogs they run with, and the coyotes, in their turn, pay them no mind. They do not threaten or attack, they merely flock together, two vastly different motives pursuing the same goal.

The coyotes are led by one large dog, an enormous male with golden eyes and fur, sleek and muscular with teeth that gleam white against the moonlight. He is running, in love, with the movement and his goal, in love, in truth, with all the world. He can see, in his furred mind, the image of her he runs to, standing tall and slim, barefoot in the mire, her long black hair nebulous around her, a dark aura, and the moonlight collecting in the pool at her feet like blood in a silver ewer.

Because he runs, because he loves her, his pack loves also. They have traveled many miles, over years and generations, to be here now. Their ancestors felt her birth; her mother's labor-pains summoned them to this lonely incarnation as clear a sign as a new star appearing in a desolate sky. They ran from their long home in the desert, and though their leader met her only recently when she was in the woods alone, they all yearn for her completely.

The dogs can sense the confused minds of the herd that runs beside them, their vapid malevolence, their deep and carnal hunger that would rend flesh and tear it without the proper rites of howled thanks or supplication, taking meat and sex as though they were their right and not a privilege of grace.

The dogs are wailing loud and wild, calling their ancestors to join in this long-awaited joy, all of the pack leaders from all of their time come forward to share in the primitive mind of this one beast, and he welcomes them. He does not run for what he can (and undoubtedly will) receive from her, but merely because it is a pleasure and a joy, rich beyond all measure, the grace of her company.

His eyes are sharp and glittering, moist in an almost human ecstasy that belies his lone two years, the eight seasons that have passed on the run to bring him to this moment, the pull, as strong of gravity, drawing him home. And his home is her.

The wind over the swampland rises, and in the distance, moving closer, the rolling thunder booms.

WOLF AND COYOTE

Matthew and his men crouch together in the storefront darkness, looking out across the cemetery towards the trees that glower around them in their masses. The sunset is gone completely now, nothing remaining of its quick passage but a thin thumbnail, the last reflected glimmering of the sun. Rose sleeps on in her corner, whining and occasionally hacking in her sleep like a dog, her long hair knotted into rattails clumped thick and heavy with the dust.

Joy is sitting by the fire, reading over the same few lines of poetry: *Sing, goddess, of Achilles ruinous anger which brought ten thousand pains to the Achaeans, and cast the souls of many stalwart heroes to Hades, and their bodies to the dogs.* She has been reading this book all day long and now, at the birth of night, has reached the beginning at the end.

Joy may look composed, but looking closely, you can see her hands are shaking. Her fingers tremble against the moist and yellowed paper of her father's book, and her head burns with the bright voice of the muse.

Matthew is crouched down, gun-drawn, at the peep hole they left in the boarded window. He has used the muzzle to clear the last remaining jags of glass, leaving him with a clear shot across the street. His powder-loaded .45 Colt, bought from a laughing pawn man in his first few hours off the boat, has a bullet that will travel a thousand feet per second and the strength to launch a shell propelling forward into the stilt-posts of the manse if he chose and found that he aimed true.

He has never fired a gun in his life, nor held one before that moment a few weeks ago when he landed in New York.

His men, three of them, are similarly armed; the other two

have bolas, long knives, and they all carry machetes. They carry enough bullets between them to bring an army down, provided the powder has not moistened and the bullets fire. They were expecting to have to do some shooting when it came time to clear the land, expecting to fill their larders with gator meat and plenty of deer. Well, they'll be shooting vermin, true enough, though some of them could be loosely defined as men.

Matthew has pushed his new leather Stetson back, exposing his forehead, and is looking out into the gloam so focused he does not even feel himself chewing on his tongue, a habit he inherited from his father and is not proud of, knowing as he does that it makes him resemble a beef steer masticating cud. Not that he cares, right now.

There is thunder, in the distance but drawing closer, and the thick black clouds obscure malevolent stars.

Holata clicks the rifle's forestock back, takes careful aim. 'Look there, on the tree-line. Something coming.'

Suddenly windows are filled with the bodies of six pressing men, the cycloptic black sights looking out towards the woods.

The undergrowth rustles, parts, the first body presses out into the lesser darkness of the clearing: a yellow dog, huge and white-tooth grinning; it walks carefully out into the manse-yard twitching its black nose as though drawn on by some delicious scent.

'Hold your fire, men,' Matthew orders, his left hand held up in its white-kid sheath of glove, 'we're hunting men, not dogs, tonight.'

Joy looks up, briefly, from her reading, firelight reflecting yellow in her black eyes. Her nostrils twitch as though scenting something familiar. Almost before Matthew has noticed her expression her eyes have returned to the pages of her book.

Across the road, the cemetery, the yard, the coyote's body tenses, head thrown back; it squats to howl and sends its wailing, mournful ululations to the black annihilating sky, its moon swathed close in scrim-clouds like a gauze. And suddenly, breaking through the mangroves, palmetto, the twisted poison oak underbrush, his pack arrives in apocalyptic numbers.

Coyotes in their hundreds, splitting out across the fading border between the wild world and the realm of men, between reason and unreason, myth and true reality, their multitudinous bodies obscure the line as they come running, howling in fury and exultation, calling out for true love, some unbelievable desire that goes deeper than mere instinct or a hunger for blood.

Joy can hear them; her heart, and the wound on her thigh, responds to them, throbbing. Her veins are forcing blood that feels like the first pressure of a freed river in the spring-time, after freezing, a sensation utterly unknown to water here in this hot climate. She is helpless before it. Her fingers numb as she rises, casting her book, unknowing, and with it, all of her known civilization into the crucible of flame.

The men are frozen, looking out at that solid mass of dogflesh, moving as one being, covering the ground, the graves, the very porch, of their hiding place in their well-muscled bodies. They seem to be searching, grinning with their sharp teeth, walking and sniffing, occasionally throwing back their pointed heads to howl.

And then, just as suddenly as they arrived, they are gone, as though summoned by some unknown signal, their bodies fleeing, galvanized, with the unified and fluid motion of a plague, moving on.

They flee into the graves, the fallen church, the empty houses all around, leaving only their eyes visible as surrogate stars that wink out in sleep, one by one, until the street is left once more in silent dark.

Joy looks around, dazed, as though she has just awoken from a vast, disturbing dream. She sees the burnt spine of her book in the ashes of the fire, but says nothing, sitting back down. She suddenly realizes that she is ravenous, and she tears into the jerky from her lover's bag like a maenad who has been flesh-starved for a week. She is thirsty, too, but not for water, or for wine.

'What the hell was that?' Miguel asks in a voice shaken, almost broken with awe. 'What was that?'

'Wolf and Coyote were brothers,' says Osceola, looking out at the night, missing stars. 'Coyote wanted man to live forever, Wolf thought death was necessary for new life. They argued about it for years until, one day, Wolf ate a poisoned rabbit and, in agony, died. He begged Coyote, "Go to Our Father and ask him to give me the water of life, for it is cold and dark here, and I am thirsty." Coyote was crying, but he still said no. "How can I ask Our Father for life for you, if Man must die? You have convinced me. If the dead were risen, there would be no room on earth for new creatures ever. But never fear, for I shall run forever with you, bringing the fallen to you for companionship." And so they do.' He shifts, moving the stock to a more comfortable place on his shoulder. 'That is not our story, but it is a good one. It comes from the Plains people. There are no wolves, here.'

'No,' Matthew grinned, out of more horror than laughter. 'Just death's escorts.'

All is silence and firelight, the thick dark outside, for a moment, until the bracken shifts again, parting to reveal two thick white bodies moving with a fluid strength. They are followed by a small army of men, mainly black but a few deep-tanned Caucasian faces, all snarling, thrown into the mix. They are armed with long knives, sickles, scythes, threshing tools, and their bodies are naked from the waist up, their nethers covered in tattered rags.

They are led by two tall men, one forward, one stalking shadow-like slightly behind, hurtling, scratched already and bleeding, across the yard and cement-hummocked graves. They move so quickly, sweat-shined limbs flashing in the gathering storm light, that no one could give their number accurate count.

Matthew throws his hammer back; his men, the armed ones, follow suit. 'This is it.'

No one notices that Rose is up now, braced against the wall, turning and turning the latch of the locked door at her back. No one hears the lock begin to give, their senses are too much directed forward, except for Joy who sits, head tilted on the floor, as though listening to some strange, undeniable music that no one else can hear.

The men are rushing for their stronghold, sweat pouring from their backs like a thin film of slime.

Matthew gives the order to fire.

There are a series of empty mechanical clicks, followed by silence.

The powder has all wet through. They have no fire, now.

With a grimness that is close to maniacal, Matthew loosens his long knife from the scabbard at his thigh. He looks around at his workers, hired men who never knew what they were staying for, and sees the gleam of steel on all sides.

He smiles, a genuine one this time, of no hope but true thanksgiving. The fingers of his right hand move of their own accord to thumb out the shape of a cross on his chest. Miguel offers up a Spanish prayer that seems to die, unheard, immediately in this dark. But the dead rise here.

Outside, on the backs of the approaching men who move like monsters, the strong winds rise.

The first few patter-falls of soft rain drop, strengthening.

No one has seen Rose move out through the broken door, or Joy follow, unheard, after.

The night has, finally, come to life.

ABYSS

The rain is well and truly coming down now, pouring on damned and just alike. The sound of rain falling on a rich canopy of leaves drowns out all but its own accompanying thunder and the only light now visible springs from pronging lightning that reveals, in flashes, an army both hideous and ignorant, that moves to clash against the barricaded walls of the general store. They move, these muscle-heaving, hungry men, towards the building unerringly, as though directed by some unseen force.

They are frothing at the mouth, white spittle washing down their jaws in the water-flow. One of the dark ones, who twelve hours ago was a man named Randy, is bleeding profusely out of many tiny lacerations in his skin, as though he were a flesh-mask housing a being that is too large for his stolen hide.

Mr. Johnson, the troop of workers behind him, remains unmarked as of yet; he is moving more slowly, cautiously, his skin crawling with the sensation of a man observed by many human and inhuman eyes. He knows from his visit to the manse in the woods that there are far less than twenty of the men hidden behind the barricaded storefront, maybe ten at most, but their rapid movements coupled with the shuttering, uncertain light makes their number appear much greater.

My God, he thinks, all this good land. So soon mine.

And worse.

This is not unnatural. This is not unnatural at all. This is what we all were once, and what we all could still become. These things are living appetite incarnate, nothing but hunger, rage and lust. The kind of people who get exactly what they want, when they want it. Now. Mr. Johnson is not familiar with Darwin, but nature red in tooth and claw? Yes. That holds appeal.

His employees hug the long blades to their bodies, sensing the guns behind the walls, as though they could extract some comfort from the iron, as though a knife, by the very nature of what it is, were not itself a link to the very darkness that they fear, their honed edges crying out for sacrificial blood. All knives are like the Hebrew God, in one aspect at least. They take their due in steaming flesh, not satisfied by the fruits and grain of Cain.

Above the sounds of rain and raging nature, they hear the hollow click of useless guns.

A slow, thin smile spreads across his bearded face as he looks over at his son who smiles back, in love with the actions of this night. His men are standing, armed and at the ready, and their twin guns are dry, powerful and strong.

This is going to be fun.

At the signal of his hand the men move in, to rage and pound the wood-braced door.

WAKING

When Rose woke in the fire-lit room she knew the truth at last. Ten years of dreaming and she had woken in an instant, entire and at last, never to dream at night again. David is dead, her daughter a woman, and she is dressed in rags and ashes, trapped and dying in a dead town. There is blood on her lips and she knows what that is a symptom of. One more month of life, if she takes an easy pace, after so many long years of happy oblivion.

So much time wasted. David is gone. David is gone, and her heart aches with the loss of him. And Joy, her Joy, (she recalls at last the hatred of 'Joyce') her lovely only girl, she is grown, strong, and in love, not needing her mother any longer, save perhaps to survive this strange attack and move on with her strong and sudden foreign love.

She does not intend to take it easy.

Rose does not know what force caused this sudden awakening. She was asleep one moment, and then at last, awake. As simply as if a gentle voice had whispered in her sleep. She smiles. Perhaps one did.

David.

And suddenly, as clear as anything, as simple as cliché, she knows what she must do to bring them through the night. She does not know how she will bring the matter off, but she knows that this is right, and if it is the will of God the way will be made clear for her, the path cleared.

She slides up against the wall, feeling the door at her back. They have not bothered to barricade it because the basement is flooded and, they reckon, impassable, but the lock has been

302

turned and the key withdrawn. Still, if her instinct is right and she is meant to do this, the way will be made clear.

Rose does not notice that Joy has turned her lovely face from the fire and the singed smell of burning book (throw it into the fire, girl, you will not need it anymore). Her black eyes are staring at Rose, noticing a newer clarity that is somehow present there, as though her mother has moved out of a decade-long envelope of fog.

She turns the handle, feeling the resistance, hearing the sharp crack as it gives, as the door slides open. She can see the light reflecting off of the deep water there. The storeroom is made of cement and its foundation lies a few inches beneath the ground line, and is therefore easily flooded. Ten years of neglect have not helped the situation. The flames are shining off the backs of swimming rats, vermin corpses, and the slimed scales of marauding cotton mouth moccasins that spread the stench of sliced cucumber before them in this flooded basement sea.

She will pass through it. The way will be made clear. That phrase repeating like a mantra, or an implanted prayer. Something comforting, the like the pressure of a firm and loving hand.

When she enters the dark, sinking down into the stinking, tepid water; ankle deep, shin, thigh, a bloated dead rat with silt-whitened eyes bobbing at her blue-clad breast; she does not hear her daughter following after.

She knows there is another exit down here somewhere, the wide coal shoot. There might even be steps or at the very least a substantial pile of fuel for her to stand on. And still the thought, reverberating like the distant cry of dogs, if this is a meant thing, the way will be cleared. After all, she thinks, brushing a seven-foot water moccasin out of her path as easily as she would move a strand of hair that had fallen in front of her daughter's eyes, even ten years of rot could not account for the easy breaking of a good Yale lock.

For ten years she has been blind in ignorance, walking in a dream, now she must be deaf, for Joy is splashing close behind her, and still she does not see or hear. But then, her daughter is being as quiet as she can, so maybe Rose is mistaking the splashing sound of her footsteps for the flailings of an especially large rat.

Somewhere in the profound darkness of this subterranean hell there is a door, an exit leading outward to a world where, unlike here, the darkness might have a chance of ending.

Just when it would seem that the night can last no longer, that her faith was misleading, her prayer a nonsense, she spots before her in the ceiling a thin wedge of silver light, and there, before her faltering toes, the sharp inclination of a waterlogged pile of coal. She climbs.

Her balance is precarious; rats are scrabbling everywhere, looking for whatever purchase they can to avoid an awful death by water; they cling to her skirt, her long soaking hair. She plucks one from her bodice, feeling its tiny, sharp nails tearing into her breasts. She is tempted to throw the fat body away, but she remembers the first pathetic, floating corpse and carries it with her, instead. If she escapes from here, the rat will, too.

The coal shoot is set a few feet above the floor, to allow the fuel carts to draw up directly to the door for easier unloading. There is a chain looped through the inside handles of the door, looped but not locked, and the door swings open easily, almost magically, at her touch. And suddenly she is outside, not dry (the rain is torrential now), but safe from drowning.

She stoops to let the struggling rat down on the rain-freshened soil and it runs off. Rose walks around the crumbling storefront, towards the sound of raging battle, watched (if she but knew it) by hundreds of yellow, shining eyes.

She watches the men attacking the store, tearing at the barricades with tooth and nail, curve-bladed scythes. She wonders, vaguely, why the men inside do not fire. They have guns, she knows this, she saw. And when the leaders arrive from the ragged edge of the forest, (the older one looks, in between lightning flashes, like that greedy charlatan Johnson) looking at each other and not at her, she takes the opportunity to run, as fast as her legs will carry her, towards the slow collapsing manse that was her home.

She runs, is followed step for step by one for whom the dogs cry longingly, across the cemetery, feeling a stabbing ache of sadness at the ruined state of the church that she once loved, and another for the deteriorated facade of her marital home, and makes it in a scant few seconds up the steps to her high porch.

It is there she hears, there she turns, to meet her shadow daughter. This woman who could be the older sister to the child she knew, this lovely dark creation in ragged skirt and white man's tunic, borrowed and drowning her thin body. Her breasts are fully visible beneath the drenched fabric, nipples dark as brutal wounds.

Joy can see her mother there, a new presence in eyes ten years' blank. She knows that Rose is dying, Joy knows that she is healed. There is new fire in the eyes, and it gladdens and terrifies her. She shifts the red remains of her skirt from sheer nervousness and the length of it comes away in her hand, baring her white legs, etched with dark hair, to the pleasures of the rain.

'Never mind honey,' Rose says, moving closer to her daughter, the rain pouring through like baptism from the holes in the roof of the porch, 'it doesn't matter. This will all be over soon, and then your nice young man will bring you more.'

'Mother? Mama? You know me?' Her hands are curled into her body, as though she would hug herself to comfort; she does not know if the warm water on her cheeks are rain droplets or tears.

'It's over now.' Rose is talking about a long night, but not this one. 'It will be fine.' She pulls her daughter toward her, holding her strongly, stroking Joy's long hair as though to make up in this one motion for a thousand misplaced caresses, for all the lost and unfelt love. In this, she succeeds. All is healed, all made well. 'I was gone a long time, little girl, and in a moment I may go again, but for now, this moment, I am here.'

Her lips press against Joy's forehead, leaving a thin rosette of blood. She says, 'I want you to go back, honey, go back and know that I go with you, though not in body. You carry me with you, always.' Her eyes are lucid, burning, as though to make up for years of dullness. 'Your father will be there as well.'

'Mama.' Joy is weeping openly; how can she have lost so long, only to lose again so quickly?

'Shh.' She holds the dark, narrow, lovely face in between her strong palms, feeling sharp cheek bones beneath her fingertips, seeing both an incarnation of her David and the lost face of her little girl. 'I am myself now, but not for long. I must do what I was freed for.' She pushes her daughter from her, almost violently, and struck by a sudden inspiration, almost a compulsion, she says, 'The thing you need is on the altar, beneath the veil. Watch out for the rotten beam.'

Joy tries to come back towards her, but Rose is insistent, pushing her back. 'Go to the church, go to the altar.' Another inspiration. 'You have the pen, you have what you need.'

'But Mama…'

The lightning flashes, Rose's face clouds over with rage, with hurt anger; she flings out her hand, shouts 'Go' and as though the very porch wood were obeying her, the boards give out and Joy plummets to the cushioned loam below.

When she drags her bruised but unhurt body from the soil her mother is gone, vanished inside the house to do her duty there, whatever that might be.

Looking back across the cemetery, the battered churchyard, she can see in between bright flashes of lightning that the battle is raging. The Johnsons' men are hammering at the barricaded shop door. And the wood is splintering, it cannot hold long.

She must do something to help. But what?

The thing you need is on the altar.

The church.

She does not question her mother's intuition, the things she said felt so right. Instead she picks her way across the gloom, the gluey soil, her feet coated in a thick layer of mud until she reaches the fallen sanctuary door.

There is just enough room for her to slither through the darkness, though splinters leave their marks on her and fray the edges of her borrowed shirt. It is dark inside and there is the heavy sound of breathing, though from what lungs she cannot tell, only that she is surrounded by yellow eyes and deep thick fur.

A warm, soft mouth with hard, sharp teeth takes her wrist in a gentle grip that she has felt before and draws her slowly through the murk, steering her around fallen ceiling beams and crushed pews, leading her softly on pads that are saved from silence only by the hard click of claws.

Joy is strangely unafraid, her right wrist tangled in that hot mouth, her left hand buried deep in fur; she is inexpressibly happy here, now, as though she has found, after a separation lasting eons, a forgotten favorite friend. Suddenly, in this darkness, is her wounded heart made whole.

They stop in front of the long low table that served as altar; she knows it intimately, though it has been years. The white cloth that served as veil is draped over the top of it, partially rotten but still, and always, sanctified. The mouth frees her hand here and she runs her fingers underneath the cloth until, in a scant moment, her fingers brush against the chased-silver offertory bowl.

It is heavy and right in her hands, embossed with wheat, grape vines, fish, the harvest symbols of the Lord. Suddenly, in an instant, like the lightning that forks down outside, she knows what she must do.

Her hand goes to the long pelt at her side, this friend, familiar, that knows where to go. The bowl is in her left hand, balanced on her hip; her father's ivory pen, a wand, heavy in her breast pocket, and at her side is a kind of dog, most definitely faithful. She is fully armed, flame-blessed and girded, made vestal by her presence here in this ruined but still holy church ground. The coyote, she can see him now, faintly in the moonlight beginning to filter through the dismembering clouds, leads her out to face her future, the battle, through the part-open, half-hinged door.

The tree her father hung from is before her, at the crossroads, and there is water for her bowl. It is Sunday, the day of resurrection, of hope for blooming. No night can stand up for long in the presence of the promise of that love.

Her feet are bare, her heart is holy.

She thinks, smiling, let there be fire at last.

CLARITY

Rose is hurtling through her desolation, knowing as she does that there is so little time. She knows what she must do and necessity seems now like mercy. She can see her home, at first, only in lightning flashes that grow further apart with each passing minute; the freak storm is finally dying out.

There is a lamp with a little oil in it sitting on the sideboard and a box of long matches near it, the kind that is used more frequently to light a fire on a chill night in the unadorned grate. She brings forth a small flame with a hand shaken with old grief. She cannot believe the state of the house. So much missing, rotten, changed. The Antique Rose wallpaper she chose for the stairwell is peeling off in moist strips like sunburnt skin, the carpets rotten through in patches as though with mange. Where has all of her furniture gone to? Where are the solid silver candlesticks her great-grandmother left her, the ones she kept in the niche by the stairs?

And then she knows.

Ten years of food without an income, with only those awful people for neighbors (she remembers them vaguely, somehow: grasping, unscrupulous, the kind that would force a girl to trade her birth-right for a bowl of thin stew and the false promise of aid). She would like to make them pay, and then she remembers the yellow canine shapes she saw, the flame eyes, the teeth picked out by lightning-strike, remembers the marks she saw upon her daughter's leg, and smiles. The sins of the father shall be paid out unto the son.

They shall both pay.

Rose only hopes that Joy does not think to stop by the house on the way out of the swamp, to rouse the woman, soon to be a widow, who resides there. Let her, Rose prays, live out her days alone in that place, surrounded by her stolen things and with no one left to pawn them to, wasting out her life alone. But no, food gets to them somehow. She will likely take the next wagonload out. Live her life rich.

It is better thus. Bitterness was never balm for anything, though flames might heal spoilt land for new growth. Death can be a sign of life – a stasis, never.

Oh God, her baby lived here. Among this wreck, this terrible ruin. She looks into the room where David died and feels a pang. Joy's dirty white nightgown is folded neatly on the sponge-sheeted bed. His blood still patterns small brown roses on the wall, and the sour stench of a death long coming permeates the air.

It takes a moment for Rose to realize that the odor is coming from herself, her own sick skin.

And then she is upstairs.

It seems that time has shifted, jumped somehow, though by how long she does not know. It could have been fifteen seconds, it could have been an hour. She has no memory of climbing the stairs, that barrier that sealed her for so long in her land of dreams, no memory of entering here, or sitting on the soft bed that she sits on, now.

Everything in her room is rotten, and nothing has been moved or changed. This then is the price of preservation. Defilement slathers over everything, ruining all that you would keep. Time, it seems, cannot be canned for later use; the contents all go sour.

Yet nothing has been taken from here, nothing sold. While Joy traded everything she could, she left her mother alone up here with her rotting clothes and useless jewels, in as close to comfort as she could manage to maintain for her.

Rose closes her eyes and is swept away by a guilt that moves her like grief. For all that long time, passing. For missing out on life, her daughter's and her own. The full, terrible knowledge of that lost time strikes her, as though with the flat of a hand, and it is hard. Hard.

The lamp is at her feet, but the room too waterlogged to take it. Rose feels, for a moment, the abysmal guttering of hope.

And then she thinks, in a voice both alien and her own, the way shall be made clear.

Nothing in her room has been touched, nothing moved or shifted, and a fire will blossom if there is fuel. A flame, rising hard and hot enough, would clear away everything. Even diamonds, like the one on her left ring finger, can be engulfed in flame, being as they are, as she is herself, a mere mask for carbon, disguised coal.

She slides off of the bed and feels beneath it for the cask that David put there over a decade ago, the cask of lamp oil left for the hard storms, the hurricanes which once-yearly wreck this coast. In the darkness, when she is beginning to despair, her fingers fumble against the catch and she hauls the three-foot barrel to her lap.

The guilt comes again: awful, implacable. Her daughter could have used this, surely, over the years. Might have, therefore, been able to save something for herself.

But then, she thinks, for the first time smiling since this errand began, sometimes Providence behaves strangely. This way, the loved and the valued things are out of the house, and can therefore somehow be redeemed. And if Joy had found the oil, it would have made her life easier for a while, surely, but it would not be here to do its duty now.

And, thank God, the seal on the barrel has held completely. She opens it now, as though it were a sacrament. The oil is thick and clear, somehow sweet-smelling. She pours it out, slowly and evenly, anointing the bedroom, the mind of her madness, the calm decaying center of the dead town's insanity. The oil, the sheen of it, makes everything appear almost new. Gleaming. Ready for its rebirth in flame.

As an afterthought that hits her like a gasp, she pries the twin rings from her fingers, the band and diamond both, binds them together with a length of blue ribbon, heaven-tinted, that she tears from the jagged remnants of her skirt, and hurls them, together, out of her broken, rusted-open window, the place she used to sit for hours, waiting for him who gave them to her, David, who she goes to now.

The wind is dying, the oil is spread, and the eye of the moon looks down on her through scattering clouds. Her bed is made, and ready, waiting for her. Her groom is ready, out there, waiting for her. Her daughter, her lovely daughter, does not need her anymore.

And somehow she knows that this is a *meant* thing, the right thing, a sigul. The thought is there with the conviction of religion.

She takes the long match in her newly-barren left hand, strikes it, and lets the dancing tip down into the gleam that waits for it, on curtains, floor, on wall. And the flames rise up to meet her hand, blooming; oh Rose of Sharon, oh lily that blooms in Mary's colors, oh the sweet scent of sacrifice rising on air… She is, here engulfed in her hour of death, alive at last. Alive. Living for once and dying, to be reborn again from the foul ashes of this earth, from the terror and the pain, into a new, clean world, that shining beacon on the hill.

She closes her eyes, her long hair crisping, curling, going up in white smoke, a smile of beatitude spreading, touching eyes and mouth.

She is finally, finally, going home.

And it is good.

HECATE IN THE MOONTIME

Joy is walking through the breaking rain, underneath a bright, unclouding sky; the moon shining down upon her like a great staring eye and the flames rising up behind her in a crucible of gold. The coyote walks beside her, as gentle as any domesticated animal. Its shoulder moves in tandem with the motion of her thigh, fur against tooth-marked skin. The light is silver, marred by the shadows of passing clouds, and the bowl that had been used for offerings, and will be so used again, is the oily color of tarnish. The embossed harvest signs alone are clear still, raised threads of white metal against the oxidized night-hue of the ewer.

She can see the battle raging just ahead of her, those terrible figures that run there, throwing themselves against the barricaded wall, and never mind the blood that flows from hides lacerated by splinters and the knife points the workmen thrust through the sight holes they left open the wall, where the windows used to be.

The noise is awful, shrieks of pain from the slave men, cries of fear from within, the impotent click of guns colliding with wet gunpowder; acts of the desperate fighting off ruin.

They have not noticed her yet, coming to the T-shaped crossroads in front of the shop. Joy is standing behind the tree her father hanged from; in a moment she will walk around it, coming face to face, unavoidably, with the savages that attack her love. The dog is calm beside her, moving steadily, and she draws strength from its fidelity, reaching down to touch the thick golden pelt.

She knows, somehow, what she must do. The knowledge sits inside her like a compulsion, a drive implanted from some other, stranger source. She has the ewer, a wide, shallow bowl of solid, blackened silver. There is the crossroads to serve for the place where all roads diverge and come together, and the dark tree from which her father hanged, his body bound in Mother's fabric, to twist in the wind in a movement like writhing. And the moon, that bright lady, is out and full to bursting, looking down.

And there, beneath a scrim of windswept leaves, there is the final thing she needs, save one. A long knife, curved, almost a sickle, shows its keen-edged blade to starlight. She stoops down without breaking stride and scoops the handle up.

Ready to do battle at last.

She can see the horrors moving, so close that their greenish veins are visible, throbbing, between their straining muscles and their skin. Their faces strained and sweat-drenched, twisted by the ever-pulsing lust for freedom mingling with rage. Their hearts are beating behind their ribs, feeding their exhausted, overwrought bodies, until they more closely resemble the workings of outmatches and driven horses than men, beaten to froth.

Joy moves from her hiding place in shadows into her position where the road meets the gnarled roots of the tree, the coyote moving with her, seeming to know better than his mistress what beauty, and horror, will follow. She bends and places the bowl between her toes.

The moon is beating down like sunlight, the knife and pen are in her hands and the bowl is at her feet. It is time, at last, for peace.

The slave men see her now, as do their masters, those grasping beasts. The slave men turn, knives barred, slathering, to face her, their teeth bared in grimaces, ready to tear and rend, no longer caring for whatever goals they came here for, to consume her in the flood of their carnality, in a bloody hunger that is itself a form of lust.

The coyote's hackles are raised, its black lips pulled back from new, strong fangs, growling.

The men move towards her, slowly first, circling, their black masters in the lead.

And then the monsters run.

They are only a few yards away, in a moment she will smell their sour-sweet breath and their teeth will stove themselves into the soft flesh of her neck.

And then she brings the sharp knife down, drawing the curved blade swift against her pale palm.

The smell of her strong blood stops them, for a minute, for long enough. It pools, collecting in the silver ewer bowl, until it has flowed deep enough to hold the moon in its reflection, her face caught, held, on the warm surface of her freely-offered sacrifice.

Joy, or the body that held that name once, drops the ivory pen into the bowl and allows the blade to clatter softly there, at her feet.

There is a great heat rising now behind her eyes, a pressure awful and enormous, as though her face had become a mask for some other, larger thing, a thing somehow stronger, more solidly real, than the girl-face it is wearing, a thing that fills up all her empty corners, but does not break the mold it loads.

The men are running again, hurtling towards her again and at full throttle, as though they cannot see or register this new force in her, rising up, implacable and natural as the tide.

And then the dog begins to howl.

And the bodies fall.

But these are sights better described by other, human, eyes.

A CLEAR AND CLEANSING
STARLIT NIGHT

The men are crouched behind the barricade, peering out into the slaughter in the murk. They see the Johnsons and their men dismembered, and Matthew is the only one who realizes the significance of the dark creature who bit the final stroke. The blood of the father, the sin of the son, paid out between the generations. They sit in silence for a while, cowering, tongues as useless as their sodden bullets in their guns.

They see this all in the stuttering light of lightning flashes, though the storm is fading out as quickly as it came. First they see the slaves turn and throw themselves at the boarded store (though none of their vestigial minds can, any longer, identify the cause) as though determined to drink their fill of those men crouched waiting, within. The lightning is over, the moon coming out, providing light enough to show the beings that slink like wolves, enjoying their hunt.

There is the sound of deep concussion, a sudden flash of yellow light, as though a great charge were exploding close enough for them to hear the sound of a pocket of oxygen consumed in an infernal blast. The manse blossoms into great, florid flame that flickers and dances in spite of wet, half-rotten wood, its stilts becoming hilltop, and it the shining beacon on it. It glows like a torch, purifying, somehow free, in this dark, wind-torn night.

The explosion, quiet as it was, distracts the approaching creatures and interrupts their attack. But the force of shock is deceptive, their fear shall feed their hunger, and in a matter of moments the slow lope has become again a rage. They hurl their bodies against the rotting wall, ignoring their injuries, never feeling their torn and bleeding hides, in their bloodlust, in their determination to break through the wall that stands before them. They hammer at the soft wood with their scythes. The barricade has already begun to give. Osceola is the one who asks the pertinent question, 'Who set that flame?'

Matthew looks around, praying quickly for what he shall not find. The woman and the girl are gone, their corner empty and the storeroom door wide open, leading on to flood and vermin. He can only hope, against all evidence, that his love at least is free from the explosion and the flame.

Holata signals to Miguel and they move to block the doorway closed, pushing a barrel full of rust that was once nails to brace shut the door, but Matthew prevents them, in the faint hope that Joy will come back through that way, and that the slave men or their masters will not discover where this entrance lies. The workers are reluctant, but he is even now the boss, and in the end they give way to his discretion, but Holata keeps his weather eye locked on the open door.

They hold the creatures off for a moment, sticking out their knives and daggers through the sight holes they intended for their guns. There is not much room for movement here, four holes left open at the base of the glassless windows. The men who stand near them flail out with their machetes and bowie knives, avoiding as best they can the attacking ifrit hoard, not to mention the blades that are gripped in their strong, work-hardened hands.

The soaking boards, pulpy when the assault began, are crumbling now, giving in to the unceasing assault of hard fists on decomposing planks. All is overwhelming noise, the animal shouts from the outer darkness, pained wailings from within, resembling, in the end, nothing so much as utter silence, as though the sound has cancelled out itself.

This false quiet is followed by the thing itself, when Osceola lifts his voice in prayer, and Matthew joins in after, two men praying the 'Our Father'.

When the assault on the dooryard stops, the men attribute it, at first, to this. And who can tell what prayers have wrought?

But then they see the girl, the ghost, the woman who walks clad in short white shift, lock-step with a large coyote, with the flames rising up behind her, a giant hand inscribing the air.

Her eyes are silver in the moonlight, and she walks like one possessed, her knife and ewer in her hand like what they are, objects of a long forgotten, alien rite.

The slave men stop and gather round her, their tongues lolling in anticipation of their feast of blood. She pays the coyote more mind than she gives to them, those broken creatures of fungus and night.

Matthew can tell, but only just, that it is Joy.

It is as though her body has become somehow more solid than the landscape that surrounds it, as though she has been taken up and worn like a cloak, her body a living mask for something infinitely real, to which the flesh creatures that surround her (for it is female, this vast, inhabiting thing) are as intangible as air.

The shock those greed-driven creatures feel passes off in an instant, the feelings of the men inside the shop are longer lasting. Three of the men inside the store cross themselves sincerely, two married men with wives at home unashamedly hold hands. And then the Johnsons cry out their raging order, and the slaves fall upon her.

She drops the bowl between her feet, and the ivory pen inside it; her back is placed upon the bark of that gnarled hangman's tree, wind howling round her terrible and loud, freeing the moon, the ecstatic stars from their imprisoning clouds, transforming her long loose hair into something mystical and wild.

The sugar baron's servants set out to spring as she draws the light blade down along her lifeline, sending a dark quantity of blood pouring down like the guise of life itself, collecting in the bowl.

She looks up and a thin but genuine smile alights on her lips.

The slaves and their dark masters crowd close around her, breathing in anticipation of their feast, saliva flowing down their jowls, slicking on their chops; wet and chips of wood stand bright against their blades.

Joy calls out the dogs.

They flow around her body like the flames that burn high up behind her, this rich and golden hoard, composed entirely of sharp teeth, bright pelts, and eyes as yellow as the sun that set so long ago. They swirl and eddy all around her, a vast and living tide, flame-colored and implacable. Her own dog, her good friend, stays ever faithful at her side, his shoulder pressing into her thigh. The others; they have been waiting for this, for centuries, eons, years on years, since the passing of their first, more real, mistress into the place where living dogs can no longer go.

And now she has come again at last, for one moment.

They rejoice in her arrival: summoned by silver, the moonlight, the blood.

The violence is intense, and over in a moment. The dogs, who have been waiting, consuming, like the Lord of Hosts, all traces of darkness and disease. Those poor children, blighted by evil, driven by the crimes of others and themselves are returned again in dying to what they always were: loose carapaces of wasted flesh.

The senior Mr. Johnson is consumed in a flurry, though he used a strong man for his human shield. The man, who came here running from a charge of rape, goes down fast and silent from a bite to carotid and another to his jugular, leaving Johnson naked and alone in that dark night, but not for long. The growls and the claws undo him quickly, and leave the small scant remnants for the ever-hungry ground.

Randolph is the last to go, eaten down by the hoard from coccyx to skull, the stringy contents of the latter lapped up as though composed of cream; seeing his own destruction, though uncomprehending, until even the bare minimum for housing life are eaten and the dark infernal light, that raging hunger, that lit his eyes has entirely gone.

And then, as suddenly as they arrived, the dogs are gone, save for one who will remain where he is until his life has fled him. And even that will occur some fourteen years hence, in a city in the North, where he and his mistress will dwell in comfort.

The coyotes vanish as they came, in a golden swirl of canine flesh, howling out their joy, fulfilled at last.

The woman, or the girl, returns to herself in a great and silent flash of light that leaves her darkened but otherwise unhurt in this roadway of bones and abandoned knives, and she falls senseless to the floor, her fingers trailing in her own spilled blood, pouring it out of its sacramental bowl. She is unconscious, dreaming story images true, innocent and wild.

The moon is out, and her dog howls.

Matthew is there beside her in an instant, having pried with bloodening fingernails the pummel-weakened long boards from the door. He lifts, but cannot rouse her, carrying her limp but radiant body into the warm close darkness of the store, where she will sleep through this last night of resurrection to waken, at long last, with the first calm light of cool blue dawn.

Resurrection

HOUSE

There is a white house buried somewhere in south Florida, a few meters from the bright Gulf. There were a tribe of people in it, twisted and perverse, who served alone the greed at the base of their own hearts, feeding on the remnants of a dead and dying town.

They are gone now; their bodies, blood, bones, all traces of them obliterated from the surface of this good, green earth, down to the smallest sliver of fingernail. And the house, which once housed enough stolen treasures to satisfy a dragon's hoard, was long ago reduced to what it always held, a few cheap Sears and Roebuck chifferobes that have long since fallen back to strangled earth, some scraps of fabric, the broken brim of an ancient leather hat.

The house itself is overgrown and falling, dragged to pieces by kudzu, sea grape, ivy, its walls crumbled, until the carved slats that composed it have long returned to the tide. If you came upon it now, it would seem almost a natural thing, spewed forth from earth. But I should warn you, before you try, the way to that cursed place is long, and terrible, green though it seems. The blood-dimmed tide is loosed underneath the sand, hidden, always, just beneath the whitened surface that served as ceremonial innocence, lost.

And even if you make it through, remember, please, remember. The bodies are gone, pulled down to earth. The greed remains. And it is hungry.

NEW LIFE

They spent the night in darkness, in a nightmare storm of violence that the dawn utterly ruined, to the joy of those who have survived the reign of Nix. The light breaks bright and blue, ringed yellow and copper gold around the rising orb, marrying that celestial body to this world that rises up before them, that seems so various and new, refreshed and cleansed of the slaughter and sorrow that painted it last night.

Joy and Matthew are curled together, enmeshed close as foeti twins, his body on the outside, hers curled within, as though he would guard her, even in sleep, from the forces that he witnessed yesterday, and that he knows he has no hope of withstanding.

It is his duty, and his will, to try.

The coyote, the new-christened 'Dog', is curled in a circle of his own, nose to tail, at their feet. The hired workers, more like brothers now, all give it wide berth. They remember what his pack did to those shivering men who struck at them so violently in that black time when the winds howled and the storms raged.

When they do wake, all of them rising nearly simultaneously as though shaking off some group hypnosis, they are awash in the light of green and gold. There is nothing in the window now, neither glass nor board, and the fires, in the grate and of the manse, have cooled to white ashes. The only light is natural, honey-yellow and delicious, warm as a bath.

No one speaks, for a long while.

They sup together on white bread, broken in long fingers, dipped in red-herb vinaigrette made from ruined wine, and eat the dark brown strips of deer meat dried last winter over celebratory flame, prayed over in gratitude of a successful hunt.

Joy slips slices to Dog. The men pretend not to notice. The silence surrounds them like a sacrament, rich and true as human blood can make it.

Osceola is the first to break the quiet. 'Well, what now? I'm guessing the farming plan is out.'

Matthew does not speak at first, his forehead constricted with unspoken worry; he looks over at his bride and sees his answer there. 'Yes, the farming is out. Here at least. Somewhere else? Who knows?' His stick turns and turns, stirring up the long-cold ashes. 'You couldn't pay me to stay here after last night. But the question of money arises.'

Joy is grooming Dog, plucking a blood-fattened tick, round as a grape, from behind the yellow ear. It bursts in her fingers, air-cooled blood painting her palms. She wipes them on her robe, getting a look from Miguel, whose shirt it was. She speaks, 'I have my inheritance, if we can get it.'

'Those antiques from the Johnsons? All of that silver?' He strokes her shoulder, possessive, as she strokes Dog. 'But how to get it, that's the thing.'

'Johnson. Singular.' Her old smile, knifelike, somehow humorous. 'There is just the one, and if she does not want to be left here all alone when we leave, abandoned as I was, she will be willing to pay well for her passage.'

'I sense a new vindictiveness in you. I like it.' Matthew's prodding stick has freed one lone spark; he leaves his wooden poker there, to let it feed, and grow. He turns to his men, loyal now, not yet talking about pay. 'Are the wagons still sound enough to take us? The mules?'

Holata answers. 'The carts look fine. They're over there by the church. As for the burros, some of the men who left tied them up underneath the columns holding up the house three doors down. I kept a weather eye on it last night. They were not molested.'

Matthew nods, relieved, not only for the animals but at no longer having to face the prospect of that long walk back. 'Good. If you men can gather up the supplies we can leave this God-forsaken place at last; pretty as it looks right now, I would be happy to leave it. The fewer words said about it the better.'

'Good plan. But first,' Joy looks at Dog, at the men that surround her, 'I must say my goodbyes.'

'Of course.' Matthew takes her by the elbow, gendered courtesy resurging in a tide. With the return of daylight, virtues blossom. 'I will travel with you. We can see to the widow Johnson on the way out of the swamp.' If there is satisfaction in his voice when he says this last, no one comments on it, though all approve.

The cemetery looks different in the daylight. The storm has worked wonders: all the graves are gone, cement-capped ones included. There are bones here, stirred up by flood and storm, and bodies, hands outstretched, reaching up in anticipation of a resurrection that will come after all who have walked there are long, long gone. And the church's roof has vanished completely, broken beam and all, leaving the altar as it should be: an open face to God.

There is nothing left at all of the place that was her prison, and her home. The ashes are stirred and scattered by wind, tramped down by new-fallen dew. There is the sweet scent of meat hovering, a creature burned in sacrifice, offered up, but of the edifice itself, there is nothing. Not a column or cornerstone, as though the vacuum where static time had been has filled at last with the vividness of life. The ghosts are exorcised, at last, the spirit freed from long possession.

The girl stands there a moment, weeping, with her lover's arms around her shoulders as the tears flow down like rivers. She cries not in sadness, but in joy.

As they turn to go, a bright flash catches her eye. Two rings, one with a diamond, glitter up at her from the ash, the mud and bracken. She bends to scoop them up and discovers that they are bound together with a torn piece of blue silk ribbon, in faded lapis. She kisses them, fervently, as one would a sacred relic from a saint, and slides them into her pocket, to ponder at another time.

By the time they return to the store, the wagons are prepared and loaded, the men ready. Dog is sitting, calm in the driver's seat, as though he did this every day, his long red tongue out hanging, as though he would drink the wind. He thumps his well-furred coyote's tail a time or two in greeting, and then as though he knows where he is headed, he looks on down the road.

They reach the Johnson farm in half an hour.

The men stay with the cart, not wishing to upset the new widow more than they have to. Matthew, Joy and Dog walk to the door. Matthew sings softly as he pulls the bell-chord: 'Henery the Eighth I am, I am! I got married to the widow next door, she'd been married seven times before. And every one was Henery.'

Joy does not know the song, but the implications are obvious; she slaps him, playfully, against his big arm, until the singing stops.

The woman who opens the door bears little resemblance to the mountainous woman she bartered with before. She is, in terms of size, the same, but looks somehow shrunken, frantic, as though a part of her brain had been stolen in the night, taking with it the capacity to understand that new bereavement. She stares at the three, uncomprehending.

She grabs Joy, ungently, when the recognition comes and her voice, when she uses it, is a rough whine. 'Where is Randolph? Where is my husband, my boy?' Asking for two bodies and one name.

She is shaking the girl now, violently, her eyes unfocused and unseeing. Matthew steps in and unclasps hands that leave bruises forming on the thin shoulders of the girl. When he does this, all her vast strength flees and her massive body crumples, like a child, to the floor.

They try to rouse her, for a while, but they know before they begin that it is hopeless. She is gone from them, whatever mind she had, utterly lost.

Joy knows that she has family in Miami. The least they can do, she tells her fiancé, is buy her a ticket there, and hire a temporary nurse, to make sure that she reaches the other end alive and in possession of whatever money they send her with.

As for the rest of the items in the house, she does not need them anymore (throw it to the fire). They lead her, somnambulant, unprotesting, to the second cart and lay her down among the farm tools and their few sacks of food.

The rest of the contents of the building they take as Joy's inheritance, moving through the empty, tasteless rooms, scooping up whatever they can of value, a process that takes hours. There is a lot of silver there, as well as several total pounds of gold, and, in a discovery that brings on a sort of drunkenness, Matthew uncovers two hundred thousand dollars in fifty-dollar bills lining the inside of a badly-mended guestroom mattress. He felt the odd, somehow greasy crunch of folding money when he sat down on the bed to rest.

Fifty pounds of greenbacks that they shove, like criminals, into a sack. Half will travel with Mrs. Johnson to Miami, in custody of her nurse.

The rest is enough for them to purchase good coal-land in Kentucky, in the county that will eventually be known as Bloody Harlan, where the barons are. Joy and Matthew will avoid that mess, all the coming trouble with the unions, by buying a small mine of their own and hiring workers who will be granted percentage shares in the company they've founded. A process that will see them through the crash of twenty-nine, will see their family brought to life in the soil of rich, dry land.

THE SACRED GROVE

Before they left the swamp behind forever for the panhandle grasslands and Georgia beyond it, Joy and Matthew spurred their cart-mules forward and left the workmen, and Dog riding with them, a few miles back, with orders to move slowly but eventually catch up with them. They rode in silence through the morning, the third one spent sleeping chastely in tents since choosing this road, each one thinking how to begin.

As the daylight faded on towards afternoon and there was as yet no sign of the men, they decided to stop and take their lunch from supplies in their packs, each hoping that in the meantime the right words would come. They came at last to a small grove where the light was sent down in waves, all green and gold. They parked underneath the spreading boughs of an orange tree, locked in the vestments of scent and blossom, spreading their blanket at its roots. The air was scented with sweet citrus and a deeper note of musk and moss, the ground beneath them as soft as a young girl's breast, and deliciously cool at this hot hour.

Matthew was a brave man, and very much in love, but he had seen the girl beside him burning with a strange, inhuman light, some foreign genius which the mortal flesh of man may look upon and live, but must never dare to touch. And yet the body beside him was winsome and human, undoubtedly warm.

He looked at her sitting there, head down and silent, her bare arms locked in a circle around her skirt-covered knees, the fabric trailing right down to her bare, muddy toes. There were white blossoms, delicate and sweetly-scented, caught in her loose writhing tendrils of glossy black hair, and the face that was framed by those tendrils? God did not have an angel so sad, or so sweet.

And yet, she had such fearsome strength.

Matthew felt unmanned before her, yet her bare touch could give him back his sword again. Oh, if she would but touch him, running her cool hand over his fever-burned skin. Why, he wondered, would she not?

He was not the only one afraid.

Yes, she thought, I could entrance him in the desolate places, among the bracken and the mire, but how could he ever hope to love me in that world, so vast and wide, where I have never been? He would leave me there, I think, for some girl so soft and tame, golden-colored like my mother when young, while I am strange, feral, and tinted with blood. Joy could not stand to face him then, watching instead her toe's excavation in the loam, her meat and bread untouched beside her, hardening in air.

They could have sat there all day long, miserable and silent, their hopes slowly wasted, were it not for the spider that crawled, dragging its body, black-shining, bloated, its swag belly marked out with the red hourglass that tells only of death. She spooled her poison down on many-jointed legs, descending on a thread of silk, stronger for its size than steel, from the upper branches of the orange to settle on the girl's white cheek.

Joy could see it, mark its slow decent from the corner of her eye, and knew its appearance there meant choosing either stillness or a terrible death. She chose to be still, and spent a painful several minutes waiting for Matthew to meet her eyes. Stillness meant, in this case, silence, and so she sat there without word or cry.

Eventually, he did try to rouse her into conversation, opening his mouth before he understood her trouble. 'Joy, I,' he turned to try to meet her eye, 'my God, what is that thing?'

There are no such poisonous spiders in England, or at any rate, such species whereby death is so sure, but he recognized death's colors on her skin, and understood the fear that radiated from

Joy's blazing eyes. But he was a man who knew and loved the nature of things, so long as that nature was true, and found great beauty even in danger.

And so, moving calmly, he allowed his forefinger to rest against the soft curve of his love's cheek, and allow death's small messenger to tie its thread to him.

The spider came gladly, resting warm in the palm of his hand. Joy turned to watch him, watching as he lowered it to the mossy ground, her fingers pressed in wonder against the place the widow landed, and yet remained no more. Its small body trundled off Matthew's fingertip as gently as a tear slides from a wounded eye, making its slow way back to its home in the moss.

'Thank you,' the girl said softly, looking at him from wide, dark eyes, her red lips trembling.

And with that look, the rift was healed.

Matthew took her right hand in his own, placed his left somewhere a little closer to the fertile earth, and then their lips were pressed together, open, their tongues, sinuous, together and tasting, discovering new worlds.

Another minute and her back was armored by the earth, his curving spine guarded strongly by the blue shield of sky as they moved together making sounds that could be singing, married here, now and forever, in this forest church, the blood spilling, transforming green moss, a sealed testament to their union and an offering given up in rapture to glade's unknown god.

When their men caught up with them, after several sweet hours, with Dog running barking up ahead, they found them curled together, purified, naked, their faces as light and innocent as one only found in the countenances of new-born children.

That night, they slept together in a single tent, the next day moving into the grasslands unified as man and wife, with running, delirious Dog running up ahead.